A CENTURY OF MYSTERY
1980-1989

EDITED BY
MARCIA MULLER
AND BILL PRONZINI

THE GREATEST STORIES
OF THE DECADE

MJF BOOKS
NEW YORK

Published by MJF Books
Fine Communications
Two Lincoln Square
60 West 66th Street
New York, NY 10023

Library of Congress Catalog Card Number 96-78813
ISBN 1-56731-155-5

Manufactured in the United States of America on acid-free paper

MJF Books and the MJF colophon are trademarks of Fine Creative Media, Inc.

10   9   8   7   6   5   4   3   2   1

A Century of Mystery: 1980-1989
Edited by Marcia Muller and Bill Pronzini

Introduction

by Edward D. Hoch

The 1980s were a decade of transition for the mystery and crime story, for readers, writers and publishers. Perhaps nowhere is this more clearly visible than in two specific areas—the resurrection of the private eye novel and the rise of a new generation of women mystery writers.

Let us go back for a moment and see what the situation was in 1980, at the beginning of the decade. The lifeblood of the private eye novel, its claim to a distinctive American voice that blended hard-edged realism with literary merit, was based almost exclusively on the writings of three men. They were Dashiell Hammett, Raymond Chandler and Ross Macdonald. Perhaps it was not an accident that their periods of productive writing neatly overlapped. Hammett wrote in the 1920s and '30s, Chandler in the 1930s, '40s and 50s, and Macdonald from the late 1940s to the mid-1970s. Thus by 1980, for the first time in nearly sixty years, none of the three giants of the private eye novel was still active. Although critics liked to proclaim their choices for a successor almost annually, no one of the required stature came along. There was even a feeling among some writers and critics that the private eye novel as such was nothing more than a period piece, that its glory days were behind it, lost somewhere along the sun-drenched Pacific coast.

There were others who didn't believe that, who tried to keep the flame alive in their own way. One of these was New York paperback writer Bob Randisi. Late in 1981 he came up with the idea of a new writers' organization, one which would honor and promote a

1

single sub-genre of the mystery. The Mystery Writers of America had existed since 1945 and its annual Edgar awards were the only such honors in America at that time. Though both Chandler and Ross Macdonald had served as presidents of MWA, some felt that tougher, harder-edged mysteries were not getting the support they deserved.

When Randisi announced formation of the Private Eye Writers of America, authors with even a borderline interest in the genre quickly signed on. In the fall of 1982, with Bill Pronzini serving as its first president, PWA presented its initial Shamus Awards at the Bouchercon XIII fan convention in San Francisco. The awards ceremony was introduced by the president of the Mystery Writers of America in a show of unity with the new organization. In 1984 PWA published the first of several anthologies containing new stories by its members, and by 1986 the organization and St. Martin's Press had announced co-sponsorship of an annual contest for the Best First Private Eye Novel.

Private eye writers were not the only ones with grievances in the 1980s. Women mystery writers were well aware of the fact that by the beginning of 1986 MWA's Edgar Award for best novel had not gone to a lone woman in the twenty-three years since Ellis Peters won in 1963. (Maj Sjowall and her husband Per Wahloo shared the honor in 1971.) And women mystery writers were all but shut out of prime review space in the major media. (Of ninety-seven mysteries reviewed by *The New York Times* in 1987, only seven were by women authors.)

The feeling was that the time had come to begin correcting these inequities. Under the direction of founding president Sara Paretsky and other women, Sisters in Crime came into existence in 1986. Their stated goals were "to combat discrimination against women in the mystery field, educate publishers and the general public as to inequalities in the treatment of female authors, and raise the level of awareness of their contribution to the mystery field."

Unlike the Private Eye Writers of America, Sisters in Crime presented no awards of its own, but vigorously supported women writers nominated by other organizations. By the end of the decade, awards were being presented by the Bouchercon World Mystery Convention (the Anthony Awards), PWA (the Shamus Awards), Mystery Readers International (the Macavity Awards), and the annual Malice Domestic conference (the Agatha Awards). It was no longer true that most mystery awards were won by men.

Sisters in Crime did much more than encourage mystery awards for women writers. By 1989 a series of five anthologies had begun appearing, edited by Marilyn Wallace and titled *Sisters in Crime*, though they were not official publications of the organization. These were followed by collaborative anthologies with PWA, but that belongs to the following decade. What Sisters in Crime did more than anything else was to make publishers and reviewers sit up and take notice. They arranged publicity and signings for members at mystery bookshops, held meetings and seminars at various fan conventions, and even ran advertising listing books and stories by members.

By the end of the 1980s more mysteries by women were being reviewed, and though the total number of mysteries published each year had not greatly changed, a larger percentage of them were by women. For new writers especially, it was easier for a woman to find a publisher. Men, unless their books had the shock fascination of serial killings or the technical hardware male readers liked, found it much tougher going. A look at the twenty-two authors whose stories make up this book shows that only one of the sixteen men, Ed Gorman, was a writer new to the 1980s. Four of the six women included here, Susan Dunlap, Linda Barnes, Julie Smith and Sara Paretsky, began writing novels in the 1980s. Although this changed climate on the part of publishers and reviewers cannot be traced entirely to Sisters in Crime, the organization certainly played a large part in the changing attitudes of the late 1980s. Editors seemed suddenly to realize that most mystery readers were women, and they preferred to read novels by other women. In the 1980s writers like Mary Higgins Clark, already on the best-seller lists, came to greater prominence with multi-book contracts. Marcia Muller made a series character out of her private eye Sharon McCone, launching a trend that soon included Sara Paretsky's V.I. Warshawski novels and the enormously successful Kinsey Millhone novels of Sue Grafton. American writers Martha Grimes and Elizabeth George began writing about traditional British detectives. On the American scene, in addition to those mentioned above, P. M. Carlson, Joan Hess, Wendy Hornsby, Sharyn McCrumb, Nancy Pickard, Carolyn Wheat and others added their own distinctive voices.

These were the major trends of the 1980s but not the only ones.

In 1987 Scott Turow's *Presumed Innocent* hit the best-seller lists big-time and the legal thriller was launched. There had been Randolph Mason and Perry Mason long before, but Turow added something new that modern writers hastened to emulate. Soon he was followed by John Grisham and the wave of courtroom crime tales became a flood. Likewise, serial killers had always been with us under one name or another, but the success of Thomas Harris's *Red Dragon* (1981) and especially *The Silence of the Lambs* (1988) helped launch another trend in books and films.

The mystery scene in Britain during the 1980s was quite a bit different. Certainly the mysteries and thrillers that climbed the best-seller lists in America often repeated their success across the ocean, but other factors were at work there. Prime among them was a revival of the classic detective story of the so-called Golden Age, mainly the 1930s, a trend which was given a substantial boost by the popularity of limited television series there. No less than three Agatha Christie series—Poirot, Miss Marple, and Tuppence & Tommy—found success there in the '80s. So did Dorothy L. Sayers's Lord Peter Wimsey, Ngaio Marsh's Roderick Alleyn, Margery Allingham's Albert Campion, and Doyle's Sherlock Holmes, the latter in a masterful interpretation by the late actor Jeremy Brett.

The television series brought renewed interest in the Golden Age novels about these detectives, and in modern sleuths whose novels soon joined them on the screen. Fine portrayals of P.D. James's Adam Dalgleish and Colin Dexter's Inspector Morse did much to enhance the popularity of the books. Ruth Rendell's Inspector Wexford and others joined the crowd, and Jonathan Gash's Lovejoy became so popular he graduated to a regular series after the novels had all been filmed. One popular legal figure, John Mortimer's barrister Horace Rumpole, was created primarily for television and went on to a successful career in books. All of these series were shown in America, but on public television and cable channels where their impact on book sales was less than in Britain.

It could be said with some truth that the best "new" British crime writer of the 1980s was Barbara Vine, a pseudonym of Ruth Rendell. Vine's first novel *A Dark-Adapted Eye* (1986) won the Edgar Award in America, while her second, *A Fatal Inversion* (1987) and her fifth, *King Solomon's Carpet* (1991), won the Gold Dagger Award in Britain.

During the 1980s, only the Mystery Writers of America presented mystery awards in this country each year. The winners of the best novel and best short story Edgars are as follows. In each case the actual award was presented in the spring of the following year.

Edgar Award for Best Novel
1980—Dick Francis, *Whip Hand*
1981—William Bayer, *Peregrine*
1982—Rick Boyer, *Billingsgate Shoal*
1983—Elmore Leonard, *La Brava*
1984—Ross Thomas, *Briarpatch*
1985—L.R. Wright, *The Suspect*
1986—Barbara Vine, *A Dark-Adapted Eye*
1987—Aaron Elkins, *Old Bones*
1988—Stuart M. Kaminsky, *A Cold Red Sunrise*
1989—James Lee Burke, *Black Cherry Blues*

Edgar Award for Best Short Story
1980—Clark Howard, "Horn Man"
1981—Jack Ritchie, "The Absence of Emily"
1982—Frederick Forsyth, "There Are No Snakes in Ireland"
1983—Ruth Rendell, "The New Girl Friend"
1984—Lawrence Block, "By Dawn's Early Light"
1985—John Lutz—"Ride the Lightning"
1986—Robert Sampson, "Rain in Pinton County"
1987—Harlan Ellison, "Soft Monkey"
1988—Bill Crenshaw, "Flicks"
1989—Donald E. Westlake, "Too Many Crooks"

Britain's Crime Writer's Association did not start giving a short story award until 1993. Listed here are winners of the Gold Dagger for Best Novel.

Gold Dagger Award
1980—H.R.F. Keating, *The Murder of the Maharajah*
1981—Martin Cruz Smith, *Gorky Park*
1982—Peter Lovesey, *The False Inspector Dew*
1983—John Hutton, *Accidental Crimes*
1984—B.M. Gill, *The Twelfth Juror*
1985—Paula Gosling, *Monkey Puzzle*
1986—Ruth Rendell, *Live Flesh*

1987—Barbara Vine, *A Fatal Inversion*
1988—Michael Dibdin, *Ratking*
1989—Colin Dexter, *The Wench Is Dead*

But enough of history! Here, for your enjoyment, are twenty-two of the best mystery and crime stories of the 1980s. (In the notes that follow, dates are those of first publication, whether in America or Britain.)

ISAAC ASIMOV

"The Good Samaritan"

Isaac Asimov was born in Petrovichi, Russia on January 2, 1920. He graduated from Columbia University in 1939 and received his Ph.D. in chemistry there in 1948, following service in the U.S. Army during World War II. Famed as a science fiction writer, Asimov first combined his s.f. writing with the detective story in 1954 with **The Caves of Steel** *about futuristic detective Elijah Baley and his robot assistant.*

Three more Baley novels followed, along with two mysteries set in the present, **The Death Dealers** *(1958) and* **Murder at the ABA** *(1976). Asimov's success as a mystery writer rests primarily on his short stories, the well-known Black Widowers series and the Griswold stories, along with a few stories about Dr. Wendell Urth and some non-series tales. Isaac Asimov died on April 6, 1992, one of the most prolific and popular of science fiction writers.*

Asimov's early mystery short stories are collected in **Asimov's Mysteries** *(1968). His Black Widower stories are collected in five volumes, 1974-1990, and the Griswold stories are to be found in* **The Union Club Mysteries** *(1983). The best one-volume collection is* **The Best Mysteries of Isaac Asimov** *(1986). "The Good Samaritan" was first published in* **Ellery Queen's Mystery Magazine** *and reprinted in* **The Big Apple Mysteries, Banquets of the Black Widowers, The Best Mysteries of Isaac Asimov,** *and* **Manhattan Mysteries***.*

The Good Samaritan

by Isaac Asimov

The Black Widowers had learned by hard experience that when Mario Gonzalo took his turn as host of the monthly banquet, they had to expect the unusual. They had reached the point where they steeled themselves, quite automatically, for disaster. When his guest arrived there was a lightening of spirit if it turned out he had the usual quota of heads and could speak at least broken English.

When the last of the Black Widowers arrived, therefore, and when Henry's efficient setting of the table was nearly complete, Geoffrey Avalon, standing, as always, straight and tall, sounded almost light-hearted as he said, "I see that your guest has not arrived yet, Mario."

Gonzalo, whose crimson velvet jacket and lightly striped blue pants reduced everything else in the room to monochrome, said, "Well—"

Avalon said, "What's more, a quick count of the settings placed at the table by our inestimable Henry shows that six people and no more are to be seated. And since all six of us are here, I can only conclude that you have not brought a guest."

"Thank Anacreon," said Emmanuel Rubin, raising his drink, "or whatever spirit it is that presides over convivial banquets of kindred souls."

Thomas Trumbull scowled and brushed back his crisply waved white hair with one hand. "What are you doing, Mario? Saving money?"

"Well—" said Gonzalo again, staring at his own drink with a totally spurious concentration.

Roger Halsted said, "I don't know that this is so good. I like the grilling sessions."

"It won't hurt us," said Avalon, in his deepest voice, "to have a quiet conversation once in a while. If we can't amuse each other without a guest, then the Black Widowers are not what once they were and we should prepare, sorrowing, for oblivion. Shall we offer Mario a vote of thanks for his unwonted discretion?"

"Well—" said Gonzalo a third time.

James Drake interposed, stubbing out a cigarette and clearing his throat. "It seems to me, gentlemen, that Mario is trying to say something and is amazingly bashful about it. If he has something he hesitates to say, I fear we are not going to like it. May I suggest we all keep quiet and let him talk."

"Well—" said Gonzalo, and stopped. This time, though, there was a prolonged silence.

"Well—" said Gonzalo again, "I *do* have a guest," and once more he stopped.

Rubin said, "Then where the hell is he?"

"Downstairs in the main dining room—ordering dinner—at my expense, of course."

Gonzalo received five blank stares. Then Trumbull said, "May I ask what dunderheaded reason you can possibly advance for that?"

"Aside," said Rubin, "from being a congenital dunderhead?"

Gonzalo put his drink down, took a deep breath, and said firmly, "Because I thought she would be more comfortable down there."

Rubin managed to get out an "And why—" before the significance of the pronoun became plain. He seized the lapels of Gonzalo's jacket, "Did you say '*she*'?"

Gonzalo caught at the other's wrist, "Hands off, Manny. If you want to talk, use your lips, not your hands. Yes, I said 'she.' "

Henry, his sixtyish, unlined face showing a little concern, raised his voice a diplomatic notch and said, "Gentlemen! Dinner is served!"

Rubin, having released Gonzalo, waved imperiously at Henry and said, "Sorry, Henry, there may be no banquet.—Mario, you damned jackass, *no woman can attend these meetings.*"

There was, in fact, a general uproar. While no one quite achieved the anger and decibels of Rubin, Gonzalo found himself at bay with the five others around him in a semicircle. Their individual comments were lost in the general explosion of anger.

Gonzalo, waving his arms madly, leaped onto a chair and shouted, "Let me speak!" over and over until out of exhaustion, it seemed, the opposition died off into a low growl.

Gonzalo said, "She is not our guest at the banquet. She's just a woman with a problem, an old woman, and it won't do us any harm if we see her *after* dinner."

There was no immediate response and Gonzalo said, "She needn't sit at the table. She can sit in the doorway."

Rubin said, "Mario, if she comes in here I go, and if I go, damn it, I may not ever come back."

Gonzalo said, "Are you saying you'll break up the Black Widowers rather than listen to an old woman in trouble?"

Rubin said, "I'm saying rules are *rules!*"

Halsted, looking deeply troubled, said, "Manny, maybe we ought to do this. The rules weren't delivered to us from Mount Sinai."

"You, too?" said Rubin savagely. "Look, it doesn't matter what any of you say. In a matter as fundamental as this, one blackball is enough, and I cast it. Either she goes or I go and, by God, you'll never see me again. In view of that, is there anyone who wants to waste his breath?"

Henry, who still stood at the head of the table, waiting with markedly less than his usual imperturbability for the company to be seated, said, "May I have a word, Mr. Rubin?"

Rubin said, "Sorry, Henry, no one sits down till this is settled."

Gonzalo said, "Stay out, Henry. I'll fight my own battles."

It was at this point that Henry departed from his role as the epitome of all Olympian waiters and advanced on the group. His voice was firm as he said, "Mr. Rubin, I wish to take responsibility for this. Several days ago Mr. Gonzalo phoned me to ask if I would be so kind as to listen to a woman he knew who had the kind of problem he thought I might be helpful with. I asked him if it were something close to his heart. He said that the woman was a relative of someone who was very likely to give him a commission for an important piece of work—"

"Money!" sneered Rubin.

"Professional opportunity," snapped Gonzalo. "If you can understand that. And sympathy for a fellow human being, if you can understand *that*."

Henry held up his hand.

"*Please*, gentlemen! I told Mr. Gonzalo I could not help him but urged him, if he had not already arranged a guest, to bring the woman. I suggested that there might be no objection if she did not actually attend the banquet itself."

Rubin said, "And why couldn't you help her otherwise?"

Henry said, "Gentlemen, I lay no claims to superior insight. I do not compare myself, as Mr. Gonzalo occasionally does on my behalf, to Sherlock Holmes. It is only after you gentlemen have discussed a problem and eliminated what is extraneous that I seem to see what remains. Therefore—"

Drake said, "Well, look, Manny, I'm the oldest member here, and the original reason for the prohibition. We might partially waive it just this once."

"No," said Rubin flatly.

Henry said, "Mr. Rubin, it is often stated at these banquets that I am a member of the Black Widowers. If so, I wish to take the responsibility. I urged Mr. Gonzalo to do this and I spoke to the woman concerned and assured her that she would be welcomed to our deliberations after dinner. It was an impulsive act based on my estimate of the characters of the gentlemen of the club.

"If the woman is now sent away, Mr. Rubin, you understand that my position here will be an impossible one and I will be forced to resign as waiter at these banquets. I would have no choice."

Almost imperceptibly the atmosphere had changed while Henry spoke and now it was Rubin who was standing at bay. He stared at the semicircle that now surrounded him and said, rather gratingly, "I appreciate your services to the club, Henry, and I do not wish to place you in a dishonorable position. Therefore, on the stipulation that this is not to set a precedent and reminding you that you must not do this again, I will withdraw my blackball."

The banquet was the least comfortable in the history of the Black Widowers. Conversation was desultory and dull and Rubin maintained a stony silence throughout.

There was no need to clatter the water glass during the serving of the coffee, since there was no babble of conversation to override. Gonzalo simply said, "I'll go down and see if she's ready. Her name, by the way, is Mrs. Barbara Lindemann."

Rubin looked up and said, "Make sure she's had her coffee, or tea, or whatever, downstairs. She can't have anything up here."

Avalon looked disapproving. "The dictates of courtesy, my dear Manny—"

"She'll have all she wants downstairs at Mario's expense. Up here we'll listen to her. What more can she want?"

Gonzalo brought her up and led her to an armchair that Henry had obtained from the restaurant office and that he had placed well away from the table.

She was a rather thin woman, with blunt good-natured features, well dressed and with her white hair carefully set. She carried a black purse that looked new and she clutched it tightly. She glanced timidly at the faces of the Black Widowers and said, "Good evening."

There was a low chorused rumble in return and she said, "I apologize for coming here with my ridiculous story. Mr. Gonzalo explained that my appearance here is out of the ordinary and I have thought, over my dinner, that I should not disturb you. I will go if you like, and thank you for the dinner and for letting me come up here."

She made as though to rise and Avalon, looking remarkably shamefaced, said, "Madame, you are entirely welcome here and we would like very much to hear what you have to say. We cannot promise that we will be able to help you, but we can try. I'm sure that we all feel the same way about this. Don't you agree, Manny?"

Rubin shot a dark look at Avalon through his thick-lensed glasses. His sparse beard bristled and his chin lifted but he said in a remarkably mild tone, "Entirely, ma'am."

There was a short pause, and then Gonzalo said, "It's our custom, Mrs. Lindemann, to question our guests and under the circumstances, I wonder if you would mind having Henry handle that. He is our waiter, but he is a member of our group."

Henry stood motionless for a moment, then said, "I fear, Mr. Gonzalo, that—"

Gonzalo said, "You have yourself claimed the privilege of membership earlier this evening, Henry. Privilege carries with it responsibility. Put down the brandy bottle, Henry, and sit down. Anyone who wants brandy can take his own. Here, Henry, take my seat." Gonzalo rose resolutely and walked to the sideboard.

Henry sat down and said mildly to Mrs. Lindemann, "Madame, would you be willing to pretend you are on the witness stand?"

The woman looked about and her look of uneasiness dissolved

into a little laugh. "I never have been and I'm not sure I know how to behave on one. I hope you won't mind if I'm nervous."

"We won't, but you needn't be. This will be very informal and we are anxious only to help you. The members of the club have a tendency to speak loudly and excitably at times, but if they do, that is merely their way and means nothing.—First, please tell us your name."

She said, with an anxious formality, "My name is Barbara Lindemann. Mrs. Barbara Lindemann."

"And do you have any particular line of work?"

"No, sir, I am retired. I am sixty-seven years old as you can probably tell by looking at me—and a widow. I was once a schoolteacher at a junior high school."

Halsted stirred and said, "That's my profession, Mrs. Lindemann. What subject did you teach?"

"Mostly I taught American history."

Henry said, "Now, from what Mr. Gonzalo has told me, you suffered an unpleasant experience here in New York and—"

"No, pardon me," interposed Mrs. Lindemann, "it was, on the whole, a very pleasant experience. If that weren't so, I would be only too glad to forget all about it."

"Yes, of course," said Henry, "but I am under the impression that you *have* forgotten some key points and would like to remember them."

"Yes," she said earnestly. "I am so ashamed at not remembering. It must make me appear senile, but it was a very *unusual* and *frightening* thing in a way—at least parts of it were—and I suppose that's my excuse."

Henry said, "I think it would be best, then, if you tell us what happened to you in as much detail as you can, and if it will not bother you, some of us may ask questions as you go along."

"It won't bother me, I assure you," said Mrs. Lindemann. "I'll welcome it as a sign of interest. I arrived in New York City nine days ago—from the West Coast. I was going to visit my niece, among other things, but I didn't want to stay with her. That would have been uncomfortable for her and confining for me, so I took a hotel room.

"I got to the hotel at about six P.M. on Wednesday and after a small dinner, which was very pleasant, although the prices were simply awful, I phoned my niece and arranged to see her the next day when her husband would be at work and the children at school. That would give us some time to ourselves and then in the evening we could have a family outing.

"Of course, I didn't intend to hang about their necks the entire two weeks I was to be in New York. I fully intended to do things on my own. In fact, that first evening after dinner, I had nothing particular to do and I certainly didn't want to sit in my room and watch television. So I thought—well, all Manhattan is just outside, Barbara, and you've read about it all your life and seen it in the movies and now's your chance to see it in real life.

"I thought I'd just step out and wander about on my own and look at the elaborate buildings and the bright lights and the people hurrying past. I just wanted to get a *feel* of the city, before I started taking organized tours. I've done that in other cities in these recent years when I've been traveling and I've always so enjoyed it."

Trumbull said, "You weren't afraid of getting lost, I suppose."

"Oh, *no*," said Mrs. Lindemann. "I have an excellent sense of direction and even if I were caught up in my sightseeing and didn't notice where I had gone, I had a map of Manhattan and the streets are all in a rectangular grid and numbered—not like Boston, London, or Paris, and I was never lost in those cities. Besides, I could always get in a taxi and give the driver the name of my hotel. Besides, I was sure anyone would give me directions if I asked."

Rubin emerged from his trough of despond to deliver himself of a ringing, "In Manhattan? Hah!"

"Why, certainly," said Mrs. Lindemann, with mild reproof. "I've always heard that Manhattanites are unfriendly, but I have not found it so. I have been the recipient of many kindnesses—not the least of which is the manner in which you gentlemen have welcomed me even though I am quite a stranger to you."

Rubin found it necessary to stare intently at his fingernails.

Mrs. Lindemann said, "In any case, I did go off on my little excursion and stayed out much longer than I had planned. Everything was so colorful and busy and the weather was so mild and pleasant. Eventually, I realized I was terribly tired and I had reached a rather quiet street and was ready to go back. I looked in one of the outer pockets of my purse for my map—"

Halsted interrupted. "I take it, Mrs. Lindemann, you were alone on this excursion."

"Oh, yes," said Mrs. Lindemann. "I always travel alone since my husband died. To have a companion means a perpetual state of compromise as to when to arise, what to eat, where to go. No, no, I want to be my own woman."

"I didn't mean quite that, Mrs. Lindemann," said Halsted. "I mean to ask whether you were alone on this particular outing in a strange city—at night—with a purse."

"Yes, sir, I'm afraid so."

Halsted said, "Had no one told you that the streets of New York aren't always safe at night—particularly, excuse me, for older women with purses who look, as you do, gentle and harmless?"

"Oh, dear, of *course* I've been told that. I've been told that of every city I've visited. My own town has districts that aren't safe. I've always felt, though, that all life is a gamble, that a no-risk situation is an impossible dream, and I wasn't going to deprive myself of pleasant experiences because of fear. And I've gone about in all sorts of places without harm."

Trumbull said, "Until that first evening in Manhattan, I take it."

Mrs. Lindemann's lips tightened and she said, "Until then. It was an experience I remember only in flashes, so to speak. I suppose that because I was so tired, and then so frightened, and the surroundings were so new to me, that much of what happened somehow didn't register properly. Little things seem to have vanished forever. That's the problem." She bit her lips and looked as though she were battling to hold back the tears.

Henry said softly, "Could you tell us what you remember?"

"Well," she said, clearing her throat and clutching at her purse, "as I said, the street was a quiet one. There were cars moving past, but no pedestrians, and I wasn't sure where I was. I was reaching for the map and looking about for a street sign when a young man seemed to appear from nowhere and said, 'Got a dollar, lady?' He couldn't have been more than fifteen years old—just a boy.

"Well, I would have been perfectly willing to let him have a dollar if I thought he needed it, but really, he seemed perfectly fit and reasonably prosperous and I didn't think it would be advisable to display my wallet, so I said, 'I'm afraid I don't, young man.'

"Of course, he didn't believe me. He came closer and said, 'Sure you do, lady. Here, let me help you look,' and he reached for my purse. Well, I wasn't going to let him have it, of course—"

Trumbull said firmly, "No 'of course' about it, Mrs. Lindemann. If it ever happens again, you surrender your purse at once. You can't save it in any case. Hoodlums think nothing of using force and there's nothing in a purse that can be worth your life."

Mrs. Lindemann sighed. "I suppose you're right, but at the time I just wasn't thinking clearly. I held on to my purse as a reflex action, I suppose, and that's when I start failing to remember. I recall engaging in a tug of war and I seem to recall other young men approaching. I don't know how many but I seemed surrounded.

"Then I heard a shout and some very bad language and the loud noise of feet. There was nothing more for a while except that my purse was gone. Then there was an anxious voice, low and polite, saying, 'Are you hurt, madam?'

"I said, 'I don't think so, but my purse is gone.' I looked about vaguely. I think I was under the impression it had fallen to the street.

"There was an older young man holding my elbow respectfully. He might have been twenty-five. He said, 'They got that, ma'am. I'd better get you out of here before they come back for some more fun. They'll probably have knives and I don't.'

"He was hurrying me away. I didn't see him clearly in the dark but he was tall and wore a sweater. He said, 'I live close by, ma'am. It's either go to my place or we'll have a battle.' I *think* I was aware of other young men in the distance, but that may have been a delusion.

"I went with the new young man quite docilely. He seemed earnest and polite and I've gotten too old to feel that I am in danger of—uh—*personal* harm. Besides, I was so confused and light-headed that I lacked any will to resist.

"The next thing I remember is being at his apartment door. I remember that it was apartment 4-F. I suppose that remains in my mind because it was such a familiar combination during World War II. Then I was inside his apartment and sitting in an upholstered armchair. It was a rather rundown apartment, I noticed, but I don't remember getting to it at all.

"The man who had rescued me had put a glass into my hand and I sipped from it. It was some kind of wine, I think. I did not particularly like the taste, but it warmed me and it seemed to make me less dizzy—rather than more dizzy, as one would suppose.

"The man appeared to be anxious about my possibly being hurt, but I reassured him. I said if he would just help me get a taxi I would get to my hotel.

"He said I had better rest a while. He offered to call the police to report the incident, but I was adamant against that. That's one of the things I remember *very* clearly. I knew the police were not likely to recover my purse and I did *not* want to become a newspaper item.

"I think I must have explained that I was from out of town because he lectured me, quite gently, on the dangers of walking on the streets of Manhattan.—I've heard so much on the subject in the last week. You should hear my niece go on and on about it.

"I remember other bits of the conversation. He wanted to know whether I'd lost much cash and I said, well, about thirty or forty dollars, but that I had traveler's checks which could, of course, be replaced. I think I had to spend some time reassuring him that I knew how to do that, and that I knew how to report my missing credit card. I had only had one in my purse.

"Finally I asked him his name so that I could speak to him properly and he laughed and said, 'Oh, first names will do for that.' He told me his and I told him mine. And I said, 'Isn't it astonishing how it all fits together, your name, and your address, and what you said back there.' I explained and he laughed and said he would never have thought of that.—So you see I knew his address.

"Then we went downstairs and it was quite late by then, at least by the clock, though, of course, it wasn't really very late by my insides. He made sure the streets were clear, then made me wait in the vestibule while he went out to hail the cab. He told me he had paid the driver to take me wherever I wanted to go and then before I could stop him he put a twenty-dollar bill in my hand because he said I mustn't be left with no money at all.

"I tried to object, but he said he loved New York, and since I had been so mistreated on my first evening there by New Yorkers, it had to be made up for by New Yorkers. So I accepted it—because I knew I would pay it back.

"The driver took me back to the hotel and he didn't try to collect any money. He even tried to give me change because he said the young man had given him a five-dollar bill, but I was pleased with his honesty and I wouldn't take the change.

"So you see although the incident began very painfully, there was the extreme kindness of the Good Samaritan young man and of the taxi driver. It was as though an act of unkindness was introduced into my life in order that I might experience other acts of kindness that would more than redress the balance. And I *still* experience them—yours, I mean.

"Of course, it was quite obvious that the young man was not well off and I strongly suspected that the twenty-five dollars he had expended on me was far more than he could afford to throw away. Nor did he ask my last name or the name of my hotel. It was as though he knew I would pay it back without having to be reminded. Naturally, I would.

"You see, I'm quite well-to-do really, and it's not just a matter of paying it back. The Bible says that if you cast your bread upon the waters it will be returned tenfold, so I think it's only fair that if he spent twenty-five dollars, he ought to get two hundred and fifty back, and I can afford it.

"I returned to my room and slept so soundly after all that; it was quite refreshing. The next morning, I arranged my affairs with respect to the credit card and the traveler's checks and then I called my niece and spent the day with her.

"I told her what had happened but just the bare essentials. After all, I had to explain why I had no bag and why I was temporarily short of cash. She went on and *on* about it. I bought a new purse—this one—and it wasn't till the end of the day when I was in bed again that I realized that I had not made it my business to repay the young man *first thing*. Being with family had just preoccupied me. And then the real tragedy struck me."

Mrs. Lindemann stopped and tried to keep her face from crumpling, but she failed. She began to weep quietly and to reach desperately into her bag for a handkerchief.

Henry said softly, "Would you care to rest, Mrs. Lindemann?"

Rubin said, just as softly, "Would you like a cup of tea, Mrs. Lindemann, or some brandy?" Then he glared about as though daring anyone to say a word.

Mrs. Lindemann said, "No, I'm all right. I apologize for behaving so, but I found I had forgotten. I don't remember the young man's address, *not at all*, though I must have known it that night because I talked about it. I don't remember his first name! I stayed awake all night trying to remember, and that just made it worse. I went out the next day to try to retrace my steps, but everything looked so different by day—and by night, I was afraid to try.

"What must the young man think of me? He's never heard from me. I took his money and just vanished with it. I am worse than those terrible young hoodlums who snatched my purse. I had never been kind to *them*. They owed *me* no gratitude."

Gonzalo said, "It's not your fault that you can't remember. You had a rough time."

"Yes, but *he* doesn't know I can't remember. He thinks I'm an ungrateful thief. Finally I told my nephew about my trouble and he was just thinking of employing Mr. Gonzalo for something and he felt that Mr. Gonzalo might have the kind of worldly wisdom that might help. Mr. Gonzalo said he would try, and in the end—well, here I am.

"But now that I've heard myself tell the story I realize how hopeless it all sounds."

Trumbull sighed.

"Mrs. Lindemann, please don't be offended at what I am about to ask, but we must eliminate some factors. Are you sure it all really happened?"

Mrs. Lindemann looked surprised, "Well, of *course* it really happened. My purse was *gone!*"

"No," said Henry, "what Mr. Trumbull means, I think, is that after the mugging you somehow got back to the hotel and then had a sleep that may have been filled with nightmares so that what you remember now is partly fact and partly dream—which would account for the imperfect memory."

"No," said Mrs. Lindemann firmly, "I remember what I do remember perfectly. It was not a dream."

"In that case," said Trumbull, shrugging, "we have very little to go on."

Rubin said, "Never mind, Tom. We're not giving up. If we choose the right name for your rescuer, Mrs. Lindemann, would you recognize it, even though you can't remember it now?"

"I hope so," said Mrs. Lindemann, "but I don't know. I've tried looking in a phone directory to see different first names, but none seemed familiar. I don't think it could have been a very common name."

Rubin said, "Then it couldn't have been Sam?"

"Oh, I'm certain that's not it."

"Why Sam, Manny?" asked Gonzalo.

"Well, the fellow was a Good Samaritan. Mrs. Lindemann called him that herself. Sam for Samaritan. His number and street may have represented the chapter and verse in the Bible where the tale of the Good Samaritan begins. You said his name and address fitted each other and that's the only clue we have."

"Wait," put in Avalon eagerly, "the first name might have been the much less common one of Luke. That's the gospel in which the parable is to be found."

"I'm afraid," said Mrs. Lindemann, "that doesn't sound right, either. Besides, I'm not *that* well acquainted with the Bible. I couldn't identify the chapter and verse of the parable."

Halsted said, "Let's not get off on impossible tangents. Mrs. Lindemann taught American history in school, so it's very likely that what struck her concerned American history. For instance, suppose the address were 1812 Madison Avenue and the young man's name was James.—James Madison was President during the War of 1812."

"Or 1492 Columbus Avenue," said Gonzalo, "and the young man was named Christopher."

"Or 1775 Lexington Avenue and the name Paul for Paul Revere," said Trumbull.

"Or 1623 Amsterdam Avenue and the name Peter," said Avalon, "for Peter Minuit, or 1609 Hudson Street and the name Henry. In fact, there are many such named streets in lower Manhattan. We can never pick an appropriate one unless Mrs. Lindemann remembers."

Mrs. Lindemann clasped her hands tightly together. "Oh, dear, oh, *dear*, nothing sounds familiar."

Rubin said, "Of course not, if we're going to guess at random. Mrs. Lindemann, I assume you are at a midtown hotel."

"I'm at the New York Hilton. Is that midtown?"

"Yes. Sixth Avenue and 53rd Street. The chances are you could not have walked more than a mile, probably less, before you grew tired. Therefore, let's stick to midtown. Hudson Street is much too far south and places like 1492 Columbus or 1812 Madison are much too far north. It would have to be midtown, probably West Side—and I can't think of anything."

Drake said, through a haze of cigarette smoke, "You're forgetting one item. Mrs. Lindemann said it wasn't just the name and address that fit but what the young man said back there—that is, at the site of the rescue. What did he say back there?"

"It's all so hazy," said Mrs. Lindemann.

"You said he called out roughly at the muggers. Can you repeat what he said?"

Mrs. Lindemann colored. "I could repeat *some* of what he said, but I don't think I want to. The young man apologized for it afterward. He said that unless he used bad language the hoodlums would not have been impressed and would not have scattered. Besides, I know I couldn't have referred to *that* at all."

Drake said thoughtfully, "That bites the dust than. Have you thought of advertising? You know, 'Will the young man who aided a woman in distress—' and so on."

"I've thought of it," said Mrs. Lindemann, "but that would be *so* dreadful. He might not see it and so many impostors might try to make a claim.—Really, this is so dreadful."

Avalon, looking distressed, turned to Henry and said, "Well, Henry, does anything occur to you?"

Henry said, "I'm not certain.—Mrs. Lindemann, you said that by the time you took the taxi it was late by the clock but not by your insides. Does that mean you arrived from the West Coast by plane so that your perception of time was three hours earlier?"

"Yes, I did," said Mrs. Lindemann.

"Perhaps from Portland, or not too far from there?" asked Henry.

"Why, yes, from just outside of Portland. Had I mentioned that?"

"No, you hadn't," interposed Trumbull. "How did you know, Henry?"

"Because it occurred to me, sir," said Henry, "that the young man's name was Eugene, which is the name of a town only about a hundred miles south of Portland."

Mrs. Lindemann rose, eyes staring. "My goodness! The name *was* Eugene! But that's marvelous. How could you possibly tell?"

Henry said, "Mr. Rubin pointed out the address had to be in mid-town Manhattan on the West Side. Dr. Drake pointed out your reference to what the young man had said at the scene of the rescue, and I recalled that one thing you reported him to have said was that you had better go to his place or there'd be a battle.

"Mr. Halsted pointed out that the address ought to have some significance in American history and so I thought it might be 54 West 40th Street, since there is the well-known election slogan of '54-40 or fight,' the election of 1844, I believe. It would be particularly meaningful to Mrs. Lindemann if she were from the Northwest since it pertained to our dispute with Great Britain over the Oregon Territory. When she said she was indeed from near Portland, Oregon, I guessed that the rescuer's name might be Eugene."

Mrs. Lindemann sat down, "To my dying day I will never forget this. That *is* the address. How could I have forgotten it when you worked it out so neatly from what little I did remember?"

And then she grew excited. She said, "But it's not too late. I must go there *at once*. I must pay him or shove an envelope under his door or something."

Rubin said, "Will you recognize the house if you see it?"

"Oh, yes," said Mrs. Lindemann. "I'm sure of that. And it's apartment 4-F. I remembered that. If I knew his last name, I would call, but, no, I want to *see* him and explain."

Rubin said mildly, "You certainly can't go yourself, Mrs. Lindemann. Not into that neighborhood at this time of night after what you've been through. Some of us will have to go with you. At the very least, I will."

Mrs. Lindemann said, "I very much dislike inconveniencing you, sir."

"Under the circumstances, Mrs. Lindemann," said Rubin, "I consider it my duty."

Henry said, "If I know the Black Widowers, I believe we will all accompany you, Mrs. Lindemann."

PETER LOVESEY

"A Man With a Fortune"

Peter Lovesey was born in Whitton, Middlesex, England on September 10, 1936. He graduated from the University of Reading at Berkshire in 1958 and served as an Education Officer in the Royal Air Force. He lectured in English at Thurrock Technical College and later served as head of the General Education Department at Hammersmith College for Further Education.

In 1970 Lovesey's first book **Wobble to Death** *won a contest as the best crime novel by a new writer, and his mystery career was launched. His first eight novels were successful Victorian mysteries about Sergeant Cribb and Constable Thackery, later televised. Feeling a change of scene was needed, he moved on to* **The False Inspector Dew** *(1982), set aboard the liner Mauretania in 1921 and winner of CWA's Gold Dagger award. Some novels that followed were non-series, like the Edgar-nominated* **Rough Cider** *(1987). Others dealt with Bertie, the future King Edward VII. Lovesey's most successful series character since the Victorian novels has been Peter Diamond, a modern police detective in the city of Bath. There have been four Diamond novels to date, notably* **The Last Detective** *(1991), winner of the Anthony Award, and* **The Summons** *(1995), winner of the CWA Silver Dagger and an Edgar nominee.*

Lovesey's short stories have been collected in **Butchers and Other Stories of Crime** *(1985) and* **The Crime of Miss Oyster Brown** *and Other Stories (1994). An uncollected story, "The Pushover," won first prize in a contest marking the 50th anniversary of Mystery Writers of America in 1995. "A Man With a Fortune" was published in* **Ellery Queen's Mystery Magazine** *and reprinted in* **Best Detective Stories of the Year-1981, Ellery Queen's Media Favorites** *and* **Criminal Elements***.*

A Man With a Fortune

By Peter Lovesey

M ost of the passengers were looking to the right, treating themselves to the breath-catching view of San Francisco Bay the captain of the 747 had invited them to enjoy. Not Eva. Her eyes were locked on the lighted NO SMOKING sign and the order to fasten seatbelts. Until that was switched off she could not think of relaxing. She knew the takeoff was the most dangerous part of the flight, and it was a delusion to think you were safe the moment the plane was airborne. She refused to be distracted. She would wait for the proof that the takeoff had been safely accomplished: the switching off of that small, lighted sign.

"Your first time?" The man on her left spoke with a West Coast accent. She had sensed that he had been waiting to speak since they took their seats, darting glances her way. Probably he was just friendly like most San Franciscans she had met on the trip, but she couldn't possibly start a conversation now.

Without turning, she mouthed a negative.

"I mean your first time to England," he went on. "Anyone can see you've flown before, the way you put your hand luggage under the seat before they even asked us, and fixed your belt. I just wondered if this is your first trip to England."

She didn't want to seem ungracious. He was obviously trying to put her at ease. She smiled at the NO SMOKING sign and nodded. It was, after all, her first flight in this direction. The fact that she was English and had just been on a business trip to California was too much to explain.

"Mine, too," he said. "I've promised myself this for years. My people came from England, you see, forty, fifty years back. All dead now, the old folk. I'm the only one of my family left, and I ain't so fit myself." He planted his hand on his chest. "Heart condition."

Eva gave a slight start as an electronic signal sounded, and the light went off on the panel she was watching. A stewardess's voice announced that seatbelts could be unfastened and it was now permissible to smoke in the seats reserved for smoking, to the right of the cabin. Eva closed her eyes a moment and felt the tension ease.

"The doctor says I could go any time," her companion continued. "I could have six months or six years. You know how old I am? Forty-two. When you hear something like that at my age it kind of changes your priorities. I figured I should do what I always promised myself—go to England and see if I had any people left over there. So here I am, and I feel like a kid again. Terrific."

She smiled, mainly from the sense of release from her anxiety at the takeoff, but also at the discovery that the man she was seated beside was as generous and open in expression as he was in conversation. In no way was he a predatory male. She warmed to him—his shining blue eyes in a round, tanned face topped with a patch of hair like cropped corn, his small hands holding tight to the armrests, his Levi shirt bulging over the seatbelt he had not troubled to unclasp. "Are you on a vacation too?" he asked.

She felt able to respond now. "Actually I live in England."

"You're English? How about that!" He made it sound like one of the more momentous discoveries of his life, oblivious that there must have been at least a hundred Britons on the flight. "You've been on vacation to California, and now you're traveling home?"

There was a ten-hour flight ahead of them, and Eva's innately shy personality flinched at the prospect of an extended conversation, but the man's candor deserved an honest reply. "Not exactly a vacation. I work in the electronics industry. My company wants to make a big push in the production of microcomputers. They sent me to see the latest developments in your country."

"Around Santa Clara?"

"That's right," said Eva, surprised that he should know. "Are you by any chance in electronics?"

He laughed. "No, I'm just one of the locals. The place is known as Silicon Valley, did you know that? I'm in farming, and I take an interest in the way the land is used. Excuse me for saying this:

You're pretty young to be representing your company on a trip like this."

"Not so young really. I'm twenty-eight." But she understood his reaction. She herself had been amazed when the Director of Research had called her into his office and asked her to make the trip. Some of her colleagues were equally astonished. The most incredulous was her flatmate, Janet—suave, sophisticated Janet, who was on the editorial side at the *Sunday Telegraph*, and had been on assignments to Dublin, Paris, and Geneva, and was always telling Eva how deadly dull it was to be confined to an electronics lab.

"I wish I were twenty-eight," said her fellow traveler. "That was the year I was married. Patty was a wonderful wife to me. We had some great times."

He paused in a way that begged Eva's next question. "Something went wrong?"

"She went missing three years back. Just disappeared. No note, nothing. I came home one night and she was gone."

"That's terrible."

"It broke me up. There was no accounting for it. We were very happily married."

"Did you tell the police?"

"Yes, but they have hundreds of missing persons in their files. They got nowhere. I have to presume she's dead. Patty was happy with me. We had a beautiful home and more money than we could spend. I own two vineyards—big ones. We had grapes in California before silicon chips, you know."

She smiled, and as it seemed that he didn't want to speak anymore about his wife she said, "People try to grow grapes in England, but you wouldn't think much of them. When I left London the temperature was in the low fifties, and that's our so-called summer."

"I'm not interested in the weather. I just want to find the place where all the records of births, marriages, and deaths are stored, so I can find if I have any family left."

Eva understood now. This was not just the trip to England to acquire a few generations of ancestors and a family coat of arms. Here was a desperately lonely man. He had lost his wife and abandoned hope of finding her. But he was still searching for someone he could call his own. "Would that be Somerset House?"

His question broke through her thoughts.

"Yes. That is to say, I think the records are kept now in a building in Kingsway, just a few minutes' walk from there. If you asked at Somerset House, they'd tell you."

"And is it easy to look someone up?"

"It should be, if you have names and dates."

"I figured I'd start with my grandfather. He was born in a village called Edgecombe in Dorset in 1868, and he had three older brothers. Their names were Matthew, Mark, and Luke, and I'm offering no prize for guessing what Grandfather was called. My pa was given the same name and so was I. Each of us was an only child. I'd like to find out if any of Grandfather's brothers got married and had families. If they did, it's possible that I have some second cousins alive somewhere. Do you think I could get that information?"

"Well, it should all be there somewhere," said Eva.

"Does it take long?"

"That's up to you. You have to find the names in the index first. That can take some time, depending how common the name is. Unfortunately, they're not computerized. You just have to work through the lists."

"You're serious?"

"Absolutely. There are hundreds of enormous bound books full of names."

For the first time in the flight, his brow creased into a frown.

"Is something wrong?" asked Eva.

"Just that my name happens to be Smith."

Janet thought it was hilarious when Eva told her. "All those Smiths! How long has he got, for heaven's sake?"

"Here in England? Three weeks, I think."

"He could spend the whole time working through the index and still get nowhere. Darling, have you ever been there? The scale of the thing beggars description. I bet he gives up on the first day."

"Oh, I don't think he will. This is very important to him."

"Whatever for? Does he hope to get a title out of it? Lord Smith of San Francisco?"

"I told you. He's alone in the world. His wife disappeared. And he has a weak heart. He expects to die soon."

"Probably when he tries to lift one of those index volumes off the shelf," said Janet. "He must be out of his mind." She could never fathom why other people didn't conform to her ideas of the way life should be conducted.

"He's no fool," said Eva. "He owns two vineyards, and in California that's big business."

"A rich man?" There was a note of respect in Janet's voice.

"Very."

"That begins to make sense. He wants his fortune to stay in the family—if he has one."

"He didn't say that, exactly."

"Darling, it's obvious. He's over here to find his people and see if he likes them enough to make them his beneficiaries." Her lower lip pouted in a way that was meant to be amusing, but might have been involuntary.

"Two vineyards in California! Someone stands to inherit all that and doesn't know a thing about it!"

"If he finds them," said Eva. "From what you say, the chance is quite remote."

"Just about impossible, the way he's going about it. You say he's starting with the grandfather and his three brothers, and hoping to draw up a family tree. It sounds beautiful in theory, but it's a lost cause. I happen to know a little about this sort of thing. When I was at Oxford I got involved in organizing an exhibition to commemorate Thomas Hughes—*Tom Brown's Schooldays*, right? I volunteered to try to find his descendants, just to see if they had any unpublished correspondence or photographs in the family. It seemed a marvelous idea at the time, but it was hopeless. I did the General Register Office bit, just like your American, and discovered you simply cannot trace people that way. You can work backward if you know the names and ages of the present generation, but it's practically impossible to do it in reverse. That was with a name like Hughes. Imagine the problems with the name Smith!"

Eva could see Janet was right. She pictured John Smith III at his impossible task and was touched with pity. "There must be some other way he could do it."

Janet grinned. "Like working through the phonebook, ringing up all the Smiths?"

"I feel really bad about this. I encouraged him."

"Darling, you couldn't have done anything else. If this was the guy's only reason for making the trip, you couldn't tell him to abandon it before the plane touched down at Heathrow. Who knows—

he might have incredible luck and actually chance on the right name."

"That *would* be incredible."

Janet took a sip of the California wine Eva had brought back as duty free. "Actually, there is another way."

"What's that?"

"Through parish records. He told you his grandfather was born somewhere in Dorset?"

"Edgecombe."

"And the four brothers were named after the gospel writers, so it's a good bet they were Church of England. Did all the brothers live in Edgecombe?"

"I think so."

"Then it's easy! Start with the baptisms. When was the grandfather born?"

"1868."

"Right. Look up the Edgecombe baptisms for 1868. There can't be so many John Smiths in a small Dorset village. You'll get the father's name in the register—he signs it, you see—and then you can start looking through other years for the brothers' entries. That's only the beginning. There are the marriage registers and the banns. If the Edgecombe register doesn't have them, they could be in an adjoining parish."

"Hold on, Janet. You're talking as if I'm going off to Dorset myself."

Janet's eyes shone. "Eva, you don't need to go there. The Society of Genealogists in Kensington has copies of thousands of parish registers. Anyone can go there and pay a fee for a few hours in the library. I've got the address somewhere." She got up and went to her bookshelf.

"Don't bother," said Eva. "It's John Smith who needs the information, not me, and I wouldn't know how to find him now. He didn't tell me where he's staying. Even if I knew, I'd feel embarrassed getting in contact again. It was just a conversation on a plane."

"Eva, I despair of you. When it comes to the point, you're so deplorably shy. I can tell you exactly where to find him: in the General Register Office in Kingsway, working through the Smiths. He'll be there for the next three weeks if someone doesn't help him out."

"Meaning me?"

"No, I can see it's not your scene. Let's handle this another way.

Tomorrow I'll take a long lunch break and pop along to the Society of Genealogists to see if they have a copy of the parish registers for Edgecombe. If they haven't, or there's no mention of the Smith family, we'll forget the whole thing."

"And if you *do* find something?"

"Then we'll consider what to do next." Casually, Janet added, "You know, I wouldn't mind telling him myself."

"But you don't know him."

"You could tell me what he looks like."

"How would you introduce yourself?"

"Eva, you're so stuffy! It's easy in a place like that where everyone is shoulder to shoulder at the indexes."

"You make it sound like a cocktail bar."

"Better."

Eva couldn't help smiling.

"Besides," said Janet. "I do have something in common with him. My mother's maiden name was Smith."

The search rooms of the General Register Office were filled with the steady sound of index volumes being lifted from the shelves, deposited on the reading tables, and then returned. There was an intense air of industry as the searchers worked up and down the columns of names, stopping only to note some discovery that usually was marked by a moment of reflection, followed by redoubled activity.

Janet had no trouble recognizing John Smith. He was where she expected to find him: at the indexes of births for 1868. He was the reader with one volume open in front of him that he had not exchanged in ten minutes. Probably not all morning. His stumpy right hand, wearing three gold rings, checked the rows of Victorian copperplate at a rate appropriate to a marathon effort. But when he turned a page he shook his head and sighed.

Eva had described him accurately enough without really conveying the total impression he made on Janet. Yes, he was short and slightly overweight, and his hair was cut to within a half inch of his scalp; yet he had a teddy-bear quality that would definitely help Janet to be warm toward him. Her worry had been that he would be too pitiable.

She waited for the person next to him to return a volume then moved to his side, put down the notebook she had brought, and asked him, "Would you be so kind as to keep my place while I look for a missing volume? I think someone must have put it back in the wrong place."

He looked up, quite startled to be addressed. "Why, sure."

Janet thanked him and walked round to the next row of shelves.

In a few minutes she was back. "I can't find it, I must have spent twenty minutes looking for it, and my lunch hour will be over soon."

He kept his finger against the place of birth he had reached and said, "Maybe I could help. Which one are you looking for, miss?"

"Could you? It's P-to-S for the second quarter of 1868."

"*Really*? I happen to have it right here."

"Oh, I didn't realize—" Janet managed to blush a little.

"Please." He slid the book in front of her. "Go ahead—I have all day for this. Your time is more valuable than mine."

"Well, thank you." She turned a couple of pages. "Oh dear, this is going to be much more difficult than I imagined. Why did my mother have to be born with a name as common as Smith?"

"Your name is Smith?" He beamed at the discovery, then nodded. "I guess it's not such a coincidence."

"My mother's name actually. I'm Janet Murdoch."

"John Smith." He held out his hand. "I'm a stranger here myself, but if I can help in any way—"

Janet said, "I'm interested in tracing my ancestors, but looking at this I think I'd better give up. My great-grandfather's name was Matthew Smith, and there are pages and pages of them. I'm not even sure of the year he was born. It was either 1868 or 1869."

"Do you know the place he was born?"

"Somewhere in Dorset. Wait, I've got it written here." She opened the notebook to the page where she had made her notes at the Society of Genealogists. "Edgecombe."

"May I see that?" John Smith held it and his hand shook. "Janet, I'm going to tell you something that you'll find hard to believe."

He took her to lunch at the Wig and Pen. It tested her nerve as he questioned her about Matthew Smith of Edgecombe, but she was well prepared. She said she knew there had been four brothers, but she was deliberately vague about their names. Two, she said, had married, and she was the solitary survivor of Matthew's line.

John Smith ate very little lunch. Most of the time, he sat staring at Janet and grinning. He was very like a teddy bear. She found it pleasing at first, because it seemed to show he was a little light-headed at the surprise she had served him, but as the meal went on it made her feel slightly uneasy, as if he had something in mind that she hadn't foreseen.

"I have an idea," he said just before they got up to leave, "only I hope you won't get me wrong, Janet. What I would like is to go out to Dorset at the weekend and find Edgecombe, and have you come with me. Maybe we could locate the church and see if they still have a record of our people. *Would* you come with me?"

It suited her perfectly. The parish registers would confirm everything she had copied at the Society of Genealogists. Any doubts John Smith might have of her integrity would be removed. And if her information on the Smiths of Edgecombe was shown to be correct, no suspicion need arise that she was not related to them at all. John Smith would accept her as his sole surviving relative. He would return to California in three weeks with his quest accomplished. And sooner or later Janet would inherit two vineyards and a fortune.

"It's a wonderful idea!" she said, "I'll be delighted to come."

Nearly a fortnight passed before Eva started to be anxious about Janet's absence. Once or twice before she had gone away on assignments for the newspaper without saying she was going. Eva suspected she did it to make her work seem more glamorous—the sudden flight to an undisclosed destination on a mission so delicate it could not be whispered to a friend—but this time the *Sunday Telegraph* called to ask why Janet had not been seen at the office for over a week.

When they called again a day or two later, and Eva still had no news, she decided she had no choice but to make a search of Janet's room for some clue as to her whereabouts. At least she'd see which clothes Janet had taken—whether she had packed for a fortnight's absence. With luck she might find a note of the flight number.

The room was in its usual disorder, as if Janet had just gone for a shower and would sweep in at any moment in her white Dior bathrobe. By the phone, Eva found the calendar Janet used to jot down appointments. There was no entry for the last fortnight. On the dressing table was her passport. The suitcase she always took on trips of a week or more was still on the top of the wardrobe.

Janet was not the sort of person you worried over, but this was becoming a worry. Eva systematically searched the room and found no clue. She phoned the *Sunday Telegraph* and told them she was sorry she couldn't help. As she put down the phone, her attention was taken by the letters beside it. She had put them there herself, the dozen or so items of mail that had arrived for Janet.

Opening someone else's private correspondence was a step on from searching her room, and she hesitated. What right had she to do such a thing? She could tell by the envelopes that two were from the Inland Revenue and she put them back by the phone. Then she noticed one addressed by hand. It was postmarked Edgecombe, Dorset.

Her meeting with the friendly Californian named John Smith had been pushed to the edge of her memory by more immediate matters, and it took a few moments' thought to recall the significance of Edgecombe. Even then, she was baffled. Janet had told her that Edgecombe was a dead end. She had checked it at the Society of Genealogists. It had no parish register because there was no church there. They had agreed to drop their plan to help John Smith trace his ancestors.

But why should Janet receive a letter from Edgecombe?

Eva decided to open it.

The address on the headed notepaper was The Vicarage, Edgecombe, Dorset.

Dear Miss Murdoch,

I must apologize for the delay in replying to your letter. I fear that this may arrive after you have left for Dorset. However, it is only to confirm that I shall be pleased to show you the entries in our register pertaining to your family, although I doubt if we have anything you have not seen at the Society of Genealogists.

Yours sincerely,
Denis Harcourt, Vicar

A dead end? No church in Edgecombe?

Eva decided to go there herself.

The vicar of Edgecombe had no difficulty in remembering Janet's visit. "Yes, Miss Murdoch called on a Saturday afternoon. At the time I was conducting a baptism, but they waited until it was over and I took them to the vicarage for a cup of tea."

"She had someone with her?"

"Her cousin."

"Cousin?"

"Well, I gather he was not a first cousin, but they were related in some way. He was from America, and his name was John Smith. He was very appreciative of everything I showed him. You see, his father and his grandfather were born here, so I was able to look up their baptisms and their marriages in the register. It goes back to the sixteenth century. We're very proud of our register."

"I'm sure you must be. Tell me, did Janet—Miss Murdoch—claim to be related to the Smiths of Edgecombe?"

"Certainly. Her great-grandfather, Matthew Smith, is buried in the churchyard. He was the brother of the American gentleman's grandfather, if I have it right."

Eva felt the anger like a kick in the stomach. Not only had Janet Murdoch deceived her, she had committed an appalling fraud on a sweet-natured man. And Eva herself had passed on the information that enabled her to do it. She would never forgive her for this.

"That's the only Smith grave we have in the churchyard," the vicar continued. "When I first got Miss Murdoch's letter, I had hopes of locating the stones of the two John Smiths, the father and grandfather of our American visitor, but it was not to be. They were buried elsewhere."

Something in the vicar's tone made Eva ask, "Do you know where they were buried?"

"Yes, indeed. I got it from Mr. Harper, the sexton. He's been here much longer than I."

There was a pause.

"Is it confidential?" Eva asked.

"Not really." The vicar eased a finger round his collar, as if it were uncomfortable. "It was information that I decided in the circumstances not to volunteer to Miss Murdoch and Mr. Smith. You are not one of the family yourself?"

"Absolutely not."

"Then I might as well tell you. It appears that the first John Smith developed some form of insanity. He was given to fits of violence and became quite dangerous. He was committed to a private asylum in London and died there a year or two later. His only son, the second John Smith, also ended his life in distressing circumstances. He was convicted of murdering two local girls by strangulation, and there was believed to have been a third, but the charge was never brought. He was found guilty but insane and sent to Broadmoor. To compound the tragedy, he had a wife and baby son. They went to America after the trial." The vicar gave a shrug. "Who knows whether the child was ever told the truth about his father—or his grandfather, for that matter? Perhaps you can understand why I was silent on the matter when Mr. Smith and Miss Murdoch were here. I may be old-fashioned, but I think the psychiatrists make too much of heredity, don't you? If you took it seriously, you'd think no woman was safe with Mr. Smith."

From the vicarage, Eva went straight to the house of the Edgecombe police constable and told her story.

The officer listened patiently. When Eva had finished, he said, "Right, miss. I'll certainly look into it. Just for the record, this American—what did he say his name was?"

FREDERICK FORSYTH

"There Are No Snakes in Ireland"

*Frederick Forsyth was born in Ashford, Kent, England in 1938. After service in the Royal Air Force he was a reporter for Reuters and the BBC for several years, before publishing his acclaimed first novel **The Day of the Jackal** in 1971. That book was a best-seller and a successful motion picture, and won the MWA Edgar Award as the best novel of the year.*

*It was followed by **The Odessa File** (1972), also a best-seller and a motion picture. Forsyth has published only eight suspense thrillers to date, but each has been highly successful and several have been filmed. All reflect his journalistic training and sense of a well-told story.*

*His short stories carry the same feeling of reality as his novels. They have been collected as **No Comebacks** (1982). The classic "There Are No Snakes in Ireland" won the MWA Edgar Award as best short story of the year. It first appeared in **No Comebacks** and has been reprinted in **The Year's Best Mystery and Suspense Stories - 1983**, **Ellery Queen's Mystery Magazine** and **The New Edgar Winners**.*

There Are No Snakes in Ireland

by Frederick Forsyth

McQueen looked across his desk at the new applicant for a job with some scepticism. He had never employed such a one before. But he was not an unkind man, and if the job-seeker needed the money and was prepared to work, McQueen was not averse to giving him a chance.

"You know it's damn hard work?" he said in his broad Belfast accent.

"Yes, sir," said the applicant.

"It's a quick in-and-out job, ye know. No questions, no pack drill. You'll be working on the lump. Do you know what that means?"

"No, Mr. McQueen."

"Well, it means you'll be paid well but you'll be paid in cash. No red tape. Geddit?"

What he meant was there would be no income tax paid, no National Health contributions deducted at source. He might also have added that there would be no National Insurance cover and that the Health and Safety standards would be completely ignored. Quick profits for all were the order of the day, with a fat slice off the top for himself as the contractor. The job-seeker nodded his head to indicate he had "goddit" though in fact he had not. McQueen looked at him speculatively.

"You say you're a medical student, in your last year at the Royal Victoria?" Another nod. "On the summer vacation?"

Another nod. The applicant was evidently one of those students who needed money over and above his grant to put himself through medical school. McQueen, sitting in his dingy Bangor officer running a hole-and-corner business as a demolition contractor with assets consisting of a battered truck and a ton of second-hand sledgehammers, considered himself a self-made man and heartily approved of the Ulster Protestant work ethic. He was not one to put down another such thinker, whatever he looked like.

"All right," he said, "you'd better take lodgings here in Bangor. You'll never get from Belfast and back in time each day. We work from seven in the morning until sundown. It's work by the hour, hard but well paid. Mention one word to the authorities and you'll lose the job like shit off a shovel. OK?"

"Yes, sir. Please, when do I start and where?"

"The truck picks the gang up at the main station yard every morning at six-thirty. Be there Monday morning. The gang foreman is Big Billie Cameron. I'll tell him you'll be there."

"Yes, Mr. McQueen." The applicant turned to go.

"One last thing," said McQueen, pencil poised. "What's your name?"

"Harkishan Ram Lal," said the student. McQueen looked at his pencil, the list of names in front of him and the student.

"We'll call you Ram," he said, and that was the name he wrote down on the list.

The student walked out into the bright July sunshine of Bangor, on the north coast of County Down, Northern Ireland.

By that Saturday evening he had found himself cheap lodgings in a dingy boarding house halfway up Railway View Street, the heart of Bangor's bed-and-breakfast land. At least it was convenient to the main station from which the works truck would depart every morning just after sun-up. From the grimy window of his room he could look straight at the side of the shored embankment that carried the trains from Belfast into the station.

It had taken him several tries to get a room. Most of those houses with a B-and-B notice in the window seemed to be fully booked when he presented himself on the doorstep. But then it was true that a lot of casual labor drifted into the town in the height of summer. True also that Mrs. McGurk was a Catholic and she still had rooms left.

He spent Sunday morning bringing his belongings over from Belfast, most of them medical textbooks. In the afternoon he lay on his bed and thought of the bright hard light on the brown hills of his native Punjab. In one more year he would be a qualified physician, and after another year of intern work he would return home to cope with the sicknesses of his own people. Such was his dream. He calculated he could make enough money this summer to tide himself through to his finals and after that he would have a salary of his own.

On the Monday morning he rose at a quarter to six at the bidding of his alarm clock, washed in cold water and was in the station yard just after six. There was time to spare. He found an early-opening café and took two cups of black tea. It was his only sustenance. The battered truck, driven by one of the demolition gang, was there at a quarter past six and a dozen men assembled near it. Harkishan Ram Lal did not know whether to approach them and introduce himself, or wait at a distance. He waited.

At twenty-five past the hour the foreman arrived in his own car, parked it down a side road and strode up to the truck. He had McQueen's list in his hand. He glanced at the dozen men, recognized them all and nodded. The Indian approached. The foreman glared at him.

"Is youse the darkie McQueen has put on the job?" he demanded.

Ram Lal stopped in his tracks. "Harkishan Ram Lal," he said. "Yes."

There was no need to ask how Big Billie Cameron had earned his name. He stood 6 feet and 3 inches in his stockings but was wearing enormous nail-studded steel-toed boots. Arms like tree trunks hung from huge shoulders and his head was surmounted by a shock of ginger hair. Two small, pale-lashed eyes stared down balefully at the slight and wiry Indian. It was plain he was not best pleased. He spat on the ground.

"Well, get in the fecking truck," he said.

On the journey out to the work site Cameron sat up in the cab which had no partition dividing it from the back of the lorry, where the dozen laborers sat on two wooden benches down the sides. Ram Lal was near the tailboard next to a small, nut-hard man with bright blue eyes, whose name turned out to be Tommy Burns. He seemed friendly.

"Where are youse from?" he asked with genuine curiosity.

"India," said Ram Lal. "The Punjab."

"Well, which?" said Tommy Burns.

Ram Lal smiled. "The Punjab is a part of India," he said.

Burns thought about this for a while. "You Protestant or Catholic?" he asked at length.

"Neither," said Ram Lal patiently. "I am a Hindu."

"You mean you're not a Christian?" asked Burns in amazement.

"No. Mine is the Hindu religion."

"Hey," said Burns to the others, "your man's not a Christian at all." He was not outraged, just curious, like a small child who has come across a new and intriguing toy.

Cameron turned from the cab up front. "Aye," he snarled, "a heathen."

The smile dropped off Ram Lal's face. He stared at the opposite canvas wall of the truck. By now they were well south of Bangor, clattering down the motorway towards Newtownards. After a while Burns began to introduce him to the others. There was a Craig, a Munroe, a Patterson, a Boyd and two Browns. Ram Lal had been long enough in Belfast to recognize the names as being originally Scottish, the sign of the hard Presbyterians who make up the backbone of the Protestant majority of the Six Counties. The men seemed amiable and nodded back at him.

"Have you not got a lunch box, laddie?" asked the elderly man called Patterson.

"No," said Ram Lal, "it was too early to ask my landlady to make one up."

"You'll need lunch," said Burns, "aye, and breakfast. We'll be making tay ourselves on a fire."

"I will make sure to buy a box and bring some food tomorrow," said Ram Lal.

Burns looked at the Indian's rubber-soled soft boots. "Have you not done this kind of work before?" he asked.

Ram Lal shook his head.

"You'll need a pair of heavy boots. To save your feet, you see."

Ram Lal promised he would also buy a pair of heavy ammunition boots from a store if he could find one open late at night. They were through Newtownards and still heading south on the A21 towards the small town of Comber. Craig looked across at him.

"What's your real job?" he asked.

"I'm a medical student at the Royal Victoria in Belfast," said Ram Lal. "I hope to quality next year."

Tommy Burns was delighted. "That's near to being a real doctor," he said. "Hey, Big Billie, if one of us gets a knock young Ram could take care of it."

Big Billie grunted. "He's not putting a finger on me," he said.

That killed further conversation until they arrived at the work site. The driver had pulled northwest out of Comber and two miles up the Dundonald road he bumped down a track to the right until they came to a stop where the trees ended and saw the building to be demolished.

It was a huge old whiskey distillery, a sheer-sided, long derelict. It had been one of two in these parts that had once turned out good Irish whiskey but had gone out of business years before. It stood beside the River Comber, which had once powered its great water-wheel as it flowed down from Dundonald to Comber and on to empty itself in Strangford Lough. The malt had arrived by horse-drawn cart down the track and the barrels of whiskey had left the same way. The sweet water that had powered the machines had also been used in the vats. But the distillery had stood alone, abandoned and empty for years.

Of course the local children had broken in and found it an ideal place to play. Until one had slipped and broken a leg. Then the county council had surveyed it, declared it a hazard and the owner found himself with a compulsory demolition order.

He, scion of an old family of squires who had known better days, wanted the job done as cheaply as possible. That was where Mc-Queen came in. It could be done faster but more expensively with heavy machinery; Big Billie and his team would do it with sledges and crowbars. McQueen had even lined up a deal to sell the best timbers and the hundreds of tons of mature bricks to a jobbing builder. After all, the wealthy nowadays wanted their new houses to have "style" and that meant looking old. So there was a premium on antique sun-bleached old bricks and genuine ancient timber beams to adorn the new-look-old "manor" houses of the top executives. McQueen would do all right.

"Right lads," said Big Billie as the truck rumbled away back to Bangor. "There it is. We'll start with the roof tiles. You know what to do."

The group of men stood beside their pile of equipment. There were great sledgehammers with 7-pound heads; crowbars 6 feet long and over an inch thick; nailbars a yard long with curved split tips for extracting nails; short-handled, heavy-headed lump hammers and a variety of timber saws. The only concessions to human safety were a number of webbing belts with dogclips and hundreds of feet of rope. Ram Lal looked up at the building and swallowed. It was four storeys high and he hated heights. But scaffolding is expensive.

One of the men unbidden went to the building, prised off a plank door, tore it up like a playing card and started a fire. Soon a billycan of water from the river was boiling away and tea was made. They all had their enamel mugs except Ram Lal. He made a mental note to buy that also. It was going to be thirsty, dusty work. Tommy Burns finished his own mug and offered it, refilled, to Ram Lal.

"Do they have tea in India?" he asked.

Ram Lal took the proffered mug. The tea was ready-mixed, sweet and off-white. He hated it.

They worked through the first morning perched high on the roof. The tiles were not to be salvaged, so they tore them off manually and hurled them to the ground away from the river. There was an instruction not to block the river with falling rubble. So it all had to land on the other side of the building, in the long grass, weeds, broom and gorse which covered the area round the distillery. The men were roped together so that if one lost his grip and began to slither down the roof, the next man would take the strain. As the tiles disappeared, great yawning holes appeared between the rafters. Down below them was the floor of the top storey, the malt store.

At ten they came down the rickety internal stairs for breakfast on the grass, with another billycan of tea. Ram Lal ate no breakfast. At two they broke for lunch. The gang tucked into their piles of thick sandwiches. Ram Lal looked at his hands. They were nicked in several places and bleeding. His muscles ached and he was very hungry. He made another mental note about buying some heavy work gloves.

Tommy Burns held up a sandwich from his own box. "Are you not hungry, Ram?" he asked. "Sure, I have enough here."

"What do you think you're doing?" asked Big Billie from where he sat across the circle round the fire.

Burns looked defensive. "Just offering the lad a sandwich," he said.

"Let the darkie bring his own fecking sandwiches," said Cameron. "You look after yourself."

The men looked down at their lunch boxes and ate in silence. It was obvious no one argued the toss with Big Billie.

"Thank you, I am not hungry," said Ram Lal to Burns. He

walked away and sat by the river where he bathed his burning hands.

By sundown when the truck came to collect them half the tiles on the great roof were gone. One more day and they would start on the rafters, work for saw and nailbar.

Throughout the week the work went on, and the once proud building was stripped of its rafters, planks and beams until it stood hollow and open, its gaping windows like open eyes staring at the prospect of its imminent death. Ram Lal was unaccustomed to the arduousness of this kind of labor. His muscles ached endlessly, his hands were blistered, but he toiled on for the money he needed so badly.

He had acquired a tin lunch box, enamel mug, hard boots and a pair of heavy gloves, which no one else wore. Their hands were hard enough from years of manual work. Throughout the week Big Billie Cameron needled him without let-up, giving him the hardest work and positioning him on the highest points once he had learned Ram Lal hated heights. The Punjabi bit on his anger because he needed the money. The crunch came on the Saturday.

The timbers were gone and they were working on the masonry. The simplest way to bring the edifice down away from the river would have been to plant explosive charges in the corners of the side wall facing the open clearing. But dynamite was out of the question. It would have required special licences in Northern Ireland of all places, and that would have alerted the tax man. McQueen and all his gang would have been required to pay substantial sums in income tax, and McQueen in National Insurance contributions. So they were chipping the walls down in square-yard chunks, standing hazardously on sagging floors as the supporting walls splintered and cracked under the hammers.

During lunch Cameron walked round the building a couple of times and came back to the circle round the fire. He began to describe how they were going to bring down a sizable chunk of one outer wall at third-floor level. He turned to Ram Lal.

"I want you up on the top there," he said. "When it starts to go, kick it outwards."

Ram Lal looked up at the section of wall in question. A great crack ran along the bottom of it.

"That brickwork is going to fall at any moment," he said evenly. "Anyone sitting on top there is going to come down with it."

Cameron stared at him, his face suffusing, his eyes pink with rage where they should have been white. "Don't you tell me my job; you do as you're told, you stupid fecking nigger." He turned and stalked away.

Ram Lal rose to his feet. When his voice came, it was in a hard-edged shout. "*Mister Cameron . . .* "

Cameron turned in amazement. The men sat openmouthed. Ram Lal walked slowly up to the big ganger.

"Let us get one thing plain," said Ram Lal, and his voice carried clearly to everyone else in the clearing. "I am from the Punjab in northern India. I am also a Kshatria, member of the warrior caste. I may not have enough money to pay for my medical studies, but my ancestors were soldiers and princes, rulers and scholars, two thousand years ago when yours were crawling on all fours dressed in skins. Please do not insult me any further."

Big Billie Cameron stared down at the Indian student. The whites of his eyes had turned a bright red. The other laborers sat in stunned amazement.

"Is that so?" said Cameron quietly. "Is that so, now? Well, things are a bit different now, you black bastard. So what are you going to do about that?"

On the last word he swung his arm, open-palmed, and his hand crashed into the side of Ram Lal's face. The youth was thrown bodily to the ground several feet away. His head sang. He heard Tommy Burns call out, "Stay down, laddie. Big Billie will kill you if you get up."

Ram Lal looked up into the sunlight. The giant stood over him, fists bunched. He realized he had not a chance in combat against the big Ulsterman. Feelings of shame and humiliation flooded over him. His ancestors had ridden, sword and lance in hand, across plains a hundred times bigger than these six counties, conquering all before them.

Ram Lal closed his eyes and lay still. After several seconds he heard the big man move away. A low conversation started among the others. He squeezed his eyes tighter shut to hold back the tears of shame. In the blackness he saw the baking plains of the Punjab and men riding over them; proud, fierce men, hook-nosed, bearded, turbaned, black-eyed, the warriors from the land of Five Rivers.

Once, long ago in the world's morning, Iskander of Macedon had ridden over these plains with his hot and hungry eyes; Alexander, the young god, whom they called The Great, who at twenty-five had wept because there were no more worlds to conquer. These riders were the descendants of his captains, and the ancestors of Harkishan Ram Lal.

He was lying in the dust as they rode by, and they looked down at him in passing. As they rode each of them mouthed one single word to him. Vengeance.

Ram Lal picked himself up in silence. It was done, and what still had to be done had to be done. That was the way of his people. He spent the rest of the day working in complete silence. He spoke to no one and no one spoke to him.

That evening in his room he began his preparations as night was about to fall. He cleared away the brush and comb from the battered dressing table and removed also the soiled doily and the mirror from its stand. He took his book of the Hindu religion and from it cut a page-sized portrait of the great goddess Shakti, she of power and justice. This he pinned to the wall above the dressing table to convert it into a shrine.

He had bought a bunch of flowers from a seller in front of the main station, and these had been woven into a garland. To one side of the portrait of the goddess he placed a shallow bowl half-filled with sand, and in the sand stuck a candle which he lit. From his suitcase he took a cloth roll and extracted half a dozen joss sticks. Taking a cheap, narrow-necked vase from the bookshelf, he placed them in it and lit the ends. The sweet, heady odor of the incense began to fill the room. Outside, big thunderheads rolled up from the sea.

When his shrine was ready he stood before it, head bowed, the garland in his fingers, and began to pray for guidance. The first rumble of thunder rolled over Bangor. He used not the modern Punjabi but the ancient Sanskrit, language of prayer. "*Devi Shakti . . . Maa . . .* Goddess Shakti . . . great mother . . ."

The thunder crashed again and the first raindrops fell. He plucked the first flower and placed it in front of the portrait of Shakti.

"I have been grievously wronged. I ask vengeance upon the wrongdoer . . ." He plucked the second flower and put it beside the first.

He prayed for an hour while the rain came down. It drummed on the tiles above his head, streamed past the window behind him. He finished praying as the storm subsided. He needed to know what form the retribution should take. He needed the goddess to send him a sign.

45

When he had finished, the joss sticks had burned themselves out and the room was thick with their scent. The candle guttered low. The flowers all lay on the lacquered surface of the dressing table in front of the portrait. Shakti stared back at him unmoved.

He turned and walked to the window to look out. The rain had stopped but everything beyond the panes dripped water. As he watched, a dribble of rain sprang from the guttering above the window and a trickle ran down the dusty glass, cutting a path through the grime. Because of the dirt it did not run straight but meandered sideways, drawing his eye farther and farther to the corner of the window as he followed its path. When it stopped he was staring at the corner of his room, where his dressing gown hung on a nail.

He noticed that during the storm the dressing-gown cord had slipped and fallen to the floor. It lay coiled upon itself, one knotted end hidden from view, the other lying visible on the carpet. Of the dozen tassels only two were exposed, like a forked tongue. The coiled dressing-gown cord resembled nothing so much as a snake in the corner. Ram Lal understood. The next day he took a train to Belfast to see the Sikh.

Ranjit Singh was also a medical student, but he was more fortunate. His parents were rich and sent him a handsome allowance. He received Ram Lal in his well-furnished room at the hostel.

"I have received word from home," said Ram Lal. "My father is dying."

"I am sorry," said Ranjit Singh, "you have my sympathies."

"He asks to see me. I am his first born. I should return."

"Of course," said Singh. "The first-born son should always be by his father when he dies."

"It is a matter of the air fare," said Ram Lal. "I am working and making good money. But I do not have enough. If you will lend me the balance I will continue working when I return and repay you."

Sikhs are no strangers to moneylending if the interest is right and repayment secure. Ranjit Singh promised to withdraw the money from the bank on Monday morning.

That Sunday evening Ram Lal visited Mr. McQueen at his home at Groomsport. The contractor was in front of his television set with a can of beer at his elbow. It was his favorite way to spend a Sunday evening. But he turned the sound down as Ram Lal was shown in by his wife.

"It is about my father," said Ram Lal. "He is dying."

"Oh, I'm sorry to hear that, laddie," said McQueen.

"I should go to him. The first-born son should be with his father at this time. It is the custom of our people."

McQueen had a son in Canada whom he had not seen for seven years.

"Aye," he said, "that seems right and proper."

"I have borrowed the money for the air fare," said Ram Lal. "If I went tomorrow I could be back by the end of the week. The point is, Mr. McQueen, I need the job more than ever now; to repay the loan and for my studies next term. If I am back by the weekend, will you keep the job open for me?"

"All right," said the contractor. "I can't pay you for the time you're away. Nor keep the job open for a further week. But if you're back by the weekend, you can go back to work. Same terms, mind."

"Thank you," said Ram, "you are very kind."

He retained his room in Railway View Street but spent the night at his hostel in Belfast. On the Monday morning he accompanied Ranjit Singh to the bank where the Sikh withdrew the necessary money and gave it to the Hindu. Ram took a taxi to Aldergrove airport and the shuttle to London where he bought an economy-class ticket on the next flight to India. Twenty-four hours later he touched down in the blistering heat of Bombay.

On the Wednesday he found what he sought in the teeming bazaar at Grant Road Bridge. Mr. Chatterjee's Tropical Fish and Reptile Emporium was almost deserted when the young student, with his textbook on reptiles under his arm, wandered in. He found the old proprietor sitting near the back of his shop in half-darkness, surrounded by his tanks of fish and glass-fronted cases in which his snakes and lizards dozed through the hot day.

Mr. Chatterjee was no stranger to the academic world. He supplied several medical centers with samples for study and dissection, and occasionally filled a lucrative order from abroad. He nodded his white-bearded head knowledgeably as the student explained what he sought.

"Ah yes," said the old Gujerati merchant, "I know the snake. You are in luck. I have one, but a few days arrived from Rajputana."

He led Ram Lal into his private sanctum and the two men stared silently through the glass of the snake's new home.

Echis carinatus, said the textbook, but of course the book had been written by an Englishman, who had used the Latin nomenclature. In English, the saw-scaled viper, smallest and deadliest of all his lethal breed.

Wide distribution, said the textbook, being found from West Africa eastwards and northwards to Iran, and on to India and Pakistan. Very adaptable, able to acclimatize to almost any environment, from the moist bush of western Africa to the cold hills of Iran in winter to the baking hills of India.

Something stirred beneath the leaves in the box.

In size, said the textbook, between 9 and 13 inches long and very slim. Olive brown in color with a few paler spots, sometimes hardly distinguishable, and a faint undulating darker line down the side of the body. Nocturnal in dry, hot weather, seeking cover during the heat of the day.

The leaves in the box rustled again and a tiny head appeared.

Exceptionally dangerous to handle, said the textbook, causing more deaths than even the more famous cobra, largely because of its size which makes it so easy to touch unwittingly with hand or foot. The author of the book had added a footnote to the effect that the small but lethal snake mentioned by Kipling in his marvelous story "Rikki-Tikki-Tavy" was almost certainly not the krait, which is about 2 feet long, but more probably the saw-scaled viper. The author was obviously pleased to have caught out the great Kipling in a matter of accuracy.

In the box, a little black forked tongue flickered towards the two Indians beyond the glass.

Very alert and irritable, the long-gone English naturalist had concluded his chapter on *Echis carinatus*. Strikes quickly without warning. The fangs are so small they make a virtually unnoticeable puncture, like two tiny thorns. There is no pain, but death is almost inevitable, usually taking between two and four hours, depending on the bodyweight of the victim and the level of his physical exertions at the time and afterwards. Cause of death is invariably a brain hemorrhage.

"How much do you want for him?" whispered Ram Lal.

The old Gujerati spread his hands helplessly. "Such a prime specimen," he said regretfully, "and so hard to come by. Five hundred rupees."

Ram Lal clinched the deal at 350 rupees and took the snake away in a jar.

For his journey back to London Ram Lal purchased a box of cigars, which he emptied of their contents and in whose lid he punctured twenty small holes for air. The tiny viper, he knew, would need no food for a week and no water for two or three days. It could breathe on an infinitesimal supply of air, so he wrapped the cigar box, resealed and with the viper inside it among his leaves, in several towels whose thick sponginess would contain enough air even inside a suitcase.

He had arrived with a handgrip, but he bought a cheap fiber suitcase and packed it with clothes from market stalls, the cigar box going in the center. It was only minutes before he left his hotel for Bombay airport that he closed and locked the case. For the flight back to London he checked the suitcase into the hold of the Boeing airliner. His hand baggage was searched, but it contained nothing of interest.

The Air India jet landed at London Heathrow on Friday morning and Ram Lal joined the long queue of Indians trying to get into Britain. He was able to prove he was a medical student and not an immigrant, and was allowed through quite quickly. He even reached the luggage carousel as the first suitcases were tumbling onto it, and saw his own in the first two dozen. He took it to the toilet, where he extracted the cigar box and put it in his handgrip.

In the Nothing-to-Declare channel he was stopped all the same, but it was his suitcase that was ransacked. The customs officer glanced in his shoulder bag and let him pass. Ram Lal crossed Heathrow by courtesy bus to Number One Building and caught the midday shuttle to Belfast. He was in Bangor by teatime and able at last to examine his import.

He took a sheet of glass from the bedside table and slipped it carefully between the lid of the cigar box and its deadly contents before opening wide. Through the glass he saw the viper going round and round inside. It paused and stared with angry black eyes back at him. He pulled the lid shut, withdrawing the pane of glass quickly as the box top came down.

"Sleep, little friend," he said, "if your breed ever sleep. In the morning you will do Shakti's bidding for her."

Before dark he bought a small screw-top jar of coffee and poured the contents into a china pot in his room. In the morning, using his heavy gloves, he transferred the viper from the box to the jar. The enraged snake bit his glove once, but he did not mind. It would have recovered its venom by midday. For a moment he studied the snake, coiled and cramped inside the glass coffee jar, before giving the top a last, hard twist and placing it in his lunch box. Then he went to catch the works truck.

Big Billie Cameron had a habit of taking off his jacket the moment he arrived at the work site, and hanging it on a convenient nail or twig. During the lunch break, as Ram Lal had observed, the giant foreman never failed to go to his jacket after eating, and from the right-hand pocket extract his pipe and tobacco pouch. The routine did not vary. After a satisfying pipe, he would knock out the dottle, rise and say, "Right, lads, back to work," as he dropped his pipe back into the pocket of his jacket. By the time he turned round everyone had to be on their feet.

Ram Lal's plan was simple but foolproof. During the morning he would slip the snake into the right-hand pocket of the hanging jacket. After his sandwiches the bullying Cameron would rise from the fire, go to his jacket and plunge his hand into the pocket. The snake would do what great Shakti had ordered that he be brought halfway across the world to do. It would be he, the viper, not Ram Lal, who would be the Ulsterman's executioner.

Cameron would withdraw his hand with an oath from the pocket, the viper hanging from his finger, its fangs deep in the flesh. Ram Lal would leap up, tear the snake away, throw it to the ground and stamp upon its head. It would by then be harmless, its venom expended. Finally, with a gesture of disgust he, Ram Lal, would hurl the dead viper far into the River Comber, which would carry all evidence away to the sea. There might be suspicion, but that was all there would ever be.

Shortly after eleven o'clock, on the excuse of fetching a fresh sledgehammer, Harkishan Ram Lal opened his lunch box, took out the coffee jar, unscrewed the lid and shook the contents into the right-hand pocket of the hanging jacket. Within sixty seconds he was back at his work, his act unnoticed.

During lunch he found it hard to eat. The men sat as usual in a circle round the fire; the dry old timber baulks crackled and spat, the billycan bubbled above them. The men joshed and joked as ever, while Big Billie munched his way through the pile of doorstep sandwiches his wife had prepared for him. Ram Lal had made a point of choosing a place in the circle near to the jacket. He forced himself to eat. In his chest his heart was pounding and the tension in him rose steadily.

Finally Big Billie crumpled the paper of his eaten sandwiches, threw it in the fire and belched. He rose with a grunt and walked towards his jacket. Ram Lal turned his head to watch. The other men took no notice. Billie Cameron reached his jacket and plunged his hand into the right-hand pocket. Ram Lal held his breath. Cameron's hand rummaged for several seconds and then withdrew his pipe and pouch. He began to fill the bowl with fresh tobacco. As he did so he caught Ram Lal staring at him.

"What are youse looking at?" he demanded belligerently.

"Nothing," said Ram Lal, and turned to face the fire. But he could not stay still. He rose and stretched, contriving to half turn as he did so. From the corner of his eye he saw Cameron replace the pouch in the pocket and again withdraw his hand with a box of matches in it. The foreman lit his pipe and pulled contentedly. He strolled back to the fire.

Ram Lal resumed his seat and stared at the flames in disbelief. Why, he asked himself, why had great Shakti done this to him? The snake had been her tool, her instrument brought at her command. But she had held it back, refused to use her own implement of retribution. He turned and sneaked another glance at the jacket. Deep down in the lining at the very hem, on the extreme left-hand side, something stirred and was still. Ram Lal closed his eyes in shock. A hole, a tiny hole in the lining, had undone all his planning. He worked the rest of the afternoon in a daze of indecision and worry.

On the truck ride back to Bangor, Big Billie Cameron sat up front as usual, but in view of the heat folded his jacket and put it on his knees. In front of the station Ram Lal saw him throw the still-folded jacket onto the back seat of his car and drive away. Ram Lal caught up with Tommy Burns as the little man waited for his bus.

"Tell me," he asked, "does Mr. Cameron have a family?"

"Sure," said the little laborer innocently, "a wife and two children."

"Does he live far from here?" said Ram Lal. "I mean, he drives a car."

"Not far," said Burns, "up on the Kilcooley estate. Ganaway Gardens, I think. Going visiting are you?"

"No, no," said Ram Lal, "see you Monday."

Back in his room Ram Lal stared at the impassive image of the goddess of justice.

"I did not mean to bring death to his wife and children," he told her. "They have done nothing to me."

The goddess from far away stared back and gave no reply.

Harkishan Ram Lal spent the rest of the weekend in an agony of anxiety. That evening he walked to the Kilcooley housing estate on the ring road and found Ganaway Gardens. It lay just off Owenroe Gardens and opposite Woburn Walk. At the corner of Woburn Walk there was a telephone kiosk, and here he waited for an hour, pretending to make a call, while he watched the short street across the road. He thought he spotted Big Billie Cameron at one of the windows and noted the house.

He saw a teenage girl come out of it and walk away to join some friends. For a moment he was tempted to accost her and tell her what demon slept inside her father's jacket, but he dared not.

Shortly before dusk a woman came out of the house carrying a shopping basket. He followed her down to the Clandeboye shopping center, which was open late for those who took their wage packets on a Saturday. The woman he thought to be Mrs. Cameron entered Stewarts supermarket and the Indian student trailed round the shelves behind her, trying to pick up the courage to approach her and reveal the danger in her house. Again his nerve failed him. He might, after all, have the wrong woman, even be mistaken about the house. In that case they would take him away as a madman.

He slept ill that night, his mind racked by visions of the saw-scaled viper coming out of its hiding place in the jacket lining to slither, silent and deadly, through the sleeping council house.

On the Sunday he again haunted the Kilcooley estate, and firmly identified the house of the Cameron family. He saw Big Billie clearly in the back garden. By mid-afternoon he was attracting attention locally and knew he must either walk boldly up to the front door and admit what he had done, or depart and leave all in the hands of the goddess. The thought of facing the terrible Cameron with the news of what deadly danger had been brought so close to his children was too much. He walked back to Railway View Street.

On Monday morning the Cameron family rose at a quarter to six, a bright and sunny August morning. By six the four of them were at breakfast in the tiny kitchen at the back of the house, the son, daughter and wife in their dressing gowns, Big Billie dressed for work. His jacket was where it had spent the weekend, in a closet in the hallway.

Just after six his daughter Jenny rose, stuffing a piece of marmaladed toast into her mouth.

"I'm away to wash," she said.

"Before ye go, girl, get my jacket from the press," said her father, working his way through a plate of cereal. The girl reappeared a few seconds later with the jacket, held by the collar. She proffered it to her father. He hardly looked up.

"Hang it behind the door," he said. The girl did as she was bid, but the jacket had no hanging tab and the hook was no rusty nail but a smooth chrome affair. The jacket hung for a moment, then fell to the kitchen floor. Her father looked up as she left the room.

"Jenny," he shouted, "pick the damn thing up."

No one in the Cameron household argued with the head of the family. Jenny came back, picked up the jacket and hung it more firmly. As she did, something thin and dark slipped from its folds and slithered into the corner with a dry rustle across the linoleum. She stared at it in horror.

"Dad, what's that in your jacket?"

Big Billie Cameron paused, a spoonful of cereal halfway to his mouth. Mrs. Cameron turned from the cooker. Fourteen-year-old Bobby ceased buttering a piece of toast and stared. The small creature lay curled in the corner by the row of cabinets, tight-bunched, defensive, glaring back at the world, tiny tongue flickering fast.

"Lord save us, it's a snake," said Mrs. Cameron.

"Don't be a bloody fool, woman. Don't you know there are no snakes in Ireland? Everyone knows that," said her husband. He put down the spoon. "What is it, Bobby?"

Though a tyrant inside and outside his house, Big Billie had a grudging respect for the knowledge of his young son, who was good at school and was being taught many strange things. The boy stared at the snake through his owlish glasses.

"It must be a slowworm, Dad," he said. "They had some at school last term for the biology class. Brought them in for dissection. From across the water."

"It doesn't look like a worm to me," said his father.

"It isn't really a worm," said Bobby. "It's a lizard with no legs."

"Then why do they call it a worm?" asked his truculent father.

"I don't know," said Bobby.

"Then what the hell are you going to school for?"

"Will it bite?" asked Mrs. Cameron fearfully.

"Not at all," said Bobby. "It's harmless."

"Kill it," said Cameron senior, and "throw it in the dustbin."

His son rose from the table and removed one of his slippers, which he held like a flyswat in one hand. He was advancing, bare-ankled towards the corner, when his father changed his mind. Big Billie looked up from his plate with a gleeful smile.

"Hold on a minute, just hold on there, Bobby," he said, "I have an idea. Woman, get me a jar."

"What kind of a jar?" asked Mrs. Cameron.

"How should I know what kind of a jar? A jar with a lid on it."

Mrs. Cameron sighed, skirted the snake and opened a cupboard. She examined her store of jars.

"There's a jamjar, with dried peas in it," she said.

"Put the peas somewhere else and give me the jar," commanded Cameron. She passed him the jar.

"What are you going to do, Dad?" asked Bobby.

"There's a darkie we have at work. A heathen man. He comes from a land with a lot of snakes in it. I have in mind to have some fun with him. A wee joke, like. Pass me that oven glove, Jenny."

"You'll not need a glove," said Bobby. "He can't bite you."

"I'm not touching the dirty thing," said Cameron.

"He's not dirty," said Bobby. "They're very clean creatures."

"You're a fool, boy, for all your school learning. Does the Good Book not say: 'On thy belly shalt thou go, and dust shalt thou eat . . .'? Aye, and more than dust, no doubt. I'll not touch him with me hand."

Jenny passed her father the oven glove. Open jamjar in his left hand, right hand protected by the glove, Big Billie Cameron stood over the viper. Slowly his right hand descended. When it dropped, it was fast; but the small snake was faster. It's tiny fangs went harmlessly into the padding of the glove at the center of the palm. Cameron did not notice, for the act was masked from his view by his own hands. In a trice the snake was inside the jamjar and the lid was on. Through the glass they watched it wriggle furiously.

"I hate them, harmless or not," said Mrs. Cameron. "I'll thank you to get it out of the house."

"I'll be doing that right now," said her husband, "for I'm late as it is."

He slipped the jamjar into his shoulder bag, already containing his lunch box, stuffed his pipe and pouch into the right-hand pocket of his jacket and took both out to the car. He arrived at the station yard five minutes late and was surprised to find the Indian student staring at him fixedly.

"I suppose he wouldn't have the second sight," thought Big Billie as they trundled south to Newtownards and Comber.

By mid-morning all the gang had been let into Big Billie's secret joke on pain of a thumping if they let on to "the darkie." There was no chance of that; assured that the slowworm was perfectly harmless, they too thought it a good leg-pull. Only Ram Lal worked on in ignorance, consumed by his private thoughts and worries.

At the lunch break he should have suspected something. The tension was palpable. The men sat in a circle around the fire as usual, but the conversation was stilted and had he not been so preoccupied he would have noticed the half-concealed grins and the looks darted in his direction. He did not notice. He placed his own lunch box between his knees and opened it. Coiled between the sandwiches and the apple, head back to strike, was the viper.

The Indian's scream echoed across the clearing, just ahead of the roar of laughter from the laborers. Simultaneously with the scream, the lunch box flew high in the air as he threw it away from himself with all his strength. All the contents of the box flew in a score of directions, landing in the long grass, the broom and gorse all around them.

Ram Lal was on his feet, shouting. The gangers rolled helplessly in their mirth, Big Billie most of all. He had not had such a laugh in months.

"It's a snake," screamed Ram Lal, "a poisonous snake. Get out of here, all of you. It's deadly."

The laughter redoubled; the men could not contain themselves. The reaction of the joke's victim surpassed all their expectations.

"Please, believe me. It's a snake, a deadly snake."

Big Billie's face was suffused. He wiped tears from his eyes, seated across the clearing from Ram Lal, who was standing looking wildly round.

"You ignorant darkie," he gasped, "don't you know? There are no snakes in Ireland. Understand? There aren't any."

His sides ached with laughing and he leaned back in the grass, his hands behind him to support him. He failed to notice the two pricks, like tiny thorns, that went into the vein on the inside of the right wrist.

The joke was over and the hungry men tucked into their lunches. Harkishan Ram Lal reluctantly took his seat, constantly glancing round him, a mug of steaming tea held ready, eating only with his left hand, staying clear of the long grass. After lunch they returned to work. The old distillery was almost down, the mountains of rubble and savable timbers lying dusty under the August sun.

At half past three Big Billie Cameron stood up from his work, rested on his pick and passed a hand across his forehead. He licked at a slight swelling on the inside of his wrist, then started work again. Five minutes later he straightened up again.

"I'm not feeling so good," he told Patterson, who was next to him. "I'm going to take a spell in the shade."

He sat under a tree for a while and then held his head in his hands. At a quarter past four, still clutching his splitting head, he gave one convulsion and toppled sideways. It was several minutes before Tommy Burns noticed him. He walked across and called to Patterson.

"Big Billie's sick," he called. "He won't answer me."

The gang broke and came over to the tree in whose shade the foreman lay. His sightless eyes were staring at the grass a few inches from his face. Patterson bent over him. He had been long enough in the laboring business to have seen a few dead ones.

"Ram," he said, "you have medical training. What do you think?"

Ram Lal did not need to make an examination, but he did. When he straightened up he said nothing, but Patterson understood.

"Stay here all of you," he said, taking command. "I'm going to phone an ambulance and call McQueen." He set off down the track to the main road.

The ambulance got there first, half an hour later. It reversed down the track and two men heaved Cameron onto a stretcher. They took him away to Newtownards General Hospital, which has the nearest casualty unit, and there the foreman was logged in as DOA—dead on arrival. An extremely worried McQueen arrived thirty minutes after that.

Because of the unknown circumstance of the death an autopsy had to be performed and it was, by the North Down area pathologist, in the Newtownards municipal mortuary to which the body had been transferred. That was on the Tuesday. By that evening the pathologist's report was on its way to the office of the coroner for North Down, in Belfast.

The report said nothing extraordinary. The deceased had been a man of forty-one years, big-built and immensely strong. There were upon the body various minor cuts and abrasions, mainly on the hands and wrists, quite consistent with the job of navvy, and none of these were in any way associated with the cause of death. The latter, beyond a doubt, had been a massive brain hemorrhage, itself probably caused by extreme exertion in conditions of great heat.

Possessed of this report, the coroner would normally not hold an inquest, being able to issue a certificate of death by natural causes to the registrar at Bangor. But there was something Harkishan Ram Lal did not know.

Big Billie Cameron had been a leading member of the Bangor council of the outlawed Ulster Volunteer Force, the hard-line Protestant paramilitary organization. The computer at Lurgan, into which all deaths in the province of Ulster, however innocent, are programmed, threw this out and someone in Lurgan picked up the phone to call the Royal Ulster Constabulary at Castlereagh.

Someone there called the coroner's office in Belfast, and a formal inquest was ordered. In Ulster death must not only be accidental; it must be seen to be accidental. For certain people, at least. The inquest was in the Town Hall at Bangor on the Wednesday. It meant a lot of trouble for McQueen, for the Inland Revenue attended. So did two quiet men of extreme Loyalist persuasion from the UVF council. They sat at the back. Most of the dead man's workmates sat near the front, a few feet from Mrs. Cameron.

Only Patterson was called to give evidence. He related the events of the Monday, prompted by the coroner, and as there was no dispute none of the other laborers was called, not even Ram Lal. The coroner read the pathologist's report aloud and it was clear enough. When he had finished, he summed up before giving his verdict.

"The pathologist's report is quite unequivocal. We have heard from Mr. Patterson of the events of that lunch break, of the perhaps rather foolish prank played by the deceased upon the Indian student. It would seem that Mr. Cameron was so amused that he laughed himself almost to the verge of apoplexy. The subsequent heavy labor with pick and shovel in the blazing sun did the rest, provoking the rupture of a large blood vessel in the brain or, as the pathologist puts it in more medical language, a cerebral hemorrhage. This court extends its sympathy to the widow and her children, and finds that Mr. William Cameron died of accidental causes."

Outside on the lawns that spread before Bangor Town Hall Mc-Queen talked to his navvies.

"I'll stand fair by you, lads," he said. "The job's still on, but I can't afford not to deduct tax and all the rest, not with the Revenue breathing down my neck. The funeral's tomorrow, you can take the day off. Those who want to go on can report on Friday."

Harkishan Ram Lal did not attend the funeral. While it was in progress at the Bangor cemetery he took a taxi back to Comber and asked the driver to wait on the road while he walked down the track. The driver was a Bangor man and had heard about the death of Cameron.

"Going to pay your respects on the spot, are you?" he asked.

"In a way," said Ram Lal.

"That the manner of your people?" asked the driver.

"You could say so," said Ram Lal.

"Aye, well, I'll not say it's any better or worse than our way, by the graveside," said the driver, and prepared to read his paper while he waited.

Harkishan Ram Lal walked down the track to the clearing and stood where the camp fire had been. He looked around at the long grass, the broom and the gorse in its sandy soil.

"Visha serp," he called out to the hidden viper. "O venomous snake, can you hear me? You have done what I brought you so far from the hills of Rajputana to achieve. But you were supposed to die. I should have killed you myself, had it all gone as I planned, and thrown your foul carcass in the river.

"Are you listening, deadly one? Then hear this. You may live a little longer but then you will die, as all things die. And you will die alone, without a female with which to mate, because there are no snakes in Ireland."

The saw-scaled viper did not hear him, or if it did, gave no hint of understanding. Deep in its hole in the warm sand beneath him, it was busy, totally absorbed in doing what nature commanded it must do.

At the base of a snake's tail are two overlapping plate-scales which obscure the cloaca. The viper's tail was erect, the body throbbed in ancient rhythm. The plates were parted, and from the cloaca, one by one, each an inch long in its transparent sac, each as deadly at birth as its parent, she was bringing her dozen babies into the world.

JANWILLEM VAN DE WETERING

"A Great Sight"

*Janwillem van de Wetering was born in Rotterdam, Netherlands, on February 12, 1931. He was educated at Delft University, the College for Service Abroad, Cambridge and the University of London. He lived in South Africa, Japan, Colombia, Peru and Australia before returning to Amsterdam in 1965 as director of a textile company. He was also a member of the Amsterdam Reserve Police and it was this experience that led to his first novel, **Outsider in Amsterdam** (1975), published at a time when he was leaving the city and moving to Maine as a member of a Buddhist group.*

*Van de Wetering's Amsterdam Cop series has continued through thirteen novels, with some like **The Maine Massacre** (1979) set far from the Netherlands. The series seemed to conclude with **Hard Rain** (1987), but in the 1990s two more novels appeared. **The Hollow-Eyed Angel** (1996) finds the commissaris on the verge of retirement but taking on one more case in New York City.*

*The short stories of Janwillem van de Wetering have been collected in **Inspector Saito's Small Satori** (1985), **The Sergeant's Cat and Other Stories** (1987) and **Mangrove Mame and Other Tropical Tales of Terror** (1995). "A Great Sight" was published in **Top Crime** and reprinted in **The Year's Best Mystery and Suspense Stories - 1984, Murder and Mystery in Maine** and **Purr-Fect Crime.***

A Great Sight

by Janwillem van de Wetering

No, it wasn't easy. It took a great deal of effortful dreaming to get where I am now. Where I am is Moose Bay, on the Maine coast, which is on the east of the United States of America, in case you haven't been looking at maps lately. Moose Bay is long and narrow, bordered by two peninsulas and holding some twenty square miles of water. I've lived on the south shore for almost thirty years now, always alone—if you don't count a couple of old cats—and badly crippled. Lost the use of my legs I have, thirty years ago, and that was my release and my ticket to Moose Bay. I've often wondered whether the mishap was really an accident. Sure enough, the fall was due to faulty equipment (a new strap that broke) and quite beyond my will. The telephone company that employed me acknowledged their responsibility easily enough, paying me handsomely so that I could be comfortably out of work for the rest of my life. But didn't I, perhaps, dream myself into that fall? You see, I wasn't exactly happy being a telephone repairman. Up one post and down another, climbing or slithering up and down forever, day after day, and not in the best of climates. For years I did that and there was no way I could see in which the ordeal would ever end. So I began to dream of a way out, and of where I would go. To be able to dream is a gift. My father didn't have the talent. No imagination the old man had, in Holland he lived, where I was born, and he had a similar job to what I would have later. He was a window-cleaner and I guess he could only visualize death, for when *he* fell it was the last thing he ever did. I survived, with mashed legs. I never dreamed of death, I dreamed of the great sights I would still see, whisking myself to a life on a rocky coast, where I would be alone, maybe with a few old cats, in a cedar log cabin with a view of the water, the sky, and a line of trees on the other shore. I would see, I dreamed, rippling waves or the mirror-like surface of a great expanse of liquid beauty on a windless day. I never gave that up, the possibility of seeing great sights, and I dreamed myself up here, where everything is as I thought it might be, only better.

Now don't get me wrong, I'm not your dreamy type. No long hair and beads for me, no debts unpaid or useless things just lying about in the house. Everything is spic-and-span with me; the kitchen works, there's an ample supply of staples, each in their own jar, I have good vegetables from the garden, an occasional bird I get with the shotgun, and fish caught off my dock. I can't walk so well, but I get about on my crutches and the pickup has been changed so that I can drive it with my hands. No fleas on the cats, either, and no smell from the outhouse. I have all I need and all within easy reach. There must be richer people in the world (don't I see them sometimes, sailing along in their hundred-foot sky-scrapers?), but I don't have to envy them. May they live happily for as long as it takes; I'll just sit here and watch the sights from my porch.

Or I watch them from the water. I have an eight-foot dory and it rows quite well in the bay if the waves aren't too high, for it *will* ship water when the weather gets rough. There's much to see when I go rowing. A herd of harbor seals lives just out of my cove and they know me well, coming to play around my boat as soon as I sing out to them. I bring them a rubber ball that they push about for a bit, and throw even, until they want to go about their own business again and bring it back. I've named them all and can identify the individuals when they frolic in the spring, or raise their tails and heads, lolling in the summer sun.

I go out most good days, for I've taken it upon myself to keep this coast clean. Garbage drifts in, thrown in by the careless, off ships I suppose, and by the city people, the unfortunates who never look at the sights. I get beer cans to pick up in my net, and every vari-ety of plastic container, boards with rusty nails in them and occa-sionally a complete vessel, made out of crumbly foam. I drag it all to the same spot and burn the rubbish. Rodney, the fellow I share Moose Bay with—he lives a mile down from me in a tar-papered shack—makes fun of me when I perform my duty. He'll come by in his smart powerboat, flat on the water and sharply pointed, with a loud engine pushing it that looks like three regular outboards stacked on top of each other. Rodney can really zip about in that thing. He's a thin, ugly fellow with a scraggly black beard and big slanted eyes above his crooked nose. He's from here, of course, and he won't let me forget his lawful nativity. Much higher up the scale than me, he claims, for what am I but some itinerant, an alien washed up from nowhere, tolerated by the locals? If I didn't happen to be an old codger, and lame, Rodney says, he would drown me like he does his kittens. Hop, into the sack, weighted down with a good boulder, and away with the mess. But being what I am, sort of human in a way, he puts up with my presence for a while, provided I don't trespass on his bit of the shore, crossing the high-tide line, for then he'll have to shoot me, with the deer rifle he now uses for poaching. Rodney has a vegetable garden, too, even though he doesn't care for greens. The garden is a trap for deer so that he can shoot them from his shack, preferably at night, after he has frozen them with a flashlight.

There are reasons for me not to like Rodney too much. He shot my friend, the killer whale that used to come here some summers ago. Killer whales are a rare sight on this coast, but they do pop up from time to time. They're supposed to be wicked animals, that will push your boat over and gobble you up when you're thrashing about, weighed down by your boots and your oilskins. Maybe they do that, but my friend didn't do it to me. He used to float alongside my dory, that he could have tipped with a single flap of his great triangular tail. He would roll over on his side, all thirty feet of him, and grin lazily from the corner of his huge curved mouth. I could see his big gleaming teeth and mirror my face in his calm, humorous eye, and I would sing to him. I haven't got a good loud voice, but I would hum away, making up a few words here and there, and he'd lift a flipper in appreciation and snort if my song wasn't long enough for his liking. Every day that killer whale came to me; I swear he was waiting for me out in the bay, for as soon as I'd splash my oars I'd see his six-foot fin cut through the waves, and a moment later his black-and-white head, always with that welcoming grin.

Now we don't have any electricity down here, and kerosene isn't as cheap as it used to be, so maybe Rodney was right when he said that he shot the whale because he needed the blubber. Blubber makes good fuel, Rodney says. Me, I think he was wrong, for he never got the blubber anyway. When he'd shot the whale, zipping past it in the powerboat, and got the animal between the eyes with his deer rifle, the whale just sank. I never saw its vast body wash up. Perhaps it didn't die straightaway and could make it to the depth of the ocean, to die there in peace.

He's a thief, too, Rodney is. He'll steal anything he can get his hands on, to begin with his welfare. There's nothing wrong with Rodney's back but he's stuffed a lot of complaints into it, enough so that the doctors pay attention. He collects his check and his food stamps, and he gets his supplies for free. There's a town, some fifty miles further along, and they employ special people there to give money to the poor, and counselors to listen to pathetic homemade tales, and there's a society that distributes gifts on holiday. Rodney even gets his firewood every year, brought by young religious men on a truck; they stack it right where Rodney points—no fee.

"Me against the world," Rodney says, "for the world owes me a living. I never asked to be born but here I am, and my hands are out." He'll be drinking when he talks like that, guzzling my Sunday bourbon on my porch, and he'll point his long finger at me. "You some sort of Kraut?"

I say I'm Dutch. The Dutch fought the Krauts during the war; I fought a bit myself until they caught me and put me in a camp. They were going to kill me, but then the Americans came. "Saved you, did we?" Rodney will say, and fill up his glass again. "So you owe us now, right? So how come you're living off the fat of this land, you with the crummy legs?" He'll raise his glass and I'll raise mine.

Rodney lost his wife. He still had her when I settled in my cabin, I got to talk to her at times and liked her fine. She would talk to Rodney, about his ways, and he would leer at her, and he was still leering when she was found at the bottom of the cliff. "Never watched where she was going," Rodney said to the sheriff, who took the corpse away. The couple had a dog, who was fond of Rodney's wife and unhappy when she was gone. The dog would howl at night and keep Rodney awake, but the dog happened to fall off the cliff, too. Same cliff. Maybe I should have reported the coincidence to the authorities, but it wasn't much more than a coincidence and, as Rodney says, accidents will happen. Look at me, I fell down a telephone post, nobody pushed *me*, right? It was a brand-new strap that snapped when it shouldn't have; a small event, quite beyond my control.

No, I never went to the sheriff and I've never stood up to Rodney. There's just the two of us on Moose Bay. He's the bad guy who'll tip his garbage into the bay and I'm the in-between guy who's silly enough to pick it up. We also have a good guy, who lives at the end of the north peninsula, at the tip, facing the ocean. Michael his name is, Michael the lobsterman. A giant of a man, Michael is, with a golden beard and flashing teeth. I can see his smile when his lobster boat enters the bay. The boat is one of these old-fashioned jobs, sturdy and white and square, puttering along at a steady ten knots in every sort of weather. Michael's got a big winch on it, for hauling up the heavy traps, and I can see him taking the lobsters out and putting the bait in and throwing them back. Michael has some thousand traps, all along the coast, but his best fishing is here in Moose Bay. Over the years we've got to know each other and I sometimes go out with him, much further than the dory can take me. Then we see the old squaws flock in, the diver ducks that look as if they've flown in from a Chinese painting, with their thin curved tailfeathers and delicately-drawn wings and necks. Or we watch the big whales, snorting and spouting, and the haze on the horizon where the sun dips, causing indefinably soft colors, or we just smell the clear air together, coming to cool the forests in summer. Michael knows Rodney, too, but he isn't the gossipy kind. He'll frown when he sees the powerboat lurking in Moose Bay and gnaw his pipe before he turns away. When Michael doesn't stop at my dock he'll wave and make some gesture, in lieu of conversation—maybe he'll hold his hands close together to show me how far he could see when he cut through the fog, or he'll point at a bird flying over us, a heron in slow flight, or a jay, hurrying from shore to shore, gawking and screeching, and I'll know what he means.

This Michael is a good guy. I knew it the first time I saw his silhouette on the lobster boat, and I've heard good stories about him, too. A knight in shining armor who has saved people about to drown in storms, or marooned and sick on the islands. A giant and a genius, for he's built his own boat, and his gear—even his house, a big sprawling structure out of driftwood on pegged beams. And he'll fight when he has to, for it isn't always cozy here. He'll be out in six-foot waves and I've seen him when the bay is frozen up, excepting the channel where the current rages, with icicles on his beard and snow driving against his bow—but he'll still haul up his traps.

I heard he was out in the last war, too, flying an airplane low above the jungle, and he still flies now, on Sundays, for the National Guard.

Rodney got worse. I don't know what devil lives in that man but the fiend must have been thrown out of the lowest hells. Rodney likes new games and he thought it would be fun to chase me a bit. My dory sits pretty low in the water, but there are enough good days here and I can get out quite a bit. When I do Rodney will wait for me, hidden behind the big rocks east of my cove, and he'll suddenly appear, revving his engine, trailing a high wake. When his curly waves hit me I have to bail for my life, and as soon as I'm done the fear will be back, for he'll be after me again.

I didn't quite know what to do then. Get a bigger boat? But then he would think of something else. There are enough games he can play. He knows my fondness for the seals, he could get them one by one, as target practice. There's my vegetable garden, too, close to the track; he could back his truck into it and get my cats as an afterthought, flattening them into the gravel, for they're slow these days, careless with old age. The fear grabbed me by the throat at night, as I watched my ceiling, remembering his dislike of my cabin and thinking how easily it would burn, being made of old cedar with a roof of shingles. I knew it was him who took the battery out of my truck, making me hitchhike to town for a new one. He was also sucking my gas, but I keep a drum of energy near the house. Oh, I'm vulnerable here all right, with the sheriff coming down only once a year. Suppose I talk to the law, suppose the law talks to Rodney, suppose *I* fall down that cliff, too?

I began to dream again, like I had done before, when I was still climbing the telephone posts like a demented monkey. I was bored then, hopelessly bored, and now I was hopelessly afraid. Hadn't I dreamed my way out once before? Tricks can be repeated.

My dream gained strength; it had to, for Rodney was getting rougher. His powerboat kept less distance, went faster. I couldn't see myself sticking to the land. I need to get out on the bay, to listen to the waves lapping the rocks, to hear the seals blow when they clear their nostrils, to hear the kingfishers and the squirrels whirr in the trees on shore, to spot the little ring-necked ducks, busily investigating the shallows, peering eagerly out of their tufted heads. There are the quiet herons stalking the mudflats and the ospreys whirling slowly; there are eagles, even, diving and splashing when the alewives run from the brooks. Would I have to potter about in the vegetable patch all the time, leaning on a crutch while pushing a hoe with my free hand?

I dreamed up a bay free of Rodney. There was a strange edge to the dream—some kind of quality there that I couldn't quite see, but it was splendid, a great sight and part of my imagination although I couldn't quite make it out.

One day, fishing off my dock, I saw Michael's lobster boat nosing into the cove: I waved and smiled and he waved back, but he didn't smile.

He moored the boat and jumped onto the jetty, light as a great cat, touching my arm. We walked up to my porch and I made some strong coffee.

"There's a thief," Michael said, "stealing my lobsters. He used to take a few, few enough to ignore maybe, but now he's taking too many."

"Oho," I said, holding my mug. Michael wouldn't be referring to me. Me? Steal lobsters? how could I ever haul up a trap? The channel is deep in the bay. A hundred feet of cable and a heavy trap at the end of it, never. I would need a winch, like Rodney has on his powerboat.

Besides, doesn't Michael leave me a lobster every now and then? Lying on my dock in the morning, its claws neatly tied with a bit of yellow string?

"Any idea?" he asked.

"Same as yours," I said, "but he's hard to catch. The powerboat is fast. He nips out of the bay before he does his work, to make sure you aren't around."

"Might get the warden," Michael said, "and then he might go to jail, and come out again, and do something bad."

I agreed. "Hard to prove, it would be," I said. "A house burns down, yours or mine. An accident maybe."

Michael left. I stayed on the porch, dreaming away, expending some power. A little power goes a long way in a dream.

It happened the next day, a Sunday it was. I was walking to the shore, for it was low tide and I wanted to see the seals on their rocks. It came about early, just after sunrise. I heard an airplane. A lot of airplanes come by here. There's the regular commuter plane from the town to the big city, and the little ones the tourists fly in summer, and the flying club. There are also big planes, dirtying up the sky, high up, some of them are Russians, they say; the National Guard has to be about, to push them back. The big planes rumble, but this sound was different, light but deadly, far away still. I couldn't see the plane, but when I did it was coming silently, ahead of its own sound, it was that fast. Then it slowed down, surveying the bay.

I've seen fighter planes during World War II, Germans and Englishmen flew them, propeller jobs that would spin around each other above the small Dutch lakes, until one of the planes came down, trailing smoke. Jet planes I only saw later, here in America. They looked dangerous enough, even while they gambolled about, and I felt happy watching them, for I was in the States and they were protecting me from the bad guys lurking in the east.

This airplane was a much-advanced version of what I had seen in the late '40s. Much longer it was, and sleek and quiet as it lost height, aiming for the channel. A baby-blue killer, with twin rudders, sticking up elegantly far behind the large gleaming canopy up front, reflecting the low sunlight. I guessed her to be seventy feet long, easily the size of the splendid yachts of the rich summer people, but there was no pleasure in her; she was all functional, programmed for swift pursuit and destruction only. I grinned when I saw her American stars, set in circles, with a striped bar sticking out at each side. When she was closer I thought I could see the pilot, all wrapped up in his tight suit and helmet, the living brain controlling this deadly superfast vessel of the sky.

I saw that the plane was armed, with white missiles attached to its slender streamlined belly. I had read about those missiles. Costly little mothers they are. Too costly to fire at Rodney's boat, busily stealing away right in front of my cove. Wouldn't the pilot have to explain the loss of one of his slick rockets? He'd surely be in terrible trouble if he returned to base incomplete.

Rodney was thinking the same way for he was jumping up and down in his powerboat, grinning and sticking two fingers at the airplane hovering above the bay.

Then the plane roared and shot away, picking up speed at an incredible rate. I was mightily impressed and grateful, visualizing the enemy confronted with such force, banking, diving, rising again at speeds much faster than sound.

The plane had gone and I was alone again, with Rodney misbehaving in the bay, taking the lobsters out as fast as he could—one trap shooting up after another, yanked up by his nastily whining little winch.

The plane came back, silently, with the roar of its twin engines well behind it. It came in low, twenty-five feet above the short choppy waves. Rodney, unaware, busy, didn't even glance over his shoulder. I was leaning on the railing of my porch, gaping stupidly. Was the good guy going to ram the bad guy? Would they go down together? This had to be the great sight I had been dreaming up. Perhaps I should have felt guilty.

Seconds it took, maybe less than one second. Is there still time at five thousand miles an hour?

Then there was the flame, just after the plane passed the power-boat. A tremendous cloud of fire, billowing, deep orange with fiery red tongues, blotting out the other shore, frayed with black smoke at the edges. The flame shot out of the rear of the plane and hung sizzling around Rodney's boat. The boat must have dissolved instantly, for I never found any debris. Fried to a cinder. Did Rodney's body whizz away inside that hellish fire? It must have, bones, teeth and all.

I didn't see where the plane went. There are low hills at the end of the bay, so it must have zoomed up immediately once the afterburners spat out the huge flame.

Michael smiled sadly when he visited me a few days later and we were having coffee on my porch again.

"You saw it happen?"

"Oh yes," I said. "A great sight indeed."

"Did he leave any animals that need taking care of?"

"Just the cat," I said. The cat was on my porch, a big marmalade tom that had settled in already.

Time has passed again since then. The bay is quiet now. We're having a crisp autumn and I'm enjoying the cool days rowing about on the bay, watching the geese gather, honking majestically as they get ready to go south.

LOREN D. ESTLEMAN

"Greektown"

*Loren D. Estleman was born in Ann Arbor, Michigan on September 15, 1952. He graduated from Eastern Michigan University in 1974 with degrees in English and journalism, becoming a reporter and staff writer on Michigan newspapers. He began writing westerns and crime novels in the late 1970s. Following two Sherlockian fantasy novels he turned to detective fiction in 1980 with **Motor City Blues**, introducing Amos Walker, the first new private eye to emerge in the decade of the '80s.*

*Estleman's 1984 Walker novel **Sugartown** won the PWA Shamus award, and two of his short stories, "Eight Mike and Dequindre" (1985) and "The Crooked Way" (1988), were also honored with Shamus Awards. His 1990 novel **Whiskey River** was an Edgar nominee.*

*The Amos Walker short stories are collected in **General Murders** (1988) and nine of Estleman's non-series stories can be found in **People Who Kill** (1993). "Greektown" was first published in **Alfred Hitchcock's Mystery Magazine** and reprinted in **The Mammoth Book of Private Eye Stories** and **General Murders**.*

Greektown

by Loren D. Estleman

The restaurant was damp and dim and showed every indication of having been hollowed out of a massive stump, with floorboards scoured as white as wood grubs and tall booths separated from the stools at the counter by an aisle just wide enough for skinny waitresses like you never see in Greektown. It was Greektown, and the only waitress in sight looked like a garage door in a uniform. She caught me checking out the booths and trundled my way, turning stools with her left hip as she came.

"You are Amos Walker?" She had a husky accent and large, dark, pretty eyes set in the rye dough of her face. I said I was, and she told me Mr. Xanthes was delayed and sat me down in a booth halfway between the door and the narrow hallway leading to the restrooms in back. Somewhere a radio turned low was playing one of those frantic Mediterranean melodies that sound like hornets set loose in the string section.

The waitress was freshening my coffee when my host arrived, extending a small right hand and a smiling observation on downtown Detroit traffic. Constantine Xanthes was a wiry five feet and ninety pounds with deep laugh lines from his narrow eyes to his broad mouth and hair as black at fifty as mine was going gray at thirty-three. His light blue tailormade suit fit him like a sheen of water. He smiled a lot, but so does every other restaurateur, and none of them means it either. When he found out I hadn't eaten he ordered egg lemon soup, bread, feta cheese, roast lamb, and a bottle of ouzo for us both. I passed on the ouzo.

"Greektown used to be more than just fine places to eat," he sighed, poking a fork at his lamb. "When my parents came it was a little Athens, with markets and pretty girls in red and white dresses at festival time and noise like I can't describe to you. It took in Macomb, Randolph, and Monroe Streets, not just one block of Monroe like now. Now those colorful old men you see drinking retsina on the stoops get up and go home to the suburbs at dark."

I washed down the last of the strong cheese with coffee. "I'm a good P.I., Mr. Xanthes, but I'm not good enough to track down and bring back the old days. What else can I do to make your life easier?"

He refilled his glass with ouzo and I watched his Adam's apple bob twice as the syrupy liquid slid down his throat. Afterwards he was still smiling, but the vertical line that had appeared between his brows when he was talking about what had happened to his neighborhood had deepened.

"I have a half brother, Joseph," he began. "He's twenty-three years younger than I am; his mother was our father's second wife. She deserted him when he was six. When Father died, my wife and I took over the job of raising Joseph, but by then I was working sixty hours a week at General Motors and he was seventeen and too much for Grace to handle with two children of our own. He ran away. We didn't hear from him until last summer, when he walked into the house unannounced, all smiles and hugs, at least for me. He and Grace never got along. He congratulated me on my success in the restaurant business and said he'd been living in Iowa for the past nine years, where he'd married and divorced twice. His first wife left him without so much as a note and had a lawyer send him papers six weeks later. The second filed suit on grounds of brutality. It seems that during quarrels he took to beating her with the cord from an iron. He was proud of that.

"He's been here fourteen months, and in that time he's held more jobs than I can count. Some he quit, some he was fired from, always for the same reason. He can't work with or for a woman. I kept him on here as a busboy until he threw a stool at one of my waitresses. She'd asked him to get a can of coffee from the storeroom and forgot to say please. I had to let him go."

He paused, and I lit a Winston to keep from having to say anything. It was all beginning to sound familiar. I wondered why.

When he saw I wasn't going to comment he drew a folded clipping from an inside breast pocket and spread it out on the table with the reluctant care of a father getting ready to punish his child. It was from that morning's *Free Press,* and it was headed PSYCHIATRIST PROFILES FIVE O'CLOCK STRANGLER.

That was the name the press had hung on the nut who had stalked and murdered four women on their way home from work on the city's northwest side on four separate evenings over the past two weeks. The women were found strangled to death in public places around quitting time, or reported missing by their families from that time and discovered later. Their ages ranged from twenty to forty-six, they had had no connection with each other in life, and they were all WASPs. One was a nurse, two were secretaries, the fourth had been something mysterious in city government. None was raped. The *Freep* had dug up a shrink who claimed the killer was between twenty-five and forty, a member of an ethnic or racial minority group, and a hater of professional women, a man who had had experiences with such women unpleasant enough to unhinge him. It was the kind of article you usually find in the science section after someone's made off with the sports and the comics, only today it had run on page one because there hadn't been any murders in a couple of days to keep the story alive. I'd read it at breakfast. I knew now what had nagged me about Xanthes' story.

"Your brother's the Five O'Clock Strangler?" I tipped half an inch of ash into the tin tray on the table.

"Half brother," he corrected. "If I was sure of that, I wouldn't have called you. Joseph could have killed that waitress, Mr. Walker. As it was he nearly broke her arm with that stool, and I had to pay for X-rays and give her a bonus to keep her from pressing charges. This article says the strangler hates working women. Joseph hates *all* women, but working women especially. His mother was a licensed practical nurse and she abandoned him. His first wife was a legal secretary and *she* left him. He told me he started beating his second wife when she started talking about getting a job. The police say that because the killer strangles women with just his hands he has to be big and strong. That description fits my half brother; he's built more like you than me, and he works out regularly."

"Does he have anything against white Anglo-Saxon Protestants?"

"I don't know. But his mother was one and so was his first wife. The waitress he hurt was of Greek descent."

72

I burned some more tobacco. "Does he have an alibi for any of the times the women were killed?"

"I asked him, in a way that wouldn't make him think I suspected him. He said he was home alone." He shifted his weight on the bench. "I didn't want to press it, but I called him one of those nights and he didn't answer. But it wasn't until I read this article that I really started to worry. It could have been written about Joseph. That's when I decided to call you. You once dug up an eyewitness to an auto accident whose testimony saved a friend of mine a bundle. He talks about you often."

"I have a license to stand in front of," I said. "If your half brother is the strangler I'll have to send him over."

"I understand that. All I ask is that you call me before you call the police. It's this not knowing, you know? And don't let him know he's being investigated. There's no telling what he'll do if he finds out I suspect him."

We took care of finances—in cash; you'll look in vain for a checkbook in Greektown—and he slid over a wallet-sized photo of a darkly handsome man in his late twenties with glossy black hair like his half brother's and big liquid eyes not at all like Xanthes' slits. "He goes by Joe Santine. You'll find him working part-time at Butsukitis' market on Brush." Joseph's home telephone number and an address on Gratiot were written on the back of the picture. That was a long way from the area where the bodies were found, but then the killer hardly ever lives in the neighborhood where he works. Not that that made any difference to the cops busy tossing every house and apartment on the northwest side.

He looked like his picture. After leaving the restaurant, I'd walked around the corner to a building with a fruit and vegetable stand out front and a faded canvas awning lettered BUTSUKITIS' FINE PRODUCE. While a beefy bald man in his sixties with fat quilting his chest under a white apron was dropping some onions into a paper sack for me, a tall young man came out the front door lugging a crate full of cabbages. He hoisted the crate onto a bare spot on the stand, swept large shiny eyes over the milling crowd of tomato-squeezers and melon-huggers, and went back inside swinging his broad shoulders.

As the grocer was ringing up the sale, a blonde wearing a navy blue business suit asked for help loading two bags of apples and cherries into her car. "Santine!" he bellowed.

The young man returned. Told to help the lady, he hesitated, then slouched forward and snatched up the bags. He stashed them on the front seat of a green Olds parked half a block down the street and swung around and walked away while she was still rummaging in her handbag for a tip. His swagger going back into the store was pronounced. I paid for my onions and left.

Back at the office I called Iowa information and got two numbers. The first belonged to a private detective agency in Des Moines. I called them, fed them the dope I had on Santine and asked them to scrape up what they could. My next call was to the Des Moines *Express*, where a reporter held me up for fifty dollars for combing the morgue for stories about non-rape female assault and murder during the last two years Santine lived in the state. They both promised to wire the information to Barry Stackpole at the Detroit *News* and I hung up and dialed Barry's number and traded a case of scotch for his cooperation. The expenses on this one were going to eat up my fee. Finally I called John Alderdyce at police headquarters. "Who's working the Five O'Clock Strangler case?" I asked him.

"Why?"

I used the dead air counting how many times he'd asked me that and dividing it by how many times I'd answered.

"DeLong," he said then. "I could just hang up because I'm busy, but you'd probably just call again."

"Probably. Is he in?"

"He's in that lot off Lahser where they found the last body. With Michael Kurof."

"The psychic?"

"No, the plumber. They're stopping there on their way to fix De-Long's toilet." He broke the connection.

The last body had been found lying in a patch of weeds in a wooded lot off Lahser just south of West Grand River by a band student taking a shortcut home from practice. I parked next to the curb behind a blue-and-white and mingled with a group of uniforms and obvious plain-clothesmen watching Kurof walk around, with Inspector DeLong nipping along at his side like a spaniel trying to keep up with a Great Dane. DeLong was a razor-faced twenty-year cop with horns of pink scalp retreating along a mouse-colored widow's peak. Kurof, a Russian-born bear of a man, bushy-haired and blue of chin even when it was still wet from shaving, bobbed his big head in time with DeLong's mile-a-minute patter for a few moments, then raised a palm, cutting him off. After that they wandered the lot in silence.

"What they looking for, rattlesnakes?" muttered a grizzled fatty in a baggy brown suit.

"Vibes," someone answered. "Emanations, the Russky calls 'em."

Lardbottom snorted. "We ran fortune-tellers in when I was in uniform."

I was nudged by a young black uniform, who winked gravely and stooped to lay a gold pencil he had taken from his shirt pocket on the ground, then backed away from it. Kurof's back was turned. Eventually he and DeLong made their way to the spot, where the psychic picked up the pencil, stroked it once between the first and second fingers of his right hand, and turned to the black cop with a broad smile, holding out the item. "You are having fun with me, officer," he announced in a deep burring voice. The uniform smiled stiffly back and accepted the pencil.

"Did you learn anything, Dr. Kurof?" DeLong wanted to know.

Kurof shook his great head slowly. "Nothing useful, I fear. Just a tangible hatred. The air is ugly everywhere here, but it is ugliest where we are standing. It crawls."

"We're standing precisely where the body was found." The inspector pushed aside a clump of thistles with his foot to expose a fresh yellow stake driven into the earth. He turned toward one of the watching uniforms. "Give our guest a lift home. Thank you, doctor. We'll be in touch when something else comes up." They shook hands and the Russian moved off slowly with his escort.

"Hatred," the fat detective growled. "Like we needed a gypsy to tell us that."

DeLong told him to shut up and go back to headquarters. As the knot of investigators loosened, I approached the inspector and introduced myself.

"Walker," he considered. "Sure, I've seen you jawing with Alderdyce. Who hired you, the family of one of the victims?"

"Just running an errand." Sometimes it's best to let a cop keep his notions. "What about what this psychiatrist said about the strangler in this morning's *Freep?* You agree with that?"

"Shrinks. Twenty years in school to tell us why some j.d. sapped an old lady and snatched her purse. I'll stick with guys like Kurof; at least he's not smug." He stuck a Tiparillo in his mouth and I lit it and a Winston for me. He sucked smoke. "My theory is the killer's unemployed and he sees all these women running out and getting themselves fulfilled by taking his job and something snaps. It isn't just coincidence that the statistics on crime against women have risen with their number in the work force."

"Is he a minority?"

"I hope so." He grinned quickly and without mirth. "No, I know what you mean. Maybe. Minorities outnumber the majority in this town in case you haven't noticed. Could be the victims are all WASPs because there are more women working who are WASPs. I'll ask him when we arrest him."

"Think you will?"

He glared at me, then he shrugged. "This is the third mass-murder case I've investigated. The one fear is that it'll just stop. I'm still hoping to wrap it up before famous criminologists start coming in from all over to give us a hand. I never liked circuses even when I was a kid."

"What are you holding back from the press on this one?"

"You expect me to answer that? Give up the one thing that'll help us differentiate between the original and all the copycats?"

"Call John Alderdyce. He'll tell you I sit on things till they hatch."

"Oh, hell." He dropped his little cigar half-smoked and crushed it out. "The guy clobbers his victims before he strangles them. One blow to the left cheek, probably with his right fist. Keeps 'em from struggling."

"Could he be a boxer?"

"Maybe. Someone used to using his dukes."

I thanked him for talking to me. He said, "I hope you are working for the family of a victim."

I got out of there without answering. Lying to a cop like DeLong can be like trying to smuggle a bicycle through customs.

It was coming up on two o'clock. If the killer was planning to strike that day, I had three hours. At the first telephone booth I came to, I excavated my notebook and called Constantine Xanthes' home number in Royal Oak. His wife answered. She had a mellow voice and no account.

"Yes, Connie told me he was going to hire you. He's not home, though. Try the restaurant."

I explained she was the one I wanted to speak with and asked if

I could come over. After a brief pause she agreed and gave me directions. I told her to expect me in half an hour.

It was a white frame house that would have been in the country when it was built, but now it was shouldered by two housing tracts with a third going up in the empty field across the street. The doorbell was answered by a tall woman on the far side of forty with black hair streaked blonde to cover the gray and a handsome oval face, the flesh shiny around the eyes and mouth from recent remodeling. She wore a dark knit dress that accentuated the slim lines of her torso and a long colored scarf to make you forget she was big enough to look down at the top of her husband's head without trying. We exchanged greetings and she let me in and hung up my hat and we walked into a dim living room furnished heavily in oak and dark leather. We sat down facing each other in a pair of horsehair-stuffed chairs.

"You're not Greek," I said.

"I hardly ever am." Her voice was just as mellow in person.

"Your husband was mourning the old Greektown at lunch and now I find out he lives in the suburbs with a woman who isn't Greek."

"Connie's ethnic standards are very high for other people."

She was smiling when she said it, but I didn't press the point. "He says you and Joseph have never been friendly. In what ways weren't you friendly when he was living here?"

"I don't suppose it's ever easy bringing up someone else's son. His having been deserted didn't help. Lord save me if I suggested taking out the garbage."

"Was he sullen, abusive, what?"

"Sullen was his best mood. 'Abusive' hardly describes his reaction to the simplest request. The children were beginning to repeat his foul language. I was relieved when he ran away."

"Did you call the police."

"Connie did. They never found him. By that time he was eighteen and technically an adult. He couldn't have been brought back without his consent anyway."

"Did he ever hit you?"

"He wouldn't dare. He worshiped Connie."

"Did he ever box?"

"You mean fight? I think so. Sometimes he came home from school with his clothes torn or a black eye, but he wouldn't talk about it. That was before he quit. Fighting is normal. We had some of the same problems with our son; he grew out of it."

I was coming to the short end. "Any scrapes with the law? Joseph, I mean."

She shook her head. Her eyes were warm and tawny. "You know, you're quite goodlooking. You have noble features."

"So does a German shepherd."

"I work in clay. I'd like to have you pose for me in my studio sometime." She waved long nails toward a door to the left. "I specialize in nudes."

"So do I. But not with clients' wives." I rose.

She lifted penciled eyebrows. "Was I that obvious?"

"Probably not, but I'm a detective." I thanked her and got my hat and let myself out.

Xanthes had told me his half brother got off at four. At ten to, I swung by the market and bought two quarts of strawberries. The beefy bald man, whom I'd pegged as Butsukitis, the owner, appeared glad to see me. Memories are long in Greektown. I said, "I just had an operation and the doc says I shouldn't lift any more than five pounds. Could your boy carry these to the car?"

"I let my boy leave early. Slow day. I will carry them."

He did, and I drove away stuck with two quarts of strawberries. They give me hives. Had Santine been around I'd planned to tail him after he punched out. Beating the steering wheel at red lights, I bucked and squirmed my way through late afternoon traffic to Gratiot, where my man kept an apartment on the second floor of a charred brick building that had housed a recording studio in the gravy days of Motown. I ditched my hat, jacket, and tie in the car and at Santine's door put on a pair of aviator's glasses in case he remembered me from the market. If he answered my knock, I was looking for another apartment. There was no answer. I considered slipping the latch and taking a look around inside, but it was too early in the round to play catch with my license. I went back down and made myself uncomfortable in my heap across the street from the entrance.

It was growing dark when a cab creaked its brakes in front of the building and Santine got out, wearing a blue wind-breaker over the clothes I'd seen him in earlier. He paid the driver and went inside. Since the window of his apartment looked out on Gratiot I let the cab go, noting its number, hit the starter, and wound my way to the company's headquarters on Woodward.

A puffy-faced black man in work clothes looked at me from behind a steel desk in an office smelling of oil. The floor tingled with the swallowed bellowing of engines in the garage below. I gave him a hinge at my investigator's photostat, placing my thumb over the "Private," and told him in an official voice I wanted information on the cab in question.

He looked back down at the ruled pink sheet he was scribbling on and said, "I been dispatcher here eleven years. You think I don't know a plastic badge when I see one?"

I licked a ten dollar bill across the sheet.

"That's Dillard," he said, watching the movement.

"He just dropped off a fare on Gratiot." I gave him the address. "I want to know where he picked him up and when."

He found the cab number on another ruled sheet attached to a clipboard on the wall and followed the line with his finger to some writing in another column. "Evergreen, between Schoolcraft and Kendall. Dillard logged it in at six twenty."

I handed him the bill without comment. The spot where Santine had entered the cab was an hour's easy walk from where the bodies of two of the murdered women had been found.

I swung past Joe Santine's apartment near Greektown on my way home. There was a light on. That night after supper I caught all the news reports on TV and looked for bulletins and wound up watching a succession of sitcoms full of single mothers shrieking at their kids about sex. There was nothing about any new stranglings. I went to bed. Eating breakfast next day I turned on the radio and read the *Free Press*. There was still nothing.

The name of the psychiatrist quoted in the last issue was Kornecki. I looked him up and called his office in the National Bank building. I expected a secretary, but I got him.

"I'd like to talk to you about someone I know," I said.

"Someone you know. I see." He spoke in Cathedral tones.

"It's not me. I have an entirely different set of neuroses."

"My consultation fee is one hundred dollars for forty minutes."

"I'll take twenty-five dollars' worth," I said.

"No, that's for forty minutes or any fraction thereof. I have a cancellation at eleven. Shall I have my secretary pencil you in when she returns from her break?"

I told him to do so, gave him my name, and rang off before I could say anything about his working out of a bank. The hundred went onto the expense sheet.

Kornecki's reception room was larger than my office by half. A redhead at a kidney-shaped desk smiled tightly at me and found my name on her calendar, and buzzed me through. The inner sanctum, pastel green with a blue carpet, dark green naugahyde couch, and a large glass-topped desk bare but for a telephone intercom, looked out on downtown through a window whose double panes swallowed the traffic noise. Behind the desk, a man about my age, wearing a blue pinstripe and steel-rimmed glasses, sat smiling at me with several thousand dollars' worth of dental work. He wore his sandy hair in bangs like Alfalfa.

We shook hands and I took charge of the customer's chair, a pedestal job upholstered in green vinyl to match the couch. I asked if I could smoke. He said whatever made me comfortable and indicated a smoking stand nearby. I lit up and laid out Santine's background without naming him. Kornecki listened.

"Is this guy capable of violence against strange women?" I finished.

He smiled again. "We all are, Mr. Walker. Every one of us men; it's our only advantage. You think your man is the strangler, is that it?"

"I guess I was absent the day they taught subtle."

"Oh, you were subtle. But you can't know how many people I've spoken with since that article appeared, wanting to be assured that their uncle or cousin or best friend isn't the killer. Hostility between the sexes is nothing new, but these last few confusing years have aggravated things. From what you've told me, though, I don't think you need to worry."

Those rich tones rumbling up from his slender chest made you want to look around to see who was talking. I waited, smoking.

"The powder is there," he went on. "But it needs a spark. If your man were to start murdering women, his second wife would have been his first victim. He wouldn't have stopped at beating her. My own theory is that the strangler suffered some real or imagined wrong at a woman's hand in his past, and that recently the wrong was repeated, either by a similar act committed by another woman, or by his coming into contact with the same woman."

"What sort of wrong?"

"It could be anything. Sexual domination is the worst because it means loss of self-esteem. Possibly she worked for a living, but it's just as likely that he equates women who work with her dominance. They would be a substitute; he would lack the courage to strike out at the actual source of his frustration."

"Suppose he ran into his mother or something like that."

He shook his head. "Too far back. I don't place as much importance on early childhood as many of my colleagues. Stale charges don't explode that easily."

"You've been a big help," I said, and we talked about sports and politics until my hundred dollars were up.

From there I went to the Detroit *News* and Barry Stackpole's cubicle, where he greeted me with the lopsided grin the silver plate in his head had left him with after some rough trade tried to blow him up in his car. He pointed to a stack of papers on his desk. I sat on one of the antique whisky crates he uses to file things in—there was a similar stack on the only other chair besides his—and went through the stuff. It had come over the wire that morning from the Des Moines agency and the *Express*, and none of it was for me. Santine had held six jobs in his last two years in Iowa, fetch-and-carry work, no brains need apply. His first wife had divorced him on grounds of marriage breakdown and he hadn't contested the action. His second had filed for extreme cruelty. The transcripts of that one were ugly but not uncommon. There were enough articles from the newspaper on violent crimes against women to make you think twice about moving there, but if there was a pattern it was lost on me. The telephone rang while I was reshuffling the papers. Barry barked his name into the receiver, paused, and held it out to me.

"I gave my service this number," I explained, accepting it.

"You bastard, you promised to call me before you called the police."

The voice belonged to Constantine Xanthes. I straightened. "Start again."

"Joseph just called me from police headquarters. They've arrested him for the stranglings."

I met Xanthes in Homicide. He was wearing the same light blue suit or one just like it and his face was pale beneath the olive pigment. "He's being interrogated now," he said stiffly. "My lawyer's with him."

"I didn't call the cops." I made my voice low. The room was alive with uniforms and detectives in shirtsleeves droning into telephones and comparing criminal anecdotes at the water cooler.

"I know. When I got here, Inspector DeLong told me that Joseph walked into some kind of trap."

On cue, DeLong entered the squad room from the hallway leading to Interrogation. His jacket was off and his shirt clung, transparent, to his narrow chest. When he saw me his eyes flamed. "You said you were representing a *victim's* family."

"I didn't," I corrected. "You did. What's this trap?"

He grinned to his molars. "It's the kind of thing you do in these things when you did everything else. Sometimes it works. We had another strangling last night."

My stomach took a dive. "It wasn't on the news."

"We didn't release it. The body was jammed into a culvert on Schoolcraft. When we got the squeal we threw wraps over it, morgued the corpse—she was a teacher at Redford High—and stuck a department store dummy in its place. These nuts like publicity; when there isn't any they might check to see if the body is still there. So Santine climbs down the bank at half past noon and takes a look inside and three officers step out of the bushes and screw their service revolvers in his ears."

"Pretty thin," I said.

"How thick does it have to be with a full confession?"

Xanthes swayed. I grabbed his arm. I was still looking at DeLong.

"He's talking to a tape recorder now," he said, filling a Dixie cup at the cooler. "He knows the details on all five murders, including the blow to the cheek."

"I'd like to see him." Xanthes was still pale, but he wasn't needing me to hold him up now.

"It'll be a couple of hours."

"I'll wait."

The inspector shrugged, drained the cup, and headed back the way he'd come, side-arming the crumpled container at a steel wastebasket already bubbling over with them. Xanthes said, "He didn't do it."

"I think he probably did." I was somersaulting a Winston back and forth across the back of my hand. "Is your wife home?"

He started slightly. "Grace? She's shopping for art supplies in Southfield. I tried to reach her after the police called, but I couldn't."

"I wonder if I could have a look at her studio."

"Why?"

"I'll tell you in the car." When he hesitated: "It beats hanging around here."

He nodded. In my crate I said, "Your father was proud of his Greek heritage, wasn't he?"

"Fiercely. He was a stonecutter in the old country and he was built like Hercules. He taught me the importance of being a man and the sanctity of womanhood. That's why I can't understand . . ." He shook his head, watching the scenery glide past his window.

"I can. When a man who's been told all his life that a man should be strong lets himself be manipulated by a woman, it does things to him. If he's smart, he'll put distance between himself and the woman. If he's weak, he'll come back and it'll start all over again. And if the woman happens to be married to his half brother, whom he worships—"

I stopped, feeling the flinty chips of his eyes on me. "Who told you that?"

"Your wife, some of it. You, some more. The rest of it I got from a psychiatrist downtown. The women's movement has changed the lives of almost everyone but the women who have the most to lose by embracing it. Your wife's been cheating on you for years."

"Liar!" He lunged across the seat at me. I spun the wheel hard and we shrieked around a corner and he slammed back against the passenger's door. A big Mercury that had been close on our tail blatted its horn and sped past. Xanthes breathed heavily, glaring.

"She propositioned me like a pro yesterday." I corrected our course. We were entering his neighborhood now. "I think she's been doing that kind of thing a long time. I think that when he was living at your place Joseph found out and threatened to tell you. That would have meant divorce from a proud man like you, and your wife would have had to go to work to support herself and the children. So she bribed Joseph with the only thing she had to bribe him with. She's still attractive, but in those days she must have been a knockout; being weak, he took the bribe, and then she had leverage. She hedged her bet by making up those stories about his incorrigible behavior so that you wouldn't believe him if he did tell you. So he got out from under. But the experience had plundered him of his self-respect and tainted his relationships with women from then on.

"Even then he might have grown out of it, but he made the mistake of coming back. Seeing her again shook something loose. He walked into your house Joe Santine and came out the Five O'Clock Strangler, victimizing seemingly independent WASP women like Grace. Who taught him how to use his fists?"

"Our father, probably. He taught me. It was part of a man's training, he said, to know how to defend himself." His voice was as dead as last year's leaves.

We pulled into his driveway and he got out, moving very slowly. Inside the house we paused before the locked door to his wife's studio. I asked him if he had a key.

"No. I've never been inside the room. She's never invited me and I respect her privacy."

I didn't. I slipped the lock with the edge of my investigator's photostat and we entered Grace Xanthes' trophy room.

It had been a bedroom, but she had erected steel utility shelves and moved in a kiln and a long library table on which stood a turning pedestal supporting a lump of red clay that was starting to look like a naked man. The shelves were lined with nude male figure studies twelve to eighteen inches high, posed in various heroic attitudes. They were all of a type, athletically muscled and wide at the shoulders, physically large, all the things the artist's husband wasn't. He walked around the room in a kind of daze, staring at each in turn. It was clear he recognized some of them. I didn't know Joseph at first, but he did. He had filled out since seventeen.

I returned two days' worth of Xanthes' three-day retainer, less expenses, despite his insistence that I'd earned it. A few weeks later court-appointed psychiatrists declared Joe Santine mentally unfit to stand trial and he was remanded for treatment to the State Forensics Center at Ypsilanti. And I haven't had a bowl of egg lemon soup or a slice of feta cheese in months.

RUTH RENDELL

"Father's Day"

Ruth Rendell was born in London on February 17, 1930. She worked as a newspaper reporter and sub-editor before publishing her first novel about Inspector Wexford, **From Doon With Death***, in 1964. From the beginning of her career she has been a prolific author, producing some of the best novels and short stories in the mystery genre. Outstanding among the Wexford novels have been* **A Sleeping Life** *(1978) and* **An Unkindness of Ravens** *(1985), both MWA Edgar nominees.*

Many critics, however, believe that Rendell's true greatness lies in her non-series novels, in modern crime classics like **A Judgement in Stone** *(1977), in books like* **A Demon in My View** *(1976) and* **Live Flesh** *(1986), both CWA Gold Dagger winners, and in* **The Tree of Hands** *(1984), a Silver Dagger winner and Edgar nominee. When she also began writing as "Barbara Vine" in 1986, she won an Edgar Award for* **A Dark-Adapted Eye** *and went on to win Gold Daggers for* **A Fatal Inversion** *(1987) and* **King Solomon's Carpet** *(1991). The Crime Writers Association presented Ruth Rendell with its Cartier Diamond Dagger in 1991, and she was awarded a CBE in the Queen's Honours List in 1996.*

As the most honored of modern mystery writers Ruth Rendell has also won two Edgar awards for her short stories "The Fallen Curtain" (1974) and "The New Girl Friend" (1983). Her first four volumes of tales have been combined into **Collected Stories** *(1987), which was followed by* **The Copper Peacock and Other Stories** *(1991) and* **BloodLines: Long and Short Stories** *(1995). "Father's Day" was first published in* **Ellery Queen's Mystery Magazine** *and has been reprinted in* **The Year's Best Mystery and Suspense Stories - 1985** *and* **Collected Stories***.*

Father's Day

by Ruth Rendell

T eddy had once read in a story written by a Victorian that a certain character liked "to have things pleasant about him." The phrase had stuck in his mind. He, too, liked to have things pleasant about him.

It was to be hoped that pleasantness would prevail while they were all away on holiday together. Teddy was beginning to be afraid they might get on each other's nerves. Anyway, it would be the last time for years the four of them would be able to go away in October, for both Emma and Andrew started school in the spring.

"A pity," Anne said. "May and October are absolutely the best times in the Greek Islands."

She and Teddy had bought the house with the money Teddy's mother had left him. The previous year they had been there twice, and again last May. They hadn't been able to go out in the evenings because they had no baby-sitter. Having Michael and Linda there would make it possible for each couple to go out every other night.

"If Michael will trust us with his children," said Teddy.

"He isn't as bad as that."

"I didn't say he was bad. He's my brother-in-law and I've got to put up with him. He's all right. It's just that he's so nuts about his kids I sometimes wonder how he dares leave them with their own mother when he goes to work."

He was recalling the time they had all spent at Chichester in July and how the evening had been spoilt by Michael's insisting on phoning the baby-sitter before the play began, during the interval, and before they began the drive home. And when he wasn't on the phone or obliged to be silent in the theater, he had talked continually about Andrew and Alison in a fretful way.

"He's under a lot of stress," Linda had whispered to her sister. "He's going through a bad patch at work."

Teddy didn't think it natural for a man to be so involved with his children. He was fond of his own children, of course he was, and anxious enough about them when he had cause, but they were little still and, let's face it, sometimes tiresome and boring. He looked forward to the time when they were older and there could be real companionship. Michael was more like a mother than a father, a mother hen. Teddy, for his sins, had occasionally changed diapers and made up formula, but Michael actually seemed to enjoy doing these things and talking about them afterwards. Teddy hoped he wouldn't be treated to too much Dr. Jolly philosophy while on Stamnos.

Just before they went, about a week before, Valerie Wilton's marriage broke up. Valerie had been at school with Anne, though just as much Linda's friend, and had written long letters to both of them, explaining everything and asking for their understanding. She had gone off with a man she met at her Commercial French evening class. Apparently the affair had been going on for a long time, but Valerie's husband had known nothing about it and her departure had come to him as a total shock. He came round and poured out his troubles to Anne and drank a lot of Scotch and broke down and cried. For all Teddy knew, he did the same at Linda's. Teddy stayed out of it—he didn't want to get involved. Liking to have things pleasant about him, he declined gently but firmly even to discuss it with Anne.

"Linda says it's really upset Michael," said Anne. "He identifies with George, you see. He's so emotional."

"I said I wasn't going to talk about it, darling, and by golly I'm not!"

During the flight, Michael had Alison on his lap and Andrew in the seat beside him. Anne remarked in a plaintive way that it was all right for Linda. Teddy saw that Linda slept most of the way. She was a beautiful girl—better-looking than Anne, most people thought, though Teddy didn't—and now that Michael was making more money she had bought a lot of new clothes and was having her hair cut in a very stylish way. Teddy, who was quite observant, especially of attractive things, noted that recently she had stopped wearing trousers. He looked appreciatively across the aisle at her long, slim legs.

They changed planes at Athens. It was a fine, clear day, and as the aircraft came in to land you could see the wine-jar shape of the island from which it took its name. Stamnos was no more than twenty miles long but the road was poor and rutted, winding up and down over low olive-clad mountains, and it took over an hour for the car to get to Votani at the wine jar's mouth. The driver, a Stamniot, was one of those Greeks who spend their youth in Australia before returning home to start a business on the money they have made. He talked all the way in a harsh, clattering Greek-Strine while his radio played bouzouki music and Alison whimpered in Michael's arms. It was hot for the time of year.

Tim, who was a bad traveler, had been carsick twice by the time they reached Votani. The car couldn't go up the narrow flagged street, so they had to get out and carry the baggage, the driver helping with a case in each hand and one on his head. Michael didn't carry a case because he had Andrew on his shoulders and Alison in his arms.

The houses of Votani covered a shallow conical hill so that it looked from a distance like a heap of pastel-colored pebbles. Close to, the buildings were neat, crowded, interlocking, hung with jasmine and bougainvillea, and the hill itself was surmounted by the ruins—extravagantly picturesque—of a Crusaders' fortress. Teddy and Anne's house was three fishermen's cottages that its previous owner had converted into one. It had a lot of little staircases on account of being built on the steep hillside. From the bedroom where the four children would sleep, you could see the eastern walls of the fortress, a dark blue expanse of sea, and, smudgy on the horizon, the Turkish coast. The dark came quickly after the sun had gone. Teddy, when abroad, always found that disconcerting after England, with its long, protracted dusks.

Within an hour of reaching Votani, he found himself walking down the main street—a stone-walled defile smelling of jasmine and lit by lamps on iron brackets—towards Agamemnon's Bar. He felt guilty about going out and leaving Anne to put the children to bed, but it had been Anne's suggestion—indeed, at Anne's insistence—that he should take Michael out for a drink before supper. A whispered colloquy had established they both thought Michael looked "washed-out" (Anne's expression) and "fed-up" (Teddy's) and no wonder, the way he had been attending to Andrew and Alison's wants all day.

Michael had needed a lot of persuading, had at first been determined to stay and help Linda, and it therefore rather surprised Teddy when he began on a grumbling tirade against women's liberation.

"I sometimes wonder what they mean, they're not 'equal,'" he said. "They have the children, don't they? We can't do that. I consider that makes them *superior* rather than inferior."

"I know *I* shouldn't like to have a baby," said Teddy irrelevantly.

"It's because of that," said Michael as if Teddy hadn't spoken, "that we need to master them. We have to, for our own sakes. Where should we be if they had the babies and the whip hand, too?"

Teddy said vaguely that he didn't know about whip hand, but someone had said that the hand which rocks the cradle rules the world. By this time they were in Agamemnon's, sitting at a table on the vine-covered terrace. The other customers were all Stamniots, some of whom recognized Teddy and nodded at him and smiled. Most of the tourists had gone by now, and all but one of the hotels were closed for the winter. Hedonistic Teddy, wanting to have things pleasant about him, hadn't cared for the turn the conversation was taking. He began telling Michael how amused he and Anne had been when they found that the proprietor of the bar was called after the great hero of classical antiquity and how ironical it had seemed, for this Agamemnon was small and fat.—Here he was forced to break off as stout, smiling Agamemnon came to take their order.

Michael had no intention of letting Teddy begin once more on the subject of Stamniot names. He spoke in a rapid, violent tone, his thin, dark face pinched with intensity.

"A man can lose his children any time, and through no fault of his own. Have you ever thought of that?"

Teddy looked at him. Notions of kidnaping, of mortal illness, came into his head. "What do you mean?"

"It could happen to you or me, to any of us. A man can lose his children overnight, and he can't do a thing about it. He may be a good, faithful husband, a good provider, a devoted father—that won't make a scrap of difference. Look at George Wilton. What did George do wrong? Nothing. But he lost his children just the same. One day they were living with him in his house, and the next they

89

were in Gerrards Cross with Valerie and that Commercial French chap and he'll be lucky if he sees them once a fortnight."

"I see what you're getting at," said Teddy. "He couldn't look after them, though, could he? He's got to go to work. I mean, I see it's unfair, but you can't take kids away from their mother, can you?"

"Apparently not. But you can take them from their father."

"I shouldn't worry about one isolated case if I were you," said Teddy, feeling very uncomfortable. "You want to forget that sort of thing while you're here. Unwind a bit."

"An isolated case is just what it isn't. There's someone at work, John Frost, you don't know him. He and his wife split up—at her wish, naturally— and she took their baby with her as a matter of course. And George told me the same thing happened in his brother's marriage a couple of years back. Three children he had. He *lived* for his children, and now he gets to take them to the zoo every other Saturday."

"Maybe," said Teddy, who had his moments of shrewdness, "if he'd lived for his wife a bit more it wouldn't have happened."

He was glad to be back in the house. In bed that night he told Anne about it. Anne said Michael was an obsessional person. When he'd first met Linda, he'd been obsessed by her and now it was Andrew and Alison. He wasn't very nice to Linda these days, she'd noticed—he was always watching her in an unpleasant way. And when Linda had suggested she take the children up to the fortress in the morning if he wanted to go down to the harbor and see the fishing boats come in, he had said: "No way am I going to allow you up there on your own with my children."

Later in the week, they all went. You had to keep your eye on the children every minute of the time, there were so many places to fall over—fissures in the walls, crumbling corners, holes that opened onto the empty blue air. But the view from the eastern walls, breached in a dozen places, where the crag fell away in an almost vertical sweep to a beach of creamy silver sand and brown rocks, was the best on Stamnos. You could see the full extent of the bay that was the lip of the wine jar and the sea with its scattering of islands and the low mountains of Turkey, behind which, Teddy thought romantically, perhaps lay the Plain of Troy. The turf up here was slippery, dry as clean combed hair. No rain had fallen on Stamnos for five months. The sky was a smooth mauvish blue, cloudless and clear. Emma and Andrew, the bigger ones, ran about on the slippery turf, enjoying it because it was slippery, falling over and slithering down the slopes.

Teddy had successfully avoided being alone with Michael since their conversation in the bar, but later that day Michael caught him. Teddy put it that way to himself but in fact it was more as if, unwittingly, he had caught Michael. He had gone down to the grocery store, had bought the red apples, the feta cheese, and the olive oil Anne wanted, and had passed into the inner room, which was a second-hand bookstore stuffed full with paperbacks in a variety of European languages, discarded by the thousand tourists who had come to Votani that summer. The room was empty but for Michael, who was standing in a far corner, having taken down from a shelf a novel whose title was its heroine's name.

"That's a Swedish translation," said Teddy gently.

"Oh, is it? Yes, I see."

"The English books are all over here."

Michael's face looked haggard in the gloom of the shop. He didn't tan easily in spite of being so dark. They came out into the sunlight, Teddy carrying his purchases in the string bag, pausing now and then to look down over a wall or through a gateway. Down there the meadows spread out to the sea, olives with the black nets laid under them to catch the harvest, cypresses thin as thorns. The shepherd's dog was bringing the flock in and the sheep bells made a distant tinkling music. Michael's shadow fell across the sunlit wall.

"I was off in a dream," said Teddy. "Beautiful, isn't it? I love it. It makes me quite sad to think we shan't come here in October again for maybe—what?—twelve or fourteen years?"

"I can't say it bothers me to have to make sacrifices for the sake of my children."

Teddy thought this reproof uncalled-for and he would have liked to rejoin with something sharp, but he wasn't very good at innuendo. And in any case, before he could come up with anything Michael had begun on quite a different subject.

"The law in Greece has relaxed a lot in the past few years in favor of women—property rights and divorce and so on."

Teddy said, not without a spark of malice, "Jolly good, isn't it?"

"Those things are the first cracks in the fabric of a society that lead to its ultimate breakdown."

"*Our* society hasn't broken down."

Michael gave a scathing laugh as if at the naivety of this comment. "Throughout the Nineteenth Century," he said in severe lecturing tones, "and a good deal of this one, if a woman left her husband the children stayed with him as a matter of course. The children were never permitted to be with the guilty party. And there was a time, not so long ago, when a man could use the law to compel his wife to return to him."

"You wouldn't want that back, would you?"

"I'll tell you something, Teddy. There's a time coming when children won't have fathers—that is, it won't matter who your father is any more. You'll know your mother, and that'll be enough. That's the way things are moving, no doubt about it. Now in the Middle Ages, men believed that in matters of reproduction the woman was merely the vessel—the man's seed was what made the child. From that we've come full circle, we've come to the nearly total supremacy of women, and men like you and me are reduced to—mere temporary agents."

Teddy said to Anne that night, "You don't think he's maybe a bit mad, do you? I mean broken down under the strain?"

"He hasn't got any strain here."

"I'll tell you the other thing I was wondering. Linda's not up to anything, is she? I mean giving some other chap a whirl? She's all dressed up these days and she's lost weight. She looks years younger. If she's got someone, that would account for poor old Michael, wouldn't it?"

It was their turn to go out in the evening and they were on their way back from the Krini Restaurant, the last one on the island to remain open after the middle of October. The night was starry, the moon three-quarters of a glowing white orb.

"There has to be a reason for him being like that. It's not normal. I don't spend my time worrying you're going to leave me and take the kids."

"Is that what it is? He's afraid Linda's going to leave him?"

"It must be. He can't be getting in a tizzy over George Wilton and Somebody Frost's problems." Sage Teddy nodded his head. "Human nature isn't like that," he said. "Let's go up to the fort, darling. We've never been up there by moonlight."

They climbed to the top of the hill, Teddy puffing a bit on account of having had rather too much ouzo at the Krini. In summer the summit was floodlit, but when the hotels closed the lights also went out. The moonlight was nearly as bright and the turf shone silver between the black shadows made by the broken walls. The

Stamniots were desperate for rain now the tourist season was over, for the final boost to swell the olive crop.

Teddy went up the one surviving flight of steps into the remains of the one surviving tower. He paused, waiting for Anne. He looked down but he couldn't see her.

"The Aegean's not always calm," came her voice. "Down here there's a current that tears in and out like a mill race."

He still couldn't see her, peering out from his lookout post. Then he did—just. She was silhouetted against the purplish starriness.

"Come back!" he shouted. "You're too near the edge!"

He had made her jump. She turned quickly and at once slipped on the turf, going into a long slide on her back, legs in the air. Teddy ran down the steps. He ran across the turf, nearly falling himself, picking her up and hugged her.

"Suppose you'd fallen the other way!"

The palms of her hands were pitted with grit and in places the skin broken, where she had ineffectually made a grab at the sides of the fissure in the wall. "I wouldn't have fallen at all if you hadn't shouted at me."

At home the children were all asleep, Linda in bed but Michael still up. There were two empty wine bottles on the table and three glasses. A man they had met the night before in Agamemnon's had come in to have a drink with them, Michael said. He was German, from Heidelberg, here on his own for a late holiday.

"He was telling us about his divorce. His wife found a younger man with better job prospects who was able to offer Werner's children a swimming pool and riding lessons. Werner tried to kill himself, but someone found him in time."

What a gloomy way to spend an evening, thought Teddy, and was trying to find something cheerful to say when a shrill yell came from the children's room. Teddy couldn't for the life of him have said which one it was, but Michael could. He knew his Alison's voice and in he went to comfort her. Teddy made a face at Anne and Anne cast up her eyes. Linda came out of her bedroom in her dressing gown.

"That awful man!" she said. "Has he gone? He looks like a toad. Why don't we seem to know anyone any more who hasn't got a broken marriage?"

"You know *us*," said Teddy.

"Yes, thank God."

*   *   *

Michael took his children down to the beach most mornings. Teddy took his children to the beach too, and would have gone to the bay on the other side of the headland except that Emma and Tim wanted to be with their cousins and Tim started bawling when Teddy demurred. So Teddy had to put up a show of being very pleased and delighted at the sight of Michael. The children were in and out of the pale clear green water. It was still very hot at noon.

"Like August," said Teddy. "By golly, it's a scorcher here in August."

"Heat and cold don't mean all that much to me," said Michael.

Resisting the temptation to say "Bully for you" or "I should be so lucky" or something on those lines, Teddy began to talk of plans for the following day—the hire car to Likythos, the visit to the monastery with the Byzantine relics, and to the temple of Apollo. Michael turned on him a face so wretched, so hag-ridden, the eyes positively screwed with pain, that Teddy, who had been disliking and resenting him with schoolboy indignation, was moved by pity to the depths of himself. The poor old boy, he thought, the poor devil. What's wrong with him?

"When Andrew and Alison are with me like they are now," Michael began in a low rapid voice, "it's not so bad. I always have that feeling, you see, that I could pick them up and run away with them and hide them." He looked earnestly at Teddy. "I'm strong— I'm young still. I could easily carry them both long distances. I could hide them. But there isn't anywhere in the civilized world you can hide for long, is there? Still, as I say, it's not so bad when they're with me, when there are just the three of us on our own. It's when I have to go out and leave them with *her*.

"I can't tell you how I feel going home. All the way in the train and walking up from the station, I'm imagining going into that house and not hearing them—just silence and a note on the mantelpiece. I dread going home, I don't mind telling you, Teddy, and yet I long for it. Of course I do. I long to see them and know they're there and still mine. I say to myself, That's another day's reprieve. Sometimes I phone home half a dozen times in the day just to know she hasn't taken them away."

Teddy was aghast. He didn't know what to say. It was as if the sun had gone in and all was cold and comfortless and hateful. The sea glittered—it looked hard and huge, an enemy.

"It hasn't been so bad while we've been here," said Michael. "Oh, I expect I've been a bore for you. I'm sorry about that, Teddy, I know what a misery I am. I keep thinking that when we get home it will all start again."

"Has Linda, then—?" Teddy stammered. "I mean, Linda isn't—?"

Michael shook his head. "Not yet, not yet. But she's young too, isn't she? She's attractive. She's got years yet ahead of her—years of torture for me, Teddy, before my kids grow up."

Anne told Teddy she had spoken to Linda about it. "She never looks at another man, she wouldn't. She's breaking her heart over Michael. She lost weight and bought those clothes because she felt she'd let herself go after Alison was born and she ought to try and be more attractive for him. This obsession of his is wearing her out. She wants him to see a psychiatrist but he won't."

"The trouble is," said Teddy, "there's a certain amount of truth behind it. There's method in his madness. If Linda met a man she liked and went off with him—I mean, Michael could drive her to it if he went on like this—she *would* take the children and Michael *would* lose them."

"Not you, too?"

"Well, no. I'm not potty like poor old Michael. I hope I'm a reasonable man. But it does make you think. A woman decides her marriage doesn't work any more and the husband can lose his kids, his home, and maybe half his income. I mean, if I were twenty-five again and hadn't ever met you I might think twice about getting married, by golly, I might."

Their last evening it was Anne and Teddy's turn to baby-sit for Michael and Linda. They were dining with Werner at the Hotel Daphne. Linda wore a green silk dress, the color of shallow seawater.

"More cozy chat about adultery and suicide, I expect," said Teddy. Liking to have things pleasant about him, he settled himself with a large ouzo on the terrace under the vine. "I shan't be altogether sorry to get home. And I'll tell you what. We could come at Easter next year, in Emma's school hols."

"On our own," said Anne.

Michael came in about ten. He was alone. Teddy saw that the palms of his hands were pitted as if he had held onto the rough surface of something stony. Anne got up.

"Where's Linda?"

He hesitated before replying. A look of cunning of the kind sane people's expressions never show spread over his face. His eyes shifted along the terrace, to the right, to the left. Then he looked at the palm of his right hand and began rubbing it with his thumb.

"At the hotel," he said. "With Werner."

Anne cottoned on before he did, Teddy could see. She took a step towards Michael.

"What on earth do you mean, with Werner?"

"She's left me. She's going home to Germany with him tomorrow."

"Michael, that just isn't true. She can't stand him, she told me so. She said he was like a toad."

"Yes, she did," said Teddy. "I heard her say that."

"All right, so she isn't with Werner. Have it your way. Did the children wake up?"

"Never mind the children, Michael, they're OK. Tell us where Linda is, please. Don't play games."

He didn't answer. He went back into the house, the bead curtain making a rattling swish as he passed through it. Anne and Teddy looked at each other.

"I'm frightened," Anne said.

"Yes, so am I frankly," said Teddy.

The curtain rattled as Michael came through, carrying his children, Andrew over his shoulder, Alison in the crook of his arm, both of them more or less asleep.

"I scraped my hands on the stones up there," he said. "The turf's as slippery as glass." He gave Anne and Teddy a great wide empty smile. "Just wanted to make sure the children were all right, I'll put them back to bed again." He began to giggle with a kind of triumphant relief. "I shan't lose them now. She won't take them from me now."

REGINALD HILL

"The Worst Crime Known to Man"

Reginald Hill was born in Hartlepool, Durham, England on April 3, 1936. He served in the British Army and graduated from St. Catherine's College, Oxford in 1960. After some years as a schoolmaster and lecturer he published his first novel **A Clubbable Woman** *in 1970. It introduced his Yorkshire policemen. Superintendent (later Chief Inspector) Andrew Dalziel and Sergeant Pascoe, who have appeared in most of his mystery novels since then. He has also published some non-series and spy novels.*

His 1990 Dalziel and Pascoe novel **Bones and Silence** *won the CWA Gold Dagger award as the best of the year. In 1995 the Crime Writers' Association presented Hill with its Cartier Diamond Dagger for lifetime achievement.*

Reginald Hill's short stories have been collected as **Pascoe's Ghost** *(1979) and* **There Are No Ghosts in the Soviet Union** *(1987). The classic tennis story "The Worst Crime Known to Man" was first published in the* **London Sunday Express** *and was reprinted in* **Ellery Queen's Mystery Magazine** *and* **The Year's Best Mystery and Suspense Stories - 1985.**

The Worst Crime Known to Man

by Reginald Hill

"A middle-aged man was removed from the Centre Court crowd yesterday for causing a disturbance during a line-call dispute."

O n summer evenings when I was young, I used to sit with Mamma on the verandah of our bungalow and watch the flamingoes gliding over the tennis court to roost on the distant lake.

This was my favorite time of day and the verandah was my favorite place. It was simply furnished with a low table, a scatter of cane chairs, and an old English farmhouse rocker with its broad seat molded and polished by long use.

This was Father's special chair. At the end of the day he would fold his great length into it, lean back with a sigh of contentment, and more often than not say, "This was your grandfather's chair, Colley, did I ever tell you that?"

"Yes, Father."

"Did I? Then probably I told you what it was my father used to tell me while sitting in this chair."

"Life is a game and you play to the rules, and cheating's the worst crime known to man," I would chant.

"Good boy," he would exclaim, laughing and glancing at Mamma, who would smile sweetly, making me smile too. I always smiled when Mamma smiled. She seemed to me then a raving beauty, and she was certainly the most attractive of the only three white women within five hundred square miles. I suppose she seemed so to many others too. "Boff" Gorton, a young District Officer from a better school than Father, used to tell her so after his third gin and tonic, and she would smile and my father would laugh. Boff came round quite a lot, ostensibly to check that all was well (there had already been the first stirrings of the Troubles) and to have a couple of sets on our lush green tennis court. I was too young to wonder how serious Boff's admiration of Mamma really was. During one of his visits, when Father had been held up in the bush, I got up in the night for a drink of water and heard a noise of violent rocking on the verandah. When I went to investigate I discovered Mamma relaxing in the rocking chair and Boff, flushed and rather breathless, sitting on the floor. Curiously, Boff's situation struck me as less remarkable than Mamma's. This was the first time in my life I had ever known her to occupy the rocker.

Father's attitude to Boff was that of an older and rather patronizingly helpful brother. Only on the tennis court did anything like passion show, and that may have been due to natural competitiveness rather than jealousy. At any rate, their games were gargantuan struggles, with Boff's youth and Father's skill in such balance that the outcome was always in doubt.

The court itself was beautiful, a rectangle of English green it had taken ten years to perfect. It was completely enclosed in a cage of wire mesh, erected more to keep wildlife out than balls in. Human entry was effected through a small, tight-fitting gate, shut at night with a heavy chain and large padlock.

Father and Boff played their last match there one spring afternoon that had all the warmth and richness of the best of English summer evenings. Mamma was away superintending the *accouchement* of our nearest female neighbor, who had foolishly delayed her transfer down-country overlong. Curiously, Mamma's absence seemed to stir things up between the two men more than her presence ever did, and Father's invitation to Boff to play tennis came out like a challenge to a duel.

Boff tried to lighten matters by saying to me, "Colley, old chum, why don't you come along and be ball boy?"

"Yes, Colley," said Father. "You come along. You can be umpire too, and see fair play."

"I say," said Boff, flushing. "Do we need an umpire? I mean, neither of us is likely to cheat, are we?"

"Life is a game and you play to the rules and cheating's the worst crime known to man," I piped up.

"How right you are, Colley," said Father, observing Boff grimly. "You umpire!"

There was no more discussion, but even in the pre-match knock-up I recognized a ferocity that both excited and disturbed me. And when the match proper began it was such a hard-fought struggle that for a long time none of us noticed the arrival of the spectators. Usually only the duty houseboy watched from a respectful distance, waiting to be summoned forward with refreshing drinks, though occasionally some nomadic tribesmen would gaze from the fringes of the bush with courteous puzzlement. But this was different. Suddenly I realized that the court was entirely surrounded. There must have been two hundred of them, all standing quietly enough, but all marked with the symbols of their intent and bearing its instruments—machetes and spears.

"Father!" I choked out.

The two men glanced toward me, then saw what I had seen. For a second no one moved; then, with a fearsome roar, the natives rushed forward. Boff hurled himself towards the gate in the fence, and for a moment I thought he was making a suicidal attempt at flight. But District Officers are trained in other schools than that, and the next minute I saw he had seized the retaining chain, pulled it round the gate post and snapped shut the padlock.

The enemy was locked out. At the same time, of course, we were locked in.

If they had been carrying guns, in, out, it would have made no difference. Fortunately they were not, and the mesh was too close for the broad heads of their throwing spears. Even so, they could soon have hacked a way through the wire had not Boff for the second time revealed the quality of his training. Father in his eagerness for the fray had come from the house unarmed, but Boff had brought his revolver, and as soon as a group of our invaders began to hack at the fence he took careful aim and shot the most enthusiastic of them between the eyes.

They fell back in panic, but only for a moment. When they realized that Boff wasn't following up his attack, they returned to the fence, but no one offered to lead another demolition attempt.

"I've got just five bullets left," murmured Boff. "The only thing holding these chaps back is that they know the first to make a move will certainly die. But eventually not even that will matter."

"Why don't we make a dash for the house?" asked Father. "It's only fifty yards. And once we get to the rifles . . ."

"For God's sake!" said Boff. "Don't you understand? Outside this fence we're finished! And please don't talk about rifles. Once one of this lot gets that idea . . ."

Suddenly there came a great cry from the direction of the bungalow and I thought someone *had* got the idea. But a puff of smoke and a sudden tongue of flame revealed the truth, at the same time better and worse. Worse, because my home was going up in flames; better, because this act of arson would destroy their only source of weaponry and might even attract attention to our plight.

Father, perhaps feeling annoyed at the lead Boff had taken in dealing with the situation, suddenly picked up his racket.

"We might as well do something till help comes," he said. "My service, I believe."

It may have started as a gesture, but very rapidly that match developed into the hard, bitter struggle it had promised to be before the attack. I stood at the net holding the revolver, at first keeping an eye on the enemy outside. But soon my judgment of line calls and lets was being required so frequently that I had to give my full attention to the game.

But the most curious thing of all was the reaction of the rebels. At first there'd been some jabbering about ways of winkling us out. Then they fell silent except for one man, some renegade houseboy, I presume, who rather self-importantly began to offer a mixture of explanation of, and commentary on, the game, till his voice too died away; and at four-all in the first set I realized they had become as absorbed in the match as the players themselves. It was quite amazing, like watching a highly sunburned Wimbledon crowd. The heads moved from side to side following the flight of the ball, and at particularly strong or clever shots they beat their spear shafts against the earth and made approving booming noises deep in their throats.

Father took the first set seven-five, and looked as if he might run away with the second. But at one-four Boff's youth began to tell, and suddenly Father was on the defensive. At four-four he seemed to fold up completely, but I guessed that he was merely admitting the inevitable and taking a rest with a view to the climax.

The policy seemed to pay off. Boff won that set six-four, but now he too seemed to have shot his bolt and neither man could gain an ascendancy in the final set. Six-six it went, seven-seven, eight-eight, nine-nine, then into double figures. The light was fading fast.

"Look," said Boff coming up to the net and speaking in a low voice. "Shall we try to keep it going as long as possible? I don't know what these fellows may do when we finish. All right?"

Father didn't answer, but returned to the base line to serve. They came hard and straight, four aces. The crowd boomed. I forgot my official neutrality and joined in the applause. Father stood back to receive service.

I don't know. Perhaps he *was* trying to keep the match going. Perhaps he just intended to give away points by lashing out wildly at Boff's far from puny service. But the result was devastating. Three times in a row the ball streaked from his racket quite unplayably, putting up baseline chalk. Love-forty. Three match points. Father settled down, Boff served. Again the flashing return, but this time Boff, driven by resentment or fear, flung himself after it and sent it floating back. Father smashed, Boff retrieved. Father smashed. Boff retrieved again.

"For God's sake!" he pleaded.

Father, at the net, drove the ball deep into the corner and Boff managed to reach this only by flinging himself full length across the grass. But what a shot he produced! A perfect lob, drifting over Father's head and making for the extreme backhand corner.

Father turned with a speed I had not believed him capable of and went in pursuit. There was topspin on the ball. Once it bounced, it would be away beyond mortal reach. The situation looked hopeless.

But Father had no intention of letting it bounce. I drew in my breath as I saw he was going to attempt that most difficult of shots, a reverse backhand volley on the run. I swear the spectating natives drew in their breath too.

Father stretched—but it wasn't enough. He leapt. He connected. It was superb. The ball floated towards Boff, who still lay prostrate on the base line, and bounced gently a couple of feet from his face.

"Out!" he called desperately.

Father's roar of triumph turned to a howl of incredulity.

"Out?" he demanded. *"Out?"*

He turned to me and flung his arms wide in appeal. Boff called to me.

"Please, Colley. It *was* out, wasn't it? It *was!*"

He spoke with all the authority of a District Officer. But I was the umpire and I knew that in this matter my powers exceeded his. I shook my head.

"In!" I called. "Game, set and match to . . ."

With a cry of triumph, Father jumped over the net. And at the same moment a big black fellow with a face painted like a Halloween lantern twisted his spear butt in the chain till it snapped, and the howling mob poured in.

They were only inside the fence for about ten seconds before the first Land Rover full of troops arrived. But in that time they managed to carve the recumbent Boff into several pieces. Father on his feet and wielding his racket like a cavalry sabre managed to get away with a few unpleasant wounds, while I—perhaps because I still held the revolver, though I was too petrified to use it—escaped without threat, let alone violence.

On her return Mamma was naturally upset. I would have thought the survival of her husband and only son would have compensated for the loss of the house, but the more this was urged, the greater waxed her grief. Later, when I told the story of the match, describing with the detail befitting a noble death how Boff had so heroically attempted to keep the final game going, she had a relapse. When she recovered, things changed. I don't think I ever saw her smile again at Father's jokes.

Not that there were many more to smile at. One of Father's wounds turned septic and he had to have his right arm amputated just above the elbow. He tried to learn to play left-handed thereafter, but it never amounted to more than pat ball, and within a twelvemonth only the metal supports rising from the luxuriant undergrowth showed where the tennis court had been.

Soon after that I was sent back to the old country for schooling, and midway through my first term the Head sent for me to tell me there'd been a tragic accident. Father had been cleaning a gun and it had gone off. Or perhaps my mother had been cleaning the gun. Or perhaps, as they both died, they'd both been cleaning guns. I never discovered any details. Out there in the old days they still knew how to draw a decent veil over such things.

I was deeply grieved, of course, but school's a good place for forgetting and I never went back. Sending me to England had been their last known wish for my future. I did not feel able to go against it, not even when I was old enough to have some freedom of choice. And I have been happy enough here with my English job, English marriage, English health. I dig my little patch of garden, read political biographies, play a bit of golf.

But no tennis. I never got interested at school somehow, and I don't suppose I would ever have bothered with tennis again if my managing director hadn't offered me a spare Centre Court ticket. Well, I had to be in town anyway, and it seemed silly to miss the chance of visiting Wimbledon.

I was enjoying it thoroughly too, enjoying the crowd and the place and the game, here, now, with never a thought for the old days, till the Australian played that deep cross-court lob which sent the short-tempered American sprawling.

Then suddenly I saw it all again.

The white ball drifting through the richly scented, darkling air.

The outstretched figure on the baseline.

The pleading, despairing look on Boff's face as he watches the ball bounce out of his reach.

And with it his youth and his hopes and his life.

I saw the same anguish on the American's face today, heard the same accusing disbelief in his voice.

Of course, it wasn't his life and hopes and youth that were at stake. But as Father used to say, life is a game, and you play to the rules, and cheating's the worst crime known to man.

And the American and Boff did have one thing in common.

Both balls were a good six inches out.

GEORGE V. HIGGINS

"A Case of Chivas Regal"

*George V. Higgins was born in Brockton, Massachusetts on November 13, 1939. Educated at Boston College and Stanford University, he received his law degree from Boston College Law School and was admitted to the Massachusetts bar in 1967. He soon became an Assistant U.S. Attorney for the Commonwealth. Drawing on his experience as a reporter while in graduate school and his legal knowledge he published his first novel **The Friends of Eddie Coyle** in 1972. Its spare descriptions and razor-sharp dialogue, with an intricate plot mixing crime and politics in the Boston area, brought Higgins instantly to the attention of readers and critics. The book was made into a successful motion picture and became the first of nearly twenty novels, most of them set in and around Boston.*

*Higgins has created only one series character, in **Kennedy for the Defense** (1980) and **Penance for Jerry Kennedy** (1985). The other books have all been non-series, sometimes told at least in part from the criminal's viewpoint.*

*Although Higgins has published a dozen or so short stories, only a few fall into the crime field and none have been collected. "A Case of Chivas Regal" first appeared in **The New Black Mask #1** and was reprinted in **Murder and Mystery in Boston**.*

A Case of
Chivas Regal

by George V. Higgins

P anda Feeney, fifty-three, was employed as a court officer. He escorted juries between the courtrooms and the rooms where they deliberated, and he made hotel and restaurant accommodations for them when they were se- questered. He fetched sandwiches and coffee for them when they were deliberating, and he delivered messages between them and the judges on their cases, when they thought of silly questions dur- ing their deliberations. "But basically," Panda would say, "my job is to take care of the judges and do what they want, all right? What the judges want."

Panda did not like all of the judges that he served. Those he dis- liked made his back hurt, so he would disappear. He would stay somewhere around the second civil session, technically on duty but a little hard to find. It was not that he feared detection, loafing; he still remembered much of what he had learned wrestling, so he was indifferent to detection.

"My back," Panda would say, rubbing it, when some assistant clerk of courts located him bent over morning papers and a cup of coffee in the vacant jury room and said: "Judge wants to see you." Panda would nod painfully, writhing slowly in his chair. "Natu- rally, he wants to see me. Could've bet on it. Never fails: my back acts up, there's some guy like him in here. What's he want, huh? You know? Can you tell me that? This damp weather, Jesus, I can hardly move."

Clerks would never know what it was that judges wanted, only that they wanted Panda and had not seen him around. Panda would nod, once, when they told him that, and grimace. "Okay," he would say, "then can you do me a favor? Tell the judge: when I fought Casey—he has heard of Crusher Casey, even if he is a moron like he acts like he is—Crusher may've been an old guy, but he still had a body slam that ruined me for life. You can get the Judge's coffee for me, can't you? Do an old, lamed-up guy a favor? Tell him that for me."

One judge that Panda especially disliked was Henry Neelon. Before Judge Neelon was relieved of trying cases so that he could spend all of his time as the administrator of the courts, he had had a run-in with Panda Feeney. Panda after a few drinks would sometimes recall the story. "Hanging Hank'd spent the morning sending guys to Walpole. Handed out about a hundred years and still he wasn't satisfied. Gets back in his chambers and he's still looking to make trouble. Sends Grayson, that pinhead, out to look for me.

"I give Grayson the routine," Panda would say, chuckling. "Grayson'd believe anything you told him. He goes down and gives the word to Hanging Hank.

"Henry blows a gasket," Panda would say, laughing now. "He does not believe what Grayson tells him I said about my back, all right? He is going to check it out.

"I am sitting there, in the jury room. I can hear old Henry coming, stomping up those iron stairs and swearing like a bastard. He is going to take my head off. 'Lazy goddamned officers. Good-for-nothing shirkers.'

"So, I think quick," Panda said. "I don't have much choice. And when old Henry comes in, I am lying on the table. 'Damn you, Feeney,' he says, when he slams the door open, and then he sees me lying there like I am all set to be the guest of honor, my own wake. Except I do not look as good as I will look when old Dave Finnerty finally gets me and lays me out in the front room. I've been holding my breath, so my face is red. And I have got a look on me like we used to use when the guy that's supposed to be the loser in the matches is pretending he is chewing on your leg, or pulling some other dirty trick that only bad guys do. Pain, you know what I mean? *Pain.* I am in agony—one look and you can see it. And Henry's jaw drops down.

"'I dunno, Judge,' I say. I have got big tears in my eyes. 'I hate to even think about it, but the pain is awful. It doesn't stop, I'm gonna have to. Even though I don't want to, go on disability and just collect the pension. I may not have any choice.'

"Does he believe me?" Panda said. "At first, I guess he does, and then when he starts to suspect something, maybe I am jerking his chain, right? But he isn't sure. And even to this day, I catch him looking at me, he still thinks I was giving him the business that day I was on the table. And if he ever gets a shot at me again, that guy is gonna take it. I can see it in his eyes."

Panda Feeney liked Judge Boyster, so his back was always fine when Andrew Boyster drew his session. "Now you take someone like Drew Boyster," Panda would tell other judges when he served them the first time. "He is my idea, a judge. Not the kind of guy, you know, where everything is hard and fast and there's no allowances for human nature, you know? Drew Boyster is the kind of guy that I'd want judging me, if I was ever in that spot, which God forbid, I should be. If we had more like Andrew Boyster this would be a better world."

Andrew Boyster always squirmed when Panda's praise got back to him. "Ahh," he'd say, looking embarrassed, "I wish Panda wouldn't do that. Every new judge comes along, Panda gives indoctrination. And all it really means, I guess, is that I am too easy. I let Panda disappear, if I don't really need him—I suppose he's sleeping, but then, Panda needs his rest. Then too, I let Panda pick the hotels when the juries are sequestered, and the ones that Panda picks are always grateful for the business. He selected the restaurants when the juries sit through dinner, and he picks out the delis when they're having sandwiches. He's probably enriching pals, but then, should he pick those who hate him? And they probably show their appreciation in ways that might be worth some money. Nothing against the law, of course—I am not suggesting that. But I bet Panda has some trouble, paying for his dinners out." He did not tell Neelon that.

Panda's explanation differed. "You know why I like Drew Boyster?" He would squint when he said that, studying the novice judge for some sign of inattention. "He thinks I am smart, is why. He does not think I am stupid. Judge Boyster doesn't come in here, like lots of these guys do—and, Christ, you come down to it, some of the broads we get are worse. He doesn't just barge in here and start throwing weight around, acting like he owns the place and everybody in it. Drew Boyster . . . well, I had one case he was involved in, before he became a judge. And that was all I needed, right? To see what kind of guy he is. This guy, he may be a lawyer and he made a lot of money before he went on the bench, although from what I heard, I guess his first wife made a big dent in that. But he has always had some class. Drew Boyster has got class. I have been here fifteen years. Judge Boyster is the best. I never ate a meal with him, or had a drink with him. It's not like we are buddies, you know? Or anything like that. It's just that, all the years I've been here, he's the best I ever saw."

He made that speech, with variations, to so many judges, that when Drew Boyster dropped dead at the age of fifty-nine, victim of a massive stroke that killed him instantly, Panda's name was mentioned by everyone who saw Judge Neelon on the morning afterward. Henry Neelon was in charge of making the arrangements for the speakers who would say a few words at Boyster's memorial, and as little as he liked the man, Henry Neelon saw the logic of including Panda Feeney.

"Look," he said, "I realize this may be hard for you. I know how you felt about Drew—everybody did."

Panda shook his head and looked down, as though he did not trust his voice to perform reliably.

"The thing of it is," Judge Neelon said to Panda, "you've been to enough of these things so you know what they are like. They are deadly, Panda—they are boring and they're dull. We get a couple lawyers who won recent cases in his court—we do not ask folks who lost. The Chief Justice declares on the record: 'He was not a pederast.' If he has one kid who can talk, we let the kid stand up—and then we all watch carefully to see if he breaks down, or displays any evidence that he's been using harmful drugs. For some reason, we don't ask surviving spouses to address us—it's probably because we're all afraid of what our own might say, if they got full attention, and we weren't there to reply. Then finally, one friend of his, if the dead guy had a friend, takes four or five long minutes to say nobody else knew him.

"You see what I mean, Panda?" Judge Neelon said pleadingly. "The last guy who gets up at those things is the only one who's right—none of the other speakers is a friend of the departed, someone who just *knew* him and enjoyed his company. No one that just *liked* him, unless he's another lawyer, ever gets a chance to speak. And we thought, since you did know Drew, and really did like him, maybe you would say a few words and do everyone a favor."

Panda looked up and he shook his head once more. "I couldn't do it, Your Honor," he said, and cracked his voice. "I would not know what to say. I'm not used to making speeches, standing up in public like that."

"Panda," Neelon said, "it could be very short. You could say . . . that case you had, the one that impressed you so much, you never forgot it? You could talk about that case, how Drew showed so much class. Look, you know Drew Boyster's history. You went back a ways with him. His family, they're not, you know, extremely happy with him, even now that he is dead. His kids, from everything I hear, they sided with the wife. You'd really help us out a lot if you saw your way clear to do it. Good Lord, Panda, all these years, you have drummed it into us. Just tell everybody once more, what a great guy Drew was."

"Your Honor," Panda said, coughing deeply as he started, "I have got to tell you—I can't talk about that case."

"Of course you can," Judge Neelon said. "It's on the public record. If it's the details that escape you, we can pull the files. We'll take care of that for you. That part will be easy."

"Judge," Panda said, "it wasn't that. It was not a case in court. Well, there *was* a case in court, that Judge Boyster was involved in. But the case I talked about . . . I can't talk about that."

"I don't follow you," the Judge said. He was starting to look grim.

"It was Chivas Regal," Panda said with difficulty. "A case of Chivas Regal, all right? That was what I meant."

"Scotch whiskey?" Neelon said. "A case of booze, you mean?"

Panda nodded. "Uh-huh," he said. "That was what it was."

"And this was back when Drew, when Drew was a lawyer?"

Panda nodded once again. "Yeah. Before he was a judge."

"Panda," Neelon said severely, "this is serious. Drew is dead now. It can't hurt him, not where he is now. But you're still escorting juries, and you still have access to them. If you influenced some verdict, back when Drew was practicing, and he gave you a case of scotch . . . well, I don't have to tell you just how serious this is. What was it you did for Drew? Tamper with a jury, or do something dumb like that?"

Panda looked indignant. "Judge," he said, "I resent that. In all the years I've been here, I have never told a jury how they should vote in a case."

"Uh-huh," Neelon said, "well, you are the first one, then. But you've raised the suspicion now, and I am forced to deal with that. If you don't tell me the truth, and tell me the truth right now, I'll have to investigate and see what you did for Drew. And until I am satisfied, you will be suspended. Without pay, I might add, until this is all cleared up. Now which will it be, Panda? This is your decision now. You can tell me what went on, or you can leave this building right now and wait to hear from the D.A."

Panda looked more sorrowful than he had looked before. He had to clear his throat again. "This won't go any further?"

"It won't if there is nothing wrong," Judge Neelon said grimly. "If I think there is something wrong, it will go further, Panda. No promises apart from that. You understand me, Panda? And I will be the judge of whether you will be reported."

Panda sighed heavily. "All right," he said, "you got me. But there is nothing wrong with this, with what I did for Drew." Judge Neelon did not comment on that.

"Over twenny years ago, I got hurt in the ring."

"I know that," Neelon said. "Get on with you and Drew."

"I'm coming to that," Panda said. "Just give me a minute, will you? The doctors told me: 'Panda,' they said, 'this is it for grappling. You get hit like that again, you'll go out in a wheelchair. You are still a young man and your heart is pretty strong. You get crippled up for life, it is going to be a long one and you will have trouble working.'

"That scared the hell right out of me," Panda told Judge Neelon. "In wrestling there's no insurance. I did not have money. I was always undercard, a couple hundred bucks. And I didn't have any trade, you know. Something I could do. But I am scared, so what I do, I take what comes along. I get into security. I become a guard.

"The first job that I had," he said, "was in the Coast Apartments. This was before it was condo. This was 1963. And since I am new and all, I am put on nights. So I do not see who goes out—I just see who goes in.

"Now, Judge," he said, "I don't know just how I should put this to you. Because I don't want to shock you, or do anything like that. But lots of the big law firms then had pads in those tall buildings. And on the tour they had me on, I'd see those guys come in. See them come in with their girlfriends? Between six and nine at night. And they would not go out again, 'fore I was through at one."

"Panda," Neelon said, "spare me. You mean: 'With their nieces they came in.' Learned counsel for rich law firms do not get so vulgar as to entertain mere girlfriends in deductible apartments."

"My mistake, Your Honor," Panda said. "Excuse me. On the tour

---

they had me on, I often saw the lawyers come in with their nieces right behind them. Now, this took me a while, before I got this figured out. I was fairly innocent, when I stopped wrestling. And when I first started in there, I did not know much. So one night, this big honcho lawyer comes with his briefcase, and it is six o'-clock or so and I am pretty stupid. And also with him, right behind him, there is this young lady. A very fine looking young lady, I might add. And she has got her handbag, but that's all she's carrying. So I assume they're visiting someone—they do not live in the building, or else they would tell me. So I ask him: 'Which apartment?' Like I was supposed to do. Coast did not want people coming in there without they had destinations, and the people they were seeing wanted to see them.

"He gets all mad at me, the guy does," Panda said to Neelon. "He tells me he belongs to this firm which keeps an apartment there. Their clients in from out of town stay overnight in it. And sometimes in the evening, if they have a lot of work, they come in with their secretaries and they work late hours themselves. And that is what he's doing, and she is his secretary. 'Gleason, Boyster and Muldoon. That is all you need to know.' And they go on upstairs.

"Well, Your Honor, nothing happened. That I got in trouble for. This guy and his secretary, they go up to work late hours and I don't know who they are, except they work for a law firm that he says he belongs to. He don't say that he is Gleason and he don't claim he is Muldoon. I do not know he is Boyster and the lady had no name. All I knew her by was her looks, and like I told you, those were fine. She also had a nice smile and she always gave it to me.

"I say 'always,' Judge," he said, "and when I say that, I mean this: 'Wednesday nights she smiled at me.' Every Wednesday night. The first night was a Wednesday and then they come back, the next one. And I naturally remember them and I don't ask no questions. And then the Wednesday after that, and the one after that, until I see this is a habit, they got going here. This guy apparently can't get his work done, any Wednesday that you name. Tuesdays he's apparently all right, when they blow the quitting whistle. Thursdays he does not show up. I had Fridays off in those days, Fridays and Saturdays. He don't come in any Sunday. He does not show up on Monday. And by now I've gotten so I know a lot of guys that have problems just like his, except their big nights are different, and their secretaries change, or else they have got whole flocks of nieces like you would not have imagined. So I am wising up a little, and I'm keeping my mouth shut. And also I am putting my name in around the city, because I am getting older and those late hours are killing me.

"Anyway, two years go by, and then things start to change. I notice that this guy has started coming in on Tuesdays. And pretty soon it's Thursdays and I'm seeing him on Mondays, and when I come in on Sunday he's been working all weekend. His secretary, too—she's in there, and they're bringing in groceries. And then this other guy gets sick, so I have to cover for him, and damned if the secretary there and her boss are not working Friday nights and Saturday nights too."

"Thriving private practice," the Judge said, nodding at him. "Envy of every practitioner. Those hours are just brutal."

"They must be," Panda said. "Well, anyway, the days go by, and one day I am sitting there, I open up the paper. And what do I see but his picture and his name is under it. This is Attorney Andrew Boyster, who's been working those long hours. And he is in the paper because his wife's suing him. She is suing him in the back and she's suing his front, too. What she wants is a nice divorce, and every dime he's got. And there's another picture, which is of Andrew Boyster's wife. And she does not look like the lady that I know."

"She looked a little older, maybe?" Henry Neelon said.

"Well, I assumed she was," Panda Feeney said. "I didn't think too much about that, just how old she might've been. What caught my eye was, you know, she alleged adultery. And I thought I might have some idea, of just who she had in mind.

"Well," Feeney said, "the papers had their usual field day. And I have got a dirty mind, so of course I read it all. And I am sitting there one night, the two of them come in, and I am looking at their pictures. They give me the great big grin, and she asks me how I like it.

"I do not know what to say. I figure they are going to tell me, I should mind my own damned business. So I mumble something at them, and they start to laugh at me. 'You're going to have to do better than that, if your name is Thomas Feeney,' Andrew Boyster says to me. And since we're never introduced, that kind of throws me, right? 'How come me?' I say to him, and that is when he tells me. I am getting a subpoena. I am going to testify.

"I say: 'Why me? What do I know?' He says his wife thinks that

I know lots. Like who's been coming in and going out the building I am guarding, and she wants to ask me that.

"Now, I figure," Panda said, "I am in the glue for fair. So I ask him: 'What do I say?' And he says: 'Tell the truth.' And they go upstairs laughing, just as happy as can be. Which at least made me feel better, that the guy's not mad at me. I just may not lose my job."

"Did you testify?" the Judge said.

"Uh-huh," Panda said.

"And did you tell the truth?" the Judge said, looking grim again.

"Absolutely," Panda said. "Told the Gospel truth. Had on my best blue suit, you know, clean shirt and everything. And they ask me, his wife's lawyers, did I work the Coast Apartments and how long did I work there. I told him those things, truthfully, and all the other junk he asked me before he comes to the point. And when he does that he decides he will be dramatic. Swings around and points to Boyster and says: 'Do you know this man?' And I say: 'Yes, I do know him. That is Andrew Boyster.' Then he shows me a picture, which is Boyster's secretary that I guess is now his widow, and he wants to know: do I know her? And I say: 'Yes, I do.'

" 'Now,' he says, like this is this great big salute he's planned, 'how long have you known these people? Will you tell His Honor that?' And I say: 'Yessir. Yes, I will.' And I turn and face the Judge there and I say: 'I have known them for two weeks.' "

"Which of course was the strict truth," Neelon said, laughing with him. "Did he ask you the next question?"

"You mean: 'When did you first see him?' " Panda asked the Judge.

"Yeah," Judge Neelon said, "that is exactly what I mean."

"No," Panda said, "he didn't. I think he was flabbergasted. He just stood there and looked at me like his mouth wouldn't work. And then when he got it working, all he could think of asking me was whether I was very sure that was my honest answer. And I said: 'Absolutely, sir.' And then I was excused. And then when Christmas came that year, I got a case of Chivas Regal, and it was from Andrew Boyster and that second wife of his who I still think's a nice lady. And then when Drew got his judgeship, my name came up on the list faster than it ever would've otherwise, and that is how I got this job here. Because Drew thought I was smart. What I said, testifying, it did not make any difference to the way the case come out—at least that is what he told me. 'But,' he told me,

'Panda, it was the one laugh that we had while all that crap was going on, and we just wanted you to know that we appreciated it.' Which is why I thought Drew Boyster was a very classy guy—because of how he treated me."

Judge Neelon studied Panda for about a half a minute. Then he nodded and said: "Okay. You are off the hook. You don't have to speak when we have services for Drew. And I will not report you."

"Thank you, Judge," Panda said.

"There's one thing, though, I'd like to know," the Judge said thoughtfully. "At least, I think I'd like to know it, so I'll tell you what it is. That day when you were on the table, up there in the jury room? The day I burst in on you and you described your back pain to me in such colorful detail?"

"I remember it, Judge," Panda Feeney said.

"If I had asked you, that day, if you had that back pain then, what would you have told me? Do you want to tell me that?"

"To be candid, Judge," Panda Feeney said, "since you're giving me that option: No, I don't think that I do."

Neelon nodded. "Uh-huh," he said. "And if I were to ask you: Have you ever lied to me? You'd tell me that you never have."

Panda Feeney nodded. "Yes. And that would be the truth."

LINDA BARNES

"Lucky Penny"

*Linda Barnes was born in Detroit, Michigan on June 6, 1949. She graduated from the Boston University School of Fine and Applied Art in 1971 with a degree in theater. After working as a teacher of theater and a drama director she published her first novel **Blood Will Have Blood** in 1982.*

*Following four novels about wealthy actor Michael Spraggue III she turned to the memorable Carlotta Carlyle, a cab-driving private investigator she first introduced in an Edgar-winning short story "Lucky Penny" (1985). Carlotta's first novel **A Trouble of Fools** (1987) won the American Mystery Award and was nominated for both the Edgar and Shamus Awards. Four more Carlotta Carlyle novels have followed.*

*Barnes has used the short story form very sparingly to date, which is surprising in view of the success of "Lucky Penny." The story first appeared in **The New Black Mask #3** and has been reprinted in **The Year's Best Mystery and Suspense Stories - 1986, Murder and Mystery in Boston, Lady on the Case** and **Sisters in Crime**.*

Lucky Penny

by Linda Barnes

Lieutenant Mooney made me dish it all out for the record. He's a good cop, if such an animal exists. We used to work the same shift before I decided—wrongly—that there was room for a lady PI in this town. Who knows? With this case under my belt, maybe business'll take a 180-degree spin, and I can quit driving a hack.

See, I've already written the official report for Mooney and the cops, but the kind of stuff they wanted: date, place, and time, cold as ice and submitted in triplicate, doesn't even start to tell the tale. So I'm doing it over again, my way.

Don't worry, Mooney. I'm not gonna file this one.

The Thayler case was still splattered across the front page of the *Boston Globe*. I'd soaked it up with my midnight coffee and was puzzling it out—my cab on automatic pilot, my mind on crime—when the mad tea party began.

"Take your next right, sister. Then pull over, and douse the lights. Quick!"

I heard the bastard all right, but it must have taken me thirty seconds or so to react. Something hard rapped on the cab's dividing shield. I didn't bother turning around. I hate staring down gun barrels.

I said, "Jimmy Cagney, right? No, your voice is too high. Let me guess, don't tell me—"

"Shut up!"

"Kill the lights, *turn off* the lights, okay. But *douse* the lights? You've been tuning in too many old gangster flicks."

"I hate a mouthy broad," the guy snarled. I kid you not.

"Broad," I said. "Christ! *Broad?* You trying to grow hair on your balls?"

"Look, I mean it, lady!"

"Lady's better. Now you wanna vacate my cab and go rob a phone booth?" My heart was beating like a tin drum, but I didn't let my voice shake, and all the time I was gabbing at him, I kept trying to catch his face in the mirror. He must have been crouching way back on the passenger side. I couldn't see a damn thing.

"I want all your dough," he said.

Who can you trust? This guy was a spiffy dresser: charcoal-gray three-piece suit and rep tie, no less. And picked up in front of the swank Copley Plaza. *I* looked like I needed the bucks more than he did, and I'm no charity case. A woman can make good tips driving a hack in Boston. Oh, she's gotta take precautions, all right. When you can't smell a disaster fare from thirty feet, it's time to quit. I pride myself on my judgment. I'm careful. I always know where the police checkpoints are, so I can roll my cab past and flash the old lights if a guy starts acting up. This dude fooled me cold.

I was ripped. Not only had I been conned, I had a considerable wad to give away. It was near the end of my shift, and like I said, I do all right. I've got a lot of regulars. Once you see me, you don't forget me—or my cab.

It's gorgeous. Part of my inheritance. A '59 Chevy, shiny as new, kept on blocks in a heated garage by the proverbial dotty old lady. It's the pits of the design world. Glossy blue with those giant chromium fins. Restrained decor: just the phone number and a few gilt curlicues on the door. I was afraid all my old pals at the police department would pull me over for minor traffic violations if I went whole hog and painted "Carlotta's Cab" in ornate script on the hood. Some do it anyway.

So where the hell were all the cops now? Where are they when you need 'em?

He told me to shove the cash through that little hole they leave for the passenger to pass the fare forward. I told him he had it backwards. He didn't laugh. I shoved bills.

"Now the change," the guy said. Can you imagine the nerve?

I must have cast my eyes up to heaven. I do that a lot these days.

"I mean it." He rapped the plastic shield with the shiny barrel of his gun. I checked it out this time. Funny how big a little .22 looks when it's pointed just right.

I fished in my pockets for change, emptied them.

"Is that all?"

"You want the gold cap on my left front molar?" I said.

"Turn around," the guy barked. "Keep both hands on the steering wheel. High."

I heard jingling, then a quick intake of breath.

"Okay," the crook said, sounding happy as a clam, "I'm gonna take my leave—"

"Good. Don't call this cab again."

"Listen!" The gun tapped. "You cool it here for ten minutes. And I mean frozen. Don't twitch. Don't blow your nose. Then take off."

"Gee, thanks."

"Thank *you*," he said politely. The door slammed.

At times like that, you just feel ridiculous. You *know* the guy isn't going to hang around, waiting to see whether you're big on insubordination. *But,* he might. And who wants to tangle with a .22 slug? I rate pretty high on insubordination. That's why I messed up as a cop. I figured I'd give him two minutes to get lost. Meantime I listened.

Not much traffic goes by those little streets on Beacon Hill at one o'clock on a Wednesday morn. Too residential. So I could hear the guy's footsteps tap along the pavement. About ten steps back, he stopped. Was he the one in a million who'd wait to see if I turned around? I heard a funny kind of *whooshing* noise. Not loud enough to make me jump, and anything much louder than the ticking of my watch would have put me through the roof. Then the footsteps patted on, straight back and out of hearing.

One minute more. The only saving grace of the situation was the location: District One. That's Mooney's district. Nice guy to talk to.

I took a deep breath, hoping it would have an encore, and pivoted quickly, keeping my head low. Makes you feel stupid when you do that and there's no one around.

I got out and strolled to the corner, stuck my head around a building kind of cautiously. Nothing, of course.

I backtracked. Ten steps, then *whoosh.* Along the sidewalk stood one of those new "Keep Beacon Hill Beautiful" trash cans, the kind with the swinging lid. I gave it a shove as I passed. I could just as easily have kicked it; I was in that kind of funk.

Whoosh, it said, just as pretty as could be.

Breaking into one of those trash cans is probably tougher than busting into your local bank vault. Since I didn't even have a dime left to fiddle the screws on the lid, I was forced to deface city property. I got the damn thing open and dumped the contents on somebody's front lawn, smack in the middle of a circle of light from one of those snooty Beacon Hill gas streetlamps.

Halfway through the whisky bottles, wadded napkins, and beer cans, I made my discovery. I was doing a thorough search. If you're going to stink like garbage anyway, why leave anything untouched, right? So I was opening all the brown bags—you know, the good old brown lunch-and-bottle bags—looking for a clue. My most valuable find so far had been the moldy rind of a bologna sandwich. Then I hit it big: one neatly creased bag stuffed full of cash.

To say I was stunned is to entirely underestimate how I felt as I crouched there, knee-deep in garbage, my jaw hanging wide. I don't know what I'd expected to find. Maybe the guy's gloves. Or his hat, if he'd wanted to get rid of it fast in order to melt back into anonymity. I pawed through the rest of the debris. My change was gone.

I was so befuddled I left the trash right on the front lawn. There's probably still a warrant out for my arrest.

District One headquarters is off the beaten path, over on New Sudbury Street. I would have called first, if I'd had a dime.

One of the few things I'd enjoyed about being a cop was gabbing with Mooney. I like driving a cab better, but, face it, most of my fares aren't scintillating conversationalists. The Red Sox and the weather usually covers it. Talking to Mooney was so much fun, I wouldn't even consider dating him. Lots of guys are good at sex, but conversation—now there's an art form.

Mooney, all six-feet-four, 240 linebacker pounds of him, gave me the glad eye when I waltzed in. He hasn't given up trying. Keeps telling me he talks even better in bed.

"Nice hat," was all he said, his big fingers pecking at the typewriter keys.

I took it off and shook out my hair. I wear an old slouch cap when I drive to keep people from saying the inevitable. One jerk even misquoted Yeats at me: "Only God, my dear, could love you for yourself alone and not your long red hair." Since I'm seated when I drive, he missed the chance to ask me how the weather is up here. I'm six-one in my stocking feet and skinny enough to make every inch count twice. I've got a wide forehead, green eyes, and a pointy chin. If you want to be nice about my nose, you say it's got character.

Thirty's still hovering in my future. It's part of Mooney's past.

I told him I had a robbery to report and his dark eyes steered me to a chair. He leaned back and took a puff of one of his low-tar cigarettes. He can't quite give 'em up, but he feels guilty as hell about 'em.

When I got to the part about the bag in the trash, Mooney lost his sense of humor. He crushed a half-smoked butt in a crowded ashtray.

"Know why you never made it as a cop?" he said.

"Didn't brown-nose enough."

"You got no sense of proportion! Always going after crackpot stuff!"

"Christ, Mooney, aren't you interested? Some guy heists a cab, at gunpoint, then tosses the money. Aren't you the least bit *intrigued*?"

"I'm a cop, Ms. Carlyle. I've got to be more than intrigued. I've got murders, bank robberies, assaults—"

"Well, excuse me. I'm just a poor citizen reporting a crime. Trying to help—"

"Want to help, Carlotta? Go away." He stared at the sheet of paper in the typewriter and lit another cigarette. "Or dig me up something on the Thayler case."

"You working that sucker?"

"Wish to hell I wasn't."

I could see his point. It's tough enough trying to solve any murder, but when your victim is *the* Jennifer (Mrs. Justin) Thayler, wife of the famed Harvard Law prof, and the society reporters are breathing down your neck along with the usual crime-beat scribblers, you got a special kind of problem.

"So who did it?" I asked.

Mooney put his size twelves up on his desk. "Colonel Mustard in the library with the candlestick! How the hell do I know? Some scumbag housebreaker. The lady of the house interrupted his haul. Probably didn't mean to hit her that hard. He must have freaked when he saw all the blood, 'cause he left some of the ritziest stereo equipment this side of heaven, plus enough silverware to blind your average hophead. He snatched most of old man Thayler's goddamn idiot artworks, collections, collectibles—whatever the hell

you call 'em—which ought to set him up for the next few hundred years, if he's smart enough to get rid of them."

"Alarm system?"

"Yeah, they had one. Looks like Mrs. Thayler forgot to turn it on. According to the maid, she had a habit of forgetting just about anything after a martini or three."

"Think the maid's in on it?"

"Christ, Carlotta. There you go again. No witnesses. No fingerprints. Servants asleep. Husband asleep. We've got word out to all the fences here and in New York that we want this guy. The pawnbrokers know the stuff's hot. We're checking out known art thieves and shady museums—"

"Well, don't let me keep you from your serious business," I said, getting up to go. "I'll give you the collar when I find out who robbed my cab."

"Sure," he said. His fingers started playing with the typewriter again.

"Wanna bet on it?" Betting's an old custom with Mooney and me.

"I'm not gonna take the few piddling bucks you earn with that ridiculous car."

"Right you are, boy. I'm gonna take the money the city pays you to be unimaginative! Fifty bucks I nail him within the week."

Mooney hates to be called "boy." He hates to be called "unimaginative." I hate to hear my car called "ridiculous." We shook hands on the deal. Hard.

Chinatown's about the only chunk of Boston that's alive after midnight. I headed over to Yee Hong's for a bowl of wonton soup.

The service was the usual low-key, slow-motion routine. I used a newspaper as a shield; if you're really involved in the *Wall Street Journal,* the casual male may think twice before deciding he's the answer to your prayers. But I didn't read a single stock quote. I tugged at strands of my hair, a bad habit of mine. Why would somebody rob me and then toss the money away?

Solution Number One: He didn't. The trash bin was some mob drop, and the money I'd found in the trash had absolutely nothing to do with the money filched from my cab. Except that it was the same amount—and that was too big a coincidence for me to swallow.

Two: The cash I'd found was counterfeit and this was a clever way of getting it into circulation. Nah. Too baroque entirely. How the hell would the guy know I was the pawing-through-the-trash type?

Three: It was a training session. Some fool had used me to perfect his robbery technique. Couldn't he learn from TV like the rest of the crooks?

Four: It was a frat hazing. Robbing a hack at gunpoint isn't exactly in the same league as swallowing goldfish.

I closed my eyes.

My face came to a fortunate halt about an inch above a bowl of steaming broth. That's when I decided to pack it in and head for home. Wonton soup is lousy for the complexion.

I checked out the log I keep in the Chevy, totaled my fares: $4.82 missing, all in change. A very reasonable robbery.

By the time I got home, the sleepiness had passed. You know how it is: one moment you're yawning, the next your eyes won't close. Usually happens when my head hits the pillow; this time I didn't even make it that far. What woke me up was the idea that my robber hadn't meant to steal a thing. Maybe he'd left me something instead. You know, something hot, cleverly concealed. Something he could pick up in a few weeks, after things cooled off.

I went over that backseat with a vengeance, but I didn't find anything besides old Kleenex and bent paperclips. My brainstorm wasn't too clever after all. I mean, if the guy wanted to use my cab as a hiding place, why advertise by pulling a five-and-dime robbery?

I sat in the driver's seat, tugged my hair, and stewed. What did I have to go on? The memory of a nervous thief who talked like a B movie and stole only change. Maybe a mad toll-booth collector.

I live in a Cambridge dump. In any other city, I couldn't sell the damned thing if I wanted to. Here, I turn real estate agents away daily. The key to my home's value is the fact that I can hoof it to Harvard Square in five minutes. It's a seller's market for tar-paper shacks within walking distance of the Square. Under a hundred thou only if the plumbing's outside.

It took me a while to get in the door. I've got about five locks on it. Neighborhood's popular with thieves as well as gentry. I'm neither. I inherited the house from my weird Aunt Bea, all paid for. I consider the property taxes my rent, and the rent's getting steeper all the time.

I slammed my log down on the dining room table. I've got rooms galore in that old house, rent a couple of them to Harvard students. I've got my own office on the second floor, but I do most of my work at the dining room table. I like the view of the refrigerator.

I started over from square one. I called Gloria. She's the late-night dispatcher for the Independent Taxi Owners Association. I've never seen her, but her voice is as smooth as mink oil and I'll bet we get a lot of calls from guys who just want to hear her say she'll pick 'em up in five minutes.

"Gloria, it's Carlotta."

"Hi, babe. You been pretty popular today."

"Was I popular at one-thirty-five this morning?"

"Huh?"

"I picked up a fare in front of the Copley Plaza at one-thirty-five. Did you hand that one out to all comers or did you give it to me solo?"

"Just a sec." I could hear her charming the pants off some caller in the background. Then she got back to me.

"I just gave him to you, babe. He asked for the lady in the '59 Chevy. Not a lot of those on the road."

"Thanks, Gloria."

"Trouble?" she asked.

"Is mah middle name," I twanged. We both laughed and I hung up before she got a chance to cross-examine me.

So. The robber wanted my cab. I wished I'd concentrated on his face instead of his snazzy clothes. Maybe it was somebody I knew, some jokester in mid-prank. I killed that idea; I don't know anybody who'd pull a stunt like that, at gunpoint and all. I don't want to know anybody like that.

Why rob my cab, then toss the dough?

I pondered sudden religious conversion. Discarded it. Maybe some robber was some perpetual screwup who'd ditched the cash by mistake.

Or . . . Maybe he got exactly what he wanted. Maybe he desperately desired my change.

Why?

Because my change was special, valuable beyond its $4.82 replacement cost.

So how would somebody know my change was valuable?

Because he'd given it to me himself, earlier in the day.

"Not bad," I said out loud. "Not bad." It was the kind of reasoning they'd bounced me off the police force for, what my so-called superiors termed the "fevered product of an overimaginative mind." I leapt at it because it was the only explanation I could think of. I do like life to make some sort of sense.

I pored over my log. I keep pretty good notes: where I pick up a fare, where I drop him, whether he's a hailer or a radio call.

First, I ruled out all the women. That made the task slightly less impossible: sixteen suspects down from thirty-five. Then I yanked my hair and stared at the blank white porcelain of the refrigerator door. Got up and made myself a sandwich: ham, Swiss cheese, salami, lettuce and tomato, on rye. Ate it. Stared at the porcelain some more until the suspects started coming into focus.

Five of the guys were just plain fat and one was decidedly on the hefty side; I'd felt like telling them all to walk. Might do them some good, might bring on a heart attack. I crossed them all out. Making a thin person look plump is hard enough; it's damn near impossible to make a fatty look thin.

Then I considered my regulars: Jonah Ashley, a tiny blond southern gent; muscle-bound "just-call-me-Harold" at Longfellow Place; Dr. Homewood getting his daily ferry from Beth Israel to MGH; Marvin of the gay bars; and Professor Dickerman, Harvard's answer to Berkeley's sixties radicals.

I crossed them all off. I could see Dickerman holding up the First Filthy Capitalist Bank, or disobeying civilly at Seabrook, even blowing up an oil company or two. But my mind boggled at the thought of the great liberal Dickerman robbing some poor cabbie. It would be like Robin Hood joining the sheriff of Nottingham on some particularly rotten peasant swindle. Then they'd both rape Maid Marian and go off pals together.

Dickerman *was* a lousy tipper. That ought to be a crime.

So what did I leave? Eleven out of sixteen guys cleared without leaving my chair. Me and Sherlock Holmes, the famous armchair detectives.

I'm stubborn; that was one of my good cop traits. I stared at that log till my eyes bugged out. I remembered two of the five pretty easily; they were handsome and I'm far from blind. The first had one of those elegant bony faces and far-apart eyes. He was taller than my bandit. I'd ceased eyeballing him when I noticed the ring on his left hand; I never fuss with the married kind. The other one was built, a weight lifter. Not an Arnold Schwarzenegger extremist, but built. I think I'd have noticed that bod on my bandit. Like I said, I'm not blind.

That left three.

Okay. I closed my eyes. Who had I picked up at the Hyatt on Memorial Drive? Yeah, that was the salesman guy, the one who looked so uncomfortable that I'd figured he'd been hoping to ask his cabbie for a few pointers concerning the best skirt-chasing areas in our fair city. Too low a voice. Too broad in the beam.

The log said I'd picked up a hailer at Kenmore Square when I'd let out the salesman. Ah, yes, a talker. The weather, mostly. Don't you think it's dangerous for you to be driving a cab? Yeah, I remembered him, all right: a fatherly type, clasping a briefcase, heading to the financial district. Too old.

Down to one. I was exhausted but not the least bit sleepy. All I had to do was remember who I'd picked up on Beacon near Charles. A hailer. Before five o'clock, which was fine by me because I wanted to be long gone before rush hour gridlocked the city. I'd gotten onto Storrow and taken him along the river into Newton Center. Dropped him off at the Bay Bank Middlesex, right before closing time. It was coming back. Little nervous guy. Pegged him as an accountant when I'd let him out at the bank. Measly, under-nourished soul. Skinny as a rail, stooped, with pits left from teenage acne.

Shit. I let my head sink down onto the dining room table when I realized what I'd done. I'd ruled them all out, every one. So much for my brilliant deductive powers.

I retired to my bedroom, disgusted. Not only had I lost $4.82 in assorted alloy metals, I was going to lose fifty dollars to Mooney. I stared at myself in the mirror, but what I was really seeing was the round hole at the end of a .22, held in a neat, gloved hand.

Somehow, the gloves made me feel better. I'd remembered another detail about my piggy-bank robber. I consulted the mirror and kept the recall going. A hat. The guy wore a hat. Not like my cap, but like a hat out of a forties gangster flick. I had one of those: I'm a sucker for hats. I plunked it on my head, jamming my hair up underneath—and I drew in my breath sharply.

A shoulder-padded jacket, a slim build, a low slouched hat. Gloves. Boots with enough heel to click as he walked away. Voice? High. Breathy, almost whispered. Not unpleasant. Accentless. No Boston *r*.

I had a man's jacket and a couple of ties in my closet. Don't ask. They may have dated from as far back as my ex-husband, but not necessarily so. I slipped into the jacket, knotted the tie, tilted the hat down over one eye.

I'd have trouble pulling it off. I'm skinny, but my build is decidedly female. Still, I wondered—enough to traipse back downstairs, pull a chicken leg out of the fridge, go back to the log, and review the feminine possibilities. Good thing I did.

Everything clicked. One lady fit the bill exactly: mannish walk and clothes, tall for a woman. And I was in luck. While I'd picked her up in Harvard Square, I'd dropped her at a real address, a house in Brookline: 782 Mason Terrace, at the top of Corey Hill.

JoJo's garage opens at seven. That gave me a big two hours to sleep.

I took my beloved car in for some repair work it really didn't need yet and sweet-talked JoJo into giving me a loaner. I needed a hack, but not mine. Only trouble with that Chevy is it's too damn conspicuous.

I figured I'd lose way more than fifty bucks staking out Mason Terrace. I also figured it would be worth it to see old Mooney's face.

She was regular as clockwork, a dream to tail. Eight-thirty-seven every morning, she got a ride to the Square with a next-door neighbor. Took a cab home at five-fifteen. A working woman. Well, she couldn't make much of a living from robbing hacks and dumping the loot in the garbage.

I was damn curious by now. I knew as soon as I looked her over that she was the one, but she seemed so blah, so *normal*. She must have been five-seven or -eight, but the way she stooped, she didn't look tall. Her hair was long and brown with a lot of blond in it, the kind of hair that would have been terrific loose and wild, like a horse's mane. She tied it back with a scarf. A brown scarf. She wore suits. Brown suits. She had a tiny nose, brown eyes under pale eyebrows, a sharp chin. I never saw her smile. Maybe what she needed was a shrink, not a session with Mooney. Maybe she'd done it for the excitement. God knows, if I had her routine, her job, I'd probably be dressing up like King Kong and assaulting skyscrapers.

See, I followed her to work. It wasn't even tricky. She trudged the same path, went in the same entrance to Harvard Yard, probably walked the same number of steps every morning. Her name was Marcia Heidegger and she was a secretary in the admissions office of the college of fine arts.

I got friendly with one of her coworkers.

There was this guy typing away like mad at a desk in her office. I could just see him from the side window. He had grad student written all over his face. Longish wispy hair. Gold-rimmed glasses. Serious. Given to deep sighs and bright velour V necks. Probably writing his thesis on "Courtly Love and the Theories of Chrétien de Troyes."

I latched onto him at Bailey's the day after I'd tracked Lady Heidegger to her Harvard lair.

Too bad Roger was so short. Most short guys find it hard to believe that I'm really trying to pick them up. They look for ulterior motives. Not the Napoleon type of short guy; he assumes I've been waiting years for a chance to dance with a guy who doesn't have to bend to stare down my cleavage. But Roger was no Napoleon. So I had to engineer things a little.

I got into line ahead of him and ordered, after long deliberation, a BLT on toast. While the guy made it up and shoved it on a plate with three measly potato chips and a sliver of pickle you could barely see, I searched through my wallet, opened my change purse, counted out silver, got to $1.60 on the last five pennies. The counterman sang out, "That'll be a buck, eighty-five." I pawed through my pockets, found a nickel, two pennies. The line was growing restive. I concentrated on looking like a damsel in need of a knight, a tough task for a woman over six feet.

Roger (I didn't know he was Roger then) smiled ruefully and passed over a quarter. I was effusive in my thanks. I sat at a table for two, and when he'd gotten his tray (ham-and-cheese and a strawberry ice cream soda), I motioned him into my extra chair.

He was a sweetie. Sitting down, he forgot the difference in our height, and decided I might be someone he could talk to. I encouraged him. I hung shamelessly on his every word. A Harvard man, imagine that. We got around slowly, ever so slowly, to his work at the admissions office. He wanted to duck it and talk about more important issues, but I persisted. I'd been thinking about getting a job at Harvard, possibly in admissions. What kind of people did he work with? Were they congenial? What was the atmosphere like? Was it a big office? How many people? Men? Women? Any soulmates? Readers? Or just, you know, office people?

According to him, every soul he worked with was brain dead. I interrupted a stream of complaint with "Gee, I know somebody who works for Harvard. I wonder if you know her."

"It's a big place," he said, hoping to avoid the whole endless business.

"I met her at a party. Always meant to look her up." I searched through my bag, found a scrap of paper and pretended to read Marcia Heidegger's name off it.

"Marcia? Geez, I work with Marcia. Same office."

"Do you think she likes her work? I mean I got some strange vibes from her," I said. I actually said "strange vibes" and he didn't laugh his head off. People in the Square say things like that and other people take them seriously.

His face got conspiratorial, of all things, and he leaned closer to me.

"You want it, I bet you could get Marcia's job."

"You mean it?" What a compliment—a place for me among the brain dead.

"She's gonna get fired if she doesn't snap out of it."

"Snap out of what?"

"It was bad enough working with her when she first came over. She's one of those crazy neat people, can't stand to see papers lying on a desktop, you know? She almost threw out the first chapter of my thesis!"

I made a suitably horrified noise and he went on.

"Well, you know, about Marcia, it's kind of tragic. She doesn't talk about it."

But he was dying to.

"Yes?" I said, as if he needed egging on.

He lowered his voice. "She used to work for Justin Thayler over at the law school, that guy in the news, whose wife got killed. You know, her work hasn't been worth shit since it happened. She's always on the phone, talking real soft, hanging up if anybody comes in the room. I mean, you'd think she was in love with the guy or something, the way she . . ."

I don't remember what I said. For all I know, I may have volunteered to type his thesis. But I got rid of him somehow and then I scooted around the corner of Church Street and found a pay phone and dialed Mooney.

"Don't tell me," he said. "Somebody mugged you, but they only took your trading stamps."

"I have just one question for you, Moon."

"I accept. A June wedding, but I'll have to break it to Mother gently."

"Tell me what kind of junk Justin Thayler collected."

I could hear him breathing into the phone.

"Just tell me," I said, "for curiosity's sake."

"You onto something, Carlotta?"

"I'm curious, Mooney. And you're not the only source of information in the world."

"Thayler collected Roman stuff. Antiques. And I mean old. Artifacts, statues—"

"Coins?"

"Whole mess of them."

"Thanks."

"Carlotta—"

I never did find out what he was about to say because I hung up. Rude, I know. But I had things to do. And it was better Mooney shouldn't know what they were, because they came under the heading of illegal activities.

When I knocked at the front door of the Mason Terrace house at 10:00 A.M. the next day, I was dressed in dark slacks, a white blouse, and my old police department hat. I looked very much like the guy who reads your gas meter. I've never heard of anyone being arrested for impersonating the gasman. I've never heard of anyone really giving the gasman a second look. He fades into the background and that's exactly what I wanted to do.

I knew Marcia Heidegger wouldn't be home for hours. Old reliable had left for the Square at her usual time, precise to the minute. But I wasn't 100 percent sure Marcia lived alone. Hence the gasman. I could knock on the door and check it out.

Those Brookline neighborhoods kill me. Act sneaky and the neighbors call the cops in twenty seconds, but walk right up to the front door, knock, talk to yourself while you're sticking a shim in the crack of the door, let yourself in, and nobody does a thing. Boldness is all.

The place wasn't bad. Three rooms, kitchen and bath, light and airy. Marcia was incredibly organized, obsessively neat, which meant I had to keep track of where everything was and put it back just so. There was no clutter in the woman's life. The smell of coffee and toast lingered, but if she'd eaten breakfast, she'd already washed, dried, and put away the dishes. The morning paper had been read and tossed in the trash. The mail was sorted in one of those plastic accordion files. I mean, she folded her underwear like origami.

Now coins are hard to look for. They're small; you can hide 'em anywhere. So this search took me one hell of a long time. Nine out of ten women hide things that are dear to them in the bedroom. They keep their finest jewelry closest to the bed, sometimes in the nightstand, sometimes right under the mattress. That's where I started.

Marcia had a jewelry box on top of her dresser. I felt like hiding it for her. She had some nice stuff and a burglar could have made quite a haul with no effort.

The next favorite place for women to stash valuables is the kitchen. I sifted through her flour. I removed every Kellogg's Rice Krispy from the giant economy-sized box—and returned it. I went through her place like no burglar ever will. When I say thorough, I mean thorough.

I found four odd things. A neatly squared pile of clippings from the *Globe* and the *Herald,* all the articles about the Thayler killing. A manila envelope containing five different safe-deposit-box keys. A Tupperware container full of superstitious junk, good luck charms mostly, the kind of stuff I'd never have associated with a straight-arrow like Marcia: rabbits' feet galore, a little leather bag on a string that looked like some kind of voodoo charm, a pendant in the shape of a cross surmounted by a hook, and, I swear to God, a pack of worn tarot cards. Oh, yes, and a .22 automatic, looking a lot less threatening stuck in an ice cube tray. I took the bullets; the loaded gun threatened a defenseless box of Breyers' mint chocolate-chip ice cream.

I left everything else just the way I'd found it and went home. And tugged my hair. And stewed. And brooded. And ate half the stuff in the refrigerator. I kid you not.

At about one in the morning, it all made blinding, crystal-clear sense.

The next afternoon, at five-fifteen, I made sure I was the cabbie who picked up Marcia Heidegger in Harvard Square. Now cabstands have the most rigid protocol since Queen Victoria; you do not grab a fare out of turn or your fellow cabbies are definitely not amused. There was nothing for it but bribing the ranks. This bet with Mooney was costing me plenty.

I got her. She swung open the door and gave the Mason Terrace number. I grunted, kept my face turned front, and took off.

Some people really watch where you're going in a cab, scared to death you'll take them a block out of their way and squeeze them for an extra nickel. Others just lean back and dream. She was a dreamer, thank God. I was almost at District One headquarters before she woke up.

"Excuse me," she said, polite as ever, "that's Mason Terrace in *Brookline.*"

"Take the next right, pull over, and douse your lights," I said in a low Bogart voice. My imitation was not that good, but it got the point across. Her eyes widened and she made an instinctive grab for the door handle.

"Don't try it, lady," I Bogied on. "You think I'm dumb enough to take you in alone? There's a cop car behind us, just waiting for you to make a move."

Her hand froze. She was a sap for movie dialogue.

"Where's the cop?" was all she said on the way up to Mooney's office.

"What cop?"

"The one following us."

"You have touching faith in our law-enforcement system," I said.

She tried to bolt, I kid you not. I've had experience with runners a lot trickier than Marcia. I grabbed her in approved cop hold number three and marched her into Mooney's office.

He actually stopped typing and raised an eyebrow, an expression of great shock for Mooney.

"Citizen's arrest," I said.

"Charges?"

"Petty theft. Commission of a felony using a firearm." I rattled off a few more charges, using the numbers I remembered from cop school.

"This woman is crazy," Marcia Heidegger said with all the dignity she could muster.

"Search her," I said. "Get a matron in here. I want my four dollars and eighty-two cents back."

Mooney looked like he agreed with Marcia's opinion of my mental state. He said, "Wait up, Carlotta. You'd have to be able to identify that four dollars and eighty-two cents as yours. Can you do that? Quarters are quarters. Dimes are dimes."

"One of the coins she took was quite unusual," I said. "I'm sure I'd be able to identify it."

"Do you have any objection to displaying the change in your purse?" Mooney said to Marcia. He got me mad the way he said it, like he was humoring an idiot.

"Of course not," old Marcia said, cool as a frozen daiquiri.

"That's because she's stashed it somewhere else, Mooney," I said patiently. "She used to keep it in her purse, see. But then she goofed. She handed it over to a cabbie in her change. She should have just let it go, but she panicked because it was worth a pile and she was just baby-sitting it for someone else. So when she got it back, she hid it somewhere. Like in her shoe. Didn't you ever carry your lucky penny in your shoe?"

"No," Mooney said. "Now, Miss—"

"Heidegger," I said clearly. "Marcia Heidegger. She used to work at Harvard Law School." I wanted to see if Mooney picked up on it, but he didn't. He went on: "This can be taken care of with a minimum of fuss. If you'll agree to be searched by—"

"I want to see my lawyer," she said.

"For four dollars and eighty-two cents?" he said. "It'll cost you more than that to get your lawyers up here."

"Do I get my phone call or not?"

Mooney shrugged wearily and wrote up the charge sheet. Called a cop to take her to the phone.

He got JoAnn, which was good. Under cover of our old-friend-long-time-no-see greetings, I whispered in her ear.

"You'll find it fifty well spent," I said to Mooney when we were alone.

JoAnn came back, shoving Marcia slightly ahead of her. She plunked her prisoner down in one of Mooney's hard wooden chairs and turned to me, grinning from ear to ear.

"Got it?" I said. "Good for you."

"What's going on?" Mooney said.

"She got real clumsy on the way to the pay phone," JoAnn said. "Practically fell on the floor. Got up with her right hand clenched tight. When we got to the phone, I offered to drop her dime for her. She wanted to do it herself. I insisted and she got clumsy again. Somehow this coin got kicked clear across the floor."

She held it up. The coin could have been a dime, except the color was off: warm, rosy gold instead of dead silver. How I missed it the first time around I'll never know.

"What the hell is that?" Mooney said.

"What kind of coins were in Justin Thayler's collection?" I asked. "Roman?"

Marcia jumped out of the chair, snapped her bag open, and drew out her little .22. I kid you not. She was closest to Mooney and she just stepped up to him and rested it above his left ear. He swallowed, didn't say a word. I never realized how prominent his Adam's apple was. JoAnn froze, hand on her holster.

Good old reliable, methodical Marcia. Why, I said to myself, *why* pick today of all days to trot your gun out of the freezer? Did you read bad luck in your tarot cards? Then I had a truly rotten thought. What if she had two guns? What if the disarmed .22 was still staring down the mint chocolate-chip ice cream?

"Give it back," Marcia said. She held out one hand, made an impatient waving motion.

"Hey, you don't need it, Marcia," I said. "You've got plenty more. In all those safe deposit boxes."

"I'm going to count to five—" she began.

"Were you in on the murder from day one? You know, from the planning stages?" I asked. I kept my voice low, but it echoed off the walls of Mooney's tiny office. The hum of everyday activity kept going in the main room. Nobody noticed the little gun in the well-dressed lady's hand. "Or did you just do your beau a favor and hide the loot after he iced his wife? In order to back up his burglary tale? I mean, if Justin Thayler really wanted to marry you, there is such a thing as divorce. Or was old Jennifer the one with the bucks?"

"I want that coin," she said softly. "Then I want the two of you"—she motioned to JoAnn and me—"to sit down facing that wall. If you yell, or do anything before I'm out of the building, I'll shoot this gentleman. He's coming with me."

"Come on, Marcia," I said, "put it down. I mean, look at you. A week ago you just wanted Thayler's coin back. You didn't want to rob my cab, right? You just didn't know how else to get your good luck charm back with no questions asked. You didn't do it for the money, right? You did it for love. You were so straight you threw away the cash. Now here you are with a gun pointed at a cop—"

"Shut up!"

I took a deep breath and said, "You haven't got the style, Marcia. Your gun's not even loaded."

Mooney didn't relax a hair. Sometimes I think the guy hasn't ever believed a word I've said to him. But Marcia got shook. She pulled the barrel away from Mooney's skull and peered at it with a puzzled frown. JoAnn and I both tackled her before she got a chance to pull the trigger. I twisted the gun out of her hand. I was almost afraid to look inside. Mooney stared at me and I felt my mouth go dry and a trickle of sweat worm its way down my back.

I looked.

No bullets. My heart stopped fibrillating, and Mooney actually cracked a smile in my direction.

So that's all. I sure hope Mooney will spread the word around that I helped him nail Thayler. And I think he will; he's a fair kind of guy. Maybe it'll get me a case or two. Driving a cab is hard on the backside, you know?

LAWRENCE BLOCK

"As Good as a Rest"

Lawrence Block was born in Buffalo, New York on June 24, 1938. He was educated at Antioch College and worked for the Scott Meredith Literary Agency in New York City. Block began publishing short mysteries in the late 1950s and paperback novels in the early '60s, under his own name and various pseudonyms. A master at creating memorable series characters, he has entertained readers with the exploits of Evan Tanner, Chip Harrison, Bernie Rhodenbarr, Martin Ehrengraf and others.

*Block's most successful series character is unlicensed private detective Matthew Scudder who has appeared in more than a dozen novels to date, including the Edgar-winning **A Dance at the Slaughterhouse** (1991). A Bernie Rhodenbarr novel, **The Burglar Who Liked to Quote Kipling** (1979) won the Nero Wolfe Award for best novel, and a Scudder novel **Eight Million Ways to Die** (1982) won the Shamus Award from the Private Eye Writers of America. Two of Block's short stories have received Edgar Awards, "By Dawn's Early Light" (1984) and "Keller's Therapy" (1993).*

*His short stories have been collected in **Sometimes They Bite** (1983), **Like a Lamb to the Slaughter** (1984) and **Ehrengraf for the Defense** (1994). "As Good as a Rest" was published in **Ellery Queen's Mystery Magazine** and reprinted in **The Year's Best Mystery and Suspense Stories - 1987**.*

As Good as a Rest

by Lawrence Block

A ndrew says the whole point of a vacation is to change your perspective of the world. A change is as good as a rest, he says, and vacations are about change, not rest. If we just wanted a rest, he says, we could stop the mail and disconnect the phone and stay home: that would add up to more of a traditional rest than traipsing all over Europe. Sitting in front of the television set with your feet up, he says, is generally considered to be more restful than climbing the forty-two thousand steps to the top of Notre Dame.

Of course, there aren't forty-two thousand steps, but it did seem like it at the time. We were with the Dattners—by the time we got to Paris the four of us had already buddied up—and Harry kept wondering aloud why the genius who'd built the cathedral hadn't thought to put in an elevator. And Sue, who'd struck me earlier as unlikely to be afraid of anything, turned out to be petrified of heights. There are two staircases at Notre Dame, one going up and one coming down, and to get from one to the other you have to walk along this high ledge. It's really quite wide, even at its narrowest, and the view of the rooftops of Paris is magnificent, but all of this was wasted on Sue, who clung to the rear wall with her eyes clenched shut.

Andrew took her arm and walked her through it, while Harry and I looked out at the City of Light. "It's high open spaces that does it to her," he told me. "Yesterday, the Eiffel Tower, no problem, because the space was enclosed. But when it's open she starts getting afraid that she'll get sucked over the side or that she'll get this sudden impulse to jump, and, well, you see what it does to her."

While neither Andrew nor I is troubled by heights, whether open or enclosed, the climb to the top of the cathedral wasn't the sort of thing we'd have done at home, especially since we'd already had a spectacular view of the city the day before from the Eiffel Tower. I'm not mad about walking stairs, but it didn't occur to me to pass up the climb. For that matter, I'm not that mad about walking generally—Andrew says I won't go anywhere without a guaranteed parking space—but it seems to me that I walked from one end of Europe to the other, and didn't mind a bit.

When we weren't walking through streets or up staircases, we were parading through museums. That's hardly a departure for me, but for Andrew it is uncharacteristic behavior in the extreme. Boston's Museum of Fine Arts is one of the best in the country, and it's not twenty minutes from our house. We have a membership, and I go all the time, but it's almost impossible to get Andrew to go.

But in Paris he went to the Louvre, and the Rodin Museum, and that little museum in the 16th arrondissement with the most wonderful collection of Monets. And in London he led the way to the National Gallery and the National Portrait Gallery and the Victoria and Albert—and in Amsterdam he spent three hours in the Rijksmuseum and hurried us to the Van Gogh Museum first thing the next morning. By the time we got to Madrid, I was museumed out. I knew it was a sin to miss the Prado but I just couldn't face it, and I wound up walking around the city with Harry while my husband dragged Sue through galleries of El Grecos and Goyas and Velasquezes.

"Now that you've discovered museums," I told Andrew, "you may take a different view of the Museum of Fine Arts. There's a show of American landscape painters that'll still be running when we get back—I think you'll like it."

He assured me he was looking forward to it. But you know he never went. Museums are strictly a vacation pleasure for him. He doesn't even want to hear about them when he's at home.

For my part, you'd think I'd have learned by now not to buy clothes when we travel. Of course, it's impossible not to—there are some genuine bargains and some things you couldn't find at home—but I almost always wind up buying something that remains unworn in my closet forever after. It seems so right in some foreign capital, but once I get it home I realize it's not me at all, and so it lives out its days on a hanger, a source in turn of fond memories and faint guilt. It's not that I lose judgment when I travel, or become wildly impulsive. It's more that I become a slightly different person in the course of the trip and the clothes I buy for that person aren't always right for the person I am in Boston.

Oh, why am I nattering on like this? You don't have to look in my closet to see how travel changes a person. For heaven's sake, just look at the Dattners.

If we hadn't all been on vacation together, we would never have come to know Harry and Sue, let alone spend so much time with them. We would never have encountered them in the first place—day-to-day living would not have brought them to Boston, or us to Enid, Oklahoma. But even if they'd lived down the street from us, we would never have become close friends at home. To put it as simply as possible, they were not our kind of people.

The package tour we'd booked wasn't one of those escorted ventures in which your every minute is accounted for. It included our charter flights over and back, all our hotel accommodations, and our transportation from one city to the next. We "did" six countries in twenty-two days, but what we did in each, and where and with whom, was strictly up to us. We could have kept to ourselves altogether, and have often done so when traveling, but by the time we checked into our hotel in London the first day we'd made arrangements to join the Dattners that night for dinner, and before we knocked off our after-dinner brandies that night it had been tacitly agreed that we would be a foursome throughout the trip—unless, of course, it turned out that we tired of each other.

"They're a pair," Andrew said that first night, unknotting his tie and giving it a shake before hanging it over the doorknob. "That y'all-come-back accent of hers sounds like syrup flowing over corn cakes."

"She's a little flashy, too," I said. "But that sport jacket of his—"

"I know," Andrew said. "Somewhere, even as we speak, a horse is shivering, his blanket having been transformed into a jacket for Harry."

"And yet there's something about them, isn't there?"

"They're nice people," Andrew said. "Not our kind at all, but what does that matter? We're on a trip. We're ripe for a change . . ."

In Paris, after a night watching a floorshow at what I'm sure was a rather disreputable little nightclub in Les Halles, I lay in bed while Andrew sat up smoking a last cigarette. "I'm glad we met the Dattners," he said. "This trip would be fun anyway, but they add to it. That joint tonight was a treat, and I'm sure we wouldn't have gone if it hadn't been for them. And do you know something? I don't think *they'd* have gone if it hadn't been for *us*."

"Where would we be without them?" I rolled onto my side. "I know where Sue would be without your helping hand. Up on top of Notre Dame, frozen with fear. Do you suppose that's how the gargoyles got there? Are they nothing but tourists turned to stone?"

"Then you'll never be a gargoyle. You were a long way from petrification whirling around the dance floor tonight."

"Harry's a good dancer. I didn't think he would be, but he's very light on his feet."

"The gun doesn't weigh him down, eh?"

I sat up. "I *thought* he was wearing a gun," I said. "How on earth does he get it past the airport scanners?"

"Undoubtedly by packing it in his luggage and checking it through. He wouldn't need it on the plane—not unless he was planning to divert the flight to Havana."

"I don't think they go to Havana any more. Why would he need it *off* the plane? I suppose tonight he'd feel safer armed. That place was a bit on the rough side."

"He was carrying it at the Tower of London, and in and out of a slew of museums. In fact, I think he carries it all the time except on planes. Most likely he feels naked without it."

"I wonder if he sleeps with it."

"I think he sleeps with her."

"Well, I know *that*."

"To their mutual pleasure, I shouldn't wonder. Even as you and I."

"Ah," I said.

And, a bit later, he said, "You like them, don't you?"

"Well, of course I do. I don't want to pack them up and take them home to Boston with us, but—"

"You like *him*."

"Harry? Oh, *I* see what you're getting at."

"Quite."

"And she's attractive, isn't she? You're attracted to her."

"At home I wouldn't look at her twice, but here—"

"Say no more. That's how I feel about him. That's exactly how I feel about him."

"Do you suppose we'll do anything about it?"

"I don't know. Do you suppose they're having this very conversation two floors below?"

"I wouldn't be surprised. If they *are* having this conversation, and if they had the same silent prelude to this conversation, they're probably feeling very good indeed."

"Mmmmm," I said dreamily. "Even as you and I."

I don't know if the Dattners had that conversation that particular evening, but they certainly had it somewhere along the way. The little tensions and energy currents between the four of us began to build until it seemed almost as though the air were crackling with electricity. More often than not we'd find ourselves pairing off on our walks. Andrew with Sue, Harry with me. I remember one moment when he took my hand crossing the street—I remember the instant but not the street or even the city—and a little shiver went right through me.

By the time we were in Madrid, with Andrew and Sue trekking through the Prado while Harry and I ate garlicky shrimp and sipped a sweetish white wine in a little cafe on the Plaza Mayor, it was clear what was going to happen. We were almost ready to talk about it.

"I hope they're having a good time," I told Harry. "I just couldn't manage another museum."

"I'm glad we're out here instead," he said, with a wave at the plaza. "But I would have gone to the Prado if you went." And he reached out and covered my hand with his.

"Sue and Andy seem to be getting along pretty good," he said.

Andy! Had anyone else ever called my husband Andy?

"And you and me, we get along all right, don't we?"

"Yes," I said, giving his hand a little squeeze. "Yes, we do."

Andrew and I were up late that night, talking and talking. The next day we flew to Rome. We were all tired our first night there and ate at the restaurant in our hotel rather than venture forth. The food was good, but I wonder if any of us really tasted it?

Andrew insisted that we all drink grappa with our coffee. It turned out to be a rather nasty brandy, clear in color and quite powerful. The men had a second round of it. Sue and I had enough work finishing our first.

Harry held his glass aloft and proposed a toast. "To good friends," he said. "To close friendship with good people." And after everyone had taken a sip he said, "You know, in a couple of days we all go back to the lives we used to lead. Sue and I go back to Oklahoma, you two go back to Boston, Mass. Andy, you go back to your investments business and I'll be doin' what I do. And we got each other's addresses and phone, and we say we'll keep in touch, and maybe we will. But if we do or we don't, either way one thing's sure. The minute we get off that plane at JFK, that's when the carriage turns into a pumpkin and the horses go back to bein' mice. You know what I mean?"

Everyone did.

"Anyway," he said, "what me an' Sue were thinkin', we thought there's a whole lot of Rome, a mess of good restaurants, and things to see and places to go. We thought it's silly to have four people all do the same things and go the same places and miss out on all the rest. We thought, you know, after breakfast tomorrow, we'd split up and spend the day separate." He took a breath. "Like Sue and Andy'd team up for the day and, Elaine, you an' me'd be together."

"The way we did in Madrid," somebody said.

"Except I mean for the whole day," Harry said. A light film of perspiration gleamed on his forehead. I looked at his jacket and tried to decide if he was wearing his gun. I'd seen it on our afternoon in Madrid. His jacket had come open and I'd seen the gun, snug in his shoulder holster. "The whole day and then the evening, too. Dinner—and after."

There was a silence that I don't suppose could have lasted nearly as long as it seemed to. Then Andrew said he thought it was a good idea, and Sue agreed, and so did I.

Later, in our hotel room, Andrew assured me that we could back out. "I don't think they have any more experience with this than we do. You saw how nervous Harry was during his little speech. He'd probably be relieved to a certain degree if we did back out."

"Is that what you want to do?"

He thought for a moment. "For my part," he said, "I'd as soon go through with it."

"So would I. My only concern is if it made some difference between us afterward."

"I don't think it will. This is fantasy, you know. It's not the real world. We're not in Boston *or* Oklahoma. We're in Rome, and you know what they say. When in Rome, do as the Romans do."

"And is this what the Romans do?"

"It's probably what they do when they go to Stockholm," Andrew said.

In the morning, we joined the Dattners for breakfast. Afterward, without anything being said, we paired off as Harry had suggested the night before. He and I walked through a sun-drenched morning to the Spanish Steps, where I bought a bag of crumbs and fed the pigeons. After that—

Oh, what does it matter what came next, what particular tourist things we found to do that day? Suffice it to say that we went interesting places and saw rapturous sights, and everything we did and saw was heightened by anticipation of the evening ahead.

We ate lightly that night, and drank freely but not to excess. The trattoria where we dined wasn't far from our hotel and the night was clear and mild, so we walked back. Harry slipped an arm around my waist. I leaned a little against his shoulder. After we'd walked a way in silence, he said very softly, "Elaine, only if you want to."

"But I do," I heard myself say.

Then he took me in his arms and kissed me.

I ought to recall the night better than I do. We felt love and lust for each other, and sated both appetites. He was gentler than I might have guessed he'd be, and I more abandoned. I could probably remember precisely what happened if I put my mind to it, but I don't think I could make the memory seem real. Because it's as if it happened to someone else. It was vivid at the time, because at the time I truly was the person sharing her bed with Harry. But that person had no existence before or after that European vacation.

There was a moment when I looked up and saw one of Andrew's neckties hanging on the knob of the closet door. It struck me that I should have put the tie away, that it was out of place there. Then I told myself that the tie was where it ought to be, that it was Harry who didn't belong here. And finally I decided that both belonged, my husband's tie and my inappropriate Oklahoma lover. Now both belonged, but in the morning the necktie would remain and Harry would be gone.

As indeed he was. I awakened a little before dawn and was alone in the room. I went back to sleep, and when I next opened my eyes Andrew was in bed beside me. Had they met in the hallway, I wondered? Had they worked out the logistics of this passage in advance? I never asked. I still don't know.

Our last day in Rome, the Dattners went their way and we went ours. Andrew and I got to the Vatican, saw the Colosseum, and wandered here and there, stopping at sidewalk cafes for espresso. We hardly talked about the previous evening, beyond assuring each other that we had enjoyed it, that we were glad it had happened, and that our feelings for one another remained unchanged—deepened, if anything, by virtue of having shared this experience, if it could be said to have been shared.

We joined Harry and Sue for dinner. And in the morning we all rode out to the airport and boarded our flight to New York. I remember looking at the other passengers on the plane, few of whom I'd exchanged more than a couple of sentences with in the course of the past three weeks. There were almost certainly couples among them with whom we had more in common than we had with the Dattners. Had any of them had comparable flings in the course of the trip?

At JFK we all collected our luggage and went through customs and passport control. Then we were off to catch our connecting flight to Boston while Harry and Sue had a four-hour wait for their TWA flight to Tulsa. We said goodbye. The men shook hands while Sue and I embraced. Then Harry and I kissed, and Sue and Andrew kissed. That woman slept with my husband, I thought. And that man—I slept with him. I had the thought that, were I to continue thinking about it, I would start laughing.

Two hours later we were on the ground at Logan, and less than an hour after that we were in our own house.

That weekend Paul and Marilyn Welles came over for dinner and heard a play-by-play account of our three-week vacation—with the exception, of course, of that second-to-last night in Rome. Paul is a business associate of Andrew's and Marilyn is a woman not unlike me, and I wondered to myself what would happen if we four traded partners for an evening.

But it wouldn't happen and I certainly didn't want it to happen. I found Paul attractive and I know Andrew had always found Marilyn attractive. But such an incident among us wouldn't be appropriate, as it had somehow been appropriate with the Dattners.

I know Andrew was having much the same thoughts. We didn't discuss it afterward, but one knows . . .

I thought of all of this just last week. Andrew was in a bank in Skokie, Illinois, along with Paul Welles and two other men. One of the tellers managed to hit the silent alarm and the police arrived as they were on their way out. There was some shooting. Paul Welles was wounded superficially, as was one of the policemen. Another of the policemen was killed.

Andrew is quite certain he didn't hit anybody. He fired his gun a couple of times, but he's sure he didn't kill the police officer.

But when he got home we both kept thinking the same thing. It could have been Harry Dattner.

Not literally, because what would an Oklahoma state trooper be doing in Skokie, Illinois? But it might as easily have been the Skokie cop in Europe with us. And it might have been Andrew who shot him—or been shot *by* him, for that matter.

I don't know that I'm explaining this properly. It's all so incredible. That I should have slept with a policeman while my husband was with a policeman's wife. That we had ever become friendly with them in the first place. I have to remind myself and keep reminding myself, that it all happened overseas. It happened in Europe, and it happened to four other people. We were not ourselves, and Sue and Harry were not themselves. It happened, you see, in another universe altogether, and so, really, it's as if it never happened at all.

TONY HILLERMAN

"Chee's Witch"

Tony Hillerman was born in Sacred Heart, Oklahoma on May 27, 1925. He attended an Indian boarding school for eight years, and after serving in the Infantry during World War II he studied at Oklahoma State University. Hillerman received a degree in journalism from the University of Oklahoma at Norman. After working as a newspaper reporter and editor he earned his masters degree in English from the University of New Mexico and became a Professor of Journalism there.

*The first of Hillerman's popular series about Navajo Tribal Police officers Joe Leaphorn and Jim Chee was **The Blessing Way** (1970), a Leaphorn novel. Chee first appeared in **People of Darkness** ten years later, and the two began combining their talents in **Skinwalkers** (1987), winner of Bouchercon's Anthony Award. **Dance Hall of the Dead** (1973), a Leaphorn novel, brought Hillerman the Edgar Award from Mystery Writers of America, and he received MWA's Grand Master Award in 1991. **A Thief of Time** (1988), often considered his best novel, won the Macavity Award from Mystery Readers International. Hillerman's highly regarded political mystery **The Fly on the Wall** (1971), an Edgar nominee, and the recent **Finding Moon** (1995) are his only non-series novels.*

*There have been very few short stories from Hillerman. "Chee's Witch" was published in **The New Black Mask** #7 and reprinted in **Felonious Assaults**.*

Chee's Witch

by Tony Hillerman

now is so important to the Eskimos they have nine nouns to describe its variations. Corporal Jimmy Chee of the Navajo Tribal Police had heard that as an anthropology student at the University of New Mexico. He remembered it now because he was thinking of all the words you need in Navajo to account for the many forms of witchcraft. The word Old Woman Tso had used was "anti'l," which is the ultimate sort, the absolute worst. And so, in fact, was the deed which seemed to have been done. Murder, apparently. Mutilation, certainly, if Old Woman Tso had her facts right. And then, if one believed all the mythology of witchery told among the fifty clans who comprised The People, there must also be cannibalism, incest, even necrophilia.

On the radio in Chee's pickup truck, the voice of the young Navajo reading a Gallup used-car commercial was replaced by Willie Nelson singing of trouble and a worried mind. The ballad fit Chee's mood. He was tired. He was thirsty. He was sticky with sweat. He was worried. His pickup jolted along the ruts in a windless heat, leaving a white fog of dust to mark its winding passage across the Rainbow Plateau. The truck was gray with it. So was Jimmy Chee. Since sunrise he had covered maybe two hundred miles of half-graded gravel and unmarked wagon tracks of the Arizona–Utah–New Mexico border country. Routine at first—a check into a witch story at the Tsossie hogan north of Teec Nos Pos to stop trouble before it started. Routine and logical. A bitter winter, a sand storm spring, a summer of rainless, desiccating heat. Hopes dying, things going wrong, anger growing, and then the witch gossip. The logical. A bitter wind, a sand storm spring, a summer awry. The trouble at the summer hogan of the Tsossies was a sick child and a water well that had turned alkaline—nothing unexpected. But you didn't expect such a specific witch. The skinwalker, the Tsossies agreed, was The City Navajo, the man who had come to live in one of the government houses at Kayenta. Why the City Navajo? Because everybody knew he was a witch. Where had they heard that, the first time? The People who came to the trading post at Mexican Water said it. And so Chee had driven westward over Tohache Wash, past Red Mesa and Rabbit Ears to Mexican Water. He had spent hours on the shady porch giving those who came to buy, and to fill their water barrels, and to visit, a chance to know who he was until finally they might risk talking about witchcraft to a stranger. They were Mud Clan, and Many Goats People, and Standing Rock Clan—foreign to Chee's own Slow Talking People—but finally some of them talked a little.

A witch was at work on the Rainbow Plateau. Adeline Etcitty's mare had foaled a two-headed colt. Hosteen Musket had seen the witch. He'd seen a man walk into a grove of cottonwoods, but when he got there an owl flew away. Rudolph Bisti's boys lost three rams while driving their flocks up into the Chuska high pastures, and when they found the bodies, the huge tracks of a werewolf were all around them. The daughter of Rosemary Nashibitti had seen a big dog bothering her horses and had shot at it with her .22 and the dog had turned into a man wearing a wolfskin and had fled, half running, half flying. The old man they called Afraid of His Horses had heard the sound of the witch on the roof of his winter hogan, and saw the dirt falling through the smoke hole as the skinwalker tried to throw in his corpse powder. The next morning the old man had followed the tracks of the Navajo Wolf for a mile, hoping to kill him. But the tracks had faded away. There was nothing very unusual in the stories, except their number and the recurring hints that City Navajo was the witch. But then came what Chee hadn't expected. The witch had killed a man.

The police dispatcher at Window Rock had been interrupting Willie Nelson with an occasional blurted message. Now she spoke directly to Chee. He acknowledged. She asked his location.

"About fifteen miles south of Dennehotso," Chee said. "Homeward bound for Tuba City. Dirty, thirsty, hungry, and tired."

"I have a message."

"Tuba City," Chee repeated, "which I hope to reach in about two hours, just in time to avoid running up a lot of overtime for which I never get paid."

"The message is FBI Agent Wells needs to contact you. Can you make a meeting at Kayenta Holiday Inn at eight P.M.?"

"What's it about?" Chee asked. The dispatcher's name was Virgie Endecheenie, and she had a very pretty voice and the first time Chee had met her at the Window Rock headquarters of the Navajo Tribal Police he had been instantly smitten. Unfortunately, Virgie was a born-into Salt Cedar Clan, which was the clan of Chee's father, which put an instant end to that. Even thinking about it would violate the complex incest taboo of the Navajos.

"Nothing on what it's about," Virgie said, her voice strictly business. "It just says confirm meeting time and place with Chee or obtain alternate time."

"Any first name on Wells?" Chee asked. The only FBI Wells he knew was Jake Wells. He hoped it wouldn't be Jake.

"Negative on the first name," Virgie said.

"All right," Chee said. "I'll be there."

The road tilted downward now into the vast barrens of erosion which the Navajos call Beautiful Valley. Far to the west, the edge of the sun dipped behind a cloud—one of the line of thunderheads forming in the evening heat over the San Francisco Peaks and the Coconino Rim. The Hopis had been holding their Niman Kachina dances, calling the clouds to come and bless them.

Chee reached Kayenta just a little late. It was early twilight and the clouds had risen black against the sunset. The breeze brought the faint smells that rising humidity carry across desert country— the perfume of sage, creosote brush, and dust. The desk clerk said that Wells was in room 284 and the first name was Jake. Chee no longer cared. Jake Wells was abrasive but he was also smart. He had the best record in the special FBI Academy class Chee had attended, a quick, tough intelligence. Chee could tolerate the man's personality for a while to learn what Wells could make of his witchcraft puzzle.

"It's unlocked," Wells said. "Come on in." He was propped against the padded headboard of the bed, shirt off, shoes on, glass in hand. He glanced at Chee and then back at the television set. He was as tall as Chee remembered, and the eyes were just as blue. He waved the glass at Chee without looking away from the set. "Mix yourself one," he said, nodding toward a bottle beside the sink in the dressing alcove.

"How you doing, Jake?" Chee asked.

Now the blue eyes reexamined Chee. The question in them abruptly went away. "Yeah," Wells said. "You were the one at the Academy." He eased himself on his left elbow and extended a hand. "Jake Wells," he said.

Chee shook the hand. "Chee," he said.

Wells shifted his weight again and handed Chee his glass. "Pour me a little more while you're at it," he said, "and turn down the sound."

Chee turned down the sound.

"About 30 percent booze," Wells demonstrated the proportion with his hands. "This is your district then. You're in charge around Kayenta? Window Rock said I should talk to you. They said you were out chasing around in the desert today. What are you working on?"

"Nothing much," Chee said. He ran a glass of water, drinking it thirstily. His face in the mirror was dirty—the lines around his mouth and eyes whitish with dust. The sticker on the glass reminded guests that the laws of the Navajo Tribal Council prohibited possession of alcoholic beverages on the reservation. He refilled his own glass with water and mixed Wells's drink. "As a matter of fact, I'm working on a witchcraft case."

"Witchcraft?" Wells laughed. "Really?" He took the drink from Chee and examined it. "How does it work? Spells and like that?"

"Not exactly," Chee said. "It depends. A few years ago a little girl got sick down near Burnt Water. Her dad killed three people with a shotgun. He said they blew corpse powder on his daughter and made her sick."

Wells was watching him. "The kind of crime where you have the insanity plea."

"Sometimes," Chee said. "Whatever you have, witch talk makes you nervous. It happens more when you have a bad year like this. You hear it and you try to find out what's starting it before things get worse."

"So you're not really expecting to find a witch?"

"Usually not," Chee said.

"Usually?"

"Judge for yourself," Chee said. "I'll tell you what I've picked up today. You tell me what to make of it. Have time?"

Wells shrugged. "What I really want to talk about is a guy

named Simon Begay." He looked quizzically at Chee. "You heard the name?"

"Yes," Chee said.

"Well, shit," Wells said. "You shouldn't have. What do you know about him?"

"Showed up maybe three months ago. Moved into one of those U.S. Public Health Service houses over by the Kayenta clinic. Stranger. Keeps to himself. From off the reservation somewhere. I figured you federals put him here to keep him out of sight."

Wells frowned. "How long you known about him?"

"Quite a while," Chee said. He'd known about Begay within a week after his arrival.

"He's a witness," Wells said. "They broke a car-theft operation in Los Angeles. Big deal. National connections. One of those where they have hired hands picking up expensive models and they drive 'em right on the ship and off-load in South America. This Begay is one of the hired hands. Nobody much. Criminal record going all the way back to juvenile, but all nickel-and-dime stuff. I gather he saw some things that help tie some big boys into the crime, so Justice made a deal with him."

"And they hide him out here until the trial?"

Something apparently showed in the tone of the question. "If you want to hide an apple, you drop it in with the other apples," Wells said. "What better place?"

Chee had been looking at Wells' shoes, which were glossy with polish. Now he examined his own boots, which were not. But he was thinking of Justice Department stupidity. The appearance of any new human in a country as empty as the Navajo Reservation provoked instant interest. If the stranger was a Navajo, there were instant questions. What was his clan? Who was his mother? What was his father's clan? Who were his relatives? The City Navajo had no answers to any of these crucial questions. He was (as Chee had been repeatedly told) unfriendly. It was quickly guessed that he was a "relocation Navajo," born to one of those hundreds of Navajo families which the federal government had tried to reestablish forty years ago in Chicago, Los Angeles, and other urban centers. He was a stranger. In a year of witches, he would certainly be suspected. Chee sat looking at his boots, wondering if that was the only basis for the charge that City Navajo was a skinwalker. Or had someone seen something? Had someone seen the murder?

"The thing about apples is they don't gossip," Chee said.

"You hear gossip about Begay?" Wells was sitting up now, his feet on the floor.

"Sure," Chee said. "I hear he's a witch."

Wells produced a pro-forma chuckle. "Tell me about it," he said.

Chee knew exactly how he wanted to tell it. Wells would have to wait a while before he came to the part about Begay. "The Eskimos have nine nouns for snow," Chee began. He told Wells about the variety of witchcraft on the reservations and its environs: about frenzy witchcraft, used for sexual conquests, of witchery distortions, of curing ceremonials, of the exotic two-heart witchcraft of the Hopi Fog Clan, of the Zuni Sorcery Fraternity, of the Navajo "chindi," which is more like a ghost than a witch, and finally of the Navajo Wolf, the anti'l witchcraft, the werewolves who pervert every taboo of the Navajo Way and use corpse powder to kill their victims.

Wells rattled the ice in his glass and glanced at his watch.

"To get to the part about your Begay," Chee said, "about two months ago we started picking up witch gossip. Nothing much, and you expect it during a drought. Lately it got to be more than usual." He described some of the tales and how uneasiness and dread had spread across the plateau. He described what he had learned today, the Tsossies's naming City Navajo as the witch, his trip to Mexican Water, of learning there that the witch had killed a man.

"They said it happened in the spring—couple of months ago. They told me the ones who knew about it were the Tso outfit." The talk of murder, Chee noticed, had revived Wells's interest. "I went up there," he continued, "and found the old woman who runs the outfit. Emma Tso. She told me her son-in-law had been out looking for some sheep, and smelled something, and found the body under some chamiso brush in a dry wash. A witch had killed him."

"How—"

Chee cut off the question. "I asked her how he knew it was a witch killing. She said the hands were stretched out like this." Chee extended his hands, palms up. "They were flayed. The skin was cut off the palms and fingers."

Wells raised his eyebrows.

"That's what the witch uses to make corpse powder," Chee explained. "They take the skin that has the whorls and ridges of the individual personality—the skin from the palms and the finger pads, and the soles of the feet. They take that, and the skin from the glans of the penis, and the small bones where the neck joins the skull, and they dry it, and pulverize it, and use it as poison."

"You're going to get to Begay any minute now," Wells said. "That right?"

"We got to him," Chee said. "He's the one they think is the witch. He's the City Navajo."

"I thought you were going to say that," Wells said. He rubbed the back of his hand across one blue eye. "City Navajo. Is it that obvious?"

"Yes," Chee said. "And then he's a stranger. People suspect strangers."

"Were they coming around him? Accusing him? Any threats? Anything like that, you think?"

"It wouldn't work that way—not unless somebody had someone in their family killed. The way you deal with a witch is hire a singer and hold a special kind of curing ceremony. That turns the witchcraft around and kills the witch."

Wells made an impatient gesture. "Whatever," he said. "I think something has made this Begay spooky." He stared into his glass, communing with the bourbon. "I don't know."

"Something unusual about the way he's acting?"

"Hell of it is I don't know how he usually acts. This wasn't my case. The agent who worked him retired or some damn thing, so I got stuck with being the delivery man." He shifted his eyes from glass to Chee. "But if it was me, and I was holed up here waiting, and the guy came along who was going to take me home again, then I'd be glad to see him. Happy to have it over with. All that."

"He wasn't?"

Wells shook his head. "Seemed edgy. Maybe that's natural, though. He's going to make trouble for some hard people."

"I'd be nervous," Chee said.

"I guess it doesn't matter much anyway," Wells said. "He's small potatoes. The guy who's handling it now in the U.S. Attorney's Office said it must have been a toss-up whether to fool with him at all. He said the assistant who handled it decided to hide him out just to be on the safe side."

"Begay doesn't know much?"

"I guess not. That, and they've got better witnesses."

"So why worry?"

Wells laughed. "I bring this sucker back and they put him on the witness stand and he answers all the questions with I don't know

153

and it makes the USDA look like a horse's ass. When a U.S. Attorney looks like that, he finds an FBI agent to blame it on." He yawned. "Therefore," he said through the yawn, "I want to ask you what you think. This is your territory. You are the officer in charge. Is it your opinion that someone got to my witness?"

Chee let the question hang. He spent a fraction of a second reaching the answer, which was they could have if they wanted to try. Then he thought about the real reason Wells had kept him working late without a meal or a shower. Two sentences in Wells's report. One would note that the possibility the witness had been approached had been checked with local Navajo Police. The next would report whatever Chee said next. Wells would have followed Federal Rule One—Protect Your Ass.

Chee shrugged. "You want to hear the rest of my witchcraft business?"

Wells put his drink on the lamp table and untied his shoe. "Does it bear on this?"

"Who knows? Anyway there's not much left. I'll let you decide. The point is we had already picked up this corpse Emma Tso's son-in-law found. Somebody had reported it weeks ago. It had been collected, and taken in for an autopsy. The word we got on the body was Navajo male in his thirties probably. No identification on him."

"How was this bird killed?"

"No sign of foul play," Chee said. "By the time the body was brought in, decay and the scavengers hadn't left a lot. Mostly bone and gristle, I guess. This was a long time after Emma Tso's son-in-law saw him."

"So why do they think Begay killed him?" Wells removed his second shoe and headed for the bathroom.

Chee picked up the telephone and dialed the Kayenta clinic. He got the night supervisor and waited while the supervisor dug out the file. Wells came out of the bathroom with his toothbrush. Chee covered the mouthpiece. "I'm having them read me the autopsy report," Chee explained. Wells began brushing his teeth at the sink in the dressing alcove. The voice of the night supervisor droned into Chee's ear.

"That all?" Chee asked. "Nothing added on? No identity yet? Still no cause?"

"That's him," the voice said.

"How about shoes?" Chee asked. "He have shoes on?"

"Just a sec," the voice said. "Yep. Size 10D. And a hat, and . . ."

"No mention of the neck or skull, right? I didn't miss that? No bones missing?"

Silence. "Nothing about neck or skull bones."

"Ah," Chee said. "Fine. I thank you." He felt great. He felt wonderful. Finally things had clicked into place. The witch was exorcised. "Jake," he said. "Let me tell you a little more about my witch case."

Wells was rinsing his mouth. He spit out the water and looked at Chee, amused. "I didn't think of this before," Wells said, "but you really don't have a witch problem. If you leave that corpse a death by natural causes, there's no case to work. If you decide it's a homicide, you don't have jurisdiction anyway. Homicide on an Indian reservation, FBI has jurisdiction." Wells grinned. "We'll come in and find your witch for you."

Chee looked at his boots, which were still dusty. His appetite had left him, as it usually did an hour or so after he missed a meal. He still hungered for a bath. He picked up his hat and pushed himself to his feet.

"I'll go home now," he said. "The only thing you don't know about the witch case is what I just got from the autopsy report. The corpse had his shoes on and no bones were missing from the base of the skull."

Chee opened the door and stood in it, looking back. Wells was taking his pajamas out of his suitcase. "So what advice do you have for me? What can you tell me about my witch case?"

"To tell the absolute truth, Chee, I'm not into witches," Wells said. "Haven't been since I was a boy."

"But we don't really have a witch case now," Chee said. He spoke earnestly. "The shoes were still on, so the skin wasn't taken from the soles of his feet. No bones missing from the neck. You need those to make corpse powder."

Wells was pulling his undershirt over his head. Chee hurried.

"What we have now is another little puzzle," Chee said. "If you're not collecting stuff for corpse powder, why cut the skin off this guy's hands?"

"I'm going to take a shower," Wells said. "Got to get my Begay back to LA tomorrow."

Outside the temperature had dropped. The air moved softly from the west, carrying the smell of rain. Over the Utah border, over the Cococino Rim, over the Rainbow Plateau, lightning flickered and glowed. The storm had formed. The storm was moving. The sky was black with it. Chee stood in the darkness, listening to the mutter of thunder, inhaling the perfume, exulting in it.

He climbed into the truck and started it. How had they set it up, and why? Perhaps the FBI agent who knew Begay had been ready to retire. Perhaps an accident had been arranged. Getting rid of the assistant prosecutor who knew the witness would have been even simpler—a matter of hiring him away from the government job. That left no one who knew this minor witness was not Simon Begay. And who was he? Probably they had other Navajos from the Los Angeles community stealing cars for them. Perhaps that's what had suggested the scheme. To most white men all Navajos looked pretty much alike, just as in his first years at college all Chee had seen in white men was pink skin, freckles, and light-colored eyes. And what would the impostor say? Chee grinned. He'd say whatever was necessary to cast doubt on the prosecution, to cast the fatal "reasonable doubt," to make—as Wells had put it—the U.S. District Attorney look like a horse's ass.

Chee drove into the rain twenty miles west of Kayenta. Huge, cold drops drummed on the pickup roof and turned the highway into a ribbon of water. Tomorrow the backcountry roads would be impassable. As soon as they dried and the washouts had been repaired, he'd go back to the Tsossie hogan, and the Tso place, and to all the other places from which the word would quickly spread. He'd tell the people that the witch was in custody of the FBI and was gone forever from the Rainbow Plateau.

SUSAN DUNLAP

"Hit-and-Run"

Susan Dunlap was born in Kew Gardens, New York on June 20, 1943. She graduated from Bucknell University in 1965 and earned her masters degree in English a year later at the University of North Carolina. She worked in social services in Baltimore, New York City and California before turning to writing in 1980. Dunlap's first novel **Karma** *(1981) introduced Berkeley homicide detective Jill Smith, one of three series characters who have appeared in her work.*

Dunlap is a founding member and past president of Sisters in Crime. In addition to Jill Smith, who has appeared in nine novels, she has produced three each about Kiernan O'Shaughnessy, a San Francisco medical examiner turned private detective, and Vejay Haskell, a California meter reader whose job brings her into contact with crime.

One of Susan Dunlap's rare short stories "The Celestial Buffet" (1990) brought her Bouchercon's Anthony Award, but her stories are uncollected thus far. "Hit-and-Run," a Jill Smith tale, appeared in **Great Modern Police Stories** *and was reprinted in* **Criminal Elements***.*

Hit-and-Run

by Susan Dunlap

I t was four-fifteen Saturday afternoon—a football Saturday at the University of California. For the moment, there was nothing in the streets leading from Memorial Stadium but rain. Sensible Berkeleyans were home, students and alumni were huddled in the stands under sheets of clear plastic, like pieces of expensive lawn furniture, as the Cal Bears and their opponents marched toward the final gun. Then the seventy-five thousand six hundred sixty-two fans would charge gleefully or trudge morosely to their cars and create a near-gridlock all over the city of Berkeley. Then only a fool, or a tourist, would consider driving across town. Then even in a black-and-white—with the pulsers on, and the siren blaring—I wouldn't be able to get to the station.

The conference beat officer Connie Pereira and I had attended— *Indications of the Pattern Behavior of the Cyclical Killer in California*—had let out at three-thirty. We'd figured we just had time to turn in the black-and-white, pick up our own cars, and get home. On the way home, I planned to stop for a pizza. That would be pushing it. But, once I got the pizza in my car, I would be going against traffic. Now, I figured, I could make good time because University Avenue would still be empty.

When the squeal came, I knew I had figured wrong. It was a hit-and-run. I hadn't handled one of those since long before I'd been assigned to Homicide. But this part of University Avenue was Pereira's beat. I looked at her questioningly; she wasn't on beat now; she could let the squeal go. But she was already reaching for the mike.

I switched on the pulser lights and the siren, and stepped on the gas. The street was deserted. The incident was two blocks ahead, below San Pablo Avenue, on University. There wasn't a car, truck, or bicycle in sight. As I crossed the intersection, I could see a man lying on his back in the street, his herringbone suit already matted with blood. Bent over him was a blond man in a white shirt and jeans.

Leaving Pereira waiting for the dispatcher's reply, I got out of the car and ran toward the two men. The blond man was breathing heavily but regularly, rhythmically pressing on the injured man's chest and blowing into his mouth. He was getting no response. I had seen enough bodies, both dead and dying, in my four years on the force to suspect that this one was on the way out. I doubted the C.P.R. was doing any good. But, once started, it couldn't be stopped until the medics arrived. And despite the lack of reaction, the blond looked like he knew what he was doing.

From across the sidewalk, the pungent smell of brown curry floated from a small, dingy storefront called the Benares Cafe, mixing with the sharp odor of the victim's urine. I turned away, took a last breath of fresh air, and knelt down by the injured man.

The blond leaned over the victim's mouth, blew breath in, then lifted back.

"Did you see the car that hit him?" I asked.

He was pressing on the victim's chest. He waited till he forced air into his mouth again and came up. "A glimpse."

"Where were you then?"

Again he waited, timing his reply with his rising. "Walking on University, a block down." He blew into the mouth again. "He didn't stop. Barely slowed down."

"What kind of car?" I asked, timing my question to his rhythm.

"Big. Silver, with a big, shiny grill."

"What make?"

"Don't know."

"Can you describe the driver?"

"No."

"Man or woman?"

"Don't know."

"Did you see any passengers?"

"No."

"Is there anything else you can tell me about the car?"

He went through an entire cycle of breathing and pressing before he said, "No."

"Thanks."

Now I looked more closely at the victim. I could see the short, gray-streaked brown hair, and the still-dark mustache. I could see the thick eyebrows and the eyes so filled with blood that it might not have been possible to detect the eye color if I hadn't already known it. I took a long look to make sure. But there was no question. Under the blood were the dark brown eyes of Graham Latham.

Behind me, the door of the black-and-white opened, letting out a burst of staccato calls from the dispatcher, then slammed shut. "Ambulance and back-up on the way, Jill," Pereira said as she came up beside me. "It wasn't easy getting anyone off Traffic on a football day."

I stood up and moved away from the body with relief. The blond man continued his work. In spite of the rain, I could see the sweat coming through his shirt.

I relayed his account of the crime, such as it was, to Pereira, then asked her, "Have you ever heard of Graham Latham?"

"Nope. Should I?"

"Maybe not. It's just ironic. When I was first on beat, I handled a hit-and-run. Only that time Latham was the driver. The victim, Katherine Hillman, was left just like he is. She lived—until last week, anyway. I saw her name in the obits. She was one of the guinea pigs they were trying a new electronic pain device on—a last resort for people with chronic untreatable pain."

Pereira nodded.

"I remember her at the trial," I said. "The pain wasn't so bad then. She could still shift around in her wheelchair and get some relief, and she had a boyfriend who helped her. But at the end it must have been bad." I looked over at the body in the street. "From the looks of Graham Latham, he'll be lucky if he can sit up in a wheelchair like she could."

"Be a hard choice," Pereira said, turning back to the black-and-white. She took the red blinkers out of the trunk, then hurried back along the empty street to put them in place.

Despite the cold rain, the sidewalks here weren't entirely empty. On the corner across University, I could see a pair of long pale female legs, shivering under stockings and black satin shorts that almost covered the curve of her buttocks—almost but not quite.

Above those shorts, a thick red jacket suggested that, from the waist up, it was winter. The wearer—young, very blonde, with wings of multicolored eye make-up visible from across the street—stood partially concealed behind the building, looking toward Latham's body as if trying to decide whether it could be scooped up, and the cops cleared off, before the free-spending alumni rambled out of Memorial Stadium and drove down University Avenue.

On the sidewalk in front of the Benares Cafe, one of Berkeley's streetpeople—a man with long, tangled, rain-soaked hair that rested on a threadbare poncho, the outermost of three or four ragged layers of clothing—clutched a brown paper bag. Behind him, a tiny woman in a *sari* peered through the cafe window. In a doorway, a man and a woman leaned against a wall, seemingly oblivious to the activity in the street.

Between the Benares Cafe and the occupied doorway was a storefront with boxes piled in the window and the name "Harris" faded on the sign above. There was no indication of what Harris offered to the public. Across the street a mom-and-pop store occupied the corner. Next to it was the Evangelical People's Church—a storefront no larger than the mom-and-pop. Here in Berkeley, there had been more gurus over the years than in most states of India, but splinter Christian groups were rare; Berkeleyans liked their religion a bit more exotic. The rest of the block was taken up by a ramshackle hotel.

I looked back at Graham Latham, still lying unmoving in his herringbone suit. It was a good suit. Latham was an architect in San Francisco, a partner in a firm that had done a stylish low-income housing project for the city. He lived high in the hills above Berkeley. The brown Mercedes parked at the curb had to be his. Graham Latham wasn't a man who should be found on the same block as the brown-bag clutcher behind him.

I walked toward the streetperson. I was surprised he'd stuck around. He wasn't one who would view the police as protectors.

I identified myself and took his name—John Eskins. "Tell me what you saw of the accident."

"Nothing."

"You were here when we arrived." I let the accusation hang.

"Khan, across the street"—he pointed to the store—"he saw it. He called you guys. Didn't have to; he just did. He said to tell you."

"Okay, but you stick around."

He shrugged.

I glanced toward Pereira. She nodded. In the distance the shriek of the ambulance siren cut through the air. On the ground the blond man was still working on Latham. His sleeves had bunched at the armpits revealing part of a tatoo—"ay" over a heart. In the rain, it looked as if the red of the letters would drip into the heart.

The ambulance screeched to a stop. Two medics jumped out.

The first came up behind the blond man. Putting a hand on his arm, he said, "Okay. We'll take over now."

The blond man didn't break his rhythm.

"It's okay," the medic said, louder. "You can stop now. You're covered."

Still he counted and pressed on Latham's chest, counted and breathed into Latham's unresponsive mouth.

The medic grabbed both arms and yanked him up. Before the blond was standing upright, the other medic was in his place.

"He'll die! Don't let him die! He can't die!" The man struggled to free himself. His hair flapped against his eyebrows; his shirt was soaked. There was blood—Latham's blood—on his face. The rain washed it down, leaving orange lines on his cheeks. "He can't die. It's not fair. You've got to save him!"

"He's getting the best care around," Pereira said.

The blond man leaned toward the action, but the medic pulled him back. Behind us, cars, limited now to one lane, drove slowly, their engines straining in first gear, headlights brightening the back of the ambulance like colorless blinkers. The rain dripped down my hair, under the collar of my jacket, collecting there in a soggy pool.

Turning to me, Pereira shrugged. I nodded. We'd both seen Good Samaritans like him, people who get so involved they can't let go.

I turned toward the store across the street. "Witness called from there. You want me to check it out?"

She nodded. It was her beat, her case. I was just doing her a favor.

I walked across University. The store was typical—a small display of apples, bananas, onions, potatoes, two wrinkled green peppers in front, and the rest of the space taken with rows of cans and boxes, a surprising number of them red, clamoring for the shoppers' notice and failing in their sameness. The shelves climbed high. There were packages of Bisquick, curry, and Garam Masala that the woman in the Benares Cafe wouldn't have been able to reach. In the back was a cooler for milk and cheese, and behind the counter by the door, the one-man bottles of vodka and bourbon—and a small, dark man, presumably Khan.

"I'm Detective Smith," I said, extending my shield. "You called us about the accident?"

"Yes," he said. "I am Farib Khan. I am owning this store. This is why I cannot leave to come to you, you see." He gestured at the empty premises.

I nodded. "But you saw the accident?"

"Yes, yes." He wagged his head side to side in that disconcerting Indian indication of the affirmative. "Mr. Latham—"

"You know him?"

"He is being my customer for a year now. Six days a week."

"Monday through Saturday?"

"Yes, yes. He is stopping on his drive from San Francisco."

"Does he work on Saturdays?" It wasn't the schedule I would have expected of a well-off architect.

"He teaches a class. After his class, he is eating lunch and driving home, you see. And stopping here."

I thought of Graham Latham in his expensive suit, driving his Mercedes. I recalled why he had hit a woman four years ago. It wasn't for curry powder that Graham Latham would be patronizing this ill-stocked store. "Did he buy liquor every day?"

"Yes, yes." Turning behind him, he took a pint bottle of vodka from the shelf. "He is buying this."

So Graham Latham hadn't changed. I didn't know why I would have assumed otherwise. "Did he open it before he left?"

"He is not a bum, not like those who come here not to buy, but to watch, to steal. Mr. Latham is a gentleman. For him, I am putting the bottle in a bag, to take home."

"Then you watched him leave? You saw the accident?"

Again the wagging of his head. "I am seeing, but it is no accident. Mr. Latham, he walks across the street, toward his big car. He is not a healthy man." Khan glanced significantly at the bottle. "So I watch. I am fearing the fall in the street, yes? But he walks straight. Then a car turns the corner, comes at him. Mr. Latham jumps back. He is fast then, you see. The car turns, comes at him. He cannot escape. He is hit. The car speeds off."

"You mean the driver was trying to hit Latham?"

"Yes, yes."

Involuntarily I glanced back to the street. Latham's body was gone now. The witnesses, John Eskin and the C.P.R. man, were standing with Pereira. A back-up unit had arrived. One of the men was checking the brown Mercedes.

Turning back to Khan, I said, "What did the car look like?"

He shrugged. "Old, middle-sized."

"Can you be more specific?"

He half-closed his eyes, trying. Finally, he said, "The day is gray, raining. The car is not new, not one I see in the ads. It is light-colored. Gray? Blue?"

"What about the driver?"

Again, he shrugged.

"Man or woman?"

It was a moment before he said, "All I am seeing is red—a sweater? Yes? A jacket?"

It took only a few more questions to discover that I had learned everything Farib Khan knew. By the time I crossed the street to the scene, Pereira had finished with the witnesses, and one of the back-up men was questioning the couple leaning in the doorway. The witnesses had seen nothing. John Eskins had been in the back of the store at the moment Latham had been hit, and the woman in the Benares Cafe—Pomilla Patel—hadn't seen anything until she heard the car hit him. And the man who stopped to give C.P.R.—Randall Sellinek—hadn't even seen the vehicle drive off. Or so they said.

They stood, a little apart from each other, as if each found the remaining two unsuitable company. Certainly they were three who would never come together in any other circumstances. John Eskin clutched his brown bag, jerking his eyes warily. Pomilla Patel glanced at him in disgust, as if he alone were responsible for the decay of the neighborhood. And Randall Sellinek just stood, letting the cold rain fall on his shirt and run down his bare arms.

I took Pereira aside and relayed what Khan had told me.

She grabbed one back-up man, telling him to call in for more help. "If it's a possible homicide we'll have to scour the area. We'll need to question everyone on this block and the ones on either side. We'll need someone to check the cars and the garbage. Get as many men as you can."

He raised an eyebrow. We all knew how many that would be.

To me, Pereira said, "You want to take Eskins or Sellinek down to the station for statements?"

I hesitated. "No. . . . Suppose we let them leave and keep an eye on them. We have the manpower."

"Are you serious, Jill? It's hardly regulations."

"I'll take responsibility."

Still, she looked uncomfortable. But she'd assisted on too many of my cases over the years to doubt me completely. "Well, okay. It's on your head." She moved toward the witnesses. "That's all, folks. Thanks for your cooperation."

Eskins seemed stunned, but not about to question his good fortune. He moved west, walking quickly, but unsteadily, toward the seedy dwellings near the bay. I shook my head. Pereira nodded to one of the back-up men, and he turned to follow Eskins.

Sellinek gave a final look at the scene of his futile effort and began walking east, toward San Pablo Avenue and the better neighborhoods beyond. He didn't seem surprised, like Eskins, but then he hadn't had the same type of contact with us. I watched him cross the street, then followed. The blocks were short. He came to San Pablo Avenue, waited for the light, then crossed. I had to run to make the light.

On the far side of University Avenue the traffic was picking up. Horns were beeping. The football game was over. The first of the revelers had made it this far. I glanced back the several blocks to the scene, wondering if the hooker had decided to wait us out. But I was too far away to tell.

Sellinek crossed another street, then another. The rain beat down on his white shirt. His blond hair clung to his head. He walked on, never turning to look back.

I let him go five blocks, just to be sure, then caught up with him. "Mr. Sellinek. You remember me, one of the police officers. I'll need to ask you a few more questions."

"Me? Listen, I just stopped to help that man. I didn't want him to die. I wanted him to live."

"I believe you. You knocked yourself out trying to save him. But that still leaves the question of why? Why were you in this neighborhood at all?"

"Just passing through."

"On foot?"

"Yeah, on foot."

"In the rain, wearing just a shirt?"

"So?"

"Tell me again why you decided to give him C.P.R."

"I saw the car hit him. It was new and silver. It had a big, shiny grill. Why are you standing here badgering me? Why aren't you out looking for that car?"

"Because it doesn't exist."

"I *saw* it."

"When?"

"When it hit him."

"But you didn't notice passengers. You couldn't describe the driver."

"The car was too far away. I was back at the corner, behind it. I told you that."

"You didn't look at it when it passed you?"

"No. I was caught up in my own thoughts. I wasn't going to cross the street. There was no reason to look at the traffic. Then the car hit him. He was dying when I got to him—I couldn't let him die."

"I believe that. You didn't intend for him to have something as easy as death."

"What?"

"There wasn't any silver car or shiny grill, Mr. Sellinek." He started to protest, but I held up a hand. "You said you were behind the car and didn't notice it until it hit Latham. You couldn't possibly have seen what kind of grill it had. *You're* the one who ran Latham down."

He didn't say anything. He just stood, letting the rain drip down his face.

"We'll check the area," I said. "We'll find the car you used—maybe not your own car, maybe hot-wired, but there'll be prints. You couldn't have had time to clean them all off. We'll find your red sweater too. When you planned to run Latham down, you never thought you'd have to stop and try to save his life, did you? And once you realized you had to go back to him, you took the sweater off because you were afraid someone might have seen it. Isn't that the way it happened, Mr. Sellinek?"

He still didn't say anything.

I looked at the tattoo on his arm. All of it was visible now—the full name above the heart. It said, "Kay."

"You were Kay Hillman's boyfriend, weren't you? That's why you ran Latham down—because she died last week and you wanted revenge."

His whole body began to shake. "Latham was drunk when he hit Kay. But he got a smart lawyer, he lied in court, he got off with a suspended sentence. What he did to Kay . . . it was just an inconvenience to him. It didn't even change his habits. He still drank when he was driving. He still stopped six days a week at the same store to pick up liquor. Sooner or later he would have run down someone else. It was just a matter of time.

"I wanted revenge, sure. But it wasn't because Kay died. It was for those four years she *lived* after he hit her. She couldn't sit without pain; she couldn't lie down. The pills didn't help. Nothing did. The pain just got worse, month after month." He closed his eyes, squeezing back tears. "I didn't want Latham to die. I wanted him to suffer like Kay did."

Now it was my turn not to say anything.

Sellinek swallowed heavily. "It's not fair," he said. "None of it is fair."

He was right. None of it was fair at all.

BRIAN GARFIELD

"King's X"

Brian Garfield was born in New York City on January 26, 1929. He served in the U.S. Army and Army Reserve, and graduated from the University of Arizona at Tucson with a masters degree in 1963. He began writing westerns and mysteries in the 1960s under his own name and a variety of pseudonyms, and was prolific in both genres through the 1970s.

*The best-known of Garfield's early crime novels was **Death Wish** (1972) which was made into a controversial film with three sequels. The author himself prefers to remember **Hopscotch** (1975), a taut espionage thriller that earned him an MWA Edgar Award as the best novel of the year. Garfield served as president of the Mystery Writers of America during 1983-84.*

*His short stories "Jode's Last Hunt" (1977) and "Scrimshaw" (1979) were nominated for Edgar Awards, and his series about aging CIA agent Charlie Dark has been collected as **Checkpoint Charlie** (1981). "King's X" appeared in **Murder California Style** and was reprinted in **The Year's Best Mystery and Suspense Stories - 1988**.*

King's X

by Brian Garfield

She found Breck on the garage floor, lying on his back with his knees up and his face hidden under the car. His striped coveralls were filthy. There was a dreadful din: he was banging on something with a tool. When there was a pause in the racket she said, "You look like a convict."

"Not this year." He slid out from under the car and blinked up at her. He looked as if he'd camouflaged his face for night maneuvers in a hostile jungle. He didn't seem surprised to see her. All he said was, "You look better than I do."

"Is that supposed to be some sort of compliment?"

"My dear, you look adorable. Beautiful. Magnificent. Ravishing." He smiled; evidently he had no idea what effect the action had on his appearance. "That better?"

"I wasn't fishing for reassurance. I need to talk to you."

He sat up. The smile crumbled; he said, "If it's anything like the last little talk we had, I'd just as soon—"

"I haven't forgotten the things we said to each other. But today's a truce. Time out, okay? King's X?"

"I'm a little busy right now, Vicky. I've got to get this car ready."

"It's important. It's serious."

"In the cosmic scheme of things how do you know it's any more important or serious than the exhaust system I'm fixing?"

She said, "It's Daddy. They've ruined him." She put her back to him and walked toward the sun. "Wash and come outside and talk. I can't stand the smell of grease."

*   *   *

The dusty yard was littered with odd-looking cars in varied conditions of disassembly. Some had numbers painted on their doors, and decal ads for automotive products. The garage was a cruddy cube of white stucco, uncompromisingly ugly.

Feeling the heat but not really minding it, she propped the rump of her jeans against the streetlight post and squinted into the California sunlight, watching pickups rattle past until Breck came out with half the oil smeared off his face. He was six four and hadn't gained an ounce since she'd last seen him three years ago: an endless long rail of a man with an angular El Greco face and bright brittle wedges of sky-blue glass for eyes.

"Shouldn't spend so much time in the sun," he said. "You'll get wrinkles."

"It's very kind of you to be concerned about my health."

"Anybody tell you lately how smashing you look?"

"Is that your devious way of asking if I'm going with someone?"

"Forget it," he said. "What do you want, then?"

"Daddy's lost everything he had. He was going to retire on his savings and the pension—now he's probably going to have to file bankruptcy. You know what that'll do to him. His pride—his blood pressure. I'm afraid he might have another stroke."

He didn't speak; he only looked at her. The sun was in her eyes and she couldn't make out his expression. Stirred by unease she blurted: "Hey—Breck, I'm not asking for myself."

"How much does he need?"

"I don't know. To pay the lawyers and get back on his feet? I don't know. Maybe seventy-five thousand dollars."

He said, "That's a little bit of money."

"Is it," she said dryly.

"I might have been more sympathetic once. But that would've been before your alimony lawyer got after me."

"You always loved Daddy. I'm asking you to help him. Not me. Him."

"What happened?"

"He was carrying diamonds and they arrested him. It was all set up. He was framed by his own boss. He's sure it was an insurance scam. We can't prove anything but we know. We just know."

"Where is he?"

"Now? Here in town, at his place. The same old apartment."

"Why don't you give him the money yourself?"

"I could, of course. But then I'd just have to get it back from you, wouldn't I?"

"You mean you haven't got that much left? What did you spend it on—aircraft carriers?"

"You have an inflated opinion of your own generosity, Breck." She smiled prettily.

He said, "I can't promise anything. But I'll talk to him. I'll finish up here about five. Tell him I'll drop by."

The old man blew his top. "I'm not some kind of charity case. I've been looking after myself for seventy-two years. Women. Can't even trust my own daughter to keep her nose out of my business. Breck, listen to me because I mean it now. I appreciate your intentions. I'm glad you came—always glad to see you. But I won't take a cent from you. Now that's all I've got to say on the subject. Finish your drink and let's talk about something less unpleasant."

The old man didn't look good. Sallow and dewlappy. His big hard voice was still vigorous but the shoulders drooped and there were sagging folds of flesh around his jaw. It had been, what, two years since Breck had seen him? The old man looked a decade older. He'd always been blustery and stubborn but you could see now by the evasiveness in his eyes that his heart wasn't in it.

Breck said, "I'm not offering you money out of my pocket. Maybe I can come up with an idea. Tell me about the man you think set you up. What's his name? Cushing?"

"Cushman. Henry Cushman."

"If he framed you for stealing the money, that suggests he's the one who actually got the money."

"Aagh," the old man said in disgust, dismissing it.

"Come on," Breck said. "Tell me about it."

"Nothing to tell. Listen—it was going to be my last run. I was going to retire. Got myself a condo picked out right on the beach down at Huntington. Buy my own little twenty-two-foot inboard, play bridge, catch fish, behave like a normal human being my age instead of flying all over the airline route maps. I wanted a home to settle down in. What've I got? You see this place? Mortgage up to here and they're going to take it away from me in six weeks if I can't make the payments."

"Come on," Breck said. "Tell me about it."

"I worked courier for that whole group of diamond merchants. I had a gun and a permit, all that stuff. No more. They took it all away. They never proved a damn thing against me but they took it all away. I carried stones forty years and never lost a one. Not even a chip. Forty years!"

Breck coaxed him: "What happened?"

"Hell. I picked up the stones in Amsterdam. I counted them in the broker's presence. They weren't anything special. Half-karat, one-karat, some chips. Three or four bigger stones but nothing spectacular. You know. Neighborhood jewelry store stuff. The amount of hijacking and armed robbery lately, they don't like to load up a courier with too much value on a single trip."

"How much were the stones worth altogether?"

"Not much. Four hundred thousand, give or take."

"To some people that's a lot."

The old man said, "It's an unattainable dream to me right now but hell, there was a time I used to carry five million at a crack. You know how much five million in really good diamonds weighs? You could get it in your hip pocket."

"Go on."

"Amsterdam, okay, the last trip. We wrapped them and packed them in the case—it's that same armored steel attaché case, the one I've carried for fifteen years. I've still got it for all the good it does. The inside's divided into small compartments lined with felt, so things don't rattle around in there. I had it made to my own design fifteen years ago. Cost me twelve hundred dollars."

"Amsterdam," Breck said gently.

"Okay, okay. We locked the case—three witnesses in the room— and we handcuffed it to my wrist and I took the noon flight over the Pole to Los Angeles. Slept part of the way. Went through customs, showed them the stones, did all the formalities. Everything routine, everything up-and-up. Met Vicky at LAX for dinner, took the night flight to Honolulu. In the morning I delivered the shipment to Cushman. Unlocked the handcuffs, unlocked the attaché case, took the packets out, and put them on his desk. He unwrapped one or two of them, looked at the stones, counted the rest of the packets, said everything was fine, said thank you very much, never looked me in the eye, signed the receipt."

"And then?"

"Nothing. I went. Next thing I know the cops are banging on my door at the hotel. Seems Cushman swore out a warrant. He said he'd taken a closer look at the stones that morning and they were no good. He claimed I'd substituted paste stones. He said the whole shipment was fakes. Said I'd stolen four hundred thousand dollars' worth of diamonds. The cops put an inquiry through Interpol and they got depositions and affidavits and God knows what-all from the brokers in Amsterdam, attesting the stones they'd given me were genuine."

Breck said, "Let me ask you a straight question then."

"No, God help me, I did not steal the damn stones."

"That's not the question."

"Then what is?"

"How come you're not in jail?"

"They couldn't prove it. It was my word against Cushman's. I said I'd delivered the proper goods. He said I delivered fakes. He had the fakes to show for it, but he couldn't prove they hadn't been substituted by himself or somebody working for him."

"Did they investigate Cushman and his employees?"

"Sure. I don't think they did an enthusiastic job of it. They figured they already knew who the culprit was, so why waste energy? They went through the motions. They didn't find anything. Cushman stuck to his story. Far as I can tell, none of his employees had access to the stones during the period of time between when I delivered them and when Cushman showed the paste fakes to the cops. So I figure it must have been Cushman."

"Did the insurance pay off?"

"They had to. They couldn't prove he'd defrauded them. Their investigator offered me a hundred thousand dollars and no questions asked if I'd turn in the stones I stole. I told him he had five seconds to get out the door before I punched him in the nose. I was an amateur light heavyweight just out of high school, you know. Nineteen thirty-one. I can handle myself."

Right now, Breck thought, he didn't look as if he could hold his own against a five-year-old in a playpen. But what he said was, "What else do you know about Cushman?"

"Snob. I don't know where he hails from but he affects that clenched-teeth North Shore of Long Island society drawl. Mingles with the million-dollar Waikiki condominium set. I guess they're his best customers for baubles."

"What'd they do to you?"

"Revoked my bond. I can't work without it. I tried to sue for defamation, this and that, but you know how these lawyers are. The case is still pending. Could be years before it's settled. The other side knows how old I am—they know all they have to do is wait a few years."

Breck said, "Maybe I'll have a talk with this Cushman."

"What's the point?"

"Maybe I can persuade him to give you back what he owes you. Don't get your hopes up. He's never going to admit he framed you—he'd go to jail himself if he did that. The best you can hope for is to get enough money out of him to pay off your debts and set you up in that retirement you talked about. The condo, the boat, the bridge games. That much I may be able to persuade him he owes you."

"Aagh."

The shop was a pricey-looking storefront at 11858 Kalakaua Avenue; the sign beside the door was discreetly engraved on a small brass plaque: CUSHMAN INTERNATIONAL DIAMOND CO.

Inside, every inch a gent in nautical whites, Breck stood looking down at several enormous diamond rings spread across a velvet background.

"My fifth wedding anniversary. I want to give my wife the most beautiful present I can find. You were recommended—they told me they were sure you'd have what I'm looking for."

The man across the counter was bald and amiable. He looked fit, as if he worked out regularly. He wore a dark suit and he'd had a manicure. "Thank you, sir. You're very kind."

"Are you Henry Cushman?"

"That's correct. May I ask who recommended me?"

"A couple of people at a party for the governor. Let me have a look at that one, will you? The emerald cut."

Cushman picked up the third ring. Breck gave him the benediction of his best smile. "Mind if I borrow your loupe?"

Clearly a trifle surprised, Cushman offered him the small magnifying glass. Screwing it into his eye, Breck examined the stone. "Very nice," he opined.

Cushman said softly, "It's flawless, sir. Excellent color. And there's not another one like it."

"How much?"

"Four hundred and fifty thousand dollars."

Breck examined the ring even more closely. Finally he said, "Make it four twenty."

"Oh, I wouldn't be at liberty to go that low, sir." The bald fellow was very smooth. "You see, diamonds at the moment—"

"Four thirty-five and that's it."

There was a considered pause before Cushman murmured, "I think I could accept that."

"I thought you could." Breck smiled again. And then, a bit amused by his own air of tremendous confidence, he went around to the proprietor's desk and took a checkbook and a gold pen from his pockets and began to write out a check. "I want it gift-wrapped—and I'll need it delivered to my suite at the Kahala Towers no later than seven o'clock tonight."

He beamed when he stood up and handed over the check, accompanied by a driver's license and a gold credit card; Cushman scribbled lengthy numbers across the top of the check and Breck didn't give the jeweler a chance to get a word in edgewise. "Of course my wife'll have to approve it, you understand. I don't want to spend this sort of money on a gift she doesn't really like. You know how women can be. But I don't really think it'll be a problem. She's a connoisseur of good stones." Then he was gone—right out the door.

He went two blocks to the beach and shoved his hands in his pockets and grinned at the ocean.

Henry Cushman stood momentarily immobilized before he came to his senses and reached for the telephone. The bank's telephone number was on the check in his hand but he didn't trust anything about that check and he looked up the bank in the directory. The telephone number was the same. He dialed it.

It was a frustrating conversation. A bank holiday, this particular Friday. "I know you're closed to the public but I've got to talk with an officer. It's important."

"I'm sorry, sir. This is the answering service. There's no one in the bank except security personnel."

Cushman hung up the phone and made a face and wasn't quite sure what to do. He paced the office for a moment, alternately pleased to have made the sale but disturbed by suspicion. Finally he picked up the telephone again.

The lobby bustled: people checking in, checking out—business people and tourists in flamboyant island colors. In this class of hotel in this high season you could estimate the fifty people in the lobby were worth approximately $20 million on the hoof. Mr. Fowler watched with satisfaction until the intercom interrupted. "Yes?"

"It's Mr. Henry Cushman, sir."

"Put him on."

"Jim?"

"How're you, Henry?"

"Puzzled. I've got a little problem."

Jim Fowler laughed. "I told you not to bet on the Lakers. Can't say I didn't warn you."

"It's serious, Jim. Listen, I've just sold a very expensive diamond ring to . . . a Mr. F. Breckenridge Baldwin. I understand he's staying at your hotel."

"Baldwin? Yes, sure he's staying here." And by the sheerest of meaningless coincidences Fowler at that moment saw the extraordinarily tall F. Breckenridge Baldwin enter through the main entrance and stride across the vast marble foyer. In turn Baldwin recognized Fowler and waved to him and Fowler waved back as Baldwin entered an elevator.

"What's that, Henry? Hell, sure, he's reputable. He and his wife have been here three weeks now. Royal Suite. They've entertained two bishops and a Rockefeller."

"How long are they staying?"

"They'll be with us at least another week. She likes the beach. I gather he has business deals in progress."

"What do you know about him? Any trouble?"

"Trouble? Absolutely not. In fact he's compulsive about keeping his account paid up."

"He gave be a damn big check on the Sugar Merchants Bank."

"If you're worried about it why don't you call Bill Yeager? He's on the board of the bank."

"Good idea. I'll do that. Thanks, Jim."

"That's all right. You're certainly welcome."

It took Henry Cushman twenty minutes and as many phone calls to find Bill Yeager. In the end he tracked him down at the Nineteenth Hole Clubhouse. There was quite a bit of background racket: a ball game of some kind on the projection TV, men's voices shouting encouragement from the bar. Yeager's voice blatted out of the phone: "You'll have to talk louder, Henry."

"Baldwin," he shouted. "F. Breckenridge Baldwin."

"Is that the big tall character, looks like Gary Cooper?"

"That's him."

"Met him the other night at a luau they threw for the senator. Nice fellow, I thought. What about him?"

"What does he do?"

"Investments, I think. Real estate mostly."

"Does he have an account with Sugar Merchants?"

"How the hell would I know?"

"You're on the board of directors, aren't you?"

"Henry, for Pete's sake, I'm not some kind of bank teller."

"It's important, Bill. I'm sorry to bother you but I really need to find out. Can you give me a home number—somebody from the bank? Somebody who might know?"

"Let me think a minute . . ."

"That's right, Mr. Cushman, he's got an account with us. Opened it several weeks ago."

"What's the balance?"

"I can't give out that kind of information on the telephone, sir."

"Let me put it this way, then. He's given me a check for four hundred and thirty-five thousand dollars. I need to know if it's good."

"I see. Then you certainly have a legitimate interest . . . If Mr. Yeager gave you my name . . . Well, all right. Based on my knowledge of that account from a few days ago, I'd say the check should be perfectly good, sir. It's an interest-bearing account, money-market rate. He's been carrying a rather large balance—it would be more than adequate to cover a four hundred and thirty-five thousand dollar check."

"Thank you very much indeed." Hanging up the phone, Henry Cushman was perspiring a bit but exhaustedly relieved. It looked as if he'd made a good sale after all.

Breck's hand placed the immaculate ring onto the woman's slender finger. Vicky admired it, turning it this way and that to catch the light, enraptured.

"It's the loveliest present of all. My darling Breck—I worship you."

He gave her a sharp look—she was laying it on a bit thick—but she moved quickly into his embrace and kissed him, at length. There was nothing he could do but go along with it. Over her shoulder he glimpsed Henry Cushman, beaming rather like a clergyman at a wedding.

Politely, Cushman averted his glance and pretended interest in the decor of the Royal Suite. If you looked down from the twelfth-story window you could see guests splashing around the enormous pool, seals performing in the man-made pond beside it, lovers walking slowly along the beach, gentle whitecaps catching the Hawaiian moonlight.

Finally she drew away and Breck turned to the room-service table; he reached for the iced champagne bottle and gestured toward Henry Cushman. "Like a drink before you go?"

"Oh, no. I'll leave you alone to enjoy your evening together. It's been a pleasure, sir. I hope we meet again."

As if at court the jeweler backed toward the door, then turned and left. Breck and Vicky stood smiling until he closed it. Then the smile disappeared from Breck's face and he walked away from her. He jerked his tie loose and flung off the evening jacket.

She said, "You might at least make an effort to be nice to me."

"Fire that alimony lawyer and let me have my money back and I'll be as nice as—"

"*Your* money? Breck, you're the most unrealistic stubborn stupid . . ."

He lifted the bottle out of the ice bucket and poured. "We're almost home with this thing. I'll keep the truce if you will. Time out? King's X?"

She lifted her champagne in toast. "King's X. To Daddy."

He drank to that. "Your turn tomorrow, ducks."

"And then what?"

"Just think about doing your job right now."

AVAKIAN JEWELRY—BY APPOINTMENT ONLY.

It was upstairs in an old building in Waikiki village. Patina of luxury; the carpet was thick and discreet. Past the desk and through the window you could see straight down the narrow street to a segment of beach and the Pacific beyond.

There were no display cases; it wasn't that sort of place. Just an office. Somewhere in another room there would be a massive safe.

The man's name was Clayton; he'd introduced himself on the telephone when she'd made the appointment. His voice on the phone was thin and asthmatically reedy; it had led her to expect a hollow-chested cadaverous man but Clayton in person was ruddy-cheeked and thirty pounds overweight and perspiring in a three-piece seersucker suit under the slowly turning overhead fan. He was the manager. She gathered from something he said that the owner had several shops in major cities around the world and rarely set foot in any of them.

Clayton was examining the ring. "Normally I don't come in on Saturdays." He'd already told her that on the phone; she'd dropped her voice half an octave and given him the pitch about how there was quite a bit of money involved.

He turned the ring in his hand, inspecting it under the high-intensity lamp. "I suppose it's a bit cool for the beach today anyhow." His talk was the sort that suggested he was afraid of silences: he had to keep filling them with unnecessary sounds. "Raining like the devil over on the windward side of the island today, did you know that?" It made her recall how one of the things she'd always admired about Breck was his comfort with silences. Sometimes his presence was a warmth in itself; sometimes when she caught his eye the glance was as good as a kiss.

But that was long ago, as he kept reminding her.

Presently Clayton took down the loupe and glanced furtively in her direction. "It's a beautiful stone . . . shame you have to part with it . . . How much did you have in mind?"

"I want a quick sale. And I need cash. A hundred and fifty thousand dollars."

He gave her a sharp look. He knew damn well it was worth more than that. He picked up the hinged satin-lined little box. "Why don't you take it back to Henry Cushman? They'd probably give you more."

"That's my business, isn't it?"

"I may not have that much cash on the premises."

She reached for the box. "If you don't want the ring, never mind—"

He said, "No, no," accepting the rebuff. "Of course it's your business. I'm sorry." He got to his feet. "I'll see what I've got in the safe. If you'll excuse me a moment?"

She gave him her sweetest smile and settled into a leather armchair while the man slipped out of the office. He left the ring and the box on the desk as if to show how trustworthy he was.

She knew where he was going: a telephone somewhere. She could imagine the conversation. She wished she could see Henry Cushman's face. "That's my ring all right. What's the woman look like?"

And the manager Clayton describing her: this tall elegant

auburn-haired woman who looked like Morristown gentry from the horsey fox-hunting set. In her fantasy she could hear Cushman's pretentious lockjaw drawl: "That's the woman. I saw him put the ring on her finger. That's her. Wait—let me think this out . . ."

She waited on. *Patient, ever patient, and Joy shall be thy share.*

Henry Cushman would be working it out in his mind—suspicion first, then certainty: by now he'd be realizing he'd been had. "They set it up. They've stuck me with a bum check."

She pictured his alarm—a deep red flush suffusing his bald head. "They must have emptied out his bank account Thursday evening just before the bank closed. They knew I'd inquire about the account. But the check's no good, don't you see? I've given them one of the best stones in the islands and they've got to get rid of it before the bank opens. If you let her get away . . . by Monday morning they'll be in Hong Kong or Caracas, setting up the same scam all over again. For God's sake stall her. Just hold her right there."

She smiled when Clayton returned.

He said in an avuncular wheeze. "I'm afraid this is going to take a few minutes, madame."

"Take your time. I don't mind."

Breck sat in the back seat of a parked taxi, watching the building. He saw the police car draw up.

Two uniformed officers got out of the car. They went to the glass door of the building and pressed a button. After a moment the door was unlocked to permit them to enter.

After that it took not more than five or six minutes before Breck saw Vicky emerge from the shop, escorted by a cop on either side of her. She was shouting at them, struggling, forcing them to manhandle her. With effort the cops hauled her into the police car. It drove off.

In the taxi, Breck settled back. "We can go now."

Henry Cushman looked up at him. Cushman's eyes were a little wild. The smooth surface of his head glistened with sweat.

"A terrible blunder, Mr. Baldwin, and I can only offer my most humble apologies. I'm so *awfully* embarrassed . . ."

On the desk were the diamond ring and Breck's check.

Breck impaled him on his icy stare. With virulent sarcasm he mimicked Cushman's phony accent:

"Your *awful* embarrassment, Mr. Cushman, hardly compensates for the insult and injury you've done to my wife and myself."

The quiet calm of his voice seemed nearly to shatter Cushman; the man seemed hardly able to reply. Finally he managed a whisper:

"Quite right, sir."

Breck stood in front of the desk, leaning forward, the heels of both hands against its edge; from his great height he loomed over the jeweler.

"Now let's get this straight. You called the bank this morning . . ."

"Yes, sir."

"And you found out my check's good." He pointed to it. *"Isn't* it. The money's in the bank to cover it."

Henry Cushman all but cringed. "Yes, sir."

"But because of your impulsive stupidity, my wife was *arrested.* . . . Do you have any idea what it's like for a woman of Mrs. Baldwin's breeding to spend a whole night locked up in whatever you call your local louse-infected women's house of detention?"

Cushman, squirming, was speechless.

Breck was very calm and serious. "I guess we haven't got anything more to say to each other, Mr. Cushman." He wheeled slowly and with dignity toward the door. "You'll be hearing from my lawyers."

"Please—please, Mr. Baldwin."

He stopped with his back to the jeweler, waiting.

"Mr. Baldwin, let's not be hasty. I feel sure we can find a solution to this without the expense of public litigation. . . ."

With visible reluctance Breck turned to face him. Very cold now: "What do you suggest?"

"No, sir. What do *you* suggest."

Breck gave it a great deal of visible thought. He regarded the check, then the ring. Finally he picked up the ring and squinted at it.

"For openers—this belongs to me."

He saw the Adam's apple go up and down inside Cushman's shirt collar. Cushman said, "Yes, sir."

"And I can see you haven't deposited my check yet. So here's my suggestion. You listening?"

"Yes, sir."

"I keep the ring—and you tear up that check."

Cushman stared at him. Breck loomed. "It's little enough for the insults we've had to suffer."

In acute and obvious discomfort, Cushman struggled but finally accepted defeat. Slowly, with a sickly smile, he tore up the check.

It earned the approval of Breck's cool smile. "You've made a sensible decision. Saved yourself a lot of trouble. Consider yourself lucky."

And he went.

She said, "Don't you think we make a good team?" She said it wistfully, with moonlight in her eyes and Remy Martin on her breath. "Don't you remember the time we sold the same Rembrandt three times for a million and a half each? I remember the Texan and the Iranian in Switzerland, but who was the third one?"

"Watanabe in Kyoto."

"Oh, yes. How could I have forgotten. The one with all the airplanes and the pagoda in his yard."

A breeze rattled the palm fronds overhead. He looked down into her upturned face. "I've got a race next week in Palm Springs, which means I've only got a few days to get the car in shape. Besides, you still need to learn a man doesn't like paying alimony. It feels like buying gas for a junked car."

"Don't talk to me about that. Talk to my lawyer," she said. "Are you going to kiss me or something?"

"I don't know. I seem to remember I tried that once. As I recall it didn't work out too well. Turned out kind of costly." He began to walk away.

"Hey. Breck."

Her voice pulled him around.

She said, "King's X?"

He threw up both arms: his eyes rolled upward as if seeking inspiration from the sky. And shaking his head like a man who ought to know better, he began to laugh.

SARA PARETSKY

"Skin Deep"

Sara Paretsky was born in Ames, Iowa on June 8, 1947. She graduated from the University of Kansas at Lawrence in 1967 and received her Ph.D. from the University of Chicago in 1977. Her first novel **Indemnity Only** *(1982) introduced female private detective V.I. Warshawski who has appeared in all eight of her novels to date. Paretsky was one of the founding members of Sisters in Crime and served as the organization's first president.*

Sara Paretsky's 1988 novel **Blood Shot** *won the CWA Silver Dagger under its British title* **Toxic Shock**. *In this country the book was a Shamus and Anthony nominee. She has also edited two anthologies of original stories by women mystery writers,* **A Woman's Eye** *(1990) and* **Women on the Case** *(1996). The former won Bouchercon's Anthony Award for best anthology of the year.*

The Warshawski short stories are collected in **Windy City Blues** *(1995), published in Britain as* **V.I. For Short**. *"Skin Deep" first appeared in* **The New Black Mask** #8 *and was reprinted in* **Homicidal Acts, City Sleuths and Tough Guys** *and* **Windy City Blues**.

Skin Deep

by Sara Paretsky

1

The warning bell clangs angrily and the submarine dives sharply. Everyone to battle stations. The Nazis pursuing closely, the bell keeps up its insistent clamor, loud, urgent, filling my head. My hands are wet: I can't remember what my job is in this cramped, tiny boat. If only someone would turn off the alarm bell. I fumble with some switches, pick up an intercom. The noise mercifully stops.

"Vic! Vic, is that you?"

"What?"

"I know it's late. I'm sorry to call so late, but I just got home from work. It's Sal, Sal Barthele."

"Oh, Sal. Sure." I looked at the orange clock readout. It was four-thirty. Sal owns the Golden Glow, a bar in the south Loop I patronize.

"It's my sister, Vic. They've arrested her. She didn't do it. I know she didn't do it."

"Of course not, Sal—Didn't do what?"

"They're trying to frame her. Maybe the manager . . . I don't know."

I swung my legs over the side of the bed. "Where are you?"

She was at her mother's house, 95th and Vincennes. Her sister had been arrested three hours earlier. They needed a lawyer, a good lawyer. And they needed a detective, a good detective. Whatever my fee was, she wanted me to know they could pay my fee.

"I'm sure you can pay the fee, but I don't know what you want me to do," I said as patiently as I could.

"She—they think she murdered that man. She didn't even know him. She was just giving him a facial. And he dies on her."

"Sal, give me your mother's address. I'll be there in forty minutes."

The little house on Vincennes was filled with neighbors and relatives murmuring encouragement to Mrs. Barthele. Sal is very black, and statuesque. Close to six feet tall, with a majestic carriage, she can break up a crowd in her bar with a look and a gesture. Mrs. Barthele was slight, frail, and light-skinned. It was hard to picture her as Sal's mother.

Sal dispersed the gathering with characteristic firmness, telling the group that I was here to save Evangeline and that I needed to see her mother alone.

Mrs. Barthele sniffed over every sentence. "Why did they do that to my baby?" she demanded of me. "You know the police, you know their ways. Why did they come and take my baby, who never did a wrong thing in her life?"

As a white woman, I could be expected to understand the machinations of the white man's law. And to share responsibility for it. After more of this meandering, Sal took the narrative firmly in hand.

Evangeline worked at La Cygnette, a high-prestige beauty salon on North Michigan. In addition to providing facials and their own brand-name cosmetics at an exorbitant cost, they massaged the bodies and feet of their wealthy clients, stuffed them into steam cabinets, ran them through a Bataan-inspired exercise routine, and fed them herbal teas. Signor Giuseppe would style their hair for an additional charge.

Evangeline gave facials. The previous day she had one client booked after lunch, a Mr. Darnell.

"Men go there a lot?" I interrupted.

Sal made a face. "That's what I asked Evangeline. I guess it's part of being a Yuppie—go spend a lot of money getting cream rubbed into your face."

Anyway, Darnell was to have had his hair styled before his facial, but the hairdresser fell behind schedule and asked Evangeline to do the guy's face first.

Sal struggled to describe how a La Cygnette facial worked—neither of us had ever checked out her sister's job. You sit in something like a dentist's chair, lean back, relax—you're naked from the waist up, lying under a big down comforter. The facial expert—cosmetician was Evangeline's official title—puts cream on your hands and sticks them into little electrically-heated mitts, so your hands are out of commission if you need to protect yourself. Then she puts stuff on your face, covers your eyes with heavy pads, and goes away for twenty minutes while the face goo sinks into your hidden pores.

Apparently while this Darnell lay back deeply relaxed, someone had rubbed some kind of poison into his skin. "When Evangeline came back in to clean his face, he was sick—heaving, throwing up, it was awful. She screamed for help and started trying to clean his face—it was terrible, he kept vomiting on her. They took him to the hospital, but he died around ten tonight.

"They came to get Baby at midnight—you've got to help her, V. I.—even if the guy tried something on her, she never did a thing like that—she'd haul off and slug him, maybe, but rubbing poison into his face? You go help her."

2

Evangeline Barthele was a younger, darker edition of her mother. At most times, she probably had Sal's energy—sparks of it flared now and then during our talk—but a night in the holding cells had worn her down.

I brought a clean suit and makeup for her: justice may be blind but her administrators aren't. We talked while she changed.

"This Darnell—you sure of the name?—had he ever been to the salon before?"

She shook her head. "I never saw him. And I don't think the other girls knew him either. You know, if a client's a good tipper or a bad one they'll comment on it, be glad or whatever that he's come in. Nobody said anything about this man."

"Where did he live?"

She shook her head. "I never talked to the guy, V. I."

"What about the PestFree?" I'd read the arrest report and talked briefly to an old friend in the M.E.'s office. To keep roaches and other vermin out of their posh Michigan Avenue offices, La Cygnette used a potent product containing a wonder chemical called chorpyrifos. My informant had been awe-struck—"Only an operation that didn't know shit about chemicals would leave chorpyrifos lying around. It's got a toxicity rating of five—it gets you through the skin—you only need a couple of tablespoons to kill a big man if you know where to put it."

Whoever killed Darnell had either known a lot of chemistry or been lucky—into his nostrils and mouth, with some rubbed into the face for good measure, the pesticide had made him convulsive so quickly that even if he knew who killed him he'd have been unable to talk, or even reason.

Evangeline said she knew where the poison was kept—everyone who worked there knew, knew it was lethal and not to touch it, but it was easy to get at. Just in a little supply room that wasn't kept locked.

"So why you? They have to have more of a reason than just that you were there."

She shrugged bitterly. "I'm the only black professional at La Cygnette—the other blacks working there sweep rooms and haul trash. I'm trying hard not to be paranoid, but I gotta wonder."

She insisted Darnell hadn't made a pass at her, or done anything to provoke an attack—she hadn't hurt the guy. As for anyone else who might have had opportunity, salon employees were always passing through the halls, going in and out of the little cubicles where they treated clients—she'd seen any number of people, all with legitimate business in the halls, but she hadn't seen anyone emerging from the room where Darnell was sitting.

When we finally got to bond court later that morning, I tried to argue circumstantial evidence—any of La Cygnette's fifty or so employees could have committed the crime, since all had access and no one had motive. The prosecutor hit me with a very unpleasant surprise: the police had uncovered evidence linking my client to the dead man. He was a furniture buyer from Kansas City who came to Chicago six times a year, and the doorman and the maids at his hotel had identified Evangeline without any trouble as the woman who accompanied him on his visits.

Bail was denied. I had a furious talk with Evangeline in one of the interrogation rooms before she went back to the holding cells.

"Why the hell didn't you tell me? I walked into the courtroom and got blindsided."

"They're lying," she insisted.

"Three people identified you. If you don't start with the truth

SARA PARETSKY

right now, you're going to have to find a new lawyer and a new detective. Your mother may not understand, but for sure Sal will."

"You can't tell my mother. You can't tell Sal!"

"I'm going to have to give them some reason for dropping your
case, and knowing Sal it's going to have to be the truth."

For the first time she looked really upset. "You're my lawyer. You
should believe my story before you believe a bunch of strangers
you never saw before."

"I'm telling you, Evangeline, I'm going to drop your case. I can't
represent you when I know you're lying. If you killed Darnell we
can work out a defense. Or if you didn't kill him and knew him we
can work something out, and I can try to find the real killer. But
when I know you've been seen with the guy any number of times, I
can't go into court telling people you never met him before."

Tears appeared on the ends of her lashes. "The whole reason I
didn't say anything was so Mama wouldn't know. If I tell you the
truth, you've got to promise me you aren't running back to Vincennes Avenue talking to her."

I agreed. Whatever the story was, I couldn't believe Mrs.
Barthele hadn't heard hundreds like it before. But we each make
our own separate peace with our mothers.

Evangeline met Darnell at a party two years earlier. She liked
him, he liked her—not the romance of the century, but they enjoyed spending time together. She'd gone on a two-week trip to Europe with him last year, telling her mother she was going with a
girlfriend.

"First of all, she has very strict morals. No sex outside marriage.
I'm thirty, mind you, but that doesn't count with her. Second, he's
white, and she'd murder me. She really would. I think that's why I
never fell in love with him—if we wanted to get married I'd never
be able to explain it to Mama."

This latest trip to Chicago, Darnell thought it would be fun to
see what Evangeline did for a living, so he booked an appointment
at La Cygnette. She hadn't told anyone there she knew him. And
when she found him sick and dying she'd panicked and lied.

"And if you tell my mother of this, V. I.—I'll put a curse on you.
My father was from Haiti and he knew a lot of good ones."

"I won't tell your mother. But unless they nuked Lebanon this
morning or murdered the mayor, you're going to get a lot of lines in
the paper. It's bound to be in print."

She wept at that, wringing her hands. So after watching her go

188

off with the sheriff's deputies, I called Murray Ryerson at the *Herald-Star* to plead with him not to put Evangeline's liaison in the paper. "If you do she'll wither your testicles. Honest."

"I don't know, Vic. You know the *Sun-Times* is bound to have some kind of screamer headline like DEAD MAN FOUND IN FACE-LICKING SEX ORGY. I can't sit on a story like this when all the other papers are running it."

I knew he was right, so I didn't push my case very hard.

He surprised me by saying, "Tell you what: you find the real killer before my deadline for tomorrow's morning edition and I'll keep your client's personal life out of it. The sex scoop came in too late for today's paper. The *Trib* prints on our schedule and they don't have it, and the *Sun-Times* runs older, slower presses, so they have to print earlier."

I reckoned I had about eighteen hours. Sherlock Holmes had solved tougher problems in less time.

3

Roland Darnell had been the chief buyer of living-room furnishings for Alexander Dumas, a high-class Kansas City department store. He used to own his own furniture store in the nearby town of Lawrence, but lost both it and his wife when he was arrested for drug smuggling ten years earlier. Because of some confusion about his guilt—he claimed his partner, who disappeared the night he was arrested, was really responsible—he'd only served two years. When he got out, he moved to Kansas City to start a new life.

I learned this much from my friends at the Chicago police. At least, my acquaintances. I wondered how much of the story Evangeline had known. Or her mother. If her mother didn't want her child having a white lover, how about a white ex-con, ex- (presumably) drug-smuggling lover?

I sat biting my knuckles for a minute. It was eleven now. Say they started printing the morning edition at two the next morning. I'd have to have my story by one at the latest. I could follow one line, and one line only—I couldn't afford to speculate about Mrs. Barthele—and anyway, doing so would only get me killed. By Sal. So I looked up the area code for Lawrence, Kansas, and found their daily newspaper.

The *Lawrence Daily Journal-World* had set up a special number for handling press inquiries. A friendly woman with a strong drawl told me Darnell's age (forty-four); place of birth (Eudora, Kansas); ex-wife's name (Ronna Perkins); and ex-partner's name (John Crenshaw). Ronna Perkins was living elsewhere in the country and the *Journal-World* was protecting her privacy. John Crenshaw had disappeared when the police arrested Darnell.

Crenshaw had done an army stint in Southeast Asia in the late sixties. Since much of the bamboo furniture the store specialized in came from the Far East, some people speculated that Crenshaw had set up the smuggling route when he was out there in the service. Especially since Kansas City immigration officials discovered heroin in the hollow tubes making up chair backs. If Darnell knew anything about the smuggling, he had never revealed it.

"That's all we know here, honey. Of course, you could come on down and try to talk to some people. And we can wire you photos if you want."

I thanked her politely—my paper didn't run too many photographs. Or even have wire equipment to accept them. A pity—I could have used a look at Crenshaw and Ronna Perkins.

La Cygnette was on an upper floor of one of the new marble skyscrapers at the top end of the Magnificent Mile. Tall, white doors opened onto a hushed waiting room reminiscent of a high-class funeral parlor. The undertaker, a middle-aged highly made-up woman seated at a table that was supposed to be French provincial, smiled at me condescendingly.

"What can we do for you?"

"I'd like to see Angela Carlson. I'm a detective."

She looked nervously at two clients seated in a far corner. I lowered my voice. "I've come about the murder."

"But—but they made an arrest."

I smiled enigmatically. At least I hoped it looked enigmatic. "The police never close the door on all options until after the trial." If she knew anything about the police she'd know that was a lie— once they've made an arrest you have to get a presidential order to get them to look at new evidence.

The undertaker nodded nervously and called Angela Carlson in a whisper on the house phone. Evangeline had given me the names of the key players at La Cygnette; Carlson was the manager.

She met me in the doorway leading from the reception area into the main body of the salon. We walked on thick, silver pile through a white maze with little doors opening onto it. Every now and then we'd pass a white-coated attendant who gave the manager a subdued hello. When we went by a door with a police order slapped to it, Carlson winced nervously.

"When can we take that off? Everybody's on edge and that sealed door doesn't help. Our bookings are down as it is."

"I'm not on the evidence team, Ms. Carlson. You'll have to ask the lieutenant in charge when they've got what they need."

I poked into a neighboring cubicle. It contained a large white dentist's chair and a tray covered with crimson pots and bottles, all with the cutaway swans which were the salon's trademark. While the manager fidgeted angrily I looked into a tiny closet where clients changed—it held a tiny sink and a few coat hangers.

Finally she burst out, "Didn't your people get enough of this yesterday? Don't you read your own reports?"

"I like to form my own impressions, Ms. Carlson. Sorry to have to take your time, but the sooner we get everything cleared up, the faster your customers will forget this ugly episode."

She sighed audibly and led me on angry heels to her office, although the thick carpeting took the intended ferocity out of her stride. The office was another of the small treatment rooms with a desk and a menacing phone console. Photographs of a youthful Mme. de Leon, founder of La Cygnette, covered the walls.

Ms. Carlson looked through a stack of pink phone messages. "I have an incredibly busy schedule, Officer. So if you could get to the point. . . ."

"I want to talk to everyone with whom Darnell had an appointment yesterday. Also the receptionist on duty. And before I do that I want to see their personnel files."

"Really! All these people were interviewed yesterday." Her eyes narrowed suddenly. "Are you really with the police? You're not, are you? You're a reporter. I want you out of here now. Or I'll call the real police."

I took my license photostat from my wallet. "I'm a detective. That's what I told your receptionist. I've been retained by the Barthele family. Ms. Barthele is not the murderer and I want to find out who the real culprit is as fast as possible."

She didn't bother to look at the license. "I can barely tolerate answering police questions. I'm certainly not letting some snoop for hire take up my time. The police have made an arrest on extremely good evidence. I suppose you think you can drum up a fee by getting Evangeline's family excited about her innocence, but you'll have to look elsewhere for your money."

I tried to appeal to her compassionate side, using half-forgotten arguments from my court appearances as a public defender. (Outstanding employee, widowed mother, sole support, intense family pride, no prior arrests, no motive.) No sale.

"Ms. Carlson, you the owner or the manager here?"

"Why do you want to know?"

"Just curious about your stake in the success of the place and your responsibility for decisions. It's like this: you've got a lot of foreigners working here. The immigration people will want to come by and check out their papers.

"You've got lots and lots of tiny little rooms. Are they sprinklered? Do you have emergency exits? The fire department can make a decision on that.

"And how come your only black professional employee was just arrested and you're not moving an inch to help her out? There are lots of lawyers around who'd be glad to look at a discrimination suit against La Cygnette.

"Now if we could clear up Evangeline's involvement fast, we could avoid having all these regulatory people trampling around upsetting your staff and your customers. How about it?"

She sat in indecisive rage for several minutes: how much authority did I have, really? Could I offset the munificent fees the salon and the building owners paid to various public officials just to avoid such investigations? Should she call headquarters for instruction? Or her lawyer? She finally decided that even if I didn't have a lot of power I could be enough of a nuisance to affect business. Her expression compounded of rage and defeat, she gave me the files I wanted.

Darnell had been scheduled with a masseuse, the hair expert Signor Giuseppe, and with Evangeline. I read their personnel files, along with that of the receptionist who had welcomed him to La Cygnette, to see if any of them might have hailed from Kansas City or had any unusual traits, such as an arrest record for heroin smuggling. The files were very sparse. Signor Giuseppe Fruttero hailed from Milan. He had no next-of-kin to be notified in the event of an accident. Not even a good friend. Bruna, the masseuse, was Lithuanian, unmarried, living with her mother. Other than the fact that the receptionist had been born as Jean Evans in Hammond but referred to herself as Monique from New Orleans, I saw no evidence of any kind of cover-up.

Angela Carlson denied knowing either Ronna Perkins or John Crenshaw or having any employees by either of those names. She had never been near Lawrence herself. She grew up in Evansville, Indiana, came to Chicago to be a model in 1978, couldn't cut it, and got into the beauty business. Angrily she gave me the names of her parents in Evansville and summoned the receptionist.

Monique was clearly close to sixty, much too old to be Roland Darnell's ex-wife. Nor had she heard of Ronna or Crenshaw.

"How many people knew that Darnell was going to be in the salon yesterday?"

"Nobody knew." She laughed nervously. "I mean, of course *I* knew—I made the appointment with him. And Signor Giuseppe knew when I gave him his schedule yesterday. And Bruna, the masseuse, of course, and Evangeline."

"Well, who else could have seen their schedules?"

She thought frantically, her heavily mascaraed eyes rolling in agitation. With another nervous giggle she finally said, "I suppose anyone could have known. I mean, the other cosmeticians and the makeup artists all come out for their appointments at the same time. I mean, if anyone was curious they could have looked at the other people's lists."

Carlson was frowning. So was I. "I'm trying to find a woman who'd be forty now, who doesn't talk much about her past. She's been divorced and she won't have been in the business long. Any candidates?"

Carlson did another mental search, then went to the file cabinets. Her mood was shifting from anger to curiosity and she flipped through the files quickly, pulling five in the end.

"How long has Signor Giuseppe been here?"

"When we opened our Chicago branch in 1980 he came to us from Miranda's—I guess he'd been there for two years. He says he came to the States from Milan in 1970."

"He a citizen? Has he got a green card?"

"Oh, yes. His papers are in good shape. We are very careful about that at La Cygnette." My earlier remark about the immigration department had clearly stung. "And now I really need to get back to my own business. You can look at those files in one of the consulting rooms—Monique, find one that won't be used today."

It didn't take me long to scan the five files, all uninformative.

Before returning them to Monique I wandered on through the back of the salon. In the rear a small staircase led to an upper story. At the top was another narrow hall lined with small offices and storerooms. A large mirrored room at the back filled with hanging plants and bright lights housed Signor Giuseppe. A dark-haired man with a pointed beard and a bright smile, he was ministering gaily to a thin, middle-aged woman, talking and laughing while he deftly teased her hair into loose curls.

He looked at me in the mirror when I entered. "You are here for the hair, Signora? You have the appointment?"

"No, Signor Giuseppe. Sono qui perchè la sua fama se è sparsa di fronte a lei. Milano è una bella città, non è vero?"

He stopped his work for a moment and held up a deprecating hand. "Signora, it is my policy to speak only English in my adopted country."

"Una vera stupida e ignorante usanza io direi." I beamed sympathetically and sat down on a high stool next to an empty customer chair. There were seats for two clients. Since Signor Giuseppe reigned alone, I pictured him spinning at high speed between customers, snipping here, pinning there.

"Signora, if you do not have the appointment, will you please leave? Signora Dotson here, she does not prefer the audience."

"Sorry, Mrs. Dotson," I said to the lady's chin. "I'm a detective. I need to talk to Signor Giuseppe, but I'll wait."

I strolled back down the hall and entertained myself by going into one of the storerooms and opening little pots of La Cygnette creams and rubbing them into my skin. I looked in a mirror and could already see an improvement. If I got Evangeline sprung maybe she'd treat me to a facial.

Signor Giuseppe appeared with a plastically groomed Mrs. Dotson. He had shed his barber's costume and was dressed for the street. I followed them down the stairs. When we got to the bottom I said, "In case you're thinking of going back to Milan—or even to Kansas—I have a few questions."

Mrs. Dotson clung to the hairdresser, ready to protect him.

"I need to speak to him alone, Mrs. Dotson. I have to talk to him about bamboo."

"I'll get Miss Carlson, Signor Giuseppe," his guardian offered.

"No, no, Signora. I will deal with this crazed woman myself. A million thanks. *Grazie, grazie.*"

"Remember, no Italian in your adopted America," I reminded him nastily.

Mrs. Dotson looked at us uncertainly.

"I think you should get Ms. Carlson," I said. "Also a police escort. Fast."

She made up her mind to do something, whether to get help or flee I wasn't sure, but she scurried down the corridor. As soon as she had disappeared, he took me by the arm and led me into one of the consulting rooms.

"Now, who are you and what is this?" His accent had improved substantially.

"I'm V. I. Warshawski. Roland Darnell told me you were quite an expert on fitting drugs into bamboo furniture."

I wasn't quite prepared for the speed of his attack. His hands were around my throat. He was squeezing and spots began dancing in front of me. I didn't try to fight his arms, just kicked sharply at his shin, following with my knee to his stomach. The pressure at my neck eased. I turned in a half circle and jammed my left elbow into his rib cage. He let go.

I backed to the door, keeping my arms up in front of my face and backed into Angela Carlson.

"What on earth are you doing with Signor Giuseppe?" she asked.

"Talking to him about furniture." I was out of breath. "Get the police and don't let him leave the salon."

A small crowd of white-coated cosmeticians had come to the door of the tiny treatment room. I said to them, "This isn't Giuseppe Fruttero. It's John Crenshaw. If you don't believe me, try speaking Italian to him—he doesn't understand it. He's probably never been to Milan. But he's certainly been to Thailand, and he knows an awful lot about heroin."

4

Sal handed me the bottle of Black Label. "It's yours, Vic. Kill it tonight or save it for some other time. How did you know he was Roland Darnell's ex-partner?"

"I didn't. At least not when I went to La Cygnette. I just knew it had to be someone in the salon who killed him, and it was most likely someone who knew him in Kansas. And that meant either Darnell's ex-wife or his partner. And Giuseppe was the only man on the professional staff. And then I saw he didn't know Italian—after praising Milan and telling him he was stupid in the same tone of voice and getting no response it made me wonder."

"We owe you a lot, Vic. The police would never have dug down to find that. You gotta thank the lady, Mama."

Mrs. Barthele grudgingly gave me her thin hand. "But how come those police said Evangeline knew that Darnell man? My baby wouldn't know some convict, some drug smuggler."

"He wasn't a drug smuggler, Mama. It was his partner. The police have proved all that now. Roland Darnell never did anything wrong." Evangeline, chic in red with long earrings that bounced as she spoke, made the point hotly.

She gave her sister a measuring look. "All I can say, Evangeline, is it's a good thing you never had to put your hand on a Bible in court about Mr. Darnell."

I hastily poured a drink and changed the subject.

BILL PRONZINI

"Stacked Deck"

*Bill Pronzini was born in Petaluma, California on April 13, 1943. He studied at junior college and traveled extensively in Europe, residing for a time in Majorca and West Germany. His first crime novel, **The Stalker** (1971) was nominated for an MWA Edgar Award, and his second novel **The Snatch** (1971) introduced the Nameless Detective who went on to star in some two dozen novels and forty short stories to date. He served as first president of the Private Eye Writers of America.*

*Nominated for numerous Edgar Awards for his novels, short stories and nonfiction, Pronzini won the PWA Shamus Award for his novel **Hoodwink** (1981) and his short story "Cat's Paw" (1983). In 1987 he received the organization's Life Achievement Award, The Eye. He has edited more than seventy-five anthologies, many in collaboration with his wife Marcia Muller. They have also collaborated on three novels and on **1001 Midnights** (1986), a landmark study of outstanding mystery novels and collections. Pronzini has written two highly entertaining books about bad mystery writing, **Gun in Cheek** (1982) and **Son of Gun in Cheek** (1987).*

*His western short stories are collected as **The Best Western Stories of Bill Pronzini** (1990). The Nameless stories are collected in **Casefile** (1983) and **Spadework** (1996). Pronzini's non-series stories can be found in **Graveyard Plots** (1985), **Small Felonies** (1988) and **Stacked Deck** (1991). Originally published in **The New Black Mask** #8, "Stacked Deck" has been reprinted in the collection of that name, in **The Year's Best Mystery and Suspense Stories - 1988**, and **The Mammoth Book of Pulp Fiction**.*

Stacked Deck

by Bill Pronzini

<hr>

1

rom where he stood in the shadow of a split-bole Douglas fir, Deighan had a clear view of the cabin down below. Big harvest moon tonight, and only a few streaky clouds scudding past now and then to dim its hard yellow shine. The hard yellow glistened off the surface of Lake Tahoe beyond, softened into a long silverish stripe out toward the middle. The rest of the water shone like polished black metal. All of it was empty as far as he could see, except for the red-and-green running lights of a boat well away to the north, pointed toward the neon shimmer that marked the North Shore gambling casinos.

The cabin was big, made of cut pine logs and redwood shakes. It had a railed redwood deck that overlooked the lake, mostly invisible from where Deighan was. A flat concrete pier jutted out into the moonstruck water, a pair of short wooden floats making a T at its outer end. The boat tied up there was a thirty-foot Chris-Craft with sleeping accommodations for four. Nothing but the finer things for the Shooter.

Deighan watched the cabin. He'd been watching it for three hours now, from this same vantage point. His legs bothered him a little, standing around like this, and his eyes hurt from squinting. Time was, he'd had the night vision of an owl. Not anymore. What he had now, that he hadn't had when he was younger, was patience. He'd learned that in the last three years, along with a lot of other things—patience most of all.

198

On all sides the cabin was dark, but that was because they'd put
the blackout curtains up. The six of them had been inside for better than two hours now, the same five-man nucleus as on every
Thursday night except during the winter months, plus the one
newcomer. The Shooter went to Hawaii when it started to snow. Or
Florida or the Bahamas—someplace warm. Mannlicher and
Brandt stayed home in the winter. Deighan didn't know what the
others did, and he didn't care.

A match flared in the darkness between the carport, where the
Shooter's Caddy Eldorado was slotted, and the parking area back
among the trees. That was the lookout—Mannlicher's boy. Some
lookout: he smoked a cigarette every five minutes, like clockwork,
so you always knew where he was. Deighan watched him smoke
this one. When he was done, he threw the butt away in a shower of
sparks, and then seemed to remember that he was surrounded by
dry timber and went after it and stamped it out with his shoe.
Some lookout.

Deighan held his watch up close to his eyes, pushed the little
button that lighted its dial. Ten-nineteen. Just about time. The
lookout was moving again, down toward the lake. Pretty soon he
would walk out on the pier and smoke another cigarette and ad-
mire the view for a few minutes. He apparently did that at least
twice every Thursday night—that had been his pattern on each of
the last two—and he hadn't gone through the ritual yet tonight.
He was bored, that was the thing. He'd been at his job a long time
and it was always the same; there wasn't anything for him to do
except walk around and smoke cigarettes and look at three hundred square miles of lake. Nothing ever happened. In three years
nothing had ever happened.

Tonight something was going to happen.

Deighan took the gun out of the clamshell holster at his belt. It
was a Smith & Wesson .38 wadcutter, lightweight, compact—a
good piece, one of the best he'd ever owned. He held it in his hand,
watching as the lookout performed as if on cue—walked to the pier,
stopped, then moved out along its flat surface. When the guy had
gone halfway, Deighan came out of the shadows and went down
the slope at an angle across the driveway, to the rear of the cabin.
His shoes made little sliding sounds on the needled ground, but
they weren't sounds that carried.

He'd been over this ground three times before, dry runs the last
two Thursday nights and once during the day when nobody was

around; he knew just where and how to go. The lookout was lighting up again, his back to the cabin, when Deighan reached the rear wall. He eased along it to the spare-bedroom window. The sash went up easily, noiselessly. He could hear them then, in the rec room—voices, ice against glass, the click and rattle of the chips. He got the ski mask from his jacket pocket, slipped it over his head, snugged it down. Then he climbed through the window, put his penlight on just long enough to orient himself, went straight across to the door that led into the rec room.

It didn't make a sound, either, when he opened it. He went in with the revolver extended, elbow locked. Sturgess saw him first. He said, "Jesus Christ!" and his body went as stiff as if he were suffering a stroke. The others turned in their chairs, gawking. The Shooter started up out of his.

Deighan said, fast and hard, "Sit still if you don't want to die. Hands on the table where I can see them—all of you. Do it!"

They weren't stupid; they did what they were told. Deighan watched them through a thin haze of tobacco smoke. Six men around the hexagonal poker table, hands flat on its green baize, heads lifted or twisted to stare at him. He knew five of them. Mannlicher, the fat owner of the Nevornia Club at Crystal Bay; he had Family ties, even though he was a Prussian, because he'd once done some favors for an east-coast *capo*. Brandt, Mannlicher's cousin and private enforcer, who doubled as the Nevornia's floor boss. Bellah, the quasi-legitimate real-estate developer and high roller. Sturgess, the bankroll behind the Jackpot Lounge down at South Shore. And the Shooter—hired muscle, hired gun, part-time coke runner, whose real name was Dennis D'Allesandro. The sixth man was the pigeon they'd lured in for this particular game, a lean guy in his fifties with Texas oil money written all over him and his fancy clothes—Donley or Donavan, something like that.

Mannlicher was the bank tonight; the table behind his chair was covered with stacks of dead presidents—fifties and hundreds, mostly. Deighan took out the folded-up flour sack, tossed it on top of the poker chips that littered the baize in front of Mannlicher. "All right. Fill it."

The fat man didn't move. He was no pushover; he was hard, tough, mean. And he didn't like being ripped off. Veins bulged in his neck, throbbed in his temples. The violence in him was close to the surface now, held thinly in check.

"You know who we are?" he said. "Who I am?"

"Fill it."

"You dumb bastard. You'll never live to spend it."

"Fill the sack. *Now.*"

Deighan's eyes, more than his gun, made up Mannlicher's mind for him. He picked up the sack, pushed around in his chair, began to savagely feed in the stacks of bills.

"The rest of you," Deighan said, "put your wallets, watches, jewelry on the table. Everything of value. Hurry it up."

The Texan said, "Listen heah—" and Deighan pointed the .38 at his head and said, "One more word, you're a dead man." The Texan made an effort to stare him down, but it was just to save face; after two or three seconds he lowered his gaze and began stripping the rings off his fingers.

The rest of them didn't make any fuss. Bellah was sweating; he kept swiping it out of his eyes, his hands moving in little jerks and twitches. Brandt's eyes were like dull knives, cutting away at Deighan's masked face. D'Allesandro showed no emotion of any kind. That was his trademark; he was your original iceman. They might have called him that, maybe, if he'd been like one of those old-timers who used an ice pick or a blade. As it was, with his preferences, the Shooter was the right name for him.

Mannlicher had the sack full now. The platinum ring on his left hand, with its circle of fat diamonds, made little gleams and glints in the shine from the low-hanging droplight. The idea of losing that bothered him even more than losing his money; he kept running the fingers of his other hand over the stones.

"The ring," Deighan said to him. "Take it off."

"Go to hell."

"Take it off or I'll put a third eye in the middle of your forehead. Your choice."

Mannlicher hesitated, tried to stare him down, didn't have any better luck at it than the Texan. There was a tense moment; then, because he didn't want to die over a piece of jewelry, he yanked the ring off, slammed it down hard in the middle of the table.

Deighan said, "Put it in the sack. The wallets and the rest of the stuff too."

This time Mannlicher didn't hesitate. He did as he'd been told.

"All right," Deighan said. "Now get up and go over by the bar. Lie down on the floor on your belly."

Mannlicher got up slowly, his jaw set and his teeth clenched as if to keep the violence from spewing out like vomit. He lay down on the floor. Deighan gestured at Brandt, said, "You next. Then the rest of you, one at a time."

When they were all on the floor he moved to the table, caught up the sack. "Stay where you are for ten minutes," he told them. "You move before that, or call to the guy outside, I'll blow the place up. I got a grenade in my pocket, the fragmentation kind. Anybody doubt it?"

None of them said anything.

Deighan backed up into the spare bedroom, leaving the door open so he could watch them all the way to the window. He put his head out, saw no sign of the lookout. Still down by the lake somewhere. The whole thing had taken just a few minutes.

He swung out through the window, hurried away in the shadows—but in the opposite direction from the driveway and the road above. On the far side of the cabin there was a path that angled through the pine forest to the north; he found it, followed it at a trot. Enough moonlight penetrated through the branches overhead to let him see where he was going.

He was almost to the lakefront when the commotion started back there: voices, angry and pulsing in the night, Mannlicher's the loudest of them. They hadn't waited the full ten minutes, but then he hadn't expected them to. It didn't matter. The Shooter's cabin was invisible from here, cut off by a wooded finger of land a hundred yards wide. And they wouldn't be looking for him along the water, anyway. They'd be up on the road, combing that area; they'd figure automatically that his transportation was a car.

The hard yellow-and-black gleam of the lake was just ahead, the rushes and ferns where he'd tied up the rented Beachcraft inboard. He moved across the sandy strip of beach, waded out to his calves, dropped the loaded flour sack into the boat, and then eased the craft free of the rushes before he lifted himself over the gunwhale. The engine caught with a quiet rumble the first time he turned the key.

They were still making noise back at the cabin, blundering around like fools, as he eased away into the night.

2

The motel was called the Whispering Pines. It was back off Highway 28 below Crystal Bay, a good half mile from the lake, tucked up in a grove of pines and Douglas fir. Deighan's cabin was the farthest from the office, detached from its nearest neighbor by thirty feet of open ground.

Inside he sat in darkness except for flickering light from the television. The set was an old one; the picture was riddled with snow and kept jumping every few seconds. But he didn't care; he wasn't watching it. Or listening to it: he had the sound turned off. It was on only because he didn't like waiting in the dark.

It had been after midnight when he came in—too late to make the ritual call to Fran, even though he'd felt a compulsion to do so. She went to bed at eleven-thirty; she didn't like the phone to ring after that. How could he blame her? When he was home and she was away at Sheila's or her sister's, he never wanted it to ring that late either.

It was one-ten now. He was tired, but not too tired. The evening was still in his blood, warming him, like liquor or drugs that hadn't quite worn off yet. Mannlicher's face . . . that was an image he'd never forget. The Shooter's, too, and Brandt's, but especially Mannlicher's.

Outside, a car's headlamps made a sweep of light across the curtained window as it swung in through the motel courtyard. When it stopped nearby and the lights went out, Deighan thought: It's about time.

Footsteps made faint crunching sounds on gravel. Soft knock on the door. Soft voice following: "Prince? You in there?"

"Door's open."

A wedge of moonlight widened across the floor, not quite reaching to where Deighan sat in the lone chair with the .38 wadcutter in his hand. The man who stood silhouetted in the opening made a perfect target—just a damned airhead, any way you looked at him.

"Prince?"

"I'm over here. Come on in, shut the door."

"Why don't you turn on a light?"

"There's a switch by the door."

The man entered, shut the door. There was a click and the ceiling globe came on. Deighan stayed where he was, but reached over with his left hand to turn off the TV.

Bellah stood blinking at him, running his palms along the sides of his expensive cashmere jacket. He said nervously, "For God's sake, put the gun away. What's the idea?"

"I'm the cautious type."

"Well, put it away. I don't like it."

Deighan got to his feet, slid the revolver into his belt holster. "How'd it go?"

"Hairy, damned hairy. Mannlicher was like a madman." Bellah took a handkerchief out of his pocket, wiped his forehead. His angular face was pale, shiny-damp. "I didn't think he'd take it this hard. Christ."

That's the trouble with people like you, Deighan thought. You never think. He pinched a cigarette out of his shirt pocket, lit it with the Zippo Fran had given him fifteen years ago. Fifteen years, and it still worked. Like their marriage, even with all the trouble. How long was it now? Twenty-two years in May? Twenty-three?

Bellah said, "He started screaming at D'Allesandro. I thought he was going to choke him."

"Who? Mannlicher?"

"Yeah. About the window in the spare bedroom."

"What'd D'Allesandro say?"

"He said he always keeps it locked, you must have jimmied it some way that didn't leave any traces. Mannlicher didn't believe him. He thinks D'Allesandro forgot to lock it."

"Nobody got the idea it was an inside job?"

"No."

"Okay then. Relax, Mr. Bellah. You're in the clear."

Bellah wiped his face again. "Where's the money?"

"Other side of the bed. On the floor."

"You count it?"

"No. I figured you'd want to do that."

Bellah went over there, picked up the flour sack, emptied it on the bed. His eyes were bright and hot as he looked at all the loose green. Then he frowned, gnawed at his lower lip, and poked at Mannlicher's diamond ring. "What'd you take this for? Mannlicher is more pissed about the ring than anything else. He said his mother gave it to him. It's worth ten thousand."

"That's why I took it," Deighan said. "Fifteen percent of the cash isn't a hell of a lot."

Bellah stiffened. "I set it all up, didn't I? Why shouldn't I get the lion's share?"

"I'm not arguing, Mr. Bellah. We agreed on a price; OK, that's the way it is. I'm only saying I got a right to a little something extra."

"All right, all right." Bellah was looking at the money again.

"Must be at least two hundred thousand," he said. "That Texan, Donley, brought fifty grand alone."

"Plenty in his wallet too, then."

"Yeah."

Deighan smoked and watched Bellah count the loose bills and what was in the wallets and billfolds. There was an expression on the developer's face like a man has when he's fondling a naked woman. Greed, pure and simple. Greed was what drove Lawrence Bellah; money was his best friend, his lover, his god. He didn't have enough ready cash to buy the lakefront property down near Emerald Bay—property he stood to make three or four million on, with a string of condos—and he couldn't raise it fast enough any legitimate way; so he'd arranged to get it by knocking over his own weekly poker game, even if it meant crossing some hard people. He had balls, you had to give him that. He was stupid as hell, and one of these days he was liable to end up in pieces at the bottom of the lake, but he did have balls.

He was also lucky, at least for the time being, because the man he'd picked to do his strong-arm work was Bob Prince. He had no idea the name was a phony, no idea the whole package on Bob Prince was the result of three years of careful manipulation. All he knew was that Prince had a reputation as dependable, easy to work with, not too smart or money-hungry, and that he was willing to do any kind of muscle work. Bellah didn't have an inkling of what he'd really done by hiring Bob Prince. If he kept on being lucky, he never would.

Bellah was sweating by the time he finished adding up the take. "Two hundred and thirty-three thousand and change," he said. "More than we figured on."

"My cut's thirty-five thousand," Deighan said.

"You divide fast." Bellah counted out two stacks, hundreds and fifties, to one side of the flowered bedspread. Then he said, "Count it? Or do you trust me?"

Deighan grinned. He rubbed out his cigarette, went to the bed, and took his time shuffling through the stacks. "On the nose," he said when he was done.

Bellah stuffed the rest of the cash back into the flour sack, leaving the watches and jewelry where they lay. He was still nervous, still sweating; he wasn't going to sleep much tonight, Deighan thought.

"That's it, then," Bellah said. "You going back to Chicago tomorrow?"

"Not right away. Thought I'd do a little gambling first."

"Around here? Christ, Prince. . . ."

"No. Reno, maybe. I might even go down to Vegas."

"Just get away from Tahoe."

"Sure," Deighan said. "First thing in the morning."

Bellah went to the door. He paused there to tuck the flour sack under his jacket; it made him look as if he had a tumor on his left side. "Don't do anything with that jewelry in Nevada. Wait until you get back to Chicago."

"Whatever you say, Mr. Bellah."

"Maybe I'll need you again sometime," Bellah said. "You'll hear from me if I do."

"Any time. Any old time."

When Bellah was gone, Deighan put five thousand dollars into his suitcase and the other thirty thousand into a knapsack he'd bought two days before at a South Shore sporting goods store. Mannlicher's diamond ring went into the knapsack, too, along with the better pieces among the rest of the jewelry. The watches and the other stuff were no good to him; he bundled those up in a hand towel from the bathroom, stuffed the bundle into the pocket of his down jacket. Then he had one more cigarette, set his portable alarm clock for six A.M., double-locked the door, and went to bed on the left side, with the revolver under the pillow near his right hand.

3

In the dawn light the lake was like smoky blue glass, empty except for a few optimistic fishermen anchored close to the eastern shoreline. The morning was cold, autumn-crisp, but there was no wind. The sun was just beginning to rise, painting the sky and its scattered cloud-streaks in pinks and golds. There was old snow on the upper reaches of Mount Tallac, on some of the other Sierra peaks that ringed the lake.

Deighan took the Beachcraft out half a mile before he dropped the bundle of watches and worthless jewelry overboard. Then he cut off at a long diagonal to the north that brought him to within a few hundred yards of the Shooter's cabin. He had his fishing gear out by then, fiddling with the glass rod and tackle—just another angler looking for rainbow, Mackinaw, and cutthroat trout.

There wasn't anybody out and around at the Shooter's place. Deighan glided past at two knots, angled into shore a couple of hundred yards beyond, where there were rushes and some heavy brush and trees overhanging the water. From there he had a pretty good view of the cabin, its front entrance, the Shooter's Caddy parked inside the carport.

It was eight o'clock, and the sun was all the way up, when he switched off the engine and tied up at the bole of a collapsed pine. It was a few minutes past nine-thirty when D'Allesandro came out and walked around to the Caddy. He was alone. No chippies from the casinos this morning, not after what had gone down last night. He might be going to the store for cigarettes, groceries, or to a café somewhere for breakfast. He might be going to see somebody, do some business. The important thing was, how long would he be gone?

Deighan watched him back his Caddy out of the carport, drive it away and out of sight on the road above. He stayed where he was, fishing, waiting. At the end of an hour, when the Shooter still hadn't come back, he started the boat's engine and took his time maneuvering around the wooded finger of land to the north and then into the cove where he'd anchored last night. He nosed the boat into the reeds and ferns, swung overboard, and pushed it farther in, out of sight. Then he caught up the knapsack and set off through the woods to the Shooter's cabin.

He made a slow half circle of the place, keeping to the trees. The carport was still empty. Nothing moved anywhere within the range of his vision. Finally he made his way down to the rear wall, around it and along the side until he reached the front door. He didn't like standing out here for even a little while because there was no cover; but this door was the only one into the house, except for sliding doors to the terrace and a porch on the other side, and you couldn't jimmy sliding doors easily and without leaving marks. The same was true of windows. The Shooter would have made sure they were all secure anyway.

Deighan had one pocket of the knapsack open, the pick gun in his hand, when he reached the door. He'd got the pick gun from a housebreaker named Caldwell, an old-timer who was retired now; he'd also got some other tools and lessons in how to use them on the various kinds of locks. The lock on the Shooter's door was a flush-mounted, five-pin cylinder lock, with a steel lip on the door frame to protect the bolt and strike plate. That meant it was a lock you couldn't loid with a piece of plastic or a shim. It also meant that with a pick gun you could probably have it open in a couple of minutes.

Bending, squinting, he slid the gun into the lock. Set it, working the little knob on top to adjust the spring tension. Then he pulled the trigger—and all the pins bounced free at once and the door opened under his hand.

He slipped inside, nudged the door shut behind him, put the pick gun away inside the knapsack, and drew on a pair of thin plastic gloves. The place smelled of stale tobacco smoke and stale liquor. They hadn't been doing all that much drinking last night; maybe the Shooter had nibbled a few too many after the rest of them finally left. He didn't like losing money and valuables any more than Mannlicher did.

Deighan went through the front room. Somebody'd decorated the place for D'Allesandro: leather furniture, deer and antelope heads on the walls, Indian rugs on the floors, tasteful paintings. Cocaine deals had paid for part of it; contract work, including two hits on greedy Oakland and San Francisco drug dealers, had paid for the rest. But the Shooter was still small-time. He wasn't bright enough to be anything else. Cards and dice and whores-in-training were all he really cared about.

The front room was no good; Deighan prowled quickly through the other rooms. D'Allesandro wasn't the kind to have an office or a den, but there was a big old-fashioned rolltop desk in a room with a TV set and one of those big movie-type screens. None of the desk drawers was locked. Deighan pulled out the biggest one, saw that it was loaded with Danish porn magazines, took the magazines out and set them on the floor. He opened the knapsack and transferred the thirty thousand dollars into the back of the drawer. He put Mannlicher's ring in there, too, along with the other rings and a couple of gold chains the Texan had been wearing. Then he stuffed the porn magazines in at the front and pushed the drawer shut.

On his way back to the front room he rolled the knapsack tight around the pick gun and stuffed them into his jacket pocket. He opened the door, stepped out. He'd just finished resetting the lock when he heard the car approaching on the road above.

He froze for a second, looking up there. He couldn't see the car because of a screen of trees; but then he heard its automatic transmission gear down as it slowed for the turn into the Shooter's driveway. He pulled the door shut and ran toward the lake, the only direction he could go. Fifty feet away the log-railed terrace began, raised up off the sloping ground on redwood pillars. Deighan caught one of the railings, hauled himself up and half rolled through the gap between them. The sound of the oncoming car was loud in his ears as he landed, off balance, on the deck.

He went to one knee, came up again. The only way to tell if he'd been seen was to stop and look, but that was a fool's move. Instead he ran across the deck, climbed through the railing on the other side, dropped down, and tried to keep from making noise as he plunged into the woods. He stopped moving after thirty yards, where ferns and a deadfall formed a thick concealing wall. From behind it, with the .38 wadcutter in his hand, he watched the house and the deck, catching his breath, waiting.

Nobody came up or out of the deck. Nobody showed himself anywhere. The car's engine had been shut off sometime during his flight; it was quiet now, except for birds and the faint hum of a powerboat out on the lake.

Deighan waited ten minutes. When there was still nothing to see or hear, he transcribed a slow curl through the trees to where he could see the front of the cabin. The Shooter's Caddy was back inside the carport, no sign of haste in the way it had been neatly slotted. The cabin door was shut. The whole area seemed deserted.

But he waited another ten minutes before he was satisfied. Even then, he didn't holster his weapon until he'd made his way around to the cove where the Beachcraft was hidden. And he didn't relax until he was well out on the lake, headed back toward North Shore.

4

The Nevornia was one of North Shore's older clubs, but it had undergone some recent modernizing. Outside, it had been given a glass and gaudy-neon face-lift. Inside, they'd used more glass, some cut crystal, and a wine-red decor that included carpeting, upholstery, and gaming tables.

When Deighan walked in a few minutes before two, the banks of slots and the blackjack tables were getting moderately heavy play.

That was because it was Friday; some of the small-time gamblers liked to get a jump on the weekend crowds. The craps and roulette layouts were quiet. The high rollers were like vampires: they couldn't stand the daylight, so they only came out after dark.

Deighan bought a roll of quarters at one of the change booths. There were a couple of dozen rows of slots in the main casino—flashy new ones, mostly, with a few of the old scrolled nickel-plated jobs mixed in for the sake of nostalgia. He stopped at one of the old quarter machines, fed in three dollars' worth. Lemons and oranges. He couldn't even line up two cherries for a three-coin drop. He smiled crookedly to himself, went away from the slots and into the long concourse that connected the main casino with the new, smaller addition at the rear.

There were telephone booths along one side of the concourse. Deighan shut himself inside one of them, put a quarter in the slot, pushed 0 and then the digits of his house number in San Francisco. When the operator came on he said it was a collect call; that was to save himself the trouble of having to feed in a handful of quarters. He let the circuit make exactly five burrs in his ear before he hung up. If Fran was home, she'd know now that he was all right. If she wasn't home, then she'd know it later when he made another five-ring call. He always tried to call at least twice a day, at different times, because sometimes she went out shopping or to a movie or to visit Sheila and the kids.

It'd be easier if she just answered the phone, talked to him, but she never did when he was away. Never. Sheila or anybody else wanted to get hold of her, they had to call one of the neighbors or come over in person. She didn't want anything to do with him when he was away, didn't want to know what he was doing or even when he'd be back. "Suppose I picked up the phone and it wasn't you?" she'd said. "Suppose it was somebody telling me you were dead? I couldn't stand that." That part of it didn't make sense to him. If he were dead, somebody'd come by and tell it to her face; dead was dead, and what difference did it make how she got the news? But he didn't argue with her. He didn't like to argue with her, and it didn't cost him anything to do it her way.

He slotted the quarter again and called the Shooter's number. Four rings, five, and D'Allesandro's voice said, "Yeah?"

"Mr. Carson?"

"Who?"

"Isn't this Paul Carson?"

210

"No. You got the wrong number."

"Oh, sorry," Deighan said, and rang off.

Another quarter in the slot. This time the number he punched out was the Nevornia's business line. A woman's voice answered, crisp and professional. He said, "Mr. Mannlicher. Tell him it's urgent."

"Whom shall I say is calling?"

"Never mind that. Just tell him it's about what happened last night."

"Sir, I'm afraid I can't—"

"Tell him last night's poker game, damn it. He'll talk to me."

There was a click and some canned music began to play in his ear. He lit a cigarette. He was on his fourth drag when the canned music quit and the fat man's voice said, "Frank Mannlicher. Who's this?"

"No names. Is it all right to talk on this line?"

"Go ahead, talk."

"I'm the guy who hit your game last night."

Silence for four or five seconds. Then Mannlicher said, "Is that so?" in a flat, wary voice.

"Ski mask, Smith & Wesson .38, grenade in my jacket pocket. The take was better than two hundred thousand. I got your ring— platinum with a circle of diamonds."

Another pause, shorter this time. "So why call me today?"

"How'd you like to get it all back—the money and the ring?"

"How?"

"Go pick it up. I'll tell you where."

"Yeah? Why should you do me a favor?"

"I didn't know who you were last night. I wasn't told. If I had been, I wouldn't of gone through with it. I don't mess with people like you, people with your connections."

"Somebody hired you, that it?"

"That's it."

"Who?"

"D'Allesandro."

"*What?*"

"The Shooter. D'Allesandro."

". . . Bullshit."

"You don't have to believe me. But I'm telling you—he's the one. He didn't tell me who'd be at the game, and now he's trying to screw me on the money. He says there was less than a hundred and fifty thousand in the sack; I know better."

"So now you want to screw him."

"That's right. Besides, I don't like the idea of you pushing to find out who I am, maybe sending somebody to pay me a visit someday. I figure if I give you the Shooter, you'll lose interest in me."

More silence. "Why'd he do it?" Mannlicher said in a different voice—harder, with that edge of violence it had held last night. "Hit the game like that?"

"He needs big money, fast. He's into some kind of scam back east; he wouldn't say what it is."

"Where's the money and the rest of the stuff?"

"At his cabin. We had a drop arranged in the woods; I put the sack there last night, he picked it up this morning when nobody was around. The money's in his desk—the big rolltop. Your ring, too. That's where it was an hour ago, anyhow, when I walked out."

Mannlicher said, "In his desk," as if he were biting the words off something bitter.

"Go out there, see for yourself."

"If you're telling this straight, you got nothing to worry about from me. Maybe I'll fix you up with a reward or something. Where can I get in touch?"

"You can't," Deighan said. "I'm long gone as soon as I hang up this phone."

"I'll make it five thousand. Just tell me where you—"

Deighan broke the connection.

His cigarette had burned down to the filter; he dropped it on the floor, put his shoe on it before he left the booth. On his way out of the casino he paused long enough to push another quarter into the same slot machine he'd played before. More lemons and oranges. This time he didn't smile as he moved away.

5

Narrow and twisty, hemmed in by trees, old Lake Road branched off Highway 28 and took two miles to get all the way to the lake. But it wasn't a dead-end; another road picked it up at the lakefront and looped back out to the highway. There were several nice homes hidden away in the area—it was called Pine Acres—with plenty of space between them. The Shooter's cabin was a mile and a half from the highway, off an even narrower lane called Little Cove Road. The only other cabin within five hundred yards was a summer place that the owners had already closed up for the year.

Deighan drove past the intersection with Little Cove, went two-tenths of a mile, parked on the turnout at that point. There wasn't anybody else around when he got out, nothing to see except trees and little winks of blue that marked the nearness of the lake. If anybody came along they wouldn't pay any attention to the car. For one thing, it was a '75 Ford Galaxy with nothing distinctive about it except the antenna for the GTE mobile phone. It was his—he'd driven it up from San Francisco—but the papers on it said it belonged to Bob Prince. For another thing, Old Lake Road was only a hundred yards or so from the water here, and there was a path through the trees to a strip of rocky beach. Local kids used it in the summer; he'd found that out from Bellah. Kids might have decided to stop here on a sunny autumn day as well. No reason for anybody to think otherwise.

He found the path, went along it a short way to where it crossed a little creek, dry now and so narrow it was nothing more than a natural drainage ditch. He followed the creek to the north, on a course he'd taken three days ago. It led him to a shelflike overhang topped by two chunks of granite outcrop that leaned against each other like a pair of old drunks. Below the shelf, the land fell away sharply to the Shooter's driveway some sixty yards distant. Off to the right, where the incline wasn't so steep and the trees grew in a pack, was the split-bole Douglas fir where he'd stood waiting last night. The trees were fewer and more widely spaced apart between here and the cabin, so that from behind the two outcrops you had a good look at the Shooter's property, Little Cove Road, the concrete pier, and the lake shimmering under the late-afternoon sun.

The Caddy Eldorado was still slotted inside the carport. It was the only car in sight. Deighan knelt behind where the outcrops came together to form a notch, rubbed tension out of his neck and shoulders while he waited.

He didn't have to wait long. Less than ten minutes had passed when the car appeared on Little Cove Road, slowed, turned down the Shooter's driveway. It wasn't Mannlicher's fancy limo; it was a two-year-old Chrysler—Brandt's, maybe. Brandt was driving it: Deighan had a clear view of him through the side window as the Chrysler pulled up and stopped near the cabin's front door. He could also see that the lone passenger was Mannlicher.

Brandt got out, opened the passenger door for the fat man, and the two of them went to the cabin. It took D'Allesandro ten seconds to answer Brandt's knock. There was some talk, not much; then Mannlicher and Brandt went in, and the door shut behind them.

All right, Deighan thought. He'd stacked the deck as well as he could; pretty soon he'd know how the hand—and the game—played out.

Nothing happened for maybe five minutes. Then he thought he heard some muffled sounds down there, loud voices that went on for a while, something that might have been a bang, but the distance was too great for him to be sure that he wasn't imagining them. Another four or five minutes went by. And then the door opened and Brandt came out alone, looked around, called something back inside that Deighan didn't understand. If there was an answer, it wasn't audible. Brandt shut the door, hurried down to the lake, went out onto the pier. The Chris-Craft was still tied up there. Brandt climbed on board, disappeared for thirty seconds or so, reappeared carrying a square of something gray and heavy. Tarpaulin, Deighan saw when Brandt came back up the driveway. Big piece of it—big enough for a shroud.

The Shooter's hand had been folded. That left three of them still in the game.

When Brandt had gone back inside with the tarp, Deighan stood and half ran along the creek and through the trees to where he'd left the Ford. Old Lake Road was deserted. He yanked open the passenger door, leaned in, caught up the mobile phone, and punched out the emergency number for the county sheriff's office. An efficient-sounding male voice answered.

"Something's going on on Little Cove Road," Deighan said, making himself sound excited. "That's in Pine Acres, you know? It's the cabin at the end, down on the lake. I heard shots—people shooting at each other down there. It sounds like a war."

"What's the address?"

"I don't know the address, it's the cabin right on the lake. People *shooting* at each other. You better get right out there."

"Your name, sir?"

"I don't want to get involved. Just hurry, will you?"

Deighan put the receiver down, shut the car door, ran back along the path and along the creek to the shelf. Mannlicher and Brandt were still inside the cabin. He went to one knee again behind the outcrops, drew the .38 wadcutter, held it on his thigh.

It was another two minutes before the door opened down there. Brandt came out, looked around as he had before, went back inside—and then he and Mannlicher both appeared, one at each end of a big, tarp-wrapped bundle. They started to carry it down the driveway toward the lake. Going to put it on the boat, Deighan thought, take it out now or later on, when it's dark. Lake Tahoe was sixteen hundred feet deep in the middle. The bundle wouldn't have been the first somebody'd dumped out there.

He let them get clear of the Chrysler, partway down the drive, before he poked the gun into the notch, sighted, and fired twice. The shots went where he'd intended them to, wide by ten feet and into the roadbed so they kicked up gravel. Mannlicher and Brandt froze for an instant, confused. Deighan fired a third round, putting the slug closer this time, and that one panicked them: they let go of the bundle and began scrambling.

There was no cover anywhere close by; they both ran for the Chrysler. Brandt had a gun in his hand when he reached it, and he dropped down behind the rear deck, trying to locate Deighan's position. Mannlicher kept on scrambling around to the passenger door, pulled it open, pushed himself across the seat inside.

Deighan blew out the Chrysler's near front tire. Sighted, and blew out the rear tire. Brandt threw an answering shot his way, but it wasn't even close. The Chrysler was tilting in Deighan's direction as the tires flattened. Mannlicher pushed himself out of the car, tried to make a run for the cabin door with his arms flailing, his fat jiggling. Deighan put a bullet into the wall beside the door. Mannlicher reversed himself, fell in his frantic haste, crawled back behind the Chrysler.

Reloading the wadcutter, Deighan could hear the sound of cars coming fast up on Little Cove Road. No sirens, but revolving lights made faint bloodred flashes through the trees.

From behind the Chrysler Brandt fired again, wildly. Beyond him, on the driveway, one corner of the tarp-wrapped bundle had come loose and was flapping in the wind off the lake.

A county sheriff's cruiser, its roof light slashing the air, made the turn off Little Cove onto the driveway. Another one was right behind it. In his panic, Brandt straightened up when he saw them and fired once, blindly, at the first in line.

Deighan was on his feet by then, hurrying away from the outcrops, holstering his weapon. Behind him he heard brakes squeal, another shot, voices yelling, two more shots. All the sounds faded as he neared the turnout and the Ford. By the time he pulled out onto the deserted road, there was nothing to hear but the sound of his engine, the screeching of a jay somewhere nearby.

Brandt had thrown in his hand by now; so had Mannlicher.

This pot belonged to him.

6

Fran was in the backyard, weeding her garden, when he got home late the following afternoon. He called to her from the doorway, and she glanced around and then got up, unsmiling, and came over to him. She was wearing jeans and one of his old shirts and a pair of gardening gloves, and her hair was tied in a long ponytail. Used to be a light, silky brown, her hair; now it was mostly gray. His fault. She was only forty-six. A woman of forty-six shouldn't be so gray.

She said, "So you're back." She didn't sound glad to see him, didn't kiss him or touch him at all. But her eyes were gentle on his face.

"I'm back."

"You all right? You look tired."

"Long drive. I'm fine; it was a good trip."

She didn't say anything. She didn't want to hear about it, not any of it. She just didn't want to know.

"How about you?" he asked. "Everything been okay?"

"Sheila's pregnant again."

"Christ. What's the matter with her? Why don't she get herself fixed? Or get Hank fixed?"

"She likes kids."

"I like kids too, but four's too many at her age. She's only twenty-seven."

"She wants eight."

"She's crazy," Deighan said. "What's she want to bring all those kids into a world like this for?"

There was an awkward moment. It was always awkward at first when he came back. Then Fran said, "You hungry?"

"You know me, I can always eat." Fact was, he was starved. He hadn't eaten much up in Nevada, never did when he was away. And he hadn't had anything today except an English muffin and some coffee for breakfast in Truckee.

"Come into the kitchen," Fran said. "I'll fix you something."

They went inside. He got a beer out of the refrigerator; she waited and then took out some covered dishes, some vegetables. He wanted to say something to her, talk a little, but he couldn't think of anything. His mind was blank at times like this. He carried his beer into the living room.

The goddamn trophy case was the first thing he saw. He hated that trophy case; but Fran wouldn't get rid of it, no matter what he said. For her it was like some kind of shrine to the dead past. All the mementoes of his years on the force—twenty-two years, from beat patrolman in North Beach all the way up to inspector on the narcotics squad. The certificate he'd won in marksmanship competition at the police academy, the two citations from the mayor for bravery, other crap like that. Bones, that's all they were to him. Pieces of a rotting skeleton. What was the sense in keeping them around, reminding both of them of what he'd been, what he'd lost?

His fault he'd lost it, sure. But it was their fault too, goddamn them. The laws, the lawyers, the judges, the *system*. No convictions on half of all the arrests he'd ever made—half! Turning the ones like Mannlicher and Brandt and D'Allesandro loose, putting them right back on the street, letting them make their deals and their hits, letting them screw up innocent lives. Sheila's kids, his grandkids—lives like that. How could they blame him for being bitter? How could they blame him for taking too many drinks now and then?

He sat down on the couch, drank some of his beer, lit a cigarette. Ah Christ, he thought, it's not them. You know it wasn't them. It was *you,* you dumb bastard. They warned you twice about drinking on duty. And you kept on doing it, you were hog-drunk the night you plowed the departmental sedan into that vanload of teenagers. What if one of *those* kids had died? You were lucky, by God. You got off easy.

Sure, he thought. Sure. But he'd been a good cop, damn it, a cop inside and out; it was all he knew how to be. What was he supposed to do after they threw him off the force? Live on his half-pension? Get a job as a part-time security guard? Forty-four years old, no skills, no friends outside the department—what the hell was he supposed to do?

He'd invented Bob Prince, that was what he'd done. He'd gone into business for himself.

Fran didn't understand. "You'll get killed one of these days," she'd said in the beginning. "It's vigilante justice," she'd said. "You think you're Rambo, is that it?" she'd said. She just didn't understand. To him it was the same job he'd always done, the only one he was any good at, only now *he* made up some of the rules. He was no Rambo, one man up against thousands, a mindless killing machine; he hated that kind of phony flag-waving crap. It wasn't real. What he was doing, that was real. It meant something. But a hero? No. Hell, no. He was a sniper, that was all, picking off a weak or a vulnerable enemy here and there, now and then. Snipers weren't heroes, for Christ's sake. Snipers were snipers, just like cops were cops.

He finished his beer and his cigarette, got up, went into Fran's sewing room. The five thousand he'd held out of the poker-game take was in his pocket—money he felt he was entitled to because his expenses ran high sometimes, and they had to eat, they had to live. He put the roll into her sewing cabinet, where he always put whatever money he made as Bob Prince. She'd spend it when she had to, parcel it out, but she'd never mention it to him or anyone else. She'd told Sheila once that he had a sales job, he got paid in cash a lot, that was why he was away from home for such long periods of time.

When he walked back into the kitchen she was at the sink, peeling potatoes. He went over and touched her shoulder, kissed the top of her head. She didn't look at him; stood there stiffly until he moved away from her. But she'd be all right in a day or two. She'd be fine until the next time Bob Prince made the right kind of connection.

He wished it didn't have to be this way. He wished he could roll back the clock three years, do things differently, take the gray out of her hair and the pain out of her eyes. But he couldn't. It was just too late.

You had to play the cards you were dealt, no matter how lousy they were. The only thing that made it tolerable was that sometimes, on certain hands, you could find ways to stack the damn deck.

ROBERT BARNARD

"More Final Than Divorce"

Robert Barnard was born in Burnham-on-Crouch, Essex, England, on November 23, 1936. He graduated from Balliol College, Oxford, in 1959 and received his Ph.D. from the University of Bergen, Norway in 1972. He lectured at universities in Australia and Norway before publishing his first novel **Death of an Old Goat** in 1974.

Barnard's first eight books were non-series novels and it was not until **Sheer Torture** (1981) that he created Perry Trethowan, a Scotland Yard detective who was to make several reappearances. A Barnard book is typically a pure detective story with touches of humor, and he has been nominated several times for MWA novel and short story Edgars. **A Scandal in Belgravia** (1992) won the Nero Wolfe Award. Among Barnard's short stories "More Final Than Divorce" won the Agatha Award, "Breakfast Television" won Bouchercon's Anthony Award, and "The Woman in the Wardrobe" won the Macavity Award.

The stories collected in **Death of a Salesperson and Other Untimely Exits** (1989) are mainly ironic crime tales rather than detection. "More Final Than Divorce" first appeared in **Ellery Queen's Mystery Magazine** and was reprinted in **Under the Gun**.

More Final
Than Divorce

by Robert Barnard

Gerry Porter had no desire to murder his wife. He would much have preferred simply to trade her in for a new model. But Gerry was a businessman, and he knew how to do his sums. He totted up the value of his butchery business, of their house and two cars, of the time-share villa in Spain. He knew it was no longer a question simply of paying her a pittance as alimony—that the judge would award his wife a substantial proportion of the marital estate. Every way he looked at it it was impossible for him to keep his business, a roof over his head, and a new wife. He sighed. It would have to be something more final than divorce. It would have to be murder. Personally, he told himself, he blamed these feminists. If it hadn't been for these new divorce laws Sandra would be alive today.

Well, actually Sandra *was* alive today. That was of course the problem. He didn't think Sandra had any suspicions about the newer model, but the moment she did she'd tell her friends, and therein would lie the main danger. For Gerry was determined that the police should not hear about the newer model, because he had no intention that Sandra's death should be treated as a case of murder. Everyone knew who the first suspect was when a wife or husband was murdered. No, Sandra was not going to be murdered. Sandra was going to have an accident. Or commit suicide.

Gerry went about it in a methodical way. There were always plenty of newspapers around in his butcher's shop as wrapping, and between customers he studied them avidly. Plenty of people did die by accident, and the inquests on them were reported in the local rag. Gerry began classifying them in his mind into road accidents, domestic accidents, and accidents at work. The last category was out, since Sandra did not go to work. The first category was large, and encompassed many different kinds of death in or under motor vehicles. Gerry did notice how many people seemed to die on holiday abroad, and he toyed with the idea of getting some Spaniard to run into her or run her down on some particularly dangerous stretch of Iberian road. But the thought of being in the power of some greasy wop (Gerry was neither a liberal nor a tolerant thinker) made him go off the idea. And the more he read about the advances in forensic science, the less inclined he felt to tamper with his wife's car.

But the more he thought about it, the same objection seemed to apply to domestic accidents. People did electrocute themselves; some even, apparently (God, what ignorant bastards people were!) perched electric fires on the ends of their baths. But the Porters had central heating, and Gerry doubted his ability to render their high-speed kettle lethal in a way that would fool Forensics.

Gerry was sent off on to another tack entirely one evening when he passed the living room while his wife was having coffee with a friend, and heard her say:

"Oh God, the Change! There's times I've wondered whether I'd ever get through it."

Gerry was a heavy man, with heavy footsteps, and he could not stop to hear any more. Sandra in fact went on to say that luckily she now seemed to be over the worst. Gerry had gone on to the front door, and out to the garage, and a little idea was jigging around in his mind. Gone were thoughts of accidents with car exhaust fumes, of pushing Sandra under an underground train. Suicide while the balance of her mind was disturbed. Or, to be more precise, the balance of her body.

With no plan as yet firmly formulated, he nevertheless began laying the ground next evening in the pub.

"You're thoughtful, Gerry," said Sam Eagleton to him, as he sat over his second pint. And indeed he was. It was quite a strain. Because Gerry was usually the life and soul of the Cock and Pheasant, with a steady stream of salacious, off-color or racist jokes.

"Aye. It's the wife. She's a bit under the weather . . ." After a pause, occupied with a gaze into the brown depths of his beer mug, he added: "It's the Change. It's a rotten thing to have to go through. It does things to a woman. We can count ourselves lucky we don't have anything like it."

It was a most un-Gerry-like topic of conversation. Sam Eagleton thought it a bit off to mention it at all, and not good form, as it was understood at the Cock and Pheasant. He said: "Aye, it's a bad business," and changed the subject.

They got used, in the Cock and Pheasant and other places that Gerry Porter frequented, to the topic of The Change over the next few weeks. It was supplemented by other causes of worry and distress to Sandra, for Gerry had decided that her suicide would be the result of a cumulative burden of miseries, of myriad worries that finally became too much to bear.

"The wife's mother is in a bad way," he would say. "Senile. It's a terrible burden on Sandra."

Gerry's mother-in-law was in a home, and he had in the past made ribald jokes about her increasingly erratic behavior. Now, apparently, all he could see was the distress that it must cause his wife.

"Gerry's gone all serious on us," said his friend Paul Tutin when he had gone out one evening, still long-faced.

There were other problems and vicissitudes in the Porter household that were tediously canvassed. Sandra's attempts to get O-Level English, one of the things she studied at one of her many evening classes, had hitherto been the subject of innumerable sexist jokes about the thickness of women. Now all they heard was what a terrible grief it was to her. "But she shouldn't be trying to get it now," he would say. "Not while she's going through the Change." They had no children to cause them worry, but nephews and nieces were press-ganged into service, and a brother of Sandra's who was serving a jail sentence was represented as an agonizing worry. But in the end it all came back to the Change.

"It does something to some women," Gerry would say. "You've no idea. Sometimes I wonder if it's the same woman I married. She says that every morning she dreads waking up."

One afternoon, while she was shopping in Darlington, Sandra dropped into the Cherry Tree Tea Shop, and was glad to see two of her old friends sitting in the window. They waved her over to their table.

"Hello, Sandra, how *are* you?" Mary Eagleton hailed.

"Fine," said Sandra, sitting down. "Just fine."

"Oh good. I *am* glad. Gerry was telling Sam the other night that the good old menopause was getting you down."

"A lot Gerry knows about it."

"When are you taking your O-Level again?" asked Mary, over the cream cakes.

"Next week!" said Sandra, roaring with laughter. "And I haven't opened a book since I failed last time. I bet the examiners are sharpening their pencils and licking their lips over the thought of giving me bottom grades."

"How's your mother?" asked Brenda Tutin.

"Great! Completely gaga. Doesn't even know me when I go in, so I've stopped going. It's a great relief."

"Gerry says you're very upset about it," said Brenda.

Sandra raised her eyebrows.

"What *exactly* has Gerry been saying?" she asked.

Things went on pretty much as normal in the next few weeks, Sandra took up yet another evening class—cake-decorating, of all things—and so they saw very little of each other, except at breakfast. Gerry insisted on the full menu with trimmings at breakfast-time—porridge, egg and bacon with sausage and tomato, two or three slices of toast and marmalade. He said it set him up for the day. Sandra, who had been to diet classes and keep fit classes, found cooking it rather nauseating, but she didn't have to watch him eat it, because he propped up his *Sun* newspaper against the coffee pot, and devoured its edifying contents along with the bacon and sausage.

He was back from the pub (or from the newer model) more often in the evening now when she got back from her classes. He was even rather considerate, something he had not been for many years, not since the first week of their honeymoon. When she flopped down in the armchair ("Everything seems to tire her now," he said in the pub) he offered her a vodka and tonic, and was even prepared to make her a mug of Ovaltine. Sometimes she accepted, sometimes she did not. It was certainly pleasant to have him actually doing something for her in the kitchen ("She's been desperate for sleep," Gerry planned to tell the police. "She's been trying everything.")

The crunch came nearly six months after Gerry had first made his decision. Sandra got back from evening classes and was *exhausted,* she said.

"Vodka and tonic, darling?" Gerry asked.

"That *would* be nice, Smoochie," she said, using a pet name they had almost abandoned.

When he brought it over Sandra noticed that he was not smelling of beer. She snuggled up on to the sofa in front of the roaring gas fire.

"This is the life!" she said.

Gerry was watching her as she tasted her drink, though ostensibly he was at the sideboard, getting one for himself. She gave no sign that it tasted any different, and he breathed out. She swung her feet up on the sofa, and took another sip or two of the vodka and tonic.

"Funny," she said. "I feel famished."

"Let me get you something."

"Would you, Smoochie? Just a few biscuits, and a bit of cheese."

When he got back the vodka and tonic was half drunk. Sandra ate the biscuits and cheese ravenously.

"I don't know why cake-decoration should be so *grueling,*" she said, taking a good swig at her drink. "I could almost settle down to sleep here in front of the fire."

"Why don't you?" Gerry said, sitting down by the head of the sofa and running his fingers through her hair. Sandra downed the rest of her drink.

"Lovely not to have the television on," she said, her voice seeming to come from far away. Her head dropped on to the arm of the sofa, her eyes closed. Soon Gerry heard gentle snores.

He jumped up and looked at his watch. It was just after ten. He could aim at the 10:45 or the 10:55. Both were expresses, and both were usually on time. He put in his pocket a little bottle of prepared vodka and sleeping draught ("She had it with her drink. I thought she wanted to sleep; I didn't realize she wanted it to deaden the pain," he would tell the police). He intended to force it down her throat if she should show signs of waking up. Then he went out into the drive and opened both doors of his wife's little Fiat (his own Range-Rover always had the garage). Then he went back into the sitting room, took his wife gently in his arms, and carried her through the front door and out to the car. He laid her gently in the front passenger seat, and got in beside her.

The drive to the bridge was uneventful, though Gerry was bathed in sweat by the end of it. They met no more than three or four cars going in the other direction. After only ten minutes they turned into the narrow road, scarcely more than a track, which led to the railway bridge. His heart banged with relief as he parked Sandra's car under a clump of trees.

He looked at his watch. Ten minutes to go before the 10:45 went by, if it was on time. He looked at his wife. She was breathing deeply, her head lolling to one side. The Sovipol he had got from the doctor (*"She* can't sleep, Doctor, and that means *I* don't sleep, and it's affecting the business . . .") was working like a dream. He got out of the car, leant back in, and with a butcher's strength he lifted Sandra across into the driver's seat. He wiped the steering-wheel, then put her fingers on it in two or three different positions. Then he let them fall, and pressed the little bottle of vodka and Sovipol into them.

"I was already in bed," he would tell the police. "I'd had a hard day. I was knackered. I did hear her driving off, but I thought she must have left something behind at her class. She's been getting very forgetful, since the Change started . . ."

Time to get her on to the bridge. It was an old one, dating from the time when this neglected track was an important road. He took her in his arms and carried her—almost tenderly—the hundred yards there. No sounds of a train yet. He laid her in a sitting position by the bridge and then straightened. God—he could do with a fag. But would that be wise? No—there in the distance was the regular hum of the diesel: the Intercity 125 from King's Cross to Leeds. He waited a moment. It wouldn't be here for a minute or two yet. Thank God he hadn't needed to force the contents of the bottle down her. His nerves as it was were stretched beyond bearing by the tension. He wanted to wet himself. Then, as the noise of the train grew nearer, he stretched down to the comatose figure by the bridge. He put his hands under the body.

And immediately he felt an open palm smash suddenly into his face. In a moment it was he who was on his back across the parapet of the bridge. Suddenly it was his wife who had strong hands on his shoulders, his wife who was pushing, pushing. Dimly he heard her voice.

"They were karate classes, Smoochie. Karate classes."

Then she dropped him into the path of the oncoming express.

The police were extremely sympathetic. It was child's play to them to unravel the details of Gerry's plan. They talked to his friends and heard about his change of character in his pub sessions, the conversations that had prepared the way. They found his dolly-bird in a little flat in central Darlington (though she said she would never have married him, not in a million years). They found the railway timetables in his study, analyzed the earth in the pot plant into which Sandra Porter had poured most of her drink. ("It tasted so off. I thought he'd given me gin by mistake, which I hate, and I didn't want to offend him.") They talked to the neighbor who had passed them on the road and seen that it was Gerry driving, talked to the poacher who had seen Gerry park the car and seen him press Sandra's hands to the steering-wheel. *Those* prints wouldn't have deceived a rookie constable into thinking that they were those of a woman actually driving a car. No, Gerry Porter would never have got away with it, even if he had succeeded in killing his wife.

Sandra was quite affecting. She had drunk about a quarter of her drink, she said, but had filled the glass up with tonic water so he shouldn't know. ("He could be awfully touchy," she said.) What she had drunk had sent her soundly to sleep. When she began to awake she was in the car, in the driving seat, and her husband was pressing her hands to the steering-wheel. She was confused and terrified. How had she got here? What was going on? She had feigned sleep until she had heard the train, her husband had lifted her up, and then she—terrified—had used the techniques she had learnt at self-defense classes. ("The police are always recommending that we do them, and with the number of ghastly rapes we've had around here . . .")

Only Inspector Potter of the South Yorkshire C.I.D. had doubts.

"Why weren't there more signs of struggle?" he asked. "Why did she make no attempt to immobilize him rather than kill him? Why did she take up karate classes, mid-term, after he'd started laying the ground in his pubs? Why did she take such care, driving to the Darlington Police Station, not to disturb the fake prints?"

"She *had* to kill him," said his Super. "Otherwise he'd have been stalking her through the woods. She was practically out of her mind."

"Yet she was careful not to disturb those prints . . . Oh, I grant you there's no point in nagging away at it. It's an academic exercise. We'd never secure a conviction, not even for manslaughter. Never in a million years."

But the doubts remained in his mind. He noticed that a few days after the inquest and funeral, Porter's Family Butchery was open again for business. He noted that Sandra ran it very efficiently, with the help of a stalwart chap, fifteen years her junior, whom he heard she had met at karate class. When, a year after Gerry's death, he saw in the paper that she had married him, he showed the announcement to the Super.

"We'd never have got a conviction," he repeated. "But she did it very nicely, didn't she? Got her freedom, her boyfriend, *and* the whole of the property. Beats a divorce settlement any time! He handed himself to her on a plate, did Gerry Porter. On a ruddy plate!"

CLARK HOWARD

"The Dakar Run"

Clark Howard was born in Tennessee in 1934. He served in the U.S. Marine Corps and began publishing mystery short stories in 1957. The first of a dozen crime novels appeared in 1969, but he is best known for his powerful and moving short stories and for a series of fact crime books beginning with the Edgar-nominated **Six Against the Rock** *(1977).*

Howard's 1980 short story "Horn Man" won the MWA Edgar Award as best of the year, one of a large group of powerful tales like "Animals," "McCulla's Kid," "Scalplock," "The Last One to Cry," "The Dakar Run," "The Color of Death," "Dark Conception," "The Dublin Eye," "All the Heroes Are Dead" and "Puerto Rican Blues" that appeared through the 1980s and '90s. The last two were nominated for Edgar Awards and several of the others won first prize in the **Ellery Queen's Mystery Magazine** *annual Readers Awards.*

Clark Howard's short stories have yet to be collected. "The Dakar Run" first appeared in **EQMM** *and was reprinted in* **The Year's Best Mystery and Suspense Stories - 1989** *and* **Under the Gun.**

The Dakar Run

by Clark Howard

Jack Sheffield limped out of the little Theatre Americain with John Garfield's defiant words still fresh in his mind. "What are you gonna do, kill me?" Garfield, as Charley Davis, the boxer, had asked Lloyd Gough, the crooked promoter, at the end of *Body and Soul*. Then, challengingly, smugly, with the Garfield arrogance, "Everybody dies!" And he had walked away, with Lilli Palmer on his arm.

Pausing outside to look at the *Body and Soul* poster next to the box office, Sheffield sighed wistfully. They were gone now, Garfield and Lilli Palmer, black-and-white films, the good numbers like Hazel Brooks singing "Am I Blue?" Even boxing—*real* boxing—was down the tubes. In the old days, hungry kids challenged seasoned pros. Now millionaires fought gold-medal winners.

Shaking his head at the pity of things changed, Sheffield turned up his collar against the chilly Paris night and limped up La Villette to the Place de Cluny. There was a cafe there called the Nubian, owned by a very tall Sudanese who mixed his own mustard, so hot it could etch cement. Every Tuesday night, the old-movie feature at the Theatre Americain changed and Jack Sheffield went to see it, whatever it was, and afterward he always walked to the Nubian for sausage and mustard and a double gin. Later, warm from the gin and the food, he would stroll, rain or fair, summer or winter, along the Rue de Rivoli next to the Tuileries, down to the Crazy Horse Saloon to wait for the chorus to do its last high kick so that Jane, the long-legged Englishwoman with whom he lived, could change and go home. Tuesdays never varied for Sheffield.

How many Tuesdays, he wondered as he entered the Nubian, had he been doing this exact same thing? As he pulled out a chair at the rickety little table for two at which he always sat, he tried to recall how long he had been with Jane. Was it three years or four? Catching the eye of the Sudanese, Sheffield raised his hand to signal that he was here, which was all he had to do; he never varied his order. The Sudanese nodded and walked with a camel-like gait toward the kitchen, and Sheffield was about to resume mentally backtracking his life when a young girl came in and walked directly to his table.

"Hi," she said.

He looked at her, tilting his head an inch, squinting slightly without his glasses. When he didn't respond at once, the girl gave him a wry, not totally amused look.

"I'm Chelsea," she said pointedly. "Chelsea Sheffield. Your daughter." She pulled out the opposite chair. "Don't bother to get up."

Sheffield stared at her incredulously, lips parted but no words being generated by his surprised brain.

"Mother," she explained, "said all I had to do to find you in Paris was locate a theater that showed old American movies, wait until the bill changed, and stand outside after the first show. She said if you didn't walk out, you were either dead or had been banished from France."

"Your mother was always right," he said, adding drily, "about everything."

"She also said you might be limping, after smashing up your ankle at Le Mans two years ago. Is the limp permanent?"

"More or less." He quickly changed the subject. "Your mother's well, I presume."

"Very. Like a Main Line Philadelphia doctor's wife should be. Her picture was on the society page five times last year."

"And your sister?"

"Perfect," Chelsea replied, "just as she's always been. Married to a proper young stockbroker, mother of two proper little girls, residing in a proper two-story Colonial, driving a proper Chrysler station wagon. Julie has *always* been proper. I was the foul-mouthed little girl who was too much like my race-car-driver daddy, remember?"

Sheffield didn't know whether to smile or frown. "What are you doing in Paris?" he asked.

"I came over with my boyfriend. We're going to enter the Paris-to-Dakar race."

Now it was Sheffield who made a wry face. "Are you serious?"

"You better believe it," Chelsea assured him.

"Who's your boyfriend—Parnelli Jones?"

"Funny, Father. His name is Austin Trowbridge. He's the son of Max Trowbridge."

Sheffield's eyebrows rose. Max Trowbridge had been one of the best race-car designers in the world before his untimely death in a plane crash. "Did your boyfriend learn anything from his father?" he asked Chelsea.

"He learned plenty. For two years he's been building a car for the Paris-Dakar Rally. It's finished now. You'd have to see it to believe it: part Land Rover, part Rolls-Royce, part Corvette. We've been test-driving it on the beach at Hilton Head. It'll do one hundred and ten on hard-packed sand, ninety on soft. The engine will cut sixty-six hundred R.P.M.s."

"Where'd you learn about R.P.M.s?" he asked, surprised.

Chelsea shrugged. "I started hanging out at dirt-bike tracks when I was fourteen. Gave mother fits. When I moved up to stock cars, she sent me away to boarding school. It didn't work. One summer at Daytona, I met Austin. We were both kind of lonely. His father had just been killed and mine—" she glanced away "—well, let's just say that Mother's new husband didn't quite know how to cope with Jack Sheffield's youngest."

And I wasn't around, Sheffield thought. He'd been off at Formula One tracks in Belgium and Italy and England, drinking champagne from racing helmets and Ferragamos with four-inch heels, looking for faster cars, getting older with younger women, sometimes crashing. Burning, bleeding, breaking—

"Don't get me wrong," Chelsea said, "I'm not being critical. Everybody's got to live his life the way he thinks best. I'm going my own way with Austin, so I can't fault you for going your own way without me."

But you do, Sheffield thought. He studied his daughter. She had to be nineteen now, maybe twenty—he couldn't even remember when her birthday was. She was plainer than she was pretty—her sister Julie had their mother's good looks, poor Chelsea favored him. Lifeless brown hair, imperfect complexion, a nose that didn't quite fit—yet there was something about her that he suspected could seize and hold a man, if he was the right man. Under the leather jacket she had unzipped was clearly the body of a woman, just as her direct gray eyes were obviously no longer the eyes of a child. There was no way, Sheffield knew, he could ever make up for the years he hadn't been there, but maybe he could do something to lessen the bad taste he'd left. Like talking her out of entering the Paris-Dakar Rally.

"You know, even with the best car in the world the Paris-Dakar run is the worst racing experience imaginable. Eight thousand miles across the Sahara Desert over the roughest terrain on the face of the earth, driving under the most brutal, dangerous, dreadful conditions. It shouldn't be called a rally, it's more like an endurance test. It's three weeks of hell."

"You've done it," she pointed out. "Twice."

"We already know I make mistakes. I didn't win either time, you know."

A touch of fierceness settled in her eyes. "I didn't look you up to get advice on whether to enter—Austin and I have already decided that. I came to ask if you'd go over the route map with us, maybe give us some pointers. But if you're too busy—"

"I'm not too busy," he said. Her words cut him easily.

Chelsea wrote down an address in Montmartre. "It's a rented garage. We've got two rooms above it. The car arrived in Marseilles by freighter this morning. Austin's driving it up tomorrow." She stood and zipped up her jacket. "When can we expect you?"

"Day after tomorrow okay?"

"Swell. See you then." She nodded briefly. "Good night, Father."

"Good night."

As she was walking out, Sheffield realized that he hadn't once spoken her name.

On Thursday, Sheffield took Jane with him to Montmartre, thinking at least he would have somebody on his side if Chelsea and Austin Trowbridge started making him feel guilty. It didn't work. Jane and Chelsea, who were only ten years apart in age, took to each other at once.

"Darling, you look just like him," Jane analyzed. "Same eyes, same chin. But I'm sure your disposition is much better. Jack has absolutely no sense of humor sometimes. If he wasn't so marvelous in bed, I'd leave him."

"He'll probably save you the trouble someday," Chelsea replied. "Father leaves everyone eventually."

"Why don't you two just talk about me like I'm not here?" Sheffield asked irritably.

Austin Trowbridge rescued him. "Like to take a look at the car, Mr. Sheffield?"

"Call me Jack. Yes, I would. I was a great admirer of your father, Austin. He was the best."

"Thanks. I hope I'll be half as good someday."

As soon as Sheffield saw the car, he knew Austin was already half as good, and more. It was an engineering work of art. The body was seamless, shaped not for velocity but for balance, with interchangeable balloon and radial wheels on the same axles, which had double suspension systems to lock in place for either. The steering was flexible from left-hand drive to right, the power train flexible from front to rear, side to side, corner to corner, even to individual wheels. The windshield displaced in one-eighth-inch increments to deflect glare in the daytime, while infrared sealed beams could outline night figures fifty yards distant. A primary petrol tank held one hundred liters of fuel and a backup tank carried two hundred additional liters. Everywhere Sheffield looked—carburetor, generator, distributor, voltage regulator, belt system, radiator, fuel lines—he saw imagination, innovation, improvement. The car was built for reliability and stability, power and pace. Sheffield couldn't have been more impressed.

"It's a beauty, Austin. Your dad would be proud."

"Thanks. I named it after him. I call it the 'Max One.' "

Nice kid, Sheffield thought. He'd probably been very close to his father before the tragedy. Not like Chelsea and himself.

After looking at the Max One, Sheffield took them all to lunch at a cafe on the Boulevard de la Chapelle. While they ate, he talked about the rally.

"There's no competition like it in the world," he said. "It's open to cars, trucks, motorcycles, anything on wheels. There's never any telling who'll be in—or on—the vehicle next to you: it might be a professional driver, a movie star, a millionaire, an Arab king. The run starts in Paris on New Year's Day, goes across France and Spain to Barcelona, crosses the Mediterranean by boat to Africa, then down the length of Algiers, around in a circle of sorts in Niger, across Mali, across Mauritania, up into the Spanish Sahara, then down along the Atlantic coast into Senegal to Dakar. The drivers spend fifteen to eighteen hours a day in their vehicles, then crawl into a sleeping bag for a short, badly needed rest at the end of each day's stage. From three to four hundred vehicles start the run each year. About one in ten will finish."

"We'll finish," Chelsea assured him. "We might even win."

Sheffield shook his head. "You won't win. No matter how good the car is, you don't have the experience to win."

"We don't have to win," Austin conceded. "We just have to finish well—respectably. There are some investors who financed my father from time to time. They've agreed to set me up in my own automotive-design center if I prove myself by building a vehicle that will survive Paris-Dakar. I realize, of course, that the car isn't everything—that's why I wanted to talk to you about the two rallies you ran, to get the benefit of your experience."

"You haven't been racing since you hurt your ankle," Chelsea said. "What have you been doing, Father?"

Sheffield shrugged. "Consulting, training other drivers, conducting track courses—"

"We're willing to pay you for your time to help us," she said.

Sheffield felt himself blush slightly. God, she knew how to cut.

"That won't be necessary," he said. "I'll help you all I can." He wanted to add, "After all, you *are* my daughter," but he didn't.

As he and Jane walked home, she said, "That was nice, Jack, saying you'd help them for nothing."

"Nice, maybe, but not very practical. I could have used the money. I haven't made a franc in fourteen months."

Jane shrugged. "What does that matter? I earn enough for both of us."

It mattered to Sheffield . . .

Sheffield began going to Montmartre every day. In addition to talking to Austin about the route and terrain of the rally, he also helped him make certain modifications on Max One.

"You've got to put locks on the doors, kid. There may be times when both of you have to be away from the car at once and there are places along the route where people will steal you blind."

Holes were drilled and locks placed.

"Paint a line on the steering wheel exactly where your front wheels are aligned straight. That way, when you hit a pothole and bounce, or when you speed off a dune, you can adjust the wheels and land straight. It'll keep you from flipping over. Use luminous paint so you can see the line after dark."

Luminous paint was secured and the line put on.

A lot of Sheffield's advice was practical rather than technical.

"Get rid of those blankets. It gets down to twenty degrees in the Sahara at night. Buy lightweight sleeping bags. And stock up on unsalted nuts, granola bars, high-potency vitamins, caffeine tablets. You'll need a breathing aid, too, for when you land in somebody's dust wake. Those little gauze masks painters use worked fine for me."

Most times when Sheffield went to Montmartre, Chelsea wasn't around. Austin always explained that she was running errands or doing this or that, but Sheffield could tell that he was embarrassed by the excuses. His daughter, Sheffield realized, obviously didn't want to see him any more than necessary. He tried not to let it bother him. Becoming more friendly each visit with Austin helped. The young man didn't repeat Chelsea's offer to pay him for his time, seeming to understand that it was insulting, and for that Sheffield was grateful. No one, not even Jane, knew how serious Sheffield's financial predicament was.

No one except Marcel.

One afternoon when Sheffield got back from Montmartre, Marcel was waiting for him at a table in the cafe. Sheffield had to pass through to get to his rooms. "Jack, my friend," he hailed, as if the encounter were mere chance, "come join me." Snapping his fingers at the waiter, he ordered, "Another glass here."

Sheffield sat down. At a nearby table were two thugs who accompanied the diminutive Marcel everywhere he went. One was white, with a neck like a bucket and a walk like a wrestler's. The other was cafe au lait, very slim, with obscene lips and a reputation for being deadly with a straight razor. After glancing at them, Sheffield drummed his fingers silently on the tablecloth and waited for the question Marcel invariably asked first.

"So, my friend, tell me, how are things with you?"

To which Sheffield, during the past fourteen months anyway, always answered, "The same, Marcel, the same."

Marcel assumed a sad expression. Which was not difficult since he had a serious face, anyway, and had not smiled, some said, since puberty. His round little countenance would have reminded Sheffield of Peter Lorre except that Marcel's eyes were narrow slits that, despite their owner's cordiality, clearly projected danger.

"I was going over my books last week, Jack," the Frenchman said as he poured Sheffield a Pernod, "and I must admit I was a little surprised to see how terrible your luck has run all year. I mean, horse races, dog races, prizefights, soccer matches—you seem to have forgotten what it is to pick a winner. Usually, of course, I don't let anyone run up a balance so large, but I've always had a soft spot for you, Jack."

"You know about the car in Montmartre, don't you?" Sheffield asked pointedly.

"Of course," Marcel replied at once, not at all surprised by the question. "I've known about it since it arrived in Marseilles". Putting a hand on Sheffield's arm, he asked confidentially, "What do you think of it, Jack?"

Sheffield moved his arm by raising the Pernod to his lips. "It's a fine car. One of the best I've ever seen."

"I'm glad you're being honest with me," Marcel said. "I've already had a man get into the garage at night to look at it for me. He was of the same opinion. He says it can win the rally."

Sheffield shook his head. "They're a couple of kids, Marcel. They may finish—they won't win."

Marcel looked at him curiously. "What is a young man like this Austin Trowbridge able to pay you, anyway?"

"I'm not being paid."

Marcel drew back his head incredulously. "A man in your financial situation? You work for nothing?"

"I used to know the kid's father," Sheffield said. Then he added, "I used to know his girlfriend's father, too."

Marcel studied the American for a moment. "Jack, let me be as candid with you as you are being with me. There are perhaps two dozen serious vehicles for which competition licenses have been secured for this year's rally. The car my associates and I are backing is a factory-built Peugeot driven by Georges Ferrand. A French driver in a French car. Call it national pride if you wish, call it practical economics—the fact is that we will have a great deal of money at risk on a Ferrand win. Of the two dozen or so vehicles that will seriously challenge Ferrand, we are convinced he will outdistance all but one of them. That one is the Trowbridge car. It is, as you said, a fine car. We have no statistics on it because it did not run in the optional trials at Cergy-Pontoise. And we know nothing about young Trowbridge himself as a driver: whether he's capable, has the stamina, whether he's *hungry*. The entire entry, car and driver, presents an unknown equation which troubles us."

"I've already told you, Marcel: the car can't win."

The Frenchman fixed him in an unblinking stare. "I want a

guarantee of that, Jack." He produced a small leather notebook. "Your losses currently total forty-nine thousand francs. That's about eight thousand dollars. I'll draw a line through the entire amount for a guarantee that the Max One will not outrun Ferrand's Peugeot."

"You're not concerned whether it finishes?"

"Not in the least." Marcel waved away the consideration. "First place wins, everything else loses."

Sheffield pursed his lips in brief thought, then said, "All right, Marcel. It's a bargain."

Later, in their rooms, Jane said, "I saw you in the cafe with Marcel. You haven't started gambling again, have you?"

"Of course not." It wasn't a lie. He had never stopped.

"What did he want, then?"

"He and his friends are concerned about Austin's car. They know I'm helping the kid. They want a guarantee that the Max One won't ace out the car they're backing."

Jane shook her head in disgust. "What did you tell him?"

"That he had nothing to worry about. Austin's not trying to win, he only wants to finish."

"But you didn't agree to help Marcel in any way?"

"Of course not." Sheffield looked away. He hated lying to Jane, yet he did so regularly about his gambling. This time, though, he swore to himself, he was going to quit—when the slate was wiped clean with Marcel, he had made up his mind not to bet on anything again, not racing, not boxing, not soccer, not even whether the Eiffel Tower was still standing. And he was going to find work, too— some kind of normal job, maybe in an automobile factory, so he could bring in some money, settle down, plan for some kind of future. Jane, after all, was almost thirty; she wouldn't be able to kick her heels above her head in the Crazy Horse chorus line forever.

And his bargain with Marcel wouldn't matter to Austin and Chelsea, he emphasized to his conscience. All Austin had to do to get his design center was finish the race, not win it.

That night while Jane was at the club, Sheffield went to a bookstall on the Left Bank that specialized in racing publications. He purchased an edition of the special Paris-Dakar Rally newspaper that listed each vehicle and how it had performed in the optional trials at Cergy-Pontoise. Back home, he studied the figures on Ferrand's Peugeot and on several other cars which appeared to have the proper ratios of weight-to-speed necessary for a serious run. There was a Mitsubishi that looked very good, a factory-sponsored Mercedes, a Range Rover, a Majorette, a little Russian-built Lada, and a Belgian entry that looked like a VW but was called an Ostend.

For two hours he worked and reworked the stats on a pad of paper, dividing weights by distance, by average speeds, by days, by the hours of daylight which would be available, by the average wind velocity across the Sahara, by the number of stops necessary to adjust tire pressure, by a dozen other factors that a prudent driver needed to consider. When he finished, and compared his final figures with the figures he had estimated for Austin Trowbridge's car, Sheffield reached an unavoidable conclusion: the Max One might—just *might*—actually win the rally.

Sheffield put on his overcoat and went for a walk along the Champs-Elysees and on into the deserted Tuileries. The trees in the park were wintry and forlorn, the grass gray from its nightly frost, and the late-November air thin and cold. Sheffield limped along, his hands deep in his pockets, chin down, brow pinched. Marcel had used the word "guarantee"—and that's what Sheffield had agreed to: a guarantee that the Max One wouldn't win. But the car, Sheffield now knew, was even better than he'd thought: it *could* win. In order to secure his guarantee to Marcel, Sheffield was left with but one alternative. He had to tamper with the car.

Sheffield sat on a bench in the dark and brooded about the weaknesses of character that had brought him to his present point in life. He wondered how much courage it would take to remain on the bench all night and catch pneumonia and freeze to death. The longer he thought about it, the more inviting it seemed. He sat there until he became very cold. But eventually he rose and returned to the rooms above the cafe.

The following week, after conceiving and dismissing a number of plans, Sheffield asked Austin, "What are you going to do about oil?"

"The rally supply truck sells it at the end of every stage, doesn't it? I thought I'd buy it there every night."

"That's okay in the stages where everything goes right," Sheffield pointed out. "But the rally supply truck is only there for a couple of hours and then starts an overnight drive to the next stage. If you get lost or break down or even blow a tire, you could miss the truck and have to run on used oil the entire next day. You need to carry a dozen quarts of your own oil for emergencies."

"I hate to add the weight," Austin said reluctantly.

"I know of a garage that will seal it in plastic bags so you can eliminate the cans," Sheffield said. "That'll save you a couple of pounds."

"You really think it's necessary?"

"I'd do it," Sheffield assured him. Austin finally agreed. "Tell me the grade you want and I'll get it for you," Sheffield said.

Austin wrote down the viscosity numbers of an oil density that was perfect for the Max One's engine. On his way home, Sheffield stopped by the garage of which he had spoken. Before he ordered the bags of oil, he drew a line through some of Austin's numbers and replaced them with figures of his own—lower figures which designated less constancy in the oil's lubricating quality.

Several days later, the garage delivered to the rooms above the cafe a carton containing the bagged oil. Jane was home and accepted the delivery. The garageman gave her a message for Sheffield.

"Our mechanic said to tell Monsieur that if this oil is for a rally vehicle, it should be several grades lighter. This viscosity will reduce engine efficiency as the air temperature drops."

When the garageman left, Jane saw taped to the top bag the slip of paper with the viscosity numbers altered. When Sheffield returned from Montmartre, she asked him about it.

"Yes, I changed them," he said, his tone deliberately casual. "The oil Austin specified was too light."

"Does he know you changed his figures?"

"Sure."

"Are you lying to me, Jack?" She had been exercising and was in black leotards, hands on hips, concern wrinkling her brow.

"Why would I lie about a thing like motor oil?" Sheffield asked.

"I don't know. But I've had an uneasy feeling since I saw you with Marcel. If you're in some kind of trouble, Jack—"

"I'm not in any kind of trouble," he said, forcing a smile.

"You're not trying to get back at Chelsea for the way she's acting toward you, I hope."

"Of course not."

"Jack," she said, "I called Austin and said I thought the garage made a mistake. I read him your numbers and he said they were wrong."

"You *what?*" Sheffield stared at her. The color drained from his face. Jane sighed wearily and sat down.

"I knew it. I could feel it."

Sheffield felt a surge of relief. "You didn't call Austin."

She shook her head. "No." Her expression saddened. "Why are you doing it, Jack?"

Sheffield poured himself a drink and sat down and told her the truth. He told her about the lies of the past fourteen months, the money he'd bet and lost, the circle of desperation that had slowly been closing in on him. "I saw a way out," he pleaded.

"By hurting someone who trusts you?"

"No one will be hurt," he insisted. "Austin doesn't have to win, all he has to do—"

"Is finish," she completed the statement for him. "That's not the point, Jack. It's wrong and you know it."

"Look," he tried to explain, "when Austin uses this heavier oil, all it will do is make the Max One's engine cut down a few R.P.M.s. He probably won't even notice it. The car will slow down maybe a mile an hour."

"It's wrong, Jack. Please don't do it."

"I've *got* to do it," Sheffield asserted. "I've got to get clear of Marcel."

"We can start paying Marcel. I have some savings."

"No." Sheffield stiffened. "I'm tired of being kept by you, Jane."

"*Kept* by me?"

"Yes, kept! You as much as said so yourself when you told my daughter I was marvelous in bed."

"Oh, Jack—surely you don't think Chelsea took me seriously!"

"*I* took you seriously."

Jane stared at him. "If you think you're going to shift onto me some of the responsibility for what you're doing, you're mistaken."

"I don't want you to take any of the responsibility," he made clear, "but I don't expect you to interfere, either. Just mind your own business."

Jane's eyes hardened. "I'll do that."

In the middle of December, the Crazy Horse closed for two weeks and Jane announced that she was going back to England for the holidays. "Dad's getting on," she said, "and I haven't seen my sister's children since they were toddlers. I'd invite you along but I'm afraid it would be awkward, our not being married and all."

"I understand," Sheffield said. "I'll spend Christmas with Chelsea and Austin."

"I rather thought you would." She hesitated. "Are you still determined to go through with your plan?"

"Yes, I am."

Jane shrugged and said no more.

After she was gone, Chelsea seemed to feel guilty about Sheffield being alone for Christmas. "You're welcome to come here," she said. "I'm not the greatest cook, but—"

"Actually, I'm going to England," he lied. "Jane telephoned last night and said she missed me. I'm taking the boat train on Christmas Eve."

What he actually took on Christmas Eve was a long, lonely walk around the gaily decorated Place de la Concorde, past the chic little shops staying open late along Rue Royale. All around him holiday music played, greetings were exchanged, and the usually dour faces of the Parisiennes softened a bit. When his ankle began to ache, Sheffield bought a quart of gin, a loaf of bread, and a small basket of cold meats and cheese, and trudged back to his rooms. The cafe downstairs was closed, so he had to walk around to the alley and go up the back way. A thin, cold drizzle started and he was glad it had waited until he was almost inside.

Putting the food away, he lighted the little space heater, opened the gin, and sat trying to imagine what the future held for him. The telephone rang that night and several times on Christmas Day, but he did not answer it. He was too involved wondering about the rest of his life. And he was afraid it might be a wrong number.

Sheffield finally answered the telephone the following week when he came in one evening and found it ringing. It was Jane.

"I thought I ought to tell you, I'm staying over for a few days longer. There's a new cabaret opening in Piccadilly and they're auditioning dancers the day after New Year's. I'm going to try out. Actually, I've been thinking about working closer to home for a while. Dad's—"

"Yes, I know. Well, then. I wish you luck."

"No hard feelings?"

"Of course not. You?"

"Not any more."

"Let me know how you make out."

"Sure."

After he hung up, Sheffield got the gin out again. He drank until he passed out. It was nearly twelve hours later when he heard an incessant pounding and imagined there was a little man inside his head trying to break out through his left eye with a mallet. When he forced himself to sit upright and engage his senses, he discovered that the pounding was on his door.

He opened the door and Chelsea burst in. "Austin's broken his arm!" she announced, distraught.

On their way to Montmartre, she gave him the details. "We decided to go out for dinner last night, to celebrate finishing the last of the work on the car. We went to a little cafe on rue Lacaur—"

"That's a rough section."

"Tell me about it. On the way home, we were walking past these two guys and one of them made a comment about me. Austin said something back, and before I knew it both of them jumped him. They beat him up badly and one of them used his knee to break Austin's arm like a stick of wood. It was awful!"

In the rooms over the garage, Austin was in bed with an ice compress on his face and his right arm in a cast. "Two years of work down the tubes," he said morosely.

"It could have been worse," Sheffield told him. "People have been shot and stabbed on that street."

"I thought for a minute one of them was going to slice Austin with a razor," Chelsea said.

"A razor?" Sheffield frowned. "What kind of razor?"

"One of those barber's razors. The kind that unfolds like a pocket knife."

"A straight razor," Sheffield said quietly. An image of Marcel's two bodyguards came into focus. The thin one carried a straight razor and the other one looked strong enough to break arms.

Sheffield managed to keep his anger under control while he tried to reconcile Austin and Chelsea to the fact that it wasn't the end of the rally for them. He gave Austin the names of four drivers he knew who weren't signed up for Paris-Dakar this year and might consider an offer to make the run. Two were here in Paris, one was in Zurich, and the other at his home in Parma. "Call them and see what you can do," he said. "I'll go back to my place and see if I can think of any others."

As soon as he left the garage, he went to a telephone kiosk around the corner and called Marcel's office.

"You son of a bitch," he said when the Frenchman came on the line. "We had an arrangement that *I* was to keep Austin Trowbridge from winning."

"That is not precisely correct," Marcel said. "You agreed to take care of the *car*. I decided, because of the amount of money at risk, that it would be best to protect your guarantee with an additional guarantee."

"That wasn't necessary, you son of a bitch!"

"That's twice you've called me that," Marcel said, his tone icing. "I've overlooked it up to now because I know you're angry. Please refrain from doing it again, however. For your information—" his voice broke slightly "—my mother was a saint."

"I don't think you had a mother," Sheffield said coldly. "I think you crawled up out of a sewer!" Slamming down the receiver, he left the kiosk and stalked across the street to a bar. He had a quick drink to calm himself down, then another, which he drank more slowly as he tried to decide what to do. There was no way he could turn in Marcel's thugs without admitting his own complicity to Austin and Chelsea. And it was Marcel he wanted to get even with. But Marcel was always protected. How the hell did you take revenge on someone with the protection he had?

As Sheffield worried it over, the bartender brought him change from the banknote with which he'd paid for his drinks. Sheffield stared at the francs on the bar and suddenly thought: *Of course.* You didn't hurt a man like Marcel physically, you hurt him financially.

Leaving the second drink unfinished, something Sheffield hadn't done in years, he left the bar and hurried back to the rooms over the garage. Austin and Chelsea were at the telephone.

"The two drivers here turned us down," Austin said. "I'm about to call the one in Zurich."

"Forget it," Sheffield said flatly. "I'm driving the Max One for you . . ."

It wasn't yet dawn in the Place d'Armes where the race was to start, but a thousand portable spotlights created an artificial daylight that illuminated the four lines of vehicles in eerie silver light. A hundred thousand spectators jammed the early-morning boulevard on each side, waving flags, signs, and balloons, cheering select cars and select drivers, the women throwing and sometimes personally delivering kisses, the men reaching past the lines of gendarmes to slap fenders and shout, *"Bon courage!"*

Young girls, the kind who pursue rock stars, walked the lines seeking autographs and more while their younger brothers and sisters followed them throwing confetti. Everyone had to shout to be heard in the general din.

The Max One was in 182nd starting position, which put it in the forty-sixth row, the second car from the inside. Chelsea, in a racing suit, stood with Austin's good arm around her, both looking with great concern at Jack as he wound extra last-minute tape over the boot around his weak ankle.

"Are you absolutely sure about this, Jack?" the young designer asked. "It's not worth further damage to your ankle."

"I'm positive," Sheffield said. "Anyway, we'll be using Chelsea's feet whenever we can." Looking up, he grinned. "You just be in Dakar to receive the trophy."

"That trophy will be yours, Jack."

"The prize money will be mine," Sheffield corrected. "The trophy will be yours."

There was a sudden roar from the crowd and a voice announced through static in the loudspeaker that the first row of four vehicles had been waved to a start. The rally had begun.

"Kiss him goodbye and get in," Sheffield said, shaking hands with Austin, then leaving the couple alone for the moments they had left.

Presently father and daughter were side by side, buckled and harnessed in, adrenaline rushing, their bodies vibrating from the revving engine, their eyes fixed on the white-coated officials who moved down the line and with a brusque nod and a wave started each row of four vehicles five seconds apart.

Sheffield grinned over at Chelsea. "I wonder what your mother would say if she could see us now?"

"I know exactly what she'd say: 'Birds of a feather.'"

"Well, maybe we are," Sheffield said.

"Let's don't get sentimental, Father," Chelsea replied. "Driving together from Paris to Dakar doesn't make a relationship."

Looking at her determined young face, Sheffield nodded. "Whatever you say, kid."

A moment later, they were waved away from the starting line.

From Paris to Barcelona would have been 850 kilometers if the road had been straight. But it wasn't. It wound through Loiret, Cher, Creuse, Correze, Cantal, and more—as if the route had been designed by an aimless schoolboy on a bicycle. Nearly all the way, the roadsides were lined with cheering, waving, kiss-throwing well-wishers shouting, *"Bonne chance!"* From time to time, flowers were thrown into the cars as they bunched up in a village and were forced to slow down. Farther south, cups of *vin ordinaire,* slices of cheese, and hunks of bread were shared. The farther away from Paris one got, the more relaxed and cheerful were the French people.

Sheffield and Chelsea didn't talk much during the trip south. She was already missing Austin and Sheffield was concentrating on finding ways to relieve pressure on his weak ankle by holding his foot in various positions. These preoccupations and the increasingly beautiful French countryside kept them both silently contemplative. The Paris-to-Barcelona stage of the rally was a liaison—a controlled section of the route in which all positions remained as they had started—so it wasn't necessary to speed or try to pass. A few vehicles invariably broke down the first day, but for the most part it was little more than a tourist outing. The real race would not begin until they reached Africa.

It was after dark when they crossed the Spanish border and well into the late Spanish dinner hour when they reached Barcelona. As the French had done, the Spaniards lined the streets to cheer on the smiling, still fresh drivers in their shiny, unbattered vehicles. Because of the crowds, and the absence of adequate crowd control, the great caterpillar of vehicles inched its way down to the dock, where the Spanish ferry that would take them to Algiers waited. It was midnight when Sheffield and Chelsea finally drove onto the quay, had their papers examined, and boarded the boat. The first day, eighteen and a half hours long, was over.

Crossing the Mediterranean, Sheffield and Chelsea got some rest and nourishment and met some of the other drivers. Sheffield was well known by most of them already. (He had asked Chelsea ahead of time how she wanted to be introduced. "I don't have to say I'm your father if you'd rather I didn't," he told her. She had shrugged. "It makes no difference to me. Everyone knows we don't choose our parents." "Or our children," Sheffield added.) He introduced her simply as Chelsea and told everyone she was the vehicle designer's girlfriend.

Ferrand, the French driver, Vera Kursk, a shapely but formidable-looking Russian woman, and Alf Zeebrug, a Belgian, all expressed great interest in the Max One's structural configuration. They were, Sheffield remembered from his computations, the three favorites to win the rally: Ferrand in his Peugeot, Vera Kursk in a Lada, Zeebrug in the Volkswagen lookalike called an Ostend.

As they studied the Max One, Ferrand winked at Sheffield and said, "So, you've brought in—what do you Americans call it, a ringer?"

Vera nodded her head knowingly. "I see why you passed up the trial races, Jack. Foxy."

"Let us look under the hood, Jack," pressed Zeebrug, knowing Sheffield wouldn't.

In the end, Ferrand spoke for them all when he said, "Welcome back, Jack. It's good to race with you again." Vera gave him a more-than-friendly kiss on the lips.

Later Chelsea said, "They all seem like nice people."

"They are," Sheffield said. "They're here for the race, nothing else: no politics, no nationalism, no petty jealousies. Just the race." Ferrand, Sheffield was convinced, knew nothing about Marcel's machinations in favor of the Peugeot. Had he known, Ferrand—an honorable man and an honest competitor—would have withdrawn and probably sought out Marcel for physical punishment.

Another comment Chelsea made just before they docked was, "They all seem to like and respect you, Father."

"There are some quarters in which I'm not a pariah," he replied. "Believe it or not."

In Africa, the first stage was Algiers to Ghardaia. Sheffield stuck a handprinted list to the dashboard between them. It read:

> Ferrand-Peugeot
> Kursk-Lada
> Zeebrug-Ostend
> Sakai-Mitsubishi
> Gordon-Range Rover
> Smythe-Majorette

"These are the drivers and cars to beat," he told Chelsea. "I had a Mercedes on the list, too, but the driver was drinking too much on the ferry and bought a bottle of scotch to take with him when we docked. I don't think we'll have to worry about him."

Chelsea looked at him curiously. "I thought we were only in this to finish, so that Austin can get his design center."

Sheffield fixed her in a flat stare. "I'm a racer, kid. I enter races to *win*. This one is no exception. If you don't want to go along with that, you can get off here."

Chelsea shook her head determinedly. "Not on your life."

Sheffield had to look away so she wouldn't see his pleased smile.

During the first stage, it seemed to Chelsea that every car, truck, and motorcycle in the rally was passing them. "Why aren't we going faster?" she demanded.

"It's not necessary right now," Sheffield told her. "All these people passing us are the showboats—rich little boys and girls with expensive little toys. They run too fast too quickly. Most of them will burn up their engines before we get out of Algeria. Look over there—"

Chelsea looked where he indicated and saw Ferrand, Vera Kursk, and the other experienced drivers cruising along at moderate speed just as Sheffield was doing. "I guess I've got a lot to learn," she said.

At Ghardaia, their sleeping bags spread like spokes around a desert campfire, the drivers discussed the day. "Let's see," Zeebrug calculated, "three hundred forty-four vehicles started and so far one hundred eighteen have dropped out."

"Good numbers," Ferrand said.

Vera Kursk smiled. "This could turn into a race instead of a herd."

Chelsea noticed that the Russian woman and Sheffield shared a little evening brandy from the same cup and that earlier, when the sleeping bags were spread, Vera had positioned hers fairly close to Sheffield's. Commie slut, she thought. When no one was paying any attention, Chelsea moved her own sleeping bag between them.

It took a week to get out of Algeria—a week in which Sheffield and the other experienced drivers continued to drive at reasonable, safe speeds that were easy on their engines, tires, and the bodies of both car and driver. All along the route, vehicles were dropping out—throwing pistons, getting stuck in sand, blowing too many tires, sliding off soft shoulders into gullies, dropping transmissions, or the exhausted drivers simply giving up. The Mercedes quit the second day—its driver, as Sheffield had predicted, drinking too much liquor for the heat he had to endure and the stamina

247

required to drive. A surprise dropout was the Mitsubishi. Driven by the Japanese speed-racer Sakai, it had hit a sand-concealed rock and broken its front axle. "One down, five to go," Sheffield said, drawing a line through Sakai's name on the dashboard list.

By the time they crossed into Niger, an additional sixty-three vehicles had dropped out. "That leaves one hundred sixty-three in," said Smythe, the Englishman driving the Majorette, when they camped that night. He was feeling good about the dropouts. At noon the next day, he joined them when the Majorette burned up its gearbox.

"Two down, four to go," Sheffield told Chelsea, and drew another line.

After camping one night in Chirfa, Chelsea noticed the next morning that Sheffield and Ferrand and the others shook hands all around and wished each other good luck. "What was that all about?" she asked.

"Everyone will be camping alone from now on," he said. "The socializing is over." Sheffield pointed toward a band of haze on the horizon. "We go into the Tenere Desert today. Now we start racing."

The terrain they encountered that day was hell on a back burner. The Max One was in ashlike sand up to its axles, plowing along like a man walking against a gale wind. The stink of the desert decay was unexpected and appalling to Chelsea. She gagged repeatedly. Huge white rats the size of rabbits leaped at the car windows. This stage of the rally that crossed the Tenere was a nightmare in glaring daylight no newcomer was ever prepared for.

Camped alone that night in some rocks above the desert floor, Chelsea saw Sheffield massaging his foot. "How's the ankle?" she asked.

"Just a little stiff. It'll be okay."

"Let's switch places tomorrow," she suggested. "I'll drive and you relieve." Up to then, Sheffield had done eighty percent of the driving. "Tomorrow," Sheffield told her, "we go over the Azbine Plain. It's like driving across a huge corrugated roof."

"Let me drive," she said quietly. "I can manage it."

He let her drive—and she took them across the rough terrain like a pilgrim determined to get to Mecca. Along the way, they saw Zeebrug lying at the side of the road, a rally first-aid team inflating a splint on his leg. The Ostend was nearby, upside down in a ditch, one wheel gone.

"Three and three," Sheffield said. He handed Chelsea the marker and she crossed off Zeebrug's name.

Into the second week of the race, both Jack and Chelsea began to feel the strain of the collective pressures: the usually unheated, quickly eaten food that wreaked havoc with their digestion, the constant jarring and jolting of the car that pummeled their bodies, the freezing nights sleeping on the ground, the scorching, glaring sun by day, the sand and dirt in their mouths, ears, eyes, noses, the constant headaches and relentless fatigue that the short rests could not remedy. Depression set in, underscored by the begging of poverty-stricken Africans everywhere they stopped.

"Cadeau," the black children pleaded as Sheffield adjusted his tire pressure. *"Cadeau,"* they whined as Chelsea filled the radiator from a village stream.

"We have no gifts," Sheffield told them in English, in French, and by a firm shaking of his head. "Try to ignore them," he advised Chelsea, and she did try, but her eyes remained moist. As did his.

Just over the border in Mali, their physical and mental distress was displaced in priority and urgency by problems the Max One began to develop. A fuel line cracked and split, and they lost considerable petrol before Chelsea noticed the trail it was leaving behind them and they stopped to repair it. The lost fuel had to be replaced at a township pump at exorbitant cost. Later the same day, for no apparent reason, a center section of the windshield bubbled and cracked. Sheffield patched it with some of the tape he had brought for his ankle. The very next day, the odometer cable snapped and they were unable to monitor their distance to the end of the stage.

"Austin's damned car," Chelsea seethed, "is falling apart."

"It's holding up better than most." Sheffield bobbed his chin at two cars, two trucks, and a motorcycle that had dropped out at the side of the road. By then, seventy-one more vehicles had quit the rally, leaving ninety-two still in.

Near Timbuktu, Sheffield and Chelsea happened on a small water pond that no one else seemed to notice. Behind a high rise, it had a few trees, some scrub, and even a patch of Gobi grass. "We've died and gone to heaven," Chelsea said when she saw the water. She began undressing. "I hope you're not modest."

"Not if you aren't."

They took their first bath in two weeks, and when they were clean they rubbed salve on their hips and shoulders where the Max One's seatbelts and harnesses had rubbed the skin raw.

"Mother never went with you when you raced, did she?" Chelsea asked reflectively.

"No."

"Who took care of you when you got hurt?"

"Whoever was around," Sheffield said. He looked off at the distance.

Chelsea patted his head maternally. "If you get hurt in this race, *I'll* take care of you," she assured him. Then she turned away to dress, as if her words embarrassed her where her nakedness had not.

After Mali, they crossed into Mauritania. The topography of the route seemed to change every day. One stage would be a mazelike, twisting and turning trail along a dry riverbed, in turn sandy and dusty, then suddenly muddy where an unexpected patch of water appeared. Then they would encounter a long, miserable stage of deep ruts and vicious potholes, then a log-and-rock-strewn track that shook their teeth and vibrated agonizingly in Sheffield's weak ankle.

With each kilometer, his pain grew more intense. During the day he swallowed codeine tablets. At night Chelsea put wet compresses on his ankle and massaged his foot. Those days they came to a stage that was open, flat straightaway, Chelsea did the driving and Sheffield enjoyed temporary respite from the pain.

Nearly every day they caught glimpses of Ferrand, Vera Kursk, and the Australian Gordon in his Range Rover. There were no smiles, waves, or shouted greetings now—just grim nods that said, So you're still in it, are you? Well, so am I.

Into the third grueling week, the pain, fatigue, and depression evolved into recriminations. "How in hell did I let myself get into this mess anyway?" Sheffield asked as he untaped his swollen ankle one night. "I don't owe Austin Trowbridge *or* you anything."

"How did *you* get into it!" Chelsea shot back. "How did *I* get into it! I'm making the same damned mistake my mother made—getting mixed up with a man who thinks speed is some kind of religion."

"I could be back in Paris going to old movies," Sheffield lamented, "eating sausages with homemade mustard, drinking gin."

"And I could be in Philadelphia going to club meetings and playing tennis with your *other* daughter."

They caught each other's eyes in the light of the campfire and both smiled sheepishly. Chelsea came over and kneeled next to her father. "I'll do that," she said, and tended to his ankle.

Later, when he got into his sleeping bag and she was preparing to stand the first two-hour watch, flare gun at the ready, she looked very frankly at him. "You know," she said, her voice slightly hoarse from the dryness, "if we weren't blood relatives, I might find myself attracted to you."

Sheffield stayed awake most of the two hours he should have been sleeping. This was one race he would be very glad to have over—for more reasons than his swollen ankle.

From Mauritania, the route cut north across the border of the Spanish Sahara for a hundred or so kilometers of hot sand, between the wells of Tichia in the east and Bir Ganduz in the west. During that stage, with seventy-one vehicles of the original 344 still in the race, there was much jockeying for position, much cutting in, out, and around, much risky driving on soft shoulders, and much blind speeding as the dust wake of the vehicle in front reduced visibility to the length of your hood. It was a dangerous stage, driven with goggles and mouth masks, clenched jaws, white knuckles, tight sphincters, and the pedal to the metal, no quarter asked, none given.

In a one-on-one, side-by-side dash to be the first into a single lane between two enormous dunes, Chelsea at the wheel of the Max One and Gordon in his Range Rover were dead even on a thousand-yard straightaway, both pushing their vehicles to the limit, when Gordon glanced over at the Max One and smiled in his helmet at the sight of the girl, not the man, doing the driving. He had the audacity to take one hand off the wheel and wave goodbye as he inched ahead.

"You bastard," Chelsea muttered and juiced the Max One's engine by letting up on the accelerator two inches, then stomping down on it, jolting the automatic transmission into its highest gear and shooting the car forward as if catapulted. With inches to spare, she sliced in front of Gordon at the point where the dunes came together, surprising him so that he swerved, went up an embankment, and immediately slid back down, burying the Range Rover's rear end in five feet of what the nomad Arabs, translated, called "slip sand": grains that, although dry, held like wet quicksand. The Australian would, Sheffield knew, be stuck for hours, and was effectively out of the race as far as finishing up front was concerned.

"Nice work, kid," he said. Now they had only Ferrand and Vera Kursk with whom to contend.

That night they camped along with the other remaining drivers around the oasis well at Bir Ganduz. When the rally starts for the day were announced, they learned that seventeen more vehicles had fallen by the wayside on the Spanish Sahara stage, leaving fifty-four competitors: thirty-eight cars, ten trucks, and six motorcycles. Ferrand was in the lead position, one of the cyclists second, Vera Kursk third, one of the trucks fourth, another cyclist fifth, and the Max One sixth.

"Are you disappointed we aren't doing better?" Chelsea asked as they changed oil and air filters.

Sheffield shook his head. "We can pass both cyclists and the truck any time we want to. And probably will, tomorrow. It'll come down to Ferrand, Vera, and us."

"Do you think we can beat them?"

Sheffield smiled devilishly. "If we don't, we'll scare hell out of them." For a moment then he became very quiet. Presently he handed Chelsea a plastic jar. "Hustle over to the control truck and get us some distilled water."

"The battery wells aren't low—I just checked them."

"I want some extra, anyway, just in case. Go on."

As soon as she was out of sight, Sheffield reached into the car and got the flare gun. Turning to a stand of trees in deep shadows twenty feet from the car, he said, "Whoever's in there has got ten seconds to step out where I can see you or I'll light you up like the Arch of Triumph."

From out of the darkness stepped Marcel's two thugs. The one who carried a razor had a sneer on his gaunt brown face. The one with the bucket neck simply looked angry as usual. "We bring greetings from Marcel," said the thin one. "He said to tell you he is willing to be reasonable. Forget what has gone before. You and he will start fresh. He will cancel your debt and give you one hundred thousand francs if you do not overtake Ferrand."

"No deal," Sheffield replied flatly.

"I am authorized to go to a hundred and fifty thousand francs. That is twenty-five thousand dollars—"

"I can add. No deal."

The other man pointed a threatening finger. "To doublecross Marcel is not very smart—"

Sheffield cocked the flare gun. "You're the one who broke my friend's arm, aren't you? How'd you like to have a multicolored face?"

"No need for that," the thin one said quickly, holding up both hands. "We delivered Marcel's message, we have your answer. We'll go now."

"If I see you again," Sheffield warned them, "I'll tell the other drivers about you. They won't like what they hear. You'll end up either in a sandy grave or a Senegalese prison. I don't know which would be worse."

"Perhaps the young lady has an opinion," the thin man said, bobbing his chin toward the Max One, off to the side of Sheffield. It was the oldest ruse in the world, but Sheffield fell for it. He looked over to his left, and when he did the thin man leaped forward with enough speed and agility to knock the flare gun to the ground before Sheffield could resist. Then the man with the bucket neck was there, shoving him roughly until his back was against the car and driving a boot-toe hard against his painful ankle. Sheffield groaned and started to fall, but the other man held him up long enough to deliver a second brutal kick.

"That's all!" his partner said urgently. "Come on!"

They were gone, leaving Sheffield sitting on the sand clutching his ankle, tears of pain cutting lines on his dry cheeks, when Chelsea got back. She ran over to him. "My God, what happened?"

"I must had stepped in a hole. It's bad—"

The ankle swelled to thrice its normal size. For several hours, Chelsea made trips to and from the public well to draw cold water for compresses. They didn't help. By morning, Sheffield couldn't put any weight at all on the foot.

"That does it, I guess," he said resignedly. "Ferrand and Vera will have to fight it out. But at least Austin will get his design center; you can drive well enough for us to finish."

"I can drive well enough for us to win," Chelsea said. She was packing up their camp. "I proved that yesterday."

"Yesterday was on a flat desert straightaway. From here down the coast to Dakar are narrow, winding roads full of tricky curves, blind spots, loose gravel."

"I can handle it."

"You don't understand," Jack said, with the patience of a parent, "this is the final lap. This is for all the marbles—this is what the last twenty days of hell have been all about. These people still in the run are serious competitors—"

"I'm serious, too," Chelsea asserted. "I'm a racer, and I'm in this run to win. If you can't accept that, if you don't want to drive with me, drop off here."

Sheffield stared incredulously at her. "You're crazy, kid. Ferrand, Vera, and the others will run you off a cliff into the Atlantic Ocean if they have to."

"They can try." She stowed their belongings on the rear deck and closed the hatchback. "You staying here?"

"Not on your life," Sheffield growled. He hopped over to the car. The passenger side.

The last lap into Dakar was a war on wheels. All caution was left behind on the Spanish Sahara. This was the heavyweight championship, the World Series, and the Kentucky Derby. No one who got this far would give an inch of track. Anything gained had to be taken.

As soon as the stage started, the Max One dropped back to eight, losing two positions as a pair of motorcycles outdistanced them. Chelsea cursed but Sheffield told her not to worry about it. "This is a good stretch for cycles. We'll probably be passed by a few more. They start falling back when we reach Akreidil; the track softens there and they can't maneuver well. Keep your speed at a steady ninety."

Chelsea glanced over. "I don't want advice on how to finish, just how to win."

"That's what you're going to get," Sheffield assured her. "You do the driving. I'll do the navigating. Deal?"

Chelsea nodded curtly. "Deal."

Sheffield tore the piece of paper from the dash and looked at the names of Ferrand and Vera Kursk. Crumbling it, he tossed it out the window.

"Litterbug," she said.

"Shut up and drive, Chelsea."

"Yes, Daddy."

They exchanged quick smiles, then grimly turned their attention back to the track.

By midmorning the Max One was back to eleventh, but Ferrand and Vera had also fallen behind, everyone being outrun by the six daredevil cyclists still in the rally. This was their moment of glory and they knew it. They would lead the last lap of the run for three magnificent hours, then—as Sheffield had predicted—start falling behind at Akreidil. From that point on, the four-wheeled vehicles overtook and passed them one by one. Ferrand moved back into first place, Vera pressed into second, and the Max One held fourth behind a modified Toyota truck. They were all sometimes mere feet apart on the dangerous track along the Mauritanian coast.

"Blind spot," Sheffield would say as they negotiated weird hairpin turns. "Hug in," he instructed when he wanted Chelsea to keep tight to the inside of the track. "Let up," he said to slow down, "Punch it" to speed up, "Drop one" to go into a lower gear as he saw Ferrand's car suddenly nose up a grade ahead.

Two of the nine trucks behind them started crowding the track south of Mederdra, taking turns ramming into the Max One's rear bumper at ninety k.p.h. "Get ready to brake," Sheffield said. Watching in a sideview mirror, he waited for exactly the right second, then yelled, "Brake!" Chelsea hit the brake and felt a jolt as one of the trucks ricocheted off the Max One's rear fender and shot across the rocky beach into the surf.

"The other one's passed us!" Chelsea shouted.

"I wanted it to," Sheffield said. "Watch."

The truck that had displaced them in fourth place quickly drew up and challenged the truck in third. For sixty kilometers they jockeyed and swerved and slammed sides trying to assert superiority. One kilometer in front of them, Ferrand and Vera held the two lead positions; behind them, Sheffield and Chelsea kept everyone else in back of the Max One to let the trucks fight it out. Finally, on the Senegal border, the crowding truck finally forced number three off the track and moved up to take its place.

"Okay!" Sheffield yelled at Chelsea. "His body's tired but his brain is happy because he just won. The two aren't working together right now. Punch it!"

Chelsea gunned the Max One and in seconds laid it right next to the victorious truck. The driver looked over, surprised. Sheffield smiled at him. Then Sheffield put his hand over Chelsea's and jerked the steering wheel sharply. The Max One leaped to the right, the truck swerved to avoid being hit, the Max One crossed the entire track, and the truck spun around and went backward into a ditch.

"Now let's go after Vera," Sheffield said.

"With pleasure," Chelsea replied.

It became a three-car race. For more than four hundred kilometers, speeding inland along Senegal's gently undulating sandy-clay plains, the Peugeot, the Lada, and the Max One vied for position. Along straightaways, it became clear that Austin Trowbridge's car was superior in speed to both the French and Russian vehicles. Chelsea caught up with and passed them both. "Yeeee*oh!*" she yelled as she sped into the lead.

"Don't open the champagne yet," Sheffield said.

When the straightaway ended and they once again encountered a stretch of the great continental dunes, the experienced drivers again outmaneuvered and outdistanced the Max One.

"What am I doing wrong?" Chelsea pleaded.

"Hanging out with race-car drivers."

"That's not what I mean!" she stormed, her sense of humor lost in the face of her frustration.

"We'll be on a sandstone flat when we cross the Saloum River," Sheffield calmed her. "You'll have a chance to take the lead again there."

When they reached the flat, Chelsea quickly caught up with Vera Kursk and passed her, and was pressing Ferrand for first place when the accident happened. A pack of hyenas, perhaps a dozen, suddenly ran in front of the Peugeot. Seasoned professional that he was, Ferrand did not swerve an inch as he felt the impact of his grille on the animals he hit and the rumble of his tires on those he ran over. Then one of the hyenas was spun up into the wheel well and, in a mangle of flesh and blood, jammed the axle. Ferrand's front wheels locked and his vehicle flipped end over end, landing a hundred feet out on the flats, bursting into flames.

"Stop the car!" Sheffield ordered, and Chelsea skidded to a halt on the shoulder. They unharnessed and leaped out, Sheffield grabbing the portable fire extinguisher, Chelsea helping him to balance upright on his swollen ankle. As they ran, hobbling, toward the burning car, they became aware that the Lada had also stopped and Vera Kursk was getting out.

At the fiery Peugeot, Sheffield handed Chelsea the extinguisher. "Start spraying the driver's door!" Chelsea pointed the red cylinder and shot a burst of Halon up and down the door. It immediately smothered the flames on that side and Sheffield was able to reach through the window, unstrap Ferrand, and drag him out of the car. Sheffield and Chelsea each took a hand and, Sheffield limping agonizingly, dragged the unconscious man far enough away so that when the Peugeot exploded none of them were hurt.

From overhead came the sound of a rotor. Looking up, Sheffield and Chelsea saw a rally control helicopter surveying a place to land. Paramedics wearing Red Cross armbands were in an open hatch waiting for touchdown.

"They'll take care of him," Sheffield said. He stood up, holding onto Chelsea for support, and they looked across the flat at the Max One and the Lada parked side by side. Vera Kursk was beside the Lada, peering down the track, where several kilometers back came the surviving vehicles. Smiling, she threw Sheffield and Chelsea a wave and quickly got into her car. Chelsea started running, dragging Sheffield with her. "The bitch!" she said.

"I'd do the same thing in her place," Sheffield groaned.

By the time they were harnessed back into the Max One, the Lada was half a kilometer ahead and the rest of the pack was moving up behind them very quickly. "We're almost to Dakar," Sheffield told his daughter. "If you want to win, you'll have to catch her."

Chelsea got back on the track and shot the car forward like a bullet. Into the African farming communities she sped, watching for animals, people, other vehicles, always keeping the Lada in sight. "Am I gaining on her, do you think?" she asked.

"Not yet."

Through the farmland, into the nearer outskirts, past larger villages, a soap factory, a shoe factory. "Am I gaining?" she shouted.

"Not yet."

Past a power station, a cotton mill, small handicraft shops at the side of the road, a huge open-air market, increasing lines of spectators in marvelously colored native garb. "Am I gaining?"

"Not yet."

"God*damn!*"

Then into the city of Dakar itself and on to the far end of Gann Boulevard, a wide, tree-lined thoroughfare roped off a mere one hour earlier, when the control aircraft advised the city that the first of the rally vehicles was approaching. The boulevard led straight to the finish line in the Place de l'Independence. The Lada was still half a kilometer ahead. "Punch it!" Sheffield yelled. He beat his fist on the dashboard. "Punch it! Punch it!"

Chelsea punched it.

The Max One drew up dead even on the right side of the Lada. The two women exchanged quick, appraising glances, saw only unyielding determination in the other, and, as if choreographed, both leaned into their steering wheels and tried to punch their accelerators through the floorboards. "Come *on!*" Chelsea muttered through her clenched teeth.

The Max One pulled forward an inch. Then two. Then three. Vera Kursk glanced over again, desperation in her eyes. Sheffield yelled, "All right!"

The cars sped down to the finish line next to the war memorial in the great plaza. Thousands cheered them on from a vast crowd that was but a blur of color to the drivers. Stretched across the end of the boulevard, a great banner with FINIS lettered on it fluttered in the breeze. The Max One was less than a car-length ahead, the Lada's windshield even with the American vehicle's rear bumper. Then Vera punched the Lada.

"She's pulling up!" Sheffield cried.

Chelsea saw Vera's face moving closer in the sideview mirror. In seconds, the Russian woman was next to her again. Biting down hard enough on her bottom lip to draw blood, Chelsea punched the Max One again.

The Max One crossed the finish line one and a half seconds ahead of the Lada.

At the banquet that night in the Saint Louis Hotel, Chelsea and Vera Kursk hugged each other and Austin Trowbridge read everyone a cable he had received congratulating him on the Max One and advising him that a bank account had been opened for one million dollars to start the Trowbridge Automotive Design Center. "I'd like you to come back to the States and be my partner," the young man told Sheffield. "Between the two of us, we can come up with cars nobody's ever imagined."

"I'll think about it, kid," Sheffield promised.

At midnight, Sheffield rode with Chelsea and Austin in a taxi out to Grand Dakar Airport, where they watched the Max One being rolled into the cargo hold of a Boeing 747 bound for

Casablanca and New York. The young couple had seats in the passenger section of the same plane.

"Austin and I are going to be married when we get home," Chelsea told Sheffield. Austin had gone ahead, giving them time to say good-bye. "And we're going to start having babies. The first boy we have, I'm naming Jack. After a guy I recently met."

"Do yourself a favor," Sheffield said. "Raise him to be a doctor."

She shook her head. "Not on your life." She kissed him on the cheek. "Bye, Daddy."

"See you, kid."

Sheffield watched the plane rumble down the runway and climb into the starry African sky. Then he sighed and limped slowly off the observation deck and back into the terminal. When he reached the glass exit doors, he was met by the familiar face he'd been expecting.

"Hello, Marcel."

The Frenchman's two thugs were standing nearby.

"The Max One was pressing Ferrand when he crashed," Marcel accused. "You were racing to win."

"I always race to win," Sheffield replied evenly.

"Do you think you can get away with doublecrossing me?" The Frenchman's eyes were narrowed and dangerous.

Sheffield merely shrugged. "What are you going to do, Marcel, kill me?" He cocked his head in the best John Garfield tradition. "Everybody dies," he said arrogantly. And pushing through the doors, he walked painfully out into the Senegalese night.

259

EDWARD GORMAN

"The Reason Why"

Ed Gorman was born in Cedar Rapids, Iowa on November 29, 1941. He attended Coe College and worked in advertising prior to publishing his first novel **Rough Cut** *in 1985. That book introduced ex-cop and part-time actor Jack Dwyer who has appeared in several novels since then. One of the best American authors to enter the mystery field during the 1980s, Gorman also writes hard-hitting western and horror novels, edits numerous anthologies and is the founder of* **Mystery Scene** *magazine, now edited by his son.*

Gorman has created three other series characters, a private eye named Walsh, a movie critic named Tobin, and a western bounty hunter named Leo Guild. A short story "Turn Away" (1987) was winner of the PWA Shamus Award for best of the year and "Prisoners" (1990) was an Edgar nominee.

Ed Gorman's crime fiction has been collected in **Prisoners and Other Stories** *(1992),* **Dark Whispers and Other Stories** *(1993),* **Cages** *(1995), and* **Moonchasers and Other Stories** *(1996). His westerns are collected in* **Gunslinger** *(1995). "The Reason Why" was first published in* **Criminal Elements** *and reprinted in* **The Mammoth Book of Private Eye Stories, The Year's Best Mystery and Suspense Stories - 1989** *and* **Under the Gun**.

The Reason Why

by Edward Gorman

I'm scared."

"This was your idea, Karen."

"You scared?"

"No."

"You bastard."

"Because I'm not scared I'm a bastard?"

"You not being scared means you don't believe me."

"Well."

"See. I knew it."

"What?"

"Just the way you said 'Well.' You bastard."

I sighed and looked out at the big red brick building that sprawled over a quarter mile of spring grass turned silver by a fat June moon. Twenty-five years ago a 1950 Ford fastback had sat in the adjacent parking lot. Mine for two summers of grocery store work.

We were sitting in her car, a Volvo she'd cadged from her last marriage settlement, number four if you're interested, and sharing a pint of bourbon the way we used to in high school when we'd been more than friends but never quite lovers.

The occasion tonight was our twenty-fifth class reunion. But there was another occasion, too. In our senior year a boy named Michael Brandon had jumped off a steep clay cliff called Pierce Point to his death on the winding river road below. Suicide. That, anyway, had been the official version.

A month ago Karen Lane (she had gone back to her maiden

name these days, the Karen Lane-Cummings-Todd-Browne-LeMay getting a tad too long) had called to see if I wanted to go to dinner and I said yes, if I could bring Donna along, but then Donna surprised me by saying she didn't care to go along, that by now we should be at the point in our relationship where we trusted each other ("God, Dwyer, I don't even look at other men, not for very long anyway, you know?"), and Karen and I had had dinner and she'd had many drinks, enough that I saw she had a problem, and then she'd told me about something that had troubled her for a long time . . .

In senior year she'd gone to a party and gotten sick on wine and stumbled out to somebody's backyard to throw up and it was there she'd overheard the three boys talking. They were earnestly discussing what had happened to Michael Brandon the previous week and they were even more earnestly discussing what would happen to them if "anybody ever really found out the truth."

"It's bothered me all these years," she'd said over dinner a month earlier. "They murdered him and they got away with it."

"Why didn't you tell the police?"

"I didn't think they'd believe me."

"Why not?"

She shrugged and put her lovely little face down, dark hair covering her features. Whenever she put her face down that way it meant that she didn't want to tell you a lie so she'd just as soon talk about something else.

"Why not, Karen?"

"Because of where we came from. The Highlands."

The Highlands is an area that used to ring the iron foundries and factories of this city. Way before pollution became a fashionable concern, you could stand on your front porch and see a peculiarly beautiful orange haze on the sky every dusk. The Highlands had bars where men lost ears, eyes, and fingers in just garden-variety fights, and streets where nobody sane ever walked after dark, not even cops unless they were in pairs. But it wasn't the physical violence you remembered so much as the emotional violence of poverty. You get tired of hearing your mother scream because there isn't enough money for food and hearing your father scream back because there's nothing he can do about it. Nothing.

Karen Lane and I had come from the Highlands, but we were smarter and, in her case, better looking than most of the people from the area, so when we went to Wilson High School—one of those nightmare conglomerates that shoves the poorest kids in a city in with the richest—we didn't do badly for ourselves. By senior year we found ourselves hanging out with the sons and daughters of bankers and doctors and city officials and lawyers and riding around in new Impala convertibles and attending an occasional party where you saw an actual maid. But wherever we went, we'd manage for at least a few minutes to get away from our dates and talk to each other. What we were doing, of course, was trying to comfort ourselves. We shared terrible and confusing feelings— pride that we were acceptable to those we saw as glamorous, shame that we felt disgrace for being from the Highlands and having fathers who worked in factories and mothers who went to Mass as often as nuns and brothers and sisters who were doomed to punching the clock and yelling at ragged kids in the cold factory dusk. (You never realize what a toll such shame takes till you see your father's waxen face there in the years-later casket.)

That was the big secret we shared, of course, Karen and I, that we were going to get out, leave the place once and for all. And her brown eyes never sparkled more Christmas-morning bright than at those moments when it all was ahead of us, money, sex, endless thrills, immortality. She had the kind of clean good looks brought out best by a blue cardigan with a line of white button-down shirt at the top and a brown suede car coat over her slender shoulders and moderately tight jeans displaying her quietly artful ass. Nothing splashy about her. She had the sort of face that snuck up on you. You had the impression you were talking to a pretty but in no way spectacular girl, and then all of a sudden you saw how the eyes burned with sad humor and how wry the mouth got at certain times and how absolutely perfect that straight little nose was and how the freckles enhanced rather than detracted from her beauty and by then of course you were hopelessly entangled. Hopelessly.

This wasn't just my opinion, either. I mentioned four divorce settlements. True facts. Karen was one of those prizes that powerful and rich men like to collect with the understanding that it's only something you hold in trust, like a yachting cup. So, in her time, she'd been an ornament for a professional football player (her college beau), an orthodontist ("I think he used to have sexual fantasies about Barry Goldwater"), the owner of a large commuter airline ("I slept with half his pilots; it was kind of a company benefit"), and a sixty-nine-year-old millionaire who was dying of heart disease ("He used to have me sit next to his bedside and just hold his hand—the weird thing was that of all of them, I loved him, I really did—and his eyes would be closed and then every once in a while tears would start streaming down his cheeks as if he was remembering something that really filled him with remorse; he was really a sweetie, but then cancer got him before the heart disease and I never did find out what he regretted so much, I mean if it was about his son or his wife or what"), and now she was comfortably fixed for the rest of her life and if the crow's feet were a little more pronounced around eyes and mouth and if the slenderness was just a trifle too slender (she weighed, at five-three, maybe ninety pounds and kept a variety of diet books in her big sunny kitchen), she was a damn good-looking woman nonetheless, the world's absurdity catalogued and evaluated in a gaze that managed to be both weary and impish, with a laugh that was knowing without being cynical.

So now she wanted to play detective.

I had some more bourbon from the pint—it burned beautifully—and said, "If I had your money, you know what I'd do?"

"Buy yourself a new shirt?"

"You don't like my shirt?"

"I didn't know you had this thing about Hawaii."

"If I had your money, I'd just forget about all this."

"I thought cops were sworn to uphold the right and the true."

"I'm an ex-cop."

"You wear a uniform."

"That's for the American Security Agency."

She sighed. "So I shouldn't have sent the letters?"

"No."

"Well, if they're guilty, they'll show up at Pierce Point tonight."

"Not necessarily."

"Why?"

"Maybe they'll know it's a trap. And not do anything."

She nodded to the school. "You hear that?"

"What?"

"The song."

It was Bobby Vinton's "Roses Are Red."

"I remember one party when we both hated our dates and we ended up dancing to that over and over again. Somebody's basement. You remember?"

"Sort of, I guess," I said.

"Good. Let's go in the gym and then we can dance to it again."

Donna, my lady friend, was out of town attending an advertising convention. I hoped she wasn't going to dance with anybody else because it would sure make me mad.

I started to open the door and she said, "I want to ask you a question."

"What?" I sensed what it was going to be so I kept my eyes on the parking lot.

"Turn around and look at me."

I turned around and looked at her. "Okay."

"Since the time we had dinner a month or so ago I've started receiving brochures from Alcoholics Anonymous in the mail. If you were having them sent to me, would you be honest enough to tell me?"

"Yes, I would."

"Are you having them sent to me?"

"Yes, I am."

"You think I'm a lush?"

"Don't you?"

"I asked you first."

So we went into the gym and danced.

Crepe of red and white, the school colors, draped the ceiling; the stage was a cave of white light on which stood four balding fat guys with spit curls and shimmery gold lamé dinner jackets (could these be the illegitimate sons of Bill Haley?) playing guitars, drum, and saxophone; on the dance floor couples who'd lost hair, teeth, jaw lines, courage, and energy (everything, it seemed, but weight) danced to lame cover versions of "Breaking Up Is Hard To Do" and "Sheila," "Runaround Sue" and "Running Scared" (tonight's lead singer sensibly not even trying Roy Orbison's beautiful falsetto) and then, while I got Karen and myself some no-alcohol punch, they broke into a medley of dance tunes—everything from "Locomotion" to "The Peppermint Twist"—and the place went a little crazy, and I went right along with it.

"Come on," I said.

"Great."

We went out there and we burned ass. We'd both agreed not to dress up for the occasion so we were ready for this. I wore the Hawaiian shirt she found so despicable plus a blue blazer, white socks and cordovan penny-loafers. She wore a salmon-colored Merikani shirt belted at the waist and tan cotton fatigue pants and, sweet Christ, she was so adorable half the guys in the place did the kind of double-takes usually reserved for somebody outrageous or famous.

Over the blasting music, I shouted, "Everybody's watching you!"

She shouted right back, "I know! Isn't it wonderful?"

The medley went twenty minutes and could easily have been confused with an aerobics session. By the end I was sopping and wishing I was carrying ten or fifteen pounds less and sometimes feeling guilty because I was having too much fun (I just hoped Donna, probably having too much fun, too was feeling equally guilty), and then finally it ended and mate fell into the arms of mate, hanging on to stave off sheer collapse.

Then the head Bill Haley clone said, "Okay, now we're going to do a ballad medley," so then we got everybody from Johnny Mathis to Connie Francis and we couldn't resist that, so I moved her around the floor with clumsy pleasure and she moved me right back with equally clumsy pleasure. "You know something?" I said.

"We're both shitty dancers?"

"Right."

But we kept on, of course, laughing and whirling a few times, and then coming tighter together and just holding each other silently for a time, two human beings getting older and scared about getting older, remembering some things and trying to forget others and trying to make sense of an existence that ultimately made sense to nobody, and then she said, "There's one of them."

I didn't have to ask her what "them" referred to. Until now she'd refused to identify any of the three people she'd sent the letters to.

At first I didn't recognize him. He had almost white hair and a tan so dark it looked fake. He wore a black dinner jacket with a lacy shirt and a black bow tie. He didn't seem to have put on a pound in the quarter century since I'd last seen him.

"Ted Forester?"

"Forester," she said. "He's president of the same savings and loan his father was president of."

"Who are the other two?"

"Why don't we get some punch?"

"The kiddie kind?"

"You could really make me mad with all this lecturing about alcoholism."

"If you're not really a lush then you won't mind getting the kiddie kind."

"My friend, Sigmund Fraud."

We had a couple of pink punches and caught our respective breaths and squinted in the gloom at name tags to see who we were saying hello to and realized all the terrible things you realize at high school reunions, namely that people who thought they were better than you still think that way, and that all the sad little people you feared for—the ones with blackheads and low IQs and lame left legs and walleyes and lisps and every other sort of unfair infirmity people get stuck with—generally turned out to be deserving of your fear, for there was a sadness in their eyes tonight that spoke of failures of every sort, and you wanted to go up and say something to them (I wanted to go up to nervous Karl Carberry, who used to twitch—his whole body twitched—and throw my arm around him and tell him what a neat guy he was, tell him there was no reason whatsoever for his twitching, grant him peace and self-esteem and at least a modicum of hope; if he needed a woman, get him a woman, too), but of course you didn't do that, you didn't go up, you just made edgy jokes and nodded a lot and drifted on to the next piece of human carnage.

"There's number two," Karen whispered.

This one I remembered. And despised. The six-three blond movie-star looks had grown only slightly older. His blue dinner jacket just seemed to enhance his air of malicious superiority. Larry Price. His wife Sally was still perfect, too, though you could see in the lacquered blond hair and maybe a hint of face lift that she'd had to work at it a little harder. A year out of high school, at a bar that took teenage IDs checked by a guy who must have been legally blind, I'd gotten drunk and told Larry that he was essentially an asshole for beating up a friend of mine who hadn't had a chance against him. I had the street boy's secret belief that I could take anybody whose father was a surgeon and whose house included a swimming pool. I had hatred, bitterness, and rage going, right? Well, Larry and I went out into the parking lot, ringed by a lot of drunken spectators, and before I got off a single punch, Larry hit me with a shot that stood me straight up, giving him a great opportunity to hit me again. He hit me three times before I found his face and sent him a shot hard enough to push him back for a time. Before we could go at it again, the guy who checked IDs got himself between us. He was madder than either Larry or me. He ended the fight by taking us both by the ears (he must have trained with nuns) and dragging us out to the curb and telling neither of us to come back.

"You remember the night you fought him?"

"Yeah."

"You could have taken him, Dwyer. Those three punches he got in were just lucky."

"Yeah, that was my impression, too. Lucky."

She laughed. "I was afraid he was going to kill you."

I was going to say something smart, but then a new group of people came up and we gushed through a little social dance of nostalgia and lies and self-justifications. We talked success (at high school reunions, everybody sounds like Amway representatives at a pep rally) and the old days (nobody seems to remember all the kids who got treated like shit for reasons they had no control over) and didn't so-and-so look great (usually this meant they'd managed to keep their toupees on straight) and introducing new spouses (we all had to explain what happened to our original mates; I said mine had been eaten by alligators in the Amazon, but nobody seemed to find that especially believable) and in the midst of all this, Karen tugged my sleeve and said, "There's the third one."

Him I recognized, too. David Haskins. He didn't look any happier than he ever had. Parent trouble was always the explanation you got for his grief back in high school. His parents had been rich, truly so, his father an importer of some kind, and their arguments so violent that they were as eagerly discussed as who was or who was not pregnant. Apparently David's parents weren't getting along any better today because although the features of his face were open and friendly enough, there was still the sense of some terrible secret stooping his shoulders and keeping his smiles to furtive wretched imitations. He was a paunchy balding little man who might have been a church usher with a sour stomach.

"The Duke of Earl" started up then and there was no way we were going to let that pass so we got out on the floor; but by now, of course, we both watched the three people she'd sent letters to. Her instructions had been to meet the anonymous letter writer at nine-thirty at Pierce Point. If they were going to be there on time, they'd be leaving soon.

"You think they're going to go?"

"I doubt it, Karen."

"You still don't believe that's what I heard them say that night?"

"It was a long time ago and you were drunk."

"It's a good thing I like you because otherwise you'd be a distinct pain in the ass."

Which is when I saw all three of them go stand under one of the glowing red EXIT signs and open a fire door that led to the parking lot.

"They're going!" she said.

"Maybe they're just having a cigarette."

"You know better, Dwyer. You know better."

Her car was in the lot on the opposite side of the gym.

"Well, it's worth a drive even if they don't show up. Pierce Point should be nice tonight."

She squeezed against me and said, "Thanks, Dwyer. Really."

So we went and got her Volvo and went out to Pierce Point where twenty-five years ago a shy kid named Michael Brandon had fallen or been pushed to his death.

Apparently we were about to find out which.

The river road wound along a high wall of clay cliffs on the left and a wide expanse of water on the right. The spring night was impossibly beautiful, one of those moments so rich with sweet odor and even sweeter sight you wanted to take your clothes off and run around in some kind of crazed animal circles out of sheer joy.

"You still like jazz?" she said, nodding to the radio.

"I hope you didn't mind my turning the station."

"I'm kind of into Country."

"I didn't get the impression you were listening."

She looked over at me. "Actually, I wasn't. I was thinking about you sending me all those AA pamphlets."

"It was arrogant and presumptuous and I apologize."

"No, it wasn't. It was sweet and I appreciate it."

The rest of the ride, I leaned my head back and smelled flowers and grass and river water and watched moonglow through the elms and oaks and birches of this new spring. There was a Dakota Staton song, "Street of Dreams," and I wondered as always where she was and what she was doing, she'd been so fine, maybe the most underappreciated jazz singer of the entire fifties.

Then we were going up a long, twisting gravel road. We pulled up next to a big park pavilion and got out and stood in the wet grass, and she came over and slid her arm around my waist and sort of hugged me in a half-serious way. "This is all probably crazy, isn't it?"

I sort of hugged her back in a half-serious way. "Yeah, but it's a nice night for a walk so what the hell."

"You ready?"

"Yep."

"Let's go then."

So we went up the hill to the Point itself, and first we looked out at the far side of the river where white birches glowed in the gloom and where beyond you could see the horseshoe shape of the city lights. Then we looked down, straight down the drop of two hundred feet, to the road where Michael Brandon had died.

When I heard the car starting up the road to the east, I said, "Let's get in those bushes over there."

A thick line of shrubs and second-growth timber would give us a place to hide, to watch them.

By the time we were in place, ducked down behind a wide elm and a mulberry bush, a new yellow Mercedes sedan swung into sight and stopped several yards from the edge of the Point.

A car radio played loud in the night. A Top 40 song. Three men got out. Dignified Forester, matinee-idol Price, anxiety-tight Haskins.

Forester leaned back into the car and snapped the radio off. But he left the headlights on. Forester and Price each had cans of beer. Haskins bit his nails.

They looked around in the gloom. The headlights made the darkness beyond seem much darker and the grass in its illumination much greener. Price said harshly, "I told you this was just some goddamn prank. Nobody knows squat."

"He's right, he's probably right," Haskins said to Forester. Obviously he was hoping that was the case.

Forester said, "If somebody didn't know something, we would never have gotten those letters."

She moved then and I hadn't expected her to move at all. I'd been under the impression we would just sit there and listen and let them ramble and maybe in so doing reveal something useful.

But she had other ideas.

She pushed through the undergrowth and stumbled a little and got to her feet again and then walked right up to them.

"Karen!" Haskins said.

"So you did kill Michael," she said.

Price moved toward her abruptly, his hand raised. He was drunk and apparently hitting women was something he did without much trouble.

Then I stepped out from our hiding place and said, "Put your hand down, Price."

Forester said, "Dwyer."

"So," Price said, lowering his hand. "I was right, wasn't I?" He was speaking to Forester.

Forester shook his silver head. He seemed genuinely saddened. "Yes, Price, for once your cynicism is justified."

Price said, "Well, you two aren't getting a goddamned penny, do you know that?"

He lunged toward me, still a bully. But I was ready for him, wanted it. I also had the advantage of being sober. When he was two steps away, I hit him just once and very hard in his solar plexus. He backed away, eyes startled, and then he turned abruptly away.

We all stood looking at one another, pretending not to hear the sounds of violent vomiting on the other side of the splendid new Mercedes.

Forester said, "When I saw you there, Karen, I wondered if you could do it alone."

"Do what?"

"What?" Forester said. "What? Let's at least stop the games. You two want money."

"Christ," I said to Karen, who looked perplexed, "they think we're trying to shake them down."

"Shake them down?"

"Blackmail them."

"Exactly," Forester said.

Price had come back around. He was wiping his mouth with the back of his hand. In his other hand he carried a silver-plated .45, the sort of weapon professional gamblers favor.

Haskins said, "Larry, Jesus, what is that?"

"What does it look like?"

"Larry, that's how people get killed." Haskins sounded like Price's mother.

Price's eyes were on me. "Yeah, it would be terrible if Dwyer here got killed, wouldn't it?" He waved the gun at me. I didn't really think he'd shoot, but I sure was afraid he'd trip and the damn thing would go off accidentally. "You've been waiting since senior year to do that to me, haven't you, Dwyer?"

I shrugged. "I guess so, yeah."

"Well, why don't I give Forester here the gun and then you and I can try it again."

"Fine with me."

He handed Forester the .45. Forester took it all right, but what he did was toss it somewhere into the gloom surrounding the car. "Larry, if you don't straighten up here, I'll fight you myself. Do you understand me?" Forester had a certain dignity and when he spoke, his voice carried an easy authority. "There will be no more fighting, do you both understand that?"

"I agree with Ted," Karen said.

Forester, like a teacher tired of naughty children, decided to get on with the real business. "You wrote those letters, Dwyer?"

"No."

"No?"

"No. Karen wrote them."

A curious glance was exchanged by Forester and Karen. "I guess I should have known that," Forester said.

"Jesus, Ted," Karen said, "I'm not trying to blackmail you, no matter what you think."

"Then just what exactly are you trying to do?"

She shook her lovely little head. I sensed she regretted ever writing the letters, stirring it all up again. "I just want the truth to come out about what really happened to Michael Brandon that night."

"The truth," Price said. "Isn't that goddamn touching?"

"Shut up, Larry," Haskins said.

Forester said, "You know what happened to Michael Brandon?"

"I've got a good idea," Karen said. "I overheard you three talking at a party one night."

"What did we say?"

"What?"

"What did you overhear us say?"

Karen said, "You said that you hoped nobody looked into what really happened to Michael that night."

A smile touched Forester's lips. "So on that basis you concluded that we murdered him?"

"There wasn't much else to conclude."

Price said, weaving still, leaning on the fender for support, "I don't goddamn believe this."

Forester nodded to me. "Dwyer, I'd like to have a talk with Price and Haskins here, if you don't mind. Just a few minutes." He pointed to the darkness beyond the car. "We'll walk over there. You know we won't try to get away because you'll have our car. All right?"

I looked at Karen.

She shrugged.

They left, back into the gloom, voices receding and fading into the sounds of crickets and a barn owl and a distant roaring train.

"You think they're up to something?"

"I don't know," I said.

We stood with our shoes getting soaked and looked at the green green grass in the headlights.

"What do you think they're doing?" Karen asked.

"Deciding what they want to tell us."

"You're used to this kind of thing, aren't you?"

"I guess."

"It's sort of sad, isn't it?"

"Yeah. It is."

"Except for you getting the chance to punch out Larry Price after all these years."

"Christ, you really think I'm that petty?"

"I know you are. I know you are."

Then we both turned to look back to where they were. There'd been a cry and Forester shouted, "You hit him again, Larry, and I'll break your goddamn jaw." They were arguing about something and it had turned vicious.

I leaned back against the car. She leaned back against me. "You think we'll ever go to bed?"

"I'd sure like to, Karen, but I can't."

"Donna?"

"Yeah. I'm really trying to learn how to be faithful."

"That been a problem?"

"It cost me a marriage."

"Maybe I'll learn how someday, too."

Then they were back. Somebody, presumably Forester, had torn Price's nice lacy shirt into shreds. Haskins looked miserable.

Forester said, "I'm going to tell you what happened that night."

I nodded.

"I've got some beer in the back seat. Would either of you like one?"

Karen said, "Yes, we would."

So he went and got a six pack of Michelob and we all had a beer and just before he started talking he and Karen shared another one of those peculiar glances and then he said, "The four of us—myself, Price, Haskins, and Michael Brandon—had done something we were very ashamed of."

"Afraid of," Haskins said.

"Afraid that, if it came out, our lives would be ruined. Forever," Forester said.

Price said, "Just say it, Forester." He glared at me. "We raped a girl, the four of us."

"Brandon spent two months afterward seeing the girl, bringing her flowers, apologizing to her over and over again, telling her how sorry we were, that we'd been drunk and it wasn't like us to do that and—" Forester sighed, put his eyes to the ground. "In fact we had been drunk; in fact it wasn't like us to do such a thing—"

Haskins said, "It really wasn't. It really wasn't."

For a time there was just the barn owl and the crickets again, no talk, and then gently I said, "What happened to Brandon that night?"

"We were out as we usually were, drinking beer, talking about it, afraid the girl would finally turn us into the police, still trying to figure out why we'd ever done such a thing—"

The hatred was gone from Price's eyes. For the first time the matinee idol looked as melancholy as his friends. "No matter what you think of me, Dwyer, I don't rape women. But that night—" He shrugged, looked away.

"Brandon," I said. "You were going to tell me about Brandon."

"We came up here, had a case of beer or something, and talked about it some more, and that night," Forester said, "that night Brandon just snapped. He couldn't handle how ashamed he was or how afraid he was of being turned in. Right in the middle of talking—"

Haskins took over. "Right in the middle, he just got up and ran out to the Point." He indicated the cliff behind us. "And before we could stop him, he jumped."

"Jesus," Price said, "I can't forget his screaming on the way down. I can't ever forget it."

I looked at Karen. "So what she heard you three talking about outside the party that night was not that you'd killed Brandon but that you were afraid a serious investigation into his suicide might turn up the rape?"

Forester said, "Exactly." He stared at Karen. "We didn't kill Michael, Karen. We loved him. He was our friend."

But by then, completely without warning, she had started to cry and then she began literally sobbing, her entire body shaking with some grief I could neither understand nor assuage.

I nodded to Forester to get back in his car and leave. They stood and watched us a moment and then they got into the Mercedes and went away, taking the burden of years and guilt with them.

This time I drove. I went far out the river road, miles out, where you pick up the piney hills and the deer standing by the side of the road.

From the glove compartment she took a pint of J&B, and I knew better than to try and stop her.

I said, "You were the girl they raped, weren't you?"

"Yes."

"Why didn't you tell the police?"

She smiled at me. "The police weren't exactly going to believe a girl from the Highlands about the sons of rich men."

I sighed. She was right.

"Then Michael started coming around to see me. I can't say I ever forgave him, but I started to feel sorry for him. His fear—" She shook her head, and looked out the window. She said, almost to herself, "But I had to write those letters, get them there tonight, know for sure if they killed him." She paused. "You believe them?"

"That they didn't kill him?"

"Right."

"Yes, I believe them."

"So do I."

Then she went back to staring out the window, her small face childlike there in silhouette against the moonsilver river. "Can I ask you a question, Dwyer?"

"Sure."

"You think we're ever going to get out of the Highlands?"

"No," I said, and drove on faster in her fine new expensive car. "No, I don't."

JULIE SMITH

"Blood Types"

Julie Smith was born in Annapolis, Maryland on November 25, 1944. She received her degree in journalism from the University of Mississippi in 1965 and worked as a reporter in New Orleans and San Francisco. Her first novel **Death Turns a Trick** (1982) introduced District Attorney Rebecca Schwartz who starred in four more novels including **The Sourdough Wars** (1984) with its uniquely San Francisco plot involving a valuable recipe for sourdough bread.

Mystery writer Paul MacDonald appeared in two novels, but it was with New Orleans police detective Skip Langdon that Julie Smith finally found a protagonist worthy of her talents. The first Langdon novel **New Orleans Mourning** (1990) won the MWA Edgar award as best of the year and was followed by five others with titles like **The Axeman's Jazz** (1991), **Jazz Funeral** (1993) and **New Orleans Beat** (1994), all steeped in the unique atmosphere of the city Smith knew so well as a reporter.

None of Julie Smith's handful of short stories have yet been collected. "Blood Types," a Rebecca Schwartz story, appeared in **Sisters in Crime**.

Blood Types

by Julie Smith

R efresh my recollection, counselor. Are holographic wills legal in California?"

Though we'd hardly spoken in seven years or more, I recognized the voice on the phone as easily as if I'd heard it yesterday. I'd lived with its owner once. "Gary Wilder. Aren't you feeling well?"

"I feel fine. Settle a bet, okay?"

"Unless you slept through more classes than I thought, you know perfectly well they're legal."

"They used to be. It's been a long time, you know? How are you, Rebecca?"

"Great. And you're a daddy, I hear. How's Stephanie?"

"Fine."

"And the wee one?"

"Little Laurie-bear. The best thing that ever happened to me."

"You sound happy."

"Laurie's my life."

I was sorry to hear it. That was a lot of responsibility for a ten-month-old.

"So about the will," Gary continued. "Have the rules changed since we were at Boalt?"

"A bit. Remember how it could be invalidated by anything preprinted on it? Like in that case where there was a date stamped on the paper the woman used, and the whole thing was thrown out?"

"Yeah. I remember someone asked whether you could use your own letterhead."

"That was you, Gary."

"Probably. And you couldn't, it seems to me."

"But you probably could now. Now only the 'materially relevant' part has to be handwritten. And you don't have to date it."

"No? That seems odd."

"Well, you would if there were a previous dated will. Otherwise just write it out, sign it, and it's legal."

Something about the call, maybe just the melancholy of hearing a voice from the past, put me in a gray and restless mood. It was mid-December and pouring outside—perfect weather for doleful ruminations on a man I hardly knew anymore. I couldn't help worrying that if Laurie was Gary's whole life, that didn't speak well for his marriage. Shouldn't Stephanie at least have gotten a small mention? But she hadn't, and the Gary I knew could easily have fallen out of love with her. He was one of life's stationary drifters—staying in the same place but drifting from one mild interest to another, none of them very consuming and none very durable. I hoped it would be different with Laurie; it wouldn't be easy to watch your dad wimp out on you.

But I sensed it was already happening. I suspected that phone call meant little Laurie, who was his life, was making him feel tied down and he was sending out feelers to former and future lady friends.

The weather made me think of a line from a poem Gary used to quote:

Il pleure dans mon coeur
Comme il pleut sur la ville.

He was the sort to quote Paul Verlaine. He read everything, retained everything, and didn't do much. He had never finished law school, had sold insurance for a while and was now dabbling in real estate, I'd heard, though I didn't know what that meant, exactly. Probably trying to figure out a way to speculate with Stephanie's money, which, out of affection for Gary, I thanked heaven she had. If you can't make up your mind what to do with your life, you should at least marry well and waffle in comfort.

Gary died that night. Reading about it in the morning *Chronicle,* I shivered, thinking the phone call was one of those grisly coincidences. But the will came the next day.

The *Chronicle* story said Gary and Stephanie were both killed instantly when their car went over a cliff on a twisty road in a blinding rainstorm. The rains were hellish that year. It was the third day of a five-day flood.

Madeline Bell, a witness to the accident, said Gary had swerved to avoid hitting her Mercedes as she came around a curve. The car had exploded and burned as Bell watched it roll off a hill near San Anselmo, where Stephanie and Gary lived.

Even in that moment of shock I think I felt more grief for Laurie than I did for Gary, who had half lived his life at best. Only a day before, when I'd talked to Gary, Laurie had had it made—her mama was rich and her daddy good-looking. Now she was an orphan.

I wondered where Gary and Stephanie were going in such an awful storm. To a party, probably, or home from one. It was the height of the holiday season.

I knew Gary's mother, of course. Would she already be at the Wilder house, for Hanukkah, perhaps? If not, she'd be coming soon; I'd call in a day or two.

In the meantime I called Rob Burns, who had long since replaced Gary in my affections, and asked to see him that night. I hadn't thought twice of Gary in the past five years, but something was gone from my life and I needed comfort. It would be good to sleep with Rob by my side and the sound of rain on the roof—life-affirming, as we say in California. I'd read somewhere that Mark Twain, when he built his mansion in Hartford, installed a section of tin roof so as to get the best rain sounds. I could understand the impulse.

It was still pouring by mid-morning the next day, and my throat was feeling slightly scratchy, the way it does when a cold's coming on. I was rummaging for vitamin C when Kruzick brought the mail in—Alan Kruzick, incredibly inept but inextricably installed secretary for the law firm of Nicholson and Schwartz, of which I was a protesting partner. The other partner, Chris Nicholson, liked his smart-ass style, my sister Mickey was his girlfriend, and my mother had simply laid down the law—hire him and keep him.

"Any checks?" I asked.

"Nope. Nothing interesting but a letter from a dead man."

"What?"

He held up an envelope with Gary Wilder's name and address in the upper left corner. "Maybe he wants you to channel him."

The tears that popped into my eyes quelled even Kruzick.

The will was in Gary's own handwriting, signed, written on plain paper, and dated December 17, the day of Gary's death. It said: "This is my last will and testament, superseding all others. I leave everything I own to my daughter, Laurie Wilder. If my wife and I die before her 21st birthday, I appoint my brother, Michael Wilder, as her legal guardian. I also appoint my brother as executor of this will."

My stomach clutched as I realized that Gary had known when we talked that he and Stephanie were in danger. He'd managed to seem his usual happy-go-lucky self, using the trick he had of hiding his feelings that had made him hard to live with.

But if he knew he was going to be killed, why hadn't he given the murderer's identity? Perhaps he had, I realized. I was a lawyer, so I'd gotten the will. Someone else might have gotten a letter about what was happening. I wondered if my old boyfriend had gotten involved with the dope trade. After all, he lived in Marin County, which had the highest population of coke dealers outside the greater Miami area.

I phoned Gary's brother at his home in Seattle but was told he'd gone to San Anselmo. I had a client coming in five minutes, but after that, nothing pressing. And so, by two o'clock I was on the Golden Gate Bridge, enjoying a rare moment of foggy overcast, the rain having relented for a while.

It was odd about Gary's choosing Michael for Laurie's guardian. When I'd known him well he'd had nothing but contempt for his brother. Michael was a stockbroker and a go-getter; Gary was a mooner-about, a romantic, and a rebel. He considered his brother boring, stuffy, a bit crass, and utterly worthless. On the other hand, he adored his sister, Jeri, a free-spirited dental hygienist married to a good-natured sometime carpenter.

Was Michael married? Yes, I thought. At least he had been. Maybe fatherhood had changed Gary's opinions on what was important—Michael's money and stability might have looked good to him when he thought of sending Laurie to college.

I pulled up in front of the Wilder-Cooper home, a modest redwood one that had probably cost nearly half a million. Such were real-estate values in Marin County—and such was Stephanie's bank account.

At home were Michael Wilder—wearing a suit—and Stephanie's parents, Mary and Jack Cooper. Mary was a big woman, comfortable and talkative; Jack was skinny and withdrawn. He stared into space, almost sad, but mostly just faraway, and I got the feeling watching TV was his great passion in life, though perhaps he drank as well. The idea, it appeared, was simply to leave the room without anyone noticing, the means of transportation being entirely insignificant.

It was a bit awkward, my being the ex-girlfriend and showing up unexpectedly. Michael didn't seem to know how to introduce me, and I could take a hint. It was no time to ask to see him privately.

"I'd hoped to see your mother," I said.

"She's at the hospital," said Mary. "We're taking turns now that—" She started to cry.

"The hospital!"

"You don't know about Laurie?"

"She was in the accident?"

"No. She's been very ill for the last two months."

"Near death," said Mary. "What that child has been through shouldn't happen to an animal. Tiny little face just contorts itself like a poor little monkey's. Screams and screams and screams; and *rivers* flow out of her little bottom. *Rivers,* Miss Schwartz!"

Her shoulders hunched and began to shake. Michael looked helpless. Mechanically Jack put an arm around her.

"What's wrong?" I asked Michael.

He shrugged. "They don't know. Can't diagnose it."

"Now, Mary," said Jack. "She's better. The doctor said so last night."

"What hospital is she in?"

"Marin General."

I said to Michael: "I think I'll pop by and see your mother—would you mind pointing me in the right direction? I've got a map in the car."

When we arrived at the curb, I said, "I can find the hospital. I wanted to give you something."

I handed him the will. "This came in today's mail. It'll be up to you as executor to petition the court for probate." As he read, a look of utter incredulity came over his face. "But . . . I'm divorced. I can't take care of a baby."

"Gary didn't ask in advance if you'd be willing?"

"Yes, but . . . I didn't think he was going to die!" His voice got higher as reality caught up with him. "He called the day of the accident. But I thought he was just depressed. You know how people get around the holidays."

"What did he say exactly?"

"He said he had this weird feeling, that's all—like something bad might happen to him. And would I take care of Laurie if anything did."

"He didn't say he was scared? In any kind of trouble?"

"No—just feeling weird."

"Michael, he wasn't dealing, was he?"

"Are you kidding? I'd be the last to know." He looked at the ground a minute. "I guess he could have been."

Ellen Wilder was cooing to Laurie when I got to the hospital. "Ohhhh, she's much better now. She just needed her grandma's touch, that's all it was."

She spoke to the baby in the third person, unaware I was there until I announced myself, whereupon she almost dropped the precious angel-wangel and dislodged her IV. We had a tearful reunion, Gary's mother and I. We both missed Gary, and we both felt for poor Laurie.

Ellen adored the baby more than breath, to listen to her, and not only that, she possessed the healing power of a witch. She had spent the night Gary and Stephanie were killed with Laurie, and all day the next day, never even going home for a shower. And gradually the fever had broken, metaphorically speaking. With Grandma's loving attention, the baby's debilitating diarrhea had begun to ease off, and little Laurie had seemed to come back to life.

"Look, Rebecca." She tiptoed to the sleeping baby. "See those cheeks? Roses in them. She's getting her pretty color back, widdle Waurie is, yes, her is." She seemed not to realize she'd lapsed into baby talk.

She came back and sat down beside me. "Stephanie stayed with her nearly around the clock, you know. She was the best mother anyone ever—" Ellen teared up for a second and glanced around the room, embarrassed.

"Look. She left her clothes here. I'll have to remember to take them home. The *best* mother . . . she and Gary were invited to a party that night. It was a horrible, rainy, rainy night, but poor Stephanie hadn't been anywhere but the hospital in weeks—"

"How long had you been here?"

"Oh, just a few days. I came for Hanukkah—and to help out if I could. I knew Stephanie had to get out, so I offered to stay with Laurie. I was just dying to have some time with the widdle fweet fing, anyhow—" This last was spoken more or less in Laurie's direction. Ellen seemed to have developed a habit of talking to the child while carrying on other conversations.

"What happened was Gary had quite a few drinks before he brought me over. Oh, God, I never should have let him drive! We nearly had a wreck on the way over—you know how stormy it was. I kept telling him he was too drunk to drive, and he said I wanted it that way, just like I always wanted him to have strep throat when he was a kid. He said he felt fine then and he felt fine now."

I was getting lost. "You *wanted* him to have strep throat?"

She shrugged. "I don't know what he meant. He was just drunk, that's all. Oh, God, my poor baby!" She sniffed, fumbled in her purse, and blew her nose into a tissue.

"Did he seem okay that day—except for being drunk?"

"Fine. Why?"

"He called me that afternoon—about his will. And he called Michael to say he—well, I guess to say he had a premonition about his death."

"His will? He called you about a will?"

"Yes."

"But he and Stephanie had already made their wills. Danny Goldstein drew them up." That made sense, as Gary had dated his holograph. Danny had been at Boalt with Gary and me. I wondered briefly if it hurt Ellen to be reminded that all Gary's classmates had gone on to become lawyers just like their parents would have wanted.

A fresh-faced nurse popped in and took a look at Laurie. "How's our girl?"

"Like a different baby."

The nurse smiled. "She sure is. We were really worried for a while there." But the smile faded almost instantly. "It's so sad. I never saw a more devoted mother. Laurie never needed us at all—Stephanie was her nurse. One of the best I ever saw."

"I didn't know Stephanie was a nurse." The last I'd heard she was working part-time for a caterer, trying to make up her mind whether to go to chef's school. Stephanie had a strong personality, but she wasn't much more career-minded than Gary was. Motherhood, everyone seemed to think, had been her true calling.

"She didn't have any training—she was just good with infants. You should have seen the way she'd sit and rock that child for hours, Laurie having diarrhea so bad she hardly had any skin on her little butt, crying her little heart out. She must have been in agony like you and I couldn't imagine. But finally Stephanie would get her to sleep. Nobody else could."

"Nobody else could breast-feed her," I said, thinking surely I'd hit on the source of Stephanie's amazing talent.

"Stephanie couldn't, either. Didn't have enough milk." The nurse shrugged. "Anyone can give a bottle. It wasn't that."

When she left, I said, "I'd better go. Can I do anything for you?"

Ellen thought a minute. "You know what you could do? Will you be going by Gary's again?"

"I'd be glad to."

"You could take some of Stephanie's clothes and things. They're going to let Laurie out in a day or two and there's so much stuff here." She looked exasperated.

Glad to help, I gathered up clothes and began to fold them. Ellen found a canvas carryall of Stephanie's to pack them in. Zipping it open, I saw a bit of white powder in the bottom, and my stomach flopped over. I couldn't get the notion of drugs out of my mind. Gary had had a "premonition" of death, the kind you might get if you burned someone and they threatened you—and now I was looking at white powder.

I found some plastic bags in a drawer that had probably once been used to transport diapers or formula, and lined the bottom of the carryall with them, to keep the powder from sticking to Stephanie's clothes.

But instead of going to Gary's, I dropped in at my parents' house in San Rafael. It was about four o'clock and I had some phoning to do before five.

"Darling!" said Mom. "Isn't it awful about poor Gary Wilder?"

Mom had always liked Gary. She had a soft spot for ne'er-do-wells, as I knew only too well. She was the main reason Kruzick was currently ruining my life. The person for whom she hadn't a minute was the one I preferred most—the blue-eyed and dashing Mr. Rob Burns, star reporter for the San Francisco *Chronicle*.

Using the phone in my dad's study, Rob was the very person I rang up. His business was asking questions that were none of his business, and I had a few for him to ask.

Quickly explaining the will, the odd phone call to Michael, and the white powder, I had him hooked. He smelled the same rat I smelled, and more important, he smelled a story.

While he made his calls I phoned Danny Goldstein. "Becky baby."

"Don't call me that."

"Terrible about Gary, isn't it? Makes you *think,* man."

"Terrible about Stephanie too."

"I don't know. She pussy-whipped him."

"She was better than Melissa."

Danny laughed unkindly, brayed you could even say. Everyone knew Gary had left me for Melissa, who was twenty-two and a cutesy-wootsy doll-baby who couldn't be trusted to go to the store for a six-pack. Naturally everyone thought *I* had Gary pussy-whipped when the truth was, he wouldn't brush his teeth without asking my advice about it. He was a man desperate for a woman to run his life, and I was relieved to be rid of the job.

But still, Melissa had hurt my pride. I thought Gary's choosing her meant he'd grown up and no longer needed me. It was a short-lived maturity, however—within two years Stephanie had appeared on the scene. I might not see it exactly the way Danny did, but I had to admit that if he'd had any balls, she was the one to bust them.

"I hear motherhood mellowed her," I said.

"Yeah, she was born for it. Always worrying was the kid too hot, too cold, too hungry—one of those poo-poo moms."

"Huh?"

"You know. Does the kid want to go poo-poo? Did the kid already go poo-poo? Does it go poo-poo often enough? Does it go poo-poo too much? Is it going poo-poo *right now*? She could discuss color and consistency through a whole dinner party, salmon mousse to kiwi tart."

I laughed. Who didn't know the type? "Say, listen, Danny," I said. "Did you know Laurie's been in the hospital?"

"Yeah. Marina, my wife, went to see Stephanie—tried to get her to go out and get some air while she took care of the baby, but Stephanie wouldn't budge."

"I hear you drew up Gary's and Stephanie's wills."

"Yeah. God, I never thought—poor little Laurie. They asked Gary's sister to be her guardian—he hated his brother and Stephanie was an only child."

"Guess what? Gary made another will just before he died, naming the brother as Laurie's guardian."

"I don't believe it."

"Believe it. I'll send you a copy."

"There's going to be a hell of a court fight."

I wasn't so sure about that. The court, of course, wouldn't be bound by either parent's nomination. Since Stephanie's will nominated Jeri as guardian, she and Michael might choose to fight it out, but given Michael's apparent hesitation to take Laurie, I wasn't sure there'd be any argument at all.

"Danny," I said, "you were seeing a lot of him, right?"

"Yeah. We played racquetball."

"Was he dealing coke? Or something else?"

"Gary? No way. You can't be a dealer and be as broke as he was."

The phone rang almost the minute I hung up. Rob had finished a round of calls to what he called "his law-enforcement sources." He'd learned that Gary's brakes hadn't been tampered with, handily blowing my murder theory.

Or seemingly blowing it. Something was still very wrong, and I wasn't giving up till I knew what the powder was. Mom asked me to dinner, but I headed back to the city—Rob had said he could get someone to run an analysis that night.

It was raining again by the time I'd dropped the stuff off, refused Rob's dinner invitation (that was two) and gone home to solitude and split pea soup that I make up in advance and keep in the freezer for nights like this. It was the second night after Gary's death; the first night I'd needed to reassure myself I was still alive. Now I needed to mourn. I didn't plan anything fancy like sackcloth and ashes, just a quiet night home with a book, free to let my mind wander and my eyes fill up from time to time.

But first I had a message from Michael Wilder. He wanted to talk. He felt awful calling me like this, but there was no one in his family he felt he could talk to. Couldn't we meet for coffee or something?

Sure we could—at my house. Not even for Gary's brother was I going out in the rain again.

After the soup I showered and changed into jeans. Michael arrived in wool slacks and a sport coat—not even in repose, apparently, did he drop the stuffy act. Maybe life with Laurie would loosen him up. I asked if he'd thought any more about being her guardian.

It flustered him. "Not really," he said, and didn't meet my eyes.

"I found out the original wills named Jeri as guardian. If Stephanie didn't make a last-minute one, too, hers will still be in effect. Meaning Jeri could fight you if you decide you want Laurie."

"I can't even imagine being a father," he said. "But Gary must have had a good reason—" he broke off. "Poor little kid. A week ago everyone thought *she* was the one who was going to die."

"What's wrong with her—besides diarrhea?" I realized I hadn't had the nerve to ask either of the grandmothers because I knew exactly what would happen—I'd get details that would give *me* symptoms, and two hours later, maybe three or four, I'd be backing toward the door, nodding, with a glazed look on my face, watching matriarchal jaws continue to work.

But Michael only grimaced. "That's all I know about—just life-threatening diarrhea."

"Life-threatening?"

"Without an IV, a dehydrated baby can die in fifteen minutes. Just ask my mother." He shrugged. "Anyway, the doctors talked about electrolyte abnormalities, whatever they may be, and did every test in the book. But the only thing they found was what they called 'high serum sodium levels.'" He shrugged again, as if to shake something off. "Don't ask—especially don't ask my mom or Stephanie's."

We both laughed. I realized Michael had good reasons for finding sudden parenthood a bit on the daunting side.

I got us some wine and when I came back, he'd turned deadly serious. "Rebecca, something weird happened today. Look what I found." He held out a paper signed by Gary and headed "Beneficiary Designation."

"Know what that is?"

I shook my head.

"I used to be in insurance—as did my little brother. It's the form you use to change your life insurance beneficiary."

The form was dated December 16, the day before Gary's death. Michael had been named beneficiary and Laurie contingent beneficiary. Michael said, "Pretty weird, huh?"

I nodded.

"I also found both Gary's and Stephanie's policies—each for half a million dollars and each naming the other as beneficiary, with Laurie as contingent. For some reason, Gary went to see his insurance agent the day before he died and changed his. What do you make of it?"

I didn't at all like what I made of it. "It goes with the will," I said. "He named you as Laurie's guardian, so he must have wanted to make sure you could afford to take care of her."

"I could afford it. For Christ's sake!"

"He must have wanted to compensate you." I stopped for a minute. "It might be his way of saying thanks."

"You're avoiding the subject, aren't you?"

I was. "You mean it would have made more sense to leave the money to Laurie directly."

"Yes. Unless he'd provided for her some other way."

"Stephanie had money."

"I don't think Gary knew how much, though."

I took a sip of wine and thought about it, or rather thought about ways to talk about it, because it was beginning to look very ugly. "You're saying you think," I said carefully, "that he knew she was going to inherit the half million from Stephanie's policy. Because she was going to die and he was the beneficiary, and he was going to die and his new will left his own property to Laurie."

Michael was blunt: "It looks like murder-suicide, doesn't it?"

I said, "Yeah," unable to say any more.

Michael took me over ground I'd already mentally covered: "He decided to do it in a hurry, probably because it was raining so hard—an accident in the rain would be much more plausible. He made the arrangements. Then he called me and muttered about a premonition, to give himself some sort of feeble motive for suddenly getting his affairs in order; he may have said the same thing to other people as well. Finally he pretended to be drunk, made a big show of almost having an accident on the way to the hospital, picked up Stephanie, and drove her over a cliff."

Still putting things together, I mumbled, "You couldn't really be sure you'd die going over just any cliff. You'd have to pick the right cliff, wouldn't you?" And then I said, "I wonder if the insurance company will figure it out."

"Oh, who cares? He probably expected they would but wanted to make the gesture. And he knew I didn't need the money. That's not the point. The point is why?" He stood up and ran his fingers through his hair, working off excess energy. "Why kill himself, Rebecca? And why take Stephanie with him?"

"I don't know," I said. But I hadn't a doubt that that was what he'd done. There was another why—why make Michael Laurie's guardian? Why not his sister as originally planned?

The next day was Saturday, and I would have dozed happily into mid-morning if Rob hadn't phoned at eight. "You know the sinister white powder?"

"Uh-huh."

"Baking soda."

"That's all?"

"That's it. No heroin, no cocaine, not even any baby talc. Baking soda. Period."

I thanked him and turned over, but the next couple of hours were full of vaguely disquieting dreams. I woke upset, feeling oddly tainted, as if I'd collaborated in Gary's crimes. It wasn't till I was in the shower—performing my purification ritual, if you believe in such things—that things came together in my conscious mind. The part of me that dreamed had probably known it all along.

I called a doctor friend to find out if what I suspected made medical sense. It did. To a baby Laurie's age, baking soda would be a deadly poison. Simply add it to the formula and the excess sodium would cause her to develop severe, dehydrating diarrhea; it might ultimately lead to death. But she would be sick only as long as someone continued to doctor her formula. The poisoning was not cumulative; as soon as it stopped, she would begin to recover, and in only a few days she would be dramatically better.

In other words, he described Laurie's illness to a *T*. And Stephanie, the world's greatest mother, who was there around the clock, must have fed her—at any rate, would have had all the opportunity in the world to doctor her formula.

It didn't make sense. Well, part of it did. The part I could figure out was this: Gary saw Stephanie put baking soda in the formula, already knew about the high sodium reports, put two and two together, may or not have confronted her . . . no, definitely didn't confront her. Gary never confronted anyone.

He simply came to the conclusion that his wife was poisoning their child and decided to kill her, taking his own aimless life as well. That would account for the hurry—to stop the poisoning without having to confront Stephanie. If he accused her, he might be able to stop her, but things would instantly get far too messy for Gary-the-conflict-avoider. Worse, the thing could easily become a criminal case, and if Stephanie was convicted, Laurie would have to grow up knowing her mother had deliberately poisoned her. If she were acquitted, Laurie might always be in danger. I could follow his benighted reasoning perfectly.

But I couldn't, for all the garlic in Gilroy, imagine why Stephanie would want to kill Laurie. By all accounts, she was the most loving of mothers, would probably even have laid down her own life for her child's. I called a shrink friend, Elaine Alvarez.

"Of course she loved the child," Elaine explained. "Why shouldn't she? Laurie perfectly answered her needs." And then she told me some things that made me forget I'd been planning to consume a large breakfast in a few minutes. On the excuse of finally remembering to take Stephanie's clothes, I drove to Gary's house.

The family was planning a memorial service in a day or two for the dead couple; Jeri had just arrived at her dead brother's house; friends had dropped by to comfort the bereaved; yet there was almost a festive atmosphere in the house. Laurie had come home that morning.

Michael and I took a walk. "Bullshit!" he said. "Dog crap! No one could have taken better care of that baby than Stephanie. Christ, she martyred herself. She stayed up night after night—"

"Listen to yourself. Everything you're saying confirms what Elaine told me. The thing even has a name. It's called Munchausen Syndrome by Proxy. The original syndrome, plain old Munchausen, is when you hurt or mutilate yourself to get attention.

" 'By proxy' means you do it to your nearest and dearest. People say, 'Oh, that poor woman. God, what she's been through. Look how brave she is! Why, no one in the world could be a better mother.' And Mom gets off on it. There are recorded cases of it, Michael, at least one involving a mother and baby."

He was pale. "I think I'm going to throw up."

"Let's sit down a minute."

In fact, stuffy, uptight Michael ended up lying down in the dirt on the side of the road, nice flannel slacks and all, taking breaths till his color returned. And then, slowly, we walked back to the house.

Jeri was holding Laurie, her mother standing over her, Mary Cooper sitting close on the couch. "Oh, look what a baby-waby. What a darling girly-wirl. Do you feel the least bit hot? Lauriebaurie, you're not running a fever, are you?"

The kid had just gotten the thumbs-up from a hospital, and she was wrapped in half a dozen blankets. I doubted she was running a fever.

Ellen leaned over to feel the baby's face. "Ohhh, I think she might be. Give her to Grandma. Grandma knows how to fix babies, doesn't she, Laurie girl? Come to Grandma and Grandma will sponge you with alcohol, Grandma will."

She looked like a hawk coming in for a landing, ready to snare its prey and fly up again, but Mary was quicker still. Almost before you saw it happening, she had the baby away from Ellen and in her own lap. "What you need is some nice juice, don't you, Laurie-bear? And then Meemaw's going to rock you and rock you . . . oh, my goodness, you're burning up." Her voice was on the edge of panic. "Listen, Jeri, this baby's wheezing! We've got to get her breathing damp air. . . ."

She wasn't wheezing, she was gulping, probably in amazement. I felt my own jaw drop and, looking away, unwittingly caught the eye of Mary's husband, who hadn't wanted me to see the anguish there. Quickly he dropped a curtain of blandness. Beside me, I heard Michael whisper, "My God!"

I knew we were seeing something extreme. They were all excited to have Laurie home, and they were competing with each other, letting out what looked like their scariest sides if you knew what we did. But a Stephanie didn't come along every day. Laurie was in no further danger, I was sure of it. Still, I understood why Gary had had the sudden change of heart about her guardianship.

I turned to Michael. "Are you going to try to get her?"

He plucked at his sweater sleeve, staring at his wrist as if it had a treasure map on it. "I haven't decided."

An image from my fitful morning dreams came back to me: a giant in a forest, taller than all the trees and built like a mountain; a female giant with belly and breasts like boulders, dressed in white robes and carrying, draped across her outstretched arms, a dead man, head dangling on its flaccid neck.

In a few days Michael called. When he got home to Seattle, a letter had been waiting for him—a note, rather, from Gary, postmarked the day of his death. It didn't apologize, it didn't explain—it didn't even say, "Dear Michael." It was simply a quote from *Hamlet* typed on a piece of paper, not handwritten, Michael thought, because it could be construed as a confession and there was the insurance to think about.

This was the quote:

Diseases desperate grown
By desperate appliance are relieved,
Or not at all.

I didn't ask Michael again whether he intended to take Laurie. At the moment, I was too furious with one passive male to trust myself to speak civilly with another. Instead, I simmered inwardly, thinking how like Gary it was to confess to murder with a quote from Shakespeare. Thinking that, as he typed it, he probably imagined grandly that nothing in his life would become him like the leaving of it. The schmuck.

MARCIA MULLER

"Deadly Fantasies"

Marcia Muller was born in Detroit, Michigan on September 28, 1944. She graduated from the University of Michigan with a masters degree in journalism in 1971. Moving to California she held a variety of jobs before publishing her first novel **Edwin of the Iron Shoes** *in 1977. It was the first novel about a modern female private detective and by the time of Sharon McCone's second case five years later it was recognized as a landmark of detective fiction. Muller has also created two other series sleuths, museum curator Elena Oliver and art investigator Joanna Stark.*

Marcia Muller's 1989 novel **The Shape of Dread** *was a PWA Shamus nominee and winner of the American Mystery Award.* **Where Echoes Live** *(1991) was also a Shamus nominee. She received Bouchercon's Anthony Award and Edgar and Shamus nominations for* **Wolf in the Shadows**, *published in 1993. That same year the Private Eye Writers of America presented her with its Lifetime Achievement Award. She has collaborated on three novels and a dozen anthologies with her husband Bill Pronzini.*

Muller's short stories are collected in **Deceptions** *(1991) and* **The McCone Files** *(1995). "Deadly Fantasies" was published in* **Alfred Hitchcock's Mystery Magazine** *and reprinted in* **The McCone Files**.

Deadly Fantasies

by Marcia Muller

Ms. McCone, I know what you're thinking. But I'm not paranoid. One of them—my brother or my sister—*is* trying to kill me!"

"Please, call me Sharon." I said it to give myself time to think. The young woman seated across my desk at All Souls Legal Cooperative certainly sounded paranoid. My boss, Hank Zahn, had warned me about that when he'd referred her for private investigative services.

"Let me go over what you've told me, to make sure I've got it straight," I said. "Six months ago you were living here in the Mission district and working as a counselor for emotionally disturbed teenagers. Then your father died and left you his entire estate, something in the neighborhood of thirty million dollars."

Laurie Newingham nodded and blew her nose. As soon as she'd come into my office she'd started sneezing. Allergies, she'd told me. To ease her watering eyes she'd popped out her contact lenses and stored them in their plastic case; in doing that she had spilled some of the liquid that the lenses soaked in over her fingers, then nonchalantly wiped them on her faded jeans. The gesture endeared her to me because I'm sloppy, too. Frankly, I couldn't imagine this freshly scrubbed young woman—she was about ten years younger than I, perhaps twenty-five—possessing a fortune. With her trim, athletic body, tanned, snub-nosed face, and carelessly styled blonde hair, she looked like a high school cheerleader. But Winfield Newingham had owned much of San Francisco's choice real estate, and Laurie had been the developer's youngest—and apparently favorite—child.

I went on, "Under the terms of the will, you were required to move back into the family home in St. Francis Wood. You've done so. The will also stipulated that your brother Dan and sister Janet can remain there as long as they wish. So you've been living with them, and they've both been acting hostile because you inherited everything."

"Hostile? One of them wants to *kill* me! I keep having stomach cramps, throwing up—you know."

"Have you seen a doctor?"

"I *hate* doctors! They're always telling me there's nothing wrong with me, when I know there *is*."

"The police, then?"

"I like them a whole lot less than doctors. Besides, they wouldn't believe me." Now she took out an inhaler and breathed deeply from it.

Asthma, as well as allergies, I thought. Wasn't asthma sometimes psychosomatic? Could the vomiting and other symptoms be similarly rooted?

"Either Dan or Janet is trying to poison me," Laurie said, "because if I die, the estate reverts to them."

"Laurie," I said, "why did your father leave everything to you?"

"The will said it was because I'd gone out on my own and done something I believed in. Dan and Janet have always lived off him; the only jobs they've ever been able to hold down have been ones Dad gave them."

"One more question: Why did you come to All Souls?" My employer is a legal services plan for people who can't afford the going rates.

Laurie looked surprised. "I've *always* come here, since I moved to the Mission and started working as a counselor five years ago. I may be able to afford a downtown law firm, but I don't trust them any more now than I did when I inherited the money. Besides, I talked it over with Dolph, and he said it would be better to stick with a known quantity."

"Dolph?"

"Dolph Edwards. I'm going to marry him. He's director of the guidance center where I used to work—still work, as a volunteer."

"That's the Inner Mission Self-Help Center?"

She nodded. "Do you know them?"

"Yes." The center offered a wide range of social services to a mainly Hispanic clientele—including job placement, psychological counseling, and short term financial assistance. I'd heard that recently their programs had been drastically cut back due to lack of funding—as all too often happens in today's arid political climate.

"Then you know what my father meant about my having done something I believed in," Laurie said. "The center's a hopeless mess, of course; it's never been very well organized. But it's the kind of project I'd like to put my money to work for. After I marry Dolph I'll help him realize his dreams effectively—and in the right way."

I nodded and studied her for a moment. She stared back anxiously. Laurie was emotionally ragged, I thought, and needed someone to look out for her. Besides, I identified with her in a way. At her age I'd also been the cheerleader type, and I'd gone out on my own and done something I believed in, too.

"Okay," I said. "What I'll do is talk with your brother and sister, feel the situation out. I'll say you've applied for a volunteer position here, counseling clients with emotional problems, and that you gave their names as character references."

Her eyes brightened and some of the lines of strain smoothed. She gave me Dan's office phone number and Janet's private line at the St. Francis Wood house. Preparing to leave, she clumsily dropped her purse on the floor. Then she located her contact case and popped a lens into her mouth to clean it; as she fitted it into her right eye, her foot nudged the bag, and the inhaler and a bottle of time-release vitamin capsules rolled across the floor. We went for them at the same time, and our heads grazed each other's.

She looked at me apologetically. One of her eyes was now gray, the other a brilliant blue from the tint of the contact. It was like a physical manifestation of her somewhat schizoid personality: down-to-earth wholesomeness warring with what I had begun to suspect was a dangerous paranoia.

Dan Newingham said, "Why the hell does Laurie want to do that? She doesn't have to work any more, even as a volunteer. She controls all the family's assets."

We were seated in his office in the controller's department of Newingham Development, on the thirty-first floor of one of the company's financial district buildings. Dan was a big guy, with the same blond good looks as his sister, but they were spoiled by a petulant mouth and a body whose bloated appearance suggested an excess of good living.

"If she wants to work," he added, "there're plenty of positions she could fill right here. It's her company now, dammit, and she ought to take an interest in it."

"I gather her interests run more to the social services."

"More to the low life, you mean."

"In what respect?"

Dan got up and went to look out the window behind the desk. The view of the bay was blocked by an upthrusting jumble of steel and plate glass—the legacy that firms such as Newingham Development had left a once old-fashioned and beautiful town.

After a moment Dan turned. "I don't want to offend you, Ms. . . . McCone, is it?"

I nodded.

"I'm not putting down your law firm, or what you're trying to do," he went on, "but when you work on your end of the spectrum, you naturally have to associate with people who aren't quite . . . well, of our class. I wasn't aware of the kind of people Laurie was associating with during those years she didn't live at home, but now . . . her boyfriend, that Dolph, for instance. He's always around; I can't stand him. Anyway, my point is, Laurie should settle down now, come back to the real world, learn the business. Is that too much to ask in exchange for thirty million?"

"She doesn't seem to care about the money."

Dan laughed harshly. "Doesn't she? Then why did she move back into the house? She could have chucked the whole thing."

"I think she feels she can use the money to benefit people who really need it."

"Yes, and she'll blow it all. In a few years there won't *be* any Newingham Development. Oh, I know what was going through my father's mind when he made that will: Laurie's always been the strong one, the dedicated one. He thought that if he forced her to move back home, she'd eventually become involved in the business and there'd be real leadership here. Laurie can be very single-minded when she wants things to go a certain way, and that's what it takes to run a firm like this. But the sad thing is, Dad just didn't realize how far gone she is in her bleeding heart sympathies."

"That aside, what do you think about her potential for counseling our disturbed clients?"

"If you really want to know, I think she'd be terrible. Laurie's a basket case. She has psychosomatic illnesses, paranoid fantasies. She needs counseling herself."

"Can you describe these fantasies?"

He hesitated, tapping his fingers on the window frame. "No, I don't think I care to. I shouldn't have brought them up."

"Actually, Mr. Newingham, I think I have an inkling of what they are. Laurie told her lawyer that someone's trying to poison her. She seemed obsessed with the idea, which is why we decided to check her references thoroughly."

"I suppose she also told her lawyer who the alleged poisoner is?"

"In a way. She said it was either you or your sister Janet."

"God, she's worse off than I realized. I suppose she claims one of us wants to kill her so he can inherit my father's estate. That's ridiculous—I don't need the damned money. I have a good job here, and I've invested profitably." Dan paused, then added, "I hope you can convince her to get into an intensive therapy program before she tries to counsel any of your clients. Her fantasies are starting to sound dangerous."

Janet Newingham was the exact opposite of her sister: a tall brunette with a highly stylized way of moving and speaking. Her clothes were designer, her jewelry expensive, and her hair and nails told of frequent attention at the finest salons. We met at the St. Francis Wood house—a great pile of stone reminiscent of an Italian villa that sat on a double lot near the fountain that crowned the area's main boulevard. I had informed Laurie that I would be interviewing her sister, and she had agreed to absent herself from the house; I didn't want my presence to trigger an unpleasant scene between the two of them.

I needn't have worried, however. Janet Newingham was one of those cool, reserved women who may smolder under the surface but seldom display anger. She seated me in a formal parlor overlooking the strip of park that runs down the center of St. Francis Boulevard and served me coffee from a sterling silver pot. From all appearances, I might have been there to discuss the Junior League fashion show.

When I had gotten to the point of my visit, Janet leaned forward and extracted a cigarette from an ivory box on the coffee table. She took her time lighting it, then said, "*Another* volunteer position? It's bad enough she kept on working at that guidance center for nothing after they lost their federal funding last spring, but this . . . I'm surprised; I thought nothing would ever pry her away from her precious Dolph."

"Perhaps she feels it's not a good idea to stay on there, since they plan to be married."

"Did she tell you that? Laurie's always threatening to marry Dolph, but I doubt she ever will. She just keeps him around because he's her one claim to the exotic. He's one of these social reformers, you know. Totally devoted to his cause."

"And what is that?"

"Helping people. Sounds very sixties, doesn't it? That center is his *raison d'etre*. He founded it, and he's going to keep it limping along no matter what. He plays the crusader role to the hilt, Dolph does: dresses in Salvation Army castoffs, drives a motorcycle. You know the type."

"That's very interesting," I said, "but it doesn't have much bearing on Laurie's ability to fill our volunteer position. What do you think of her potential as a counselor?"

"Not a great deal. Oh, I know that's what she's been doing these past five years, but recently Laurie's been . . . a very disturbed young woman. But you know that. My brother told me of your visit to his office, and that you had already heard of her fantasy that one of us is trying to kill her."

"Well, yes. It's odd—"

"It's not just odd, it's downright dangerous. Dangerous for her to walk around in such a paranoid state, and dangerous for Dan and me. It's our reputations she's smearing."

"Because on the surface you both appear to have every reason to want her out of the way."

Janet's lips compressed—a mild reaction, I thought, to what I'd implied. "On the surface, I suppose that is how it looks," she said. "But as far as I'm concerned Laurie is welcome to our father's money. I had a good job in the public relations department in Newingham Development; I saved and invested my salary well. After my father died, I quit working there, and I'm about to open my own public relations firm."

"Did the timing of your quitting have anything to do with Laurie's inheriting the company?"

Janet picked up a porcelain ashtray and carefully stubbed her cigarette out. "I'll be frank with you, Ms. McCone: it did. Newingham Development had suddenly become not a very good place to work; people were running scared—they always do when there's no clear managerial policy. Besides . . ."

"Besides?"

"Since I'm being frank, I may as well say it. I did not want to work for my spoiled little bitch of a sister who's always had things her own way. And if that makes me a potential murderer—"

She broke off as the front door opened. We both looked that way. A man wearing a shabby tweed coat and a shocking purple scarf and aviator sunglasses entered. His longish black hair was windblown, and his sharp features were ruddy from the cold. He pocketed a key and started for the stairway.

"Laurie's not here, Dolph," Janet said.

He turned. "Where is she?"

"Gone shopping."

"Laurie hates to shop."

"Well, that's where she is. You'd better come back in a couple of hours." Janet's tone did little to mask her dislike.

Nor did the twist of his mouth mask *his* dislike of his fiancée's sister. Without a word he turned and strode out the door.

I said, "Dolph Edwards?"

"Yes. You can see what I mean."

Actually, I hadn't seen enough of him, and I decided to take the opportunity to talk to him while it was presented. I thanked Janet Newingham for her time and hurried out.

Dolph's motorcycle was parked at the curb near the end of the front walk, and he was just revving it up when I reached him. At first his narrow lips pulled down in annoyance, but when I told him who I was, he smiled and shut the machine off. He remained astride it while we talked.

"Yes, I told Laurie it would be better to stick with All Souls," he said when I mentioned the context in which I'd first heard of him. "You've got good people there, and you're more likely to take Laurie's problem seriously than some downtown law firm."

"You think someone *is* trying to kill her, then?"

"I know what I see. The woman's sick a lot lately, and those two—he motioned at the house, "—hate her guts."

"You must see a great deal of what goes on here," I said. "I noticed you have a key."

"Laurie's my fiancée," he said with a puritanical stiffness that surprised me.

"So she said. When do you plan to be married?"

I couldn't make out his eyes behind the dark aviator glasses, but the lines around them deepened. Perhaps Dolph suspected what Janet claimed: that Laurie didn't really intend to marry him. "Soon," he said curtly.

We talked for a few minutes more, but Dolph could add little to what I'd already observed about the Newingham family. Before he started his bike he said apologetically, "I wish I could help, but I'm not around them very much. Laurie and I prefer to spend our time at my apartment."

I didn't like Dan or Janet Newingham, but I also didn't believe either was trying to poison Laurie. Still, I followed up by explaining the situation to my former lover and now good friend Greg Marcus, lieutenant with the SFPD homicide detail. Greg ran a background check on Dan for me, and came up with nothing more damning than a number of unpaid parking tickets. Janet didn't even have those to her discredit. Out of curiosity, I asked him to check on Dolph Edwards, too. Dolph had a record of two arrests involving political protests in the late seventies—just what I would have expected.

At that point I reported my findings to Laurie and advised her to ask her brother and sister to move out of the house. If they wouldn't, I said, she should talk to Hank about invalidating that clause of her father's will. And in any case she should also get herself some psychological counseling. Her response was to storm out of my office. And that, I assumed, ended my involvement with Laurie Newingham's problems.

But it didn't. Two weeks later Greg called to tell me that Laurie had been taken ill during a family cocktail party and had died at the St. Francis Wood house, an apparent victim of poisoning.

I felt terrible, thinking of how lightly I had taken her fears, how easily I'd accepted her brother and sister's claims of innocence, how I'd let Laurie down when she'd needed and trusted me. So I waited until Greg had the autopsy results and then went to the office at the Hall of Justice.

"Arsenic," Greg said when I'd seated myself on his visitor's chair. "The murderer's perfect poison: widely available, no odor, little if any taste. It takes the body a long time to eliminate arsenic, and a person can be fed small amounts over a period of two or three weeks, even longer, before he or she succumbs. According to the medical examiner, that's what happened to Laurie."

"But why small amounts? Why not just one massive dose?"

"The murderer was probably stupid enough that he figured if she'd been sick for weeks we wouldn't check for poisons. But why he went on with it after she started talking about someone trying to kill her . . ."

"He? Dan's your primary suspect, then?"

"I was using 'he' generically. The sister looks good, too. They both had extremely strong motives, but we're not going to be able to charge either until we can find out how Laurie was getting the poison."

"You say extremely strong motives. Is there something besides the money?"

"Something connected to the money; each of them seems to need it more badly than they're willing to admit. The interim management of Newingham Development has given Dan his notice; there'll be a hefty severance payment, of course, but he's deeply in debt—gambling debts, to the kind of people who won't accept fifty-dollars-a-week installments. The sister had most of her savings tied up in one of those real estate investment partnerships; it went belly up, and Janet needs to raise additional cash to satisfy outstanding obligations to the other partners."

"I wish I'd known about that when I talked with them. I might have prevented Laurie's death."

Greg held up a cautioning hand. "Don't blame yourself for something you couldn't know or foresee. That should be one of the cardinal rules of your profession."

"It's one of the rules, all right, but I seem to keep breaking it. Greg, what about Dolph Edwards?"

"He didn't stand to benefit by her death. Laurie hadn't made a will, so everything reverts to the brother and sister."

"No will? I'm surprised Hank didn't insist she make one."

"According to your boss, she had an appointment with him for the day after she died. She mentioned something about a change in her circumstances, so I guess she was planning to make the will in favor of her future husband. Another reason we don't suspect Edwards."

I sighed. "So what you've got is a circumstantial case against one of two people."

"Right. And without uncovering the means by which the poison got to her, we don't stand a chance of getting an indictment against either."

"Well . . . the obvious means is in her food."

"There's a cook who prepares all the meals. She, a live-in maid, and the family basically eat the same things. On the night she died, Laurie, her brother and sister, and Dolph Edwards all had the same hors d'oeuvres with cocktails. The leftovers tested negative."

"And you checked what she drank, of course."

"It also tested negative."

"What about medications? Laurie probably took pills for her asthma. She had an inhaler—"

"We checked everything. Fortunately, I caught the call and remembered what you'd told me. I was more than thorough. Had the contents of the bedroom and bathroom inventoried, anything that could have contained poison was taken away for testing."

"What about this cocktail party? I know for a fact that neither Dan nor Janet liked Dolph. And according to Dolph, they both hated Laurie. He wasn't fond of them, either. It seems like an unlikely group for a convivial gathering."

"Apparently Laurie arranged the party. She said she had an announcement to make."

"What was it?"

"No one knows. She died before she could tell them."

Three days later Hank and I attended Laurie's funeral. It was in an old-fashioned churchyard in the little town of Tomales, near the bay of the same name northwest of San Francisco. The Newinghams had a summer home on the bay, and Laurie had wanted to be buried there.

It was one of those winter afternoons when the sky is clear and hard, and the sun is as pale as if it were filtered through water. Hank and I stood a little apart from the crowd of mourners on the knoll, near a windbreak of eucalyptus that bordered the cemetery. The people who had traveled from the city to lay Laurie to rest were an oddly assorted group: dark-suited men and women who represented San Francisco's business community; others who bore the unmistakable stamp of high society; shabbily dressed Hispanics who must have been clients of the Inner Mission Self-Help Center. Dolph Edwards arrived on his motorcycle; his inappropriate attire—the shocking purple scarf seemed several shades too festive—annoyed me.

Dan and Janet Newingham arrived in the limousine that followed the hearse and walked behind the flower-covered casket to the graveside. Their pious propriety annoyed me, too. As the service went on, the wind rose. It rustled the leaves of the eucalyptus trees and brought with it dampness and the odor of the nearby sea. During the final prayer, a strand of my hair escaped the knot I'd fastened it in and blew across my face. It clung damply there, and when I licked my lips to push it away, I tasted salt—whether from the sea air or tears, I couldn't tell.

As soon as the service was concluded, Janet and Dan went back to the limousine and were driven away. One of the Chicana women stopped to speak to Hank; she was a client; and he introduced us. When I looked around for Dolph, I found he had disappeared. By the time Hank finished chatting with his client, the only other person left at the graveside besides us and the cemetery workers was an old Hispanic lady who was placing a single rose on the casket.

Hank said, "I could use a drink." We started down the uneven stone walk, but I glanced back at the old woman, who was following us unsteadily.

"Wait," I said to Hank and went to take her arm as she stumbled.

The woman nodded her thanks and leaned on me, breathing heavily.

"Are you all right?" I asked. "Can we give you a ride back to the city?" My old MG was the only car left beyond the iron fence.

"Thank you, but no," she said. "My son brought me. He's waiting down the street, there's a bar. You were a friend of Laurie?"

"Yes." But not as good a friend as I might have been, I reminded myself. "Did you know her through the center?"

"Yes. She talked with my grandson many times and made him stay in school when he wanted to quit. He loved her, we all did."

"She was a good woman. Tell me, did you see her finacé leave?" I had wanted to give Dolph my condolences.

The woman looked puzzled.

"The man she planned to marry—Dolph Edwards."

"I thought he was her husband."

"No, although they planned to marry soon."

The old woman sighed. "They were always together. I thought they were already married. But nowadays who can tell? My son—

Laurie helped his own son, but is he grateful? No. Instead of coming to her funeral, he sits in a bar. . . ."

I was silent on the drive back to the city—so silent that Hank, who is usually oblivious to my moods, asked me twice what was wrong. I'm afraid I snapped at him, something to the effect of funerals not being my favorite form of entertainment, and when I dropped him at All Souls, I refused to have the drink he offered. Instead I went downtown to City Hall.

When I entered Greg Marcus's office at the Hall of Justice a couple of hours later, I said without preamble, "The Newingham case: you told me you inventoried the contents of Laurie's bedroom and bathroom and had anything that could have contained poison taken away for testing?"

". . . Right."

"Can I see the inventory sheet?"

He picked up his phone and asked for the file to be brought in. While he waited, he asked me about the funeral. Over the years, Greg has adopted a wait-and-see attitude toward my occasional interference in his cases. I've never been sure whether it's because he doesn't want to disturb what he considers to be my shaky thought processes, or that he simply prefers to leave the hard work to me.

When the file came, he passed it to me. I studied the inventory sheet, uncertain exactly what I was looking for. But something was missing there. What? I flipped the pages, then wished I hadn't. A photo of Laurie looked up at me, brilliant blue eyes blank and lifeless. No more cheerleader out to save the world—

Quickly I flipped back to the inventory sheet. The last item was "1 handbag, black leather, & contents." I looked over the list of things from the bathroom again and focused on the word "unopened."

"Greg," I said, "what was in Laurie's purse?"

He took the file from me and studied the list. "It should say here, but it doesn't. Sloppy work—new man on the squad."

"Can you find out?"

Without a word he picked up the phone receiver, dialed, and made the inquiry. When he hung up he read off the notes he'd made. "Wallet. Checkbook. Inhaler, sent to lab. Vitamin capsules, also sent to lab. Contact lens case. That's all."

"That's enough. The contact lens case is a two-chambered plastic receptacle holding about half an ounce of fluid for the lenses to soak in. There was a brand-new, unopened bottle of fluid on the inventory of Laurie's bathroom."

"So?"

"I'm willing to bet the contents of that bottle will test negative for arsenic; the surface of it might or might not show someone's fingerprints, but not Laurie's. That's because the murderer put it there *after* she died, but *before* your people arrived on the scene."

Greg merely waited.

"Have the lab test the liquid in that lens case for arsenic. I'm certain the results will be positive. The killer added arsenic to Laurie's soaking solution weeks ago, and then he removed that bottle and substituted the unopened one. We wondered why slow poisoning, rather than a massive dose; it was because the contact case holds so little fluid."

"Sharon, arsenic can't be ingested through the eyes—"

"Of course it can't! But Laurie had the habit, as lots of contact wearers do—you're not supposed to, of course; it can cause eye infections—of taking her lenses out of the case and putting them into her mouth to clean them before putting them on. She probably did it a lot because she had allergies and took the lenses off to rest her eyes. That's how he poisoned her, a little at a time over an extended period."

"Dan Newingham?"

"No. Dolph Edwards."

Greg waited, his expression neither doubting nor accepting.

"Dolph is a social reformer," I said. "He funded that Inner Mission Self-Help Center; it's his whole life. But its funding has been cancelled and it can't go on much longer. In Janet Newingham's words, Dolph is intent on keeping it going 'no matter what.' "

"So? He was going to marry Laurie. She could have given him plenty of money—"

"Not for the center. She told me it was a 'hopeless mess.' When she married Dolph, she planned to help him, but in the 'right way.' Laurie has been described to me by both her brother and sister as quite single-minded and always getting what she wanted. Dolph must have realized that too, and knew her money would never go for his self-help center."

"All right, I'll take your word for that. But Edwards still didn't stand to benefit. They weren't married, she hadn't made a will—"

"They *were* married. I checked that out at City Hall a while ago.

They were married last month, probably at Dolph's insistence when he realized the poisoning would soon have a fatal effect."

Greg was silent for a moment. I could tell by the calculating look in his eyes that he was taking my analysis seriously. "That's another thing we slipped up on—just like not listing the contents of her purse. What made you check?"

"I spoke with an old woman who was at the funeral. She thought they were married and made the comment that nowadays you can't tell. It got me thinking. . . . Anyway, it doesn't matter about the will because under California's community property laws, Dolph inherits automatically in the absence of one."

"It seems stupid of him to marry her so soon before she died. The husband automatically comes under suspicion—"

"But the poisoning started long *before* they were married. That automatically threw suspicion on the brother and sister."

"And Dolph had the opportunity."

"Plenty. He even tried to minimize it by lying to me: he said he and Laurie didn't spend much time at the St. Francis Wood house, but Dan described Dolph as being around all the time. And even if he wasn't he could just as easily have poisoned her lens solution at his own apartment. He told another unnecessary lie to you when he said he didn't know what the announcement Laurie was going to make at the family gathering was. It could only have been the announcement of their secret marriage. He may even have increased the dosage of poison, in the hope she'd succumb before she could reveal it."

"Why do you suppose they kept it secret?"

"I think Dolph wanted it that way. It would minimize the suspicion directed at him if he just let the fact of the marriage come out after either Dan or Janet had been charged with the murder. He probably intended to claim ignorance of the community property laws, say he'd assumed since there was no will he couldn't inherit. Why don't we ask him if I'm right?"

Greg's hand moved toward his phone. "Yes—why don't we?"

When Dolph Edwards confessed to Laurie's murder, it turned out that I'd been absolutely right. He also added an item of further interest; he hadn't been in love with Laurie at all, had had a woman on the Peninsula whom he planned to marry as soon as he could without attracting suspicion.

It was too bad about Dolph; his kind of social crusader had so much ego tied up in their own individual projects that they lost sight of the larger objective. Had Laurie lived, she would have applied her money to any number of worthy causes, but now it would merely go to finance the lifestyles of her greedy brother and sister.

But it was Laurie I felt worst about. And it was a decidedly bittersweet satisfaction that I took in solving her murder, in fulfilling my final obligation to my client.

MJF BOOKS
Is Proud to Bring You

A Century of Science Fiction
A Century of Mystery
A Century of Fantasy
A Century of Horror

The four series collects the greatest stories written during the
twentieth century in each genre. Each volume's cover is
illustrated by a well-known artist, printed on acid-free paper, and
sturdily bound to last for years. The Series Editor is Martin H.
Greenberg, America's most renowned anthologist. Mr.
Greenberg has been the Guest of Honor at the World Science
Fiction Convention and The World Fantasy Convention, and the
recipient of the Ellery Queen Award for lifetime achievement for
editing in the mystery field. He also was a member of the Board
of Advisors of the Sci-Fi Channel, a basic cable network that
launched in September 1992. To oversee the four series, he has
recruited top editors Robert Silverberg (Science Fiction and
Fantasy), David Drake (Horror), and Marcia Muller and Bill
Pronzini (Mystery).
The Century series has been conceived to offer the reader only
the very best, in collectible books of lasting value.

Available Now:

A Century of Science Fiction: 1950-1959

Featuring stories by Robert Silverberg, Fritz Leiber,
Ray Bradbury, James Blish, Walter M. Miller, Jr.,
Philip Jose Farmer, Arthur C. Clarke, Philip K. Dick,
Isaac Asimov, Theodore Sturgeon,
Marion Zimmer Bradley, and others

A Century of Mystery: 1980-1989

Featuring stories by Tony Hillerman,
Frederick Forsyth, Ruth Rendell, Janwillem van de Wetering,
George V. Higgins, Lawrence Block, Bill Pronzini,
Clark Howard, Marcia Muller, Peter Lovesey, and others

A Century of Fantasy: 1980-1989

Featuring stories by Roger Zelazny, Andre Norton,
Orson Scott Card, Harlan Ellison, Joe Haldeman,
George R.R. Martin, Ellen Kushner, Alan Dean Foster,
Larry Niven, Ursula K. Le Guin, and others

A Century of Horror: 1970-1979

Featuring stories by Richard Matheson, David Drake,
Robert Bloch, Brian Lumley, Joyce Carol Oates,
Ray Bradbury, Michael Bishop, Harlan Ellison,
Orson Scott Card, Tanith Lee, Ramsey Campbell, and others

Available At Your Local Bookstore